PERVADE
LONDON

USA TODAY BESTSELLING AUTHOR
VANESSA FEWINGS

Cover photo from Depositphoto: Artur Verkhovetskiy
Photo credit: Depositphoto: heckmannoleg, Masha Kotscur, and Verkhovetskiy, and Pixabay
Cover created by: Najla Qamber Designs

Formatted by: Champagne Book Design
Book edited by: Debbie Kuhn

ISBN-9781733774208

Sign-up for Vanessa's email newsletter.

VanessaFewings.com

For the Members of Vanessa Fewings' Romance Lounge on Facebook

"Silence is the ultimate weapon of power."

—Charles de Gaulle

Chapter 1

Present Day
The Savoy

"Y OU CAN'T GO IN THERE." THE TALL, VERY BLONDE MAÎTRE D'
blocked the entrance, preventing me from passing. I
didn't like the way she looked down her elitist nose at
me either.

"But...I saw my boyfriend go in."

This was The Savoy's posh restaurant Simpson's in the Strand, and
I knew I looked classy enough for it in my expensive Lily Charis mini-
dress layered in twinkling crystals.

Her attitude made no sense. The way I dressed hid my past. I liked
it that way. During those desolate years, I'd garnered the kind of wisdom
that meant I never talked down to anyone the way she'd done to me. I
remembered where I came from, and it was a far cry from the high-and-
mighty Strand in the heart of London.

These cocktail-laced self-reflections continued as I watched her close
the door to the restaurant in a final act of authority.

Seeing my fiancé had been a chance occurrence. I'd left my best
friend Kitty with our other girlfriends sitting at the bar sipping Cosmos
while laughing raucously. A rare Wednesday night out because it was her
birthday. And, trust me—Kitty Adair could look out for herself.

One cocktail in and we'd "left the station" as far as common sense
was concerned, but I wasn't so drunk I'd misidentify my man.

Leaving my drink at the bar, I'd gotten lost looking for the loo and
seconds later caught sight of him strolling nonchalantly through the
hotel.

He wasn't supposed to be here.

The restaurant's heavy door loomed ahead, and I weighed my options. I could go back and rejoin the others. Pretend I'd not seen him. Ask him about it later when we both got home and hope he shared the truth.

Admitting that Xander Rothschild was out of my league was not a fault-line in my confidence...not at all. Even if his Cambridge education ensured he knew the difference between Beluga and Osetra—caviar to us lesser mortals. Even if he drew a twisted pleasure from dragging me up to his elite standards, I loved him deeply. Xander was always reminding me I was the only woman who truly understood him, which was to say I was the only one who respected his foibles.

Take for example his passion for chess. Okay, it was more of an obsession. The first time I visited his place on Baker Street, I'd walked into his tastefully decorated bachelor pad and gawped at what I saw. Placed sporadically around his living room were *ten* chessboards set up with games going *at the same time*. Even now he liked to stroll from board to board moving the pieces as he challenged anonymous players online. He found it relaxing, apparently.

Tolerating this obsession and other quirks that showcased his brilliance was the price I paid to live with this extraordinary thirty-two-year-old man. As I was twenty-three, he constantly liked to remind me that he knew best—about everything. His worldliness was a reminder of how little I'd traveled and how little I'd seen. Personally, I believed he loved me because my background was the opposite of his, since he'd had a silver spoon stuck up his ass for most of his life.

We were opposites in appearances as well. Born to a Norwegian mum and a highbrow British diplomat father, neither of whom I'd met, Xander had inherited seductive looks—dark blonde hair and a sun-kissed complexion that never faded, not even during one of England's harsh winters. In contrast, I had porcelain skin that stood out against my brunette locks and green irises.

Intellectually, Xander was a match for anyone who crossed his path. He had a thing for manipulating a conversation to prove he was always right. He would throw in one of his drop-dead gorgeous smiles right before finishing off his victim during an argument, using a quip to deliver the final blow.

With me, he was just as insistent on getting his own way. When we fought, which was rare, he had no qualms about delivering an arrogant tongue-lashing. Though after he'd shown me what else he could do with that mouth I'd fallen head over heels for him.

Xander Rothschild was simply mesmerizing.

And tonight he was meant to be at home where I'd left him, sitting on the sofa reading *The Outline of History* by H. G. Wells…again. My man was a sci-fi buff, always walking around with his head in a book by the likes of Ray Bradbury, Frank Herbert or Jules Verne, to name but a few. I loved that about him. *Hell,* I loved everything about him and the thought of Xander not being in my life was unbearable.

Which was why my stomach was tied up in knots.

Until now, I'd never doubted his loyalty. The sobering thought of losing him to someone else made my palms sweat and my heart race.

Fuck it.

It's better to know.

With a Bombay Sapphire Martini onboard to lend panache to my grand entry into London's most famous restaurant, I shoved the door open and dodged the maître d'.

The interior's opulent superiority was quickly apparent. Beneath an ornate stucco ceiling, dark wood framed walls added to the grandness. Neatly stationed tables were adorned with cream-colored tablecloths and matching high-back chairs. Here and there were extravagant lush plants rising out of swanky pots, harkening back to that "old world" colonial style.

I looked around, bracing myself in case I saw Xander with another woman.

The quiet place was nearly empty.

Ten or so striking men sat around a corner table, all wearing elegant suits and each nursing a glass of bourbon as they chatted. The empty bottle of liquor sat in the middle of the table.

And there he was…my Xander in his tailored-to-perfection Savile

Row ensemble that included a pair of highly polished Oxfords. He lifted an ice-filled glass to his lips and finished off his drink in one gulp.

I saw him set his tumbler down, as though sensing me behind him.

Feeling embarrassed over gate-crashing such a formal elitist gathering, I spun around to bolt and nearly ran into the maître d'.

"I'm so sorry, sir," she said, capturing everyone's attention.

I cringed inwardly, facing them with a wave. "Hey."

Surprised disappointment flashed across Xander's face as his crystal blue gaze narrowed, and I saw dread reflected in those dazzling eyes. A chill slithered up my spine, my forearms prickling.

Xander threw a look of concern over to one of the men.

I followed his line of sight, blinking at the striking vision of the thirty-something man staring back. Complex emotions bubbled up inside me, a sense of my rising insignificance in contrast to the man's profoundness. I snapped my attention away from the glare of his raw beauty.

Then, daring to look back, I let his chestnut eyes capture mine and lost myself in what seemed like a multitude of worlds, all touched by privilege.

His hypnotic stare held me transfixed as the room and everyone around us disappeared. I studied his perfect features, his regal nose and full sensuous mouth. Raven-black hair framed his devastatingly chiseled features.

His intense scrutiny took my breath away.

He pushed to his feet with a deadly grace. He was tall, a couple of inches more than Xander's six-foot-two. Versace-clad broad shoulders made him stand out and when he tilted his head with intrigue, he held the silence hostage, commanding the room.

The way the other men deferred to him with reverence confirmed he had the authority. He was the only one not wearing a tie and his shirt collar fell open casually. For some reason that made him look all the more powerful…

He stood there, exuding power while looking my way, his voice deep and penetrating. "This must be Emily."

Chapter 2

Six Months Ago

"**A**RE YOU OKAY?" I GAVE THE MAN A NUDGE TO WAKE HIM.

He rubbed sleepiness from his eyes. "I'm fine."

No, he wasn't. I'd just found him curled up in a ball on the filthy tiled floor in a corner of the Piccadilly Circus Tube station, half-hidden behind a pillar. His fancy Burberry coat looked creased and a three-day scruff shadowed his face, matching his dark blonde hair.

Meandering tourists and evening commuters strolled by him without a glance—like he was garbage and not a person who'd fallen on hard times. Goodness knows how long he'd lain there breathing stale air while people rushed by.

It had only been when foot traffic had slowed that I'd caught sight of him from where I'd been busking. For over half an hour, I'd been playing my violin to passers-by trying to make some extra cash to supplement my student grant. Glancing over at where'd I'd been playing, I checked to make sure no one had touched my tip jar.

Turning my attention back on him, I studied his dazzling features and guessed he was probably in his early thirties. His pale blue irises were a stark contrast to his grubby face. I found his Norwegian attributes quite beautiful.

"What time is it?" His accent was pure Surrey…or close. A friendly tone balanced out his posh accent, a contrast to mine.

"It's just after nine," I told him.

"Morning or evening?"

"Evening. What's your name?"

He mulled that over. "Xander."

"Can you sit up?" I helped him, and he leaned back against the grubby tile and blinked as though re-orientating himself.

"Here." I handed him a bottle of Smart Water I'd carried over with me.

He eyed it suspiciously before accepting it. "You're a sucker for advertising, then?"

"Excuse me?"

"I mean…thank you."

"Much better." I smiled approvingly.

He mirrored my smile while unscrewing the cap. After taking a gulp, he offered it back.

"Keep it."

Xander chuckled. We both knew I wasn't drinking that now.

He searched his wrist for a watch that wasn't there, and then banged his head back against the wall in frustration.

"Were you mugged?"

He touched his scalp with elegant fingers. "They can be a little overbearing."

"Who? The muggers? We can go to the police."

"Is that your real eye color?"

An odd question. "Yes."

"It's the Tyndall effect, a scattering of light in the stroma."

"Excuse me?"

"They're an unusual green. I thought you were wearing contacts for a second."

"I thought the same about you. Are you an ophthalmologist?"

"Hardly." His eyes crinkled as he offered me a gorgeous smile, which faded as he looked down at his dirty clothes. "I don't usually sleep in Tube stations."

"What happened?"

His bright eyes roamed over my face. "Why did you do that?"

"You were out cold. I was worried about you."

"No, I mean why did you get your nose pierced?"

Brushing my nose ring self-consciously, I gave him a pass.

Homeless people were very often broken people and he didn't need the hassle of me arguing over my vanity.

His hands disappeared inside his coat. "Shit."

"Did they take your wallet?"

"They like to make a statement."

"Who?"

He shook his head, refusing to elaborate.

"Are you out of money?"

He looked concerned. "You'll miss your train."

"I'm busking over there." I gestured at the adjacent corner, expecting to see my instrument.

Ice-cold fear surged through my veins. My violin was gone, the case empty.

My legs felt like they were moving in slow motion as I pushed to my feet and scurried over to where I'd been busking.

"My violin!" I screeched. "Did anyone see anything?"

My flesh chilled as I glanced around to see if anyone had it. There were too many people, hundreds of commuters hurrying by, and I was being spectacularly ignored by everyone.

I bolted toward the exit and took two steps at a time to the street level, spilling out into the cold air and into a sea of people. Scanning the hands of pedestrians, I fought waves of lightheadedness, ready to bolt after someone as soon as I saw it. There was no way I could lose my precious instrument.

This isn't happening.

"Can I help?"

Xander joined me on the pavement.

"Do you see anyone carrying a violin?" I zeroed in on the pedestrians again, glancing left and right. Time was slipping away. "Maybe they caught the Tube?" I tried to stay focused, fearing my legs were about to crumble.

"It's my fault," he said. "I'll make it up to you."

"No, this had nothing to do with you." It was me who'd turned my attention away from where I'd set up to play. Regret made my head spin.

"Did you see the person who took it?" he asked.

"Oh, God, it's gone."

"Have faith." Xander reached into his pocket. "The fuckers didn't take my phone." He stared at it, swiping the screen.

"Are you calling the police?" I turned away to continue studying the pedestrians. There were too many people in the crowd. Too many cars lined up in rush-hour traffic, the sound of their deafening horns heightening the tension.

Heat rose from the Tube station, making the air feel oppressive.

A streak of sweat snaked down my spine. "What am I going to do?"

Xander's focus was still on his phone. I felt I was wasting time I didn't have.

"The thief got into a black cab." He raised his eyes from the screen and peered left. "Traffic's slow. I can catch him."

"You saw him? Which way did he go?"

"It's too dangerous for you."

I glared at him. "Tell me."

"I'll get it back for you if you promise to buy me a meal."

I groaned in frustration.

"I was joking. But I am pretty hungry."

I regained my composure. "Bring me my violin and I'll treat you to a three-course dinner."

"Five-course."

"Seriously?" *Go on, waste another five minutes.*

He gave me a heart-stopping grin and took off at a sprint, dodging pedestrians while scaring a few, before leaping into traffic. A car horn signaled he'd barely missed being hit.

Guilt kicked in. I'd just catapulted a homeless man into some kind of superhero mission. No good deed goes unpunished—and I'd just received the mother of all reminders.

Trudging down the steps of the Underground, I hurried over to where I'd been playing Niccolò Paganini's "Caprice No. 24," a piece no one seemed to recognize, which was one of the hardest to master. I'd literally given my violin away while attending to some homeless guy. Who was to say he wouldn't just take the violin for himself once he got it back...*if* he got it back.

After swiping away a tear, I tried not to let the floodgates open yet so as not to embarrass myself and bring any more unwanted attention my way from strangers. There was a reason you weren't supposed to talk to them.

I closed the lid on my glass jar. It had five pounds in it—the same fiver I'd put in there to entice people to give me tips. I threw the jar irreverently into my violin case and clipped the lid closed. When I hoisted it up, its lightness reminded me of my stupidity.

I couldn't remember how I'd arrived at my stop at Gloucester Street, but somehow I'd made it to the Tube station I always used to get home.

Numbness settled in my bones, but I left my coat hanging open because I deserved to be assaulted by the chill.

I trudged down the pavement, each footstep feeling unbearably heavy as I made my way past the row of terraces to the old Victorian house where I lived. The room I rented wasn't much and the plumbing was noisy, but my bedroom window overlooked the garden. I always enjoyed the view while I practiced my lessons.

How was I going to practice now?

How was I going to explain this to Mr. Penn-Rhodes, my tutor at the Royal Academy of Music, when I faced him tomorrow?

Someone might as well have ripped my right arm off. Playing that violin had gotten me a scholarship into one of the finest music academies, and though it wasn't worth much it had become my world. I'd bonded with it. Loving fingertips had traced each ripple in the wood and each flame in the maple. That instrument had warmed to me personally, too, and like an old friend it always came through.

That instrument *was* my life.

I'd also taught countless children with that precious violin. Those hour-long lessons had been their introduction to one of the most difficult instruments to master. And though teaching helped pay my rent, it also felt good to know I was making a difference.

What the hell was I going to do?

Waves of grief drenched me in sorrow. I'd suffered a terrible violation by a person who had no idea that they'd stolen part of my soul.

Three doors down, Mrs. Kaminski's golden retriever, Charlie, was barking at something. I usually didn't mind him going wild over the occasional horn or even another pet, but today it grated on my nerves.

What was I thinking leaving my precious violin unattended?

"No more Good Samaritan," I muttered.

Unlatching the brass gate that squeaked on its hinges, I continued on between the hedges, trudging down the cobbled pathway that felt uneven beneath the worn soles of my shoes. I lifted my gaze to the door.

No way.

Xander rose from where he'd been sitting on the front steps.

"Hey, Emily." My violin was in his hands. "Forget the five-course. I'm craving a curry."

"How did you…?" *Get here before me.*

He turned the instrument, showing me the front and back. "Undamaged." He held it out to me with both hands.

I set my empty case down and moved quickly to claim it, hugging the violin to my chest as though my lost child had been returned.

My cheeks flushed with relief. "How'd you get it back?"

"Trade secret." A wink of mischief was followed by a drop-dead gorgeous smile.

Wait…how the hell did he know where I lived?

Chapter 3

Six Months Ago

I THOUGHT MY LIFE WOULD FALL INTO A DOWNWARD SPIRAL AFTER MY violin was stolen. To be honest, I'd not believed this stranger could save it. Yet here he was standing in front of me, having delivered what seemed like a miracle. I'd last seen him half an hour ago outside Piccadilly Circus, when he'd sprinted off to save my violin like a beautiful angel stripped of his wings.

His eyes lit up as he grinned. "My good deed for the day. Though nothing tops yours."

I studied him. "Xander, right?"

"Right."

"I never told you my name." I narrowed my gaze on him.

"I don't want to lie to you."

"Then don't."

"You might not like the truth."

"What does that mean?"

He looked toward the gate.

"Did you set me up?" I snapped. "Were you working with the guy who stole my violin?"

"No, I've never stolen anything in my life."

"Then explain."

His crystal blue eyes held mine for what seemed like an eternity. "I'm sorry I scared you."

"I'm still calling the police."

"You can't."

"And why is that?" My foot was poised to kick him in the balls if he made one wrong move.

He let out a deep sigh. "I didn't get the man's name. Your violin thief."

I stepped back. "I need proof you're not working with him. That you didn't do all this so I would feel indebted to you, and the next thing I know you're inside my home stealing my landlord's shit."

He chewed his bottom lip, looking thoughtful.

"I've never been scared of the truth, so spill."

"Sure?"

"Don't underestimate me."

He arched a brow, and then gave a nod. "While you and I were outside the Tube station I used my phone to access the city's surveillance system, training one of the cameras positioned on the corner of Piccadilly Avenue to scan your face. Your name came up in their recognition software." Seeing my look of horror, he added, "At some point you decided to use face recognition to sign in to Facebook. The app recorded the results of your features into its database. All done legally because you clicked the terms of service without reading them. The government buys the data. I have access to it."

The air crackled around us as I processed his admission.

"And that's how you got my name?" I asked, stunned.

"Yes, and then I shifted the camera to train it in the direction I guessed the thief had run."

"How did you know he went left?"

"Most people choose the invariant right. You know, when you walk through a store you usually head right. It's mainly because you're right-handed—"

"He went left."

"His guilt contradicted his instincts."

"How would you know this?"

He shrugged it off. "It's my job to know."

"You did all this in less than a minute?"

He looked surprised at the question.

"Prove it," I said.

"Apparently, you voted Labour at the last election and you're registered to this place." He raised his chin to point to the house. "That's how I got your address. I checked the voter registration."

"No, seriously."

He looked apologetic.

"Isn't it illegal what you just did?"

"Well, you gave me permission when you asked me to get your violin back." He flashed a cute smile. "I had to find you to return it."

Okay…that logic worked, but everything else sounded like a crapshoot of weirdness.

He had me intrigued, though.

It wasn't just his compelling words, it was the way he stood there tall and alluring with those exotic eyes. I could get lost in their pale blue depths. Right now he seemed to be summing me up, too.

I gestured to his phone. "That's a little scary."

"That's nothing. I can also access your Google searches, your buying habits, and if you give me an hour, I'll have you profiled all the way down to what you like to eat and your reading preferences."

I should have been more cautious. This all sounded too far-fetched, but I'd been disarmed by him returning my violin.

He grinned, oozing a charm that could be weaponized. Those full lips were seductive.

I was so damn tired and all day tomorrow I'd be teaching my students violin lessons. I needed to get a good night's sleep. Though there was something about Xander that caused me to linger on the doorstep.

Wait…I did vote Labour.

"It was really nice meeting you, Em."

Only my mum called me that.

He pivoted and continued down the pathway toward the gate. It squeaked as he opened it.

"Where are you going now?" I called after him.

"I just upgraded myself to crazy-guy level ten." He gave a shrug. "This is where I make my exit."

I knelt and opened my violin case, removing five pounds from the jar.

I hurried over to him. "Take this."

Xander looked surprised. "I'm not taking your money." He turned and walked quickly down the pavement.

I followed him. "Xander."

He stopped, facing me. "What now?"

"Show me how you got my violin back."

He blew out a sigh.

That familiar uneasiness swept over me. "Or not."

He mulled it over. "The footage is recorded, so…"

A few swipes later and he held his iPhone up for me to see an aerial view outside Piccadilly. The camera was trained on the line of taxis not going anywhere fast. The footage had recorded us outside the Tube. There I was, looking left and right. It captured nothing of the agony I'd felt. Farther down the street was a man scurrying away with my violin. The thief ducked inside a cab.

What followed was Xander coming into frame in a sprint toward the cab, opening the door and then reappearing with my violin.

I shot Xander a look of concern. "How did you get into their system?"

"It's one of my many talents."

"Are you a hacker?"

"Not technically."

"What do you do?"

"Security." A twist of his lips hinted it was a little more complicated than that.

"Why did you lose your job?"

"Creative differences."

I hesitated only for a moment. "Okay…one night. You can sleep on the sofa."

He lit up with joy. "I'll repay you."

"You got my violin back." My eyebrows rose to let him know that was no small feat. "If I wake up dead tomorrow I'll be pissed."

Xander laughed and followed me back up the pathway. "Tomorrow, I'll have access to money. I'll be able to thank you properly."

"Trust me, you already did." I raised the violin.

Not that I didn't believe him, but we were all one day away from a lucky break that would turn us around. I certainly felt this way.

Reaching into my pocket for my door keys, I rummaged around and then looked up at him. "I rent a room here so bear that in mind."

"I'll be quiet." Xander followed me up the steps. "I appreciate this."

"Of course."

"You're talented. I may have been half asleep, but I recognized 'Caprice No. 24.'"

"You heard me play?"

"A little, yes."

The fact he recognized that piece of music added a new dimension to him in my eyes. He certainly carried himself like someone who was cultured and educated.

It didn't take me long to give him a tour of the house. He was polite enough not to make fun of the country décor with its chintz fabrics, plaid furniture and drapes. Though the kitchen was an improvement, despite my landlord's love for the French provincial style. The numerous gadgets revealed its owner was addicted to cooking shows and I often benefited from this by finding an assortment of Harold's delicious creations in the fridge.

He was away visiting his sister in Edinburgh, but Xander didn't need to know that.

While he used my bathroom to take a shower, I got to work ordering us a curry.

When the take-out arrived, I paid the deliveryman with the money I'd scrounged up. For some reason, getting Xander fed brought out my nurturing side.

I returned to the kitchen and dished out our delicious meal into bowls, placing them on the table. The scent of tomato and spices filled the air.

From the cupboard, I brought down two china plates and pulled out cutlery from the drawer. Then I filled two glasses with water.

"Hey." Xander stood in the kitchen doorway. "That smells amazing."

He looked a lot more than presentable, from his softly tanned skin to those locks of dark gold. The scruff gave him an edgy appeal. He reminded me of European royalty.

"Come sit."

He took a chair at the kitchen table. "Where did you study the violin?"

"The Royal Academy of Music." I was still there.

"That's why you're so good." He reached for a glass and gulped the water.

"Your techy skills are impressive. You'd make a dangerous enemy."

He stared at me. "Someone once told me the same thing. But I'm not like that."

"Glad to hear it."

"Could you get the thief's name?" I watched him carefully.

"Do you want me to?"

With a shake of my head, I let him know I wasn't sure. After handing him the rice dish, I set his chicken tikka masala before him.

He looked like he was saying a prayer. "Thank you. Thank you. Thank you."

"Hungry?"

"You have no idea."

I caught him looking at my nose ring. "Go on then, say it."

"I was going to say you should delete all apps from your phone."

"Hmmm, you sound paranoid."

Xander scooped several helpings of the creamy chicken onto his rice. "The problem with society is they're not paranoid enough."

"Really?"

He paused with his fork to his mouth. "The richest one percent owns more of the country's wealth now than in the last fifty years."

"I'd read that somewhere."

"But what you don't know is the extremes they'll go to in order to keep it that way."

I picked up my fork. "What do you do again…when you're employed?"

"My specialty is computers."

"But you don't hack into them?"

"Not in the way you think." He looked thoughtful. "It's about… communications."

He ate elegantly, and I marveled that a man so hungry didn't shovel in his food.

I took another bite of the chicken and rich creamy sauce and the flavors burst over my taste buds. My stomach grumbled. Usually, when I got home, I'd grab a bowl of cereal or something simple, so this was a nice treat.

I had bailed on making any money tonight by helping him. I'd have to make the cash up after classes when I went out busking again. At least I had a season pass for the Tube so I could get to the Academy.

I turned my attention back on the intriguing man opposite me who was dipping a piece of naan bread into his sauce.

He took another elegant bite and dabbed his mouth with the paper napkin. "So good."

"Who did you work for?"

"Doesn't matter now." He fixed his stare on me. "Where does your family live?

"Mum lives in Devon. Dad left when I was a baby. We don't talk."

"I'm sorry."

I shrugged. "He was in the Air Force. A dashing pilot that my mother fell head over heels in love with. He swept in and out of her life as fast as one of those jets he flew."

"That must have been hard."

I nodded. "Still, she says she has no regrets because he gave her me."

He smiled. "I was in the Army for a while."

"Where were you stationed?"

"All over." He seemed to realize he was being vague. "East Asia."

"What was that like?"

"About like you'd imagine." He turned to the window. "Is your landlord a relative?"

"No, Harold just lets me rent one of his rooms."

"This is a nice home." He looked at me as though wanting to say more.

We finished eating in silence, both of us breaking off naan bread and dipping it in our sauce and swapping appreciative smiles with each other.

Xander carried his empty plate over to the sink and washed it, then took mine from me and loaded the dishwasher.

"How did you end up at Piccadilly?" I asked, joining him at the sink.

He tapped my nose ring. "It diverts attention from your beauty."

A frisson of excitement hit my solar plexus and made me tingle. I wanted to ask him a lot more questions, the kind that would reveal more about him. But he seemed tired and I didn't want to encroach any more on his privacy.

I set Xander up in the front room on the daybed with a duvet and a pillow.

"Sorry, but the TV stopped working last week," I said. "Not sure why."

"I'm just going to crash."

"Feel free to visit the kitchen if you need anything."

"If only everyone on the planet was like you," he said, shaking his head.

"Oh, I'm a little damaged."

"How?"

"I'm an artist. We're kind of temperamental."

"You're not damaged. You're deep. There's a difference."

He didn't know me, but I didn't try to correct him.

"What inspired you to take up the violin?"

"Diana Lucia Zane," I said wistfully. "My mum took me to see her play the violin in London. I was twelve. I fell in love with the instrument that day and never looked back. Diana's my idol. She's from Vienna. Anyway, Mum and I went backstage afterward and I met her. Couldn't say anything. I was too starstruck. She knew it, too. Diana took my hands in hers and stared into my eyes and announced, "You have the hands of a violinist."

Xander remained quiet.

"Mum bought me a violin the following week and got me lessons. That concert changed my life."

The way he stared at me caught me off guard. "What?"

"Which relative of yours is deaf?"

"Why?" I sat back, surprised.

"You lip read. It's not that obvious. I see things most people don't."

"My mum."

His eyes were filled with sympathy. He didn't need to say anything—it was written on his face, his understanding that she'd never hear me play. "She encouraged you anyway."

"She's pretty special."

"That doesn't make you damaged."

"She was protective. Like, super-obsessive about me going out, or making friends, or doing anything that would place me in danger."

"Because she loves you."

"The result is I have a penchant for danger now," I said suggestively.

A rush of adrenaline hit me when he seemed to catch my drift.

He raised his glass in a toast. "Well, it benefited me so thank you, Em's mum."

Xander defused the sexual tension with a friendly smile.

I changed the subject. "She teaches, too…sign language to children."

"Too?"

"I teach violin to kids."

He looked impressed.

I headed for the door. "Good night."

"Emily."

I paused and looked over my shoulder.

"Thank you for this."

His sincerity was the kindness I needed. It felt good to help someone. And I had the sense that he understood me. There was something comforting in that.

I left him to get settled and headed to my room and locked the door.

Letting a stranger sleep under the same roof wasn't one of my better decisions, but somehow I felt like I would be able to rest better knowing I wasn't alone.

The next morning, daybreak flooded into my bedroom and I blinked awake, realizing I'd taken the mother of all risks.And I wasn't about to let my violin out of my sight again.

Wearing my pajamas, I made my way downstairs and pressed my ear to the sitting room door. Sounds of movement revealed Xander was awake. I knocked and then opened the door slightly to peer in. He was doing push-ups on the carpet and only wearing his boxers. He rose off the floor with lightning speed, his back muscles rippling as his biceps tightened. He'd gone from being my dark angel to a ripped God-like figure.

He leaped to his feet when he saw me. "Hey, Emily."

I nudged the door open farther. "How did you sleep?"

"Great. You?"

"Fine."

My gaze slid from his sculpted broad shoulders to his six-pack abs and down to that impressive bulge in his boxers. My tongue moistened my lower lip. "I'll put the kettle on." Blushing, I pivoted and hurried into the kitchen, hoping he'd not noticed me ogling his gorgeousness.

Fifteen minutes later, I left a mug of tea and a fresh egg sandwich for him on a china plate in the center of the kitchen island and returned to my room with my own favorite mug in hand.

I leaped into the shower and raised my face to the rush of hot water to try to forget the memory of seeing him half-naked downstairs.

I'd taken such a risk having a stranger here, but I was kind of lonely. Harold was a generation older and we had little in common other than our love of this place. Hanging out with someone closer to my age had brought the company I'd desperately needed.

Maybe, just maybe, we could be friends. Especially if his homelessness was only temporary. These thoughts filled me with hope as I pulled on my jeans and a blouse and then dragged a brush through my hair.

There was a knock on my bedroom door.

"Come in." I faced Xander as he entered.

"Hey, thank you for breakfast. You didn't need to do that."

"I don't want you leaving hungry."

He looked surprised at that. "I took a look at your TV. One of the cables was disconnected so I fixed it."

"Was that all, seriously?"

"Seriously. I'll put a new battery in the remote and I'll be on my way."

"In there." I pointed to my chest of drawers.

Turning to face the mirror, I checked to make sure my hair was not too unruly. When I turned back, Xander was holding my vibrator.

Oh, God.

"I'm assuming this is yours?" He smiled as he said it.

"The other drawer."

"Ah."

My face was on fire.

He turned it in his hand. "If it's made in China, there's a chance they put a listening device in it."

"Fuck off." I had to laugh.

He bit his lip suggestively. "I'll put it back."

"I don't use it." The words came out before I could stop myself.

"I didn't mean to embarrass you."

"You didn't." I lifted a shoulder. "I mean, I prefer to use it on my clit."

I wasn't scared of my sexuality, even if my flushed face contradicted this. Under different circumstances I would have led him over to my bed and explored his well-toned body. And then done more to him...so much more.

I raised my chin, wanting to shock him. "Sometimes, I put it inside and turn it up to the max."

"Well, that's fine, of course."

A spark of chemistry passed between us and I sensed a shift in his emotions. He looked intrigued.

Then I remembered how I'd met him. "Harold's going to be home."

He placed the vibrator back and closed the drawer.

Here stood a dreamy man whose presence filled the room with a rare aura that was indefinable. If he walked out the door, I'd never see him again.

"Do you have a girlfriend?" I asked.

"I'm not seeing anyone. You?"

I gave him a thin smile. "You could always hack into my bank account and see if I buy dinner for two."

"You should never pay for dinner." Xander looked around my bedroom.

I had a feeling he was trying to find out more about me.

He winked. "If your violin goes astray again. I'll get it back for you."

"How can I contact you if it does?"

"This is why my relationships don't work out. I'm too elusive, apparently."

"What happened?"

"We both wanted more...just totally different things."

"Are you still friends?"

He mulled that over. "There's a connection between us that just won't break."

Someone still had a piece of his heart and it was kind of romantic.

"I've never had that."

"You deserve to be loved entirely. Your lover should make you feel invincible."

"That would be nice."

"Personally, I'm not an easy lover to have," he admitted.

"Why not?"

"I'm into…things." He glanced down at the drawer that held my vibrator.

I wanted to ask for details as a rush of excitement swept through me, making me feel giddy. *God*, if he was into rough sex, I may have met my dream man.

"I should go," he said.

"Best of luck with everything."

"You're the kindest person I've ever met, Emily."

His words filled me with a flush of warmth—like basking in the sun on a summer day.

He moved toward the door. "Thanks again for breakfast. For all of it, really."

"Would you like to…"

Xander shut the door behind him.

Great. We'd ended things on an awkward note.

I stood there replaying our conversation, and let out a sigh of sadness when I heard the front door close. Tentatively, I went downstairs to the hallway and peered through the peephole. Xander was at the end of the garden closing the gate behind him.

I had pushed him away. My love of music had always been my priority, but now I felt a lingering loneliness. As I entered the sitting room, I cursed my coldness.

As I grabbed up the sheets I'd given him, ready to throw them into the washing machine, his soft scent wafted up around me, mixing with the vanilla aroma of my body wash he'd used last night. He smelt like good company. Like a friend I could get to like a lot.

My thoughts returned to that vision of him standing in front of the unlit fireplace, bare-chested and wearing nothing but his boxers. In a daze, my hands caressed my nipples to soothe my longing. It didn't help.

Back in the kitchen, I threw the sheets in the washing machine.

"I'm into things." His words teased me all the way back to my bedroom.

I eased off my clothes and then my panties and bra, my naked body feeling kissed by the cold air as my breaths came short and sharp with anticipation. I removed my vibrator from the chest of drawers and then ran my fingertips over where Xander had touched it. A jolt of arousal overwhelmed me, bringing on a delicious swoon as I lay upon my bed.

As my fingers trailed along myself, I felt the wetness, having been aroused from when Xander had stood only feet away. My clit throbbed as I thought about the way he'd held up my sex toy and caressed its length.

I fired it up, rubbing it along myself. The buzz went deep, making my thighs tremble.

I strummed my sensitized sex delicately at first, mesmerized by the sensations gripping me, my jaw tense, the theatre of my imagination taunting me with forbidden thoughts of Xander doing things to me that were downright dirty.

Losing control, needing to belong to *him* more than I needed my next breath, I squeezed the toy between my thighs to hold it in place and reached up and pinched my nipples, pretending it was Xander whose tongue was lashing me down there. The slow torture of his pleasure proving he possessed me completely.

The memory of him owned my orgasm as I gasped out loud, my body shuddering as I rode out the seemingly endless spasms.

My head hit the pillow as the residual vibrations began to fade. I cupped my sex to prolong the exquisite throbbing.

"I should have let you in," I thought, sending a silent message to Xander.

But it was too late—my beautiful stranger was gone.

Chapter 4

Six Months Ago

Letting Xander into Harold's home last night had been reckless.

I knew nothing about him, not even his last name. The relief I'd felt from getting my violin back had made me high and affected my judgment. It could have gone so differently.

I scanned the sitting room where Xander had slept last night. Even though I didn't know him I missed him. Over there on the carpet, I'd caught him doing those impressive push-ups like he'd stepped out of one of those scorching hot billboard ads you see for high fashion all around the city.

And the TV worked now because he'd fixed it.

I pushed my focus onto playing "Concerto No. 3" by Mozart and this cleansed my musical palate after teaching violin all morning. Three one-hour sessions for teenagers had frayed my nerves. It made me recall my old violin tutor and the patience he'd had as I'd learned to master this instrument.

Notes rose majestically as I pulled my bow across the strings to say what I couldn't say with words. I closed my eyes as the music flowed through me, soothing my soul.

The doorbell rang, snapping me back into time and place. I set down my instrument and bow and hurried to answer the door.

When I opened it, there was no one there.

My focus fell to the steps, where an antique wooden violin case lay at the bottom.

I knelt beside it to take a closer look.

Maybe there was a clue inside to reveal who the case belonged to. I taught all ages, though had one of my students turned up with this I'd have remembered it. The antique design was gorgeous and unforgettable.

I clicked the case open and inhaled sharply, blinking to clear my vision.

A Stradivarius lay within the velvet interior.

Who the hell had left this here?

I ran my fingertips reverently over the maple neck. This beautiful seventeenth century violin was famed for its astounding sound.

Confused, I looked toward the gate, hoping to find someone there who could explain this extraordinary find. I knew it was worth a fortune.

Returning my attention to the violin, I lifted it out of the case with great care. A Sotheby's auction tag was tucked beneath the fingerboard.

Could this be from *him*? The mysterious man who'd entered my life last night and then disappeared? Xander had said that he'd repay me...

It was stupid to think this had anything to do with him. There was another perfectly good explanation. No way could I continue with my day without at least trying to find the rightful owner of the Stradivarius. I knew what it felt like to lose one's most precious possession, and I didn't want anyone else to go through the same grief. Gently, I returned it to the case and shut the lid.

I grabbed the violin, locked up the house, and headed out, following my only clue—the auction tag. It was time to visit Sotheby's.

I put my ear buds in and listened to Demi Lovato sing about not holding on and letting go. With that raw truth reminding me what it was going to be like giving up this priceless violin, I rode the Tube toward Mayfair.

Don't think about keeping it.

This wasn't meant for me.

But I couldn't help but get excited over the thought of owning one of the world's finest violins. There were so few of these in existence that even playing one was a privilege.

New Bond Street reigned with its impressive architecture and decadent shops. The one I was heading for was tucked between Delvaux, a fancy boutique, and Richard Green, a high-end art store.

Above the frontage of Sotheby's hung its blue flag stating the company had been established in 1744. Inside were the kinds of experts who would come running to snatch this off my hands when I told them what was inside. The girl with a nose ring would no doubt cause a riot when she appeared with a Strad.

I stepped into the impressive foyer and was greeted by the receptionist, who glanced at the case. She led me to a door with "Charles Bisbee" stamped on the glass.

Inside the small office sat a sixty-something man wearing a tweed jacket and chatting on the phone. When he saw me, he held up a finger to tell me to wait, while he curiously considered the violin case.

He hung up. "How can I help?"

"I found a Stradivarius…" I waited for his surprised reaction, and then continued. "And I want to return it to its rightful owner."

He leaned back in his chair. "Where did you find it?"

"Outside my house, on the doorstep. I found the Sotheby's auction tag, so here I am."

I opened the case to show him the instrument. Shock settled on his face.

"So you remember it?"

"It's a Strad," he replied, his tone sarcastic.

"Can you tell me the name of the person who bought it?"

He gave me a thin smile that served as a *no*.

"Right…confidentiality. Maybe you can get a message to him?"

"If I see the gentleman again," he said.

"I'm not comfortable keeping it."

"I'm not surprised, considering it sold for a couple of million."

"Pounds?"

"No, breadsticks." He looked over my shoulder. "Are you with the other gentleman who visited after my client left?"

"Who was your client?"

He smiled. "Bravo."

I smirked at my cheekiness. "Who was the man who came after?"

"Didn't leave a name."

I turned and peered out the window with a sigh.

"It was a private sale," he said. "Details sealed."

"Was his name Xander?"

"Sealed, as in private."

"Can you at least give the buyer a message?"

He folded his arms.

I had to wonder if Xander had actually left no way of being contacted.

"Consider this an official report," I told him, snapping the case shut.

He dragged his fingers over his mouth as though thinking this through. "If the owner returns—"

"He knows where I live."

"Take care of that violin." His bushy eyebrows rose with a hint of condescension. "You have something special, young lady."

I raised the case for dramatic effect. "Circa 1645 to 1750 there was a little ice age. During that time tree growth slowed resulting in unusually dense wood. Boom, you get a violin with superior sound."

"True. The wood was also meant to come from cathedrals."

"Debunked."

He nodded, impressed. "You know your violins."

"I do, and it's a shame after talking to you I don't know more."

I headed for the door, having failed miserably to get Xander's contact info.

"Miss? I never caught your name."

I stopped and looked back. "Emily Rampling."

"Sounds like that violin was destined to find you, Emily." His eyes lit up with a smile.

"Not sure about that."

"Someone obviously thinks so."

I glanced past him to the back wall. The old black and white photos hanging in fancy frames revealed Charles Bisbee's passion for instruments. Knowing we had this interest in common, I shared a look of understanding with him before heading out.

I couldn't think of anyone other than Xander who would have given me something so priceless. I'd lost my only chance of contacting him and as my consolation prize I'd received the most incredible gift. Though I still wasn't sure keeping it was an option. Falling in love with a violin this remarkable was a bad idea.

As though part of me wasn't willing to let Xander go, I returned to the place I'd met him.

Beneath the low ceiling of Piccadilly Circus's Tube station, in the same spot I'd played the night I'd met him, I removed the Strad from its case. I made a wish that music would draw him back to me.

The notes echoed with extraordinary beauty. It was a musician's dream, holding an instrument of this quality and history. I was in awe.

It was easy to forget where I was as my soul became one with the violin. I played my heart out for Xander, savoring each note as I recalled every second spent in his company.

Although I imagined him listening to me amongst the crowd, I never saw him.

Closing my eyes, I embraced this instrument that had already stolen a piece of my heart.

The heaviness in my chest made me feel like I'd lost a friend. Of course, there was no logic to this emotional connection, and no reasonable argument why I should suffer this way. I just did.

Chapter 5

Six Months Ago

THREE NIGHTS AFTER MEETING XANDER, I WENT BACK TO THE TUBE station at Piccadilly Circus and reclaimed the exact spot in the ticket area.

I was here to play for him…and him alone.

I still wore my music school clothes—a short tartan skirt, thigh-high tights and flat shoes. I'd not even stopped off at home to change first.

The commuters passing by had no idea they were listening to a two-century old violin. I'd not been brave enough to take this instrument into class at the Academy yet. Girls like me didn't turn up with one of these without arousing suspicion.

I lowered my instrument to my side to take a break, watching the pedestrians flow by. At this time of day, I'd have better luck playing in Covent Garden. But I'd have less chance of seeing Xander.

It was a ridiculous hope, but I clung to it.

A tall man with graying temples stopped in front of me to throw a five-pound note into my case. I gave a bow of thanks and watched him walk away.

I glanced out into the stream of human traffic and glimpsed a familiar face.

Xander.

My heart skipped a beat, and then began to race.

He stood amongst the meandering crowd. Gone were his rumpled clothes. He wore what looked like designer jeans and a black blazer over a nice shirt. A scarf was wrapped around his neck in the sophisticated European style. His looks were more astonishing than I remembered.

The rush of excitement I was feeling suddenly turned into panic.

Xander had turned away and was heading through the turnstile. I watched, dismayed, as he stepped onto a descending escalator, disappearing from view.

Quickly, with trembling hands, I knelt to put my Strad and bow away.

Holding the handle of the case with a tight grip, I rushed toward the escalator that would take me into the heart of the Tube station. I leapt onto the moving escalator, my heart pounding over the fear I was close to losing him.

Xander stepped off the escalator and turned sharply into a tunnel leading to a platform.

I ran beneath the same arch until I made it onto the platform, drawing in sharp breaths when I saw him hop onto a waiting carriage, the doors beginning to close.

I bolted forwards, sprinting through the doors directly in front of me. Even though I'd not be on his carriage, I'd make his train.

Holding onto the handrail and balancing the violin case with my other hand, I felt the Tube rock beneath my feet as it headed down the track. It was soon swallowed up by a tunnel, plunging us into darkness.

When the lights flickered back on, I hurried down the center aisle, peering through the glass divider into Xander's carriage.

As though sensing my stare, he turned his head and looked at me.

This man had been a constant in my thoughts since he'd walked out of my bedroom and I was too caught up in the mystery of him to walk away.

This chase was exhilarating.

A jolt and a shudder signaled the train was changing tracks. It took off down another tunnel. From the worried expressions of the other passengers, I could tell they weren't expecting this either. This wasn't the train's regular route.

Xander stared back at me, raising his phone.

No, I was imagining it. Surely he'd not just changed our direction with his phone.

The train squealed to a stop at a deserted station. Light bulbs flickered like in some old horror movie where you know things were about to go wrong.

The overhead announcement informed passengers that this was not a working platform and it was closed to the public. There had been a "technical glitch" and we were "being re-routed."

With my jaw taut with tension, I watched Xander tap the screen of his phone. The doors in front of him opened and he took a leap onto the abandoned station's platform.

With a whoosh the doors before me parted as well.

Glancing back at the other passengers, my heart jack-hammered over what I was being coaxed to do. From halfway down the platform, Xander held my stare as though challenging me to join him.

I didn't want to see the expressions of anyone witnessing my leap onto the platform with my violin in tow. I ducked, hoping to avoid being seen by the train's driver, and hid behind a pillar, inhaling a steadying breath.

The train pulled away with a screech and headed off into the tunnel. I was left standing alone, the silence only interrupted by the far-off sounds of trains flying by on distant tracks. The echo of the Underground clanged around me.

Xander was gone.

A shimmering vaulted ceiling stretched overhead. My addled mind knew this station had been built in the early part of the nineteenth century. I noticed old stains on the walls from water damage, but the rusted arches above were still spectacular.

Xander reappeared on the track about twenty feet away and I let out a sigh of relief. I hurried towards him, wondering why the hell he was making this so difficult.

I closed in on him. "Did you change the destination of our train?" Even as I spoke those words, I didn't really believe them.

He gave me a provocative smile, which looked a lot like a *yes*.

"Why?"

"Why not?"

"Because those people need to get to their destination."

"A bit of adventure never hurt anyone."

"I'm serious."

"They need to be shaken from their routine. They need to know that one person can make a difference."

Maybe he was some kind of vigilante?

I raised the violin case.

"You deserve even more than that," he said.

"Xander, it's too much!"

He shook his head. "What you did for me—"

"One night on the sofa."

"Emily, you saw me. The real me."

I studied his face. "So…would you like to be friends?"

Though after that trick he'd claimed to pull on the train, he would make a dangerous ex.

He looked conflicted. "A good friend of mine once told me I'm like one of those priceless Ming Dynasty vases. Seemingly perfect, with an invisible crack running through me that makes me deeply complicated."

"Why would she say such a thing?"

"Because *he* knows me."

"I don't believe that about you."

"Don't let this be the good advice you didn't take."

"You're asking me to walk away?"

He pointed. "The exit."

"I made it this far, right?"

"You don't scare easily, do you?"

I ignored that. "You heard me play?"

"It was selfish of me."

"You gave me a Stradivarius."

"Hearing you play makes everything worth it."

"What do you mean?"

He shook his head to avoid answering. "It had to be equal to the kindness you showed."

"That's silly. This violin is worth millions."

"Perhaps I should have done more."

"Oh, stop. Now I owe *you*, Xander."

He looked thoughtful. "This is where we part ways."

"Why?"

"You are everything that is good."

"And I believe that about you."

"My life is...complex."

I wasn't ready to let him walk out of mine. "Did you find somewhere to live?" I asked.

"I did."

"You have enough to eat?"

"Yes, I have access to money now." His gaze roamed over the violin case in my hand. "I'm so happy you kept it."

"I went to Sotheby's."

"I know."

"Did Mr. Bisbee contact you?"

He didn't answer.

"I feel like you and me...we could be more..." There, I dared to say it.

He let out a sigh of frustration. "You may not like my brand of friendship."

"Why?"

He gestured with his chin to an archway. "You'll be able to make it to the street from there."

"Maybe I want to stay down here with you?"

Xander hesitated. "I'm not sure I can give you what you want."

"You've seen how and where I live. My life is simple. I don't need anything other than music."

His expression changed. "We are deliciously wrong for each other."

"How do you mean?"

"We're opposites."

"Doesn't mean we can't be there for each other."

"I like you too much."

"That makes no sense."

"Goodbye, Em." He leaped onto the track, barely missing an electrical rail, and walked away.

Go home. Forget him.

Yet I couldn't keep myself from following him. I clambered onto the track, avoiding the rails. The steel rods could change any second and pin my foot in between, so I leaned on the side and continued on. One misstep and I'd be electrocuted.

I just couldn't lose him again...

Inside the dark tunnel, I saw Xander leaning against the wall as though waiting for me. Shadows danced over his face. This wasn't the most daring thing I had done lately. That was inviting a homeless man back to my place a few nights ago. But this was a close second.

"What point are you trying to make?" I asked, my voice echoing around us.

"I come with a catch."

"What catch?" My flesh tingled at his insinuation that maybe, just maybe, we could be together.

Or maybe I should heed his earlier warning.

Yet he was the adrenaline rush I'd yearned for. The apex of an aliveness I'd long craved.

"Are you a criminal?"

He looked amused. "Other end of the spectrum."

I gestured around us. "Is this a metaphor for how things will be if we're friends?"

"It is."

"When you derailed that train—"

"Didn't derail it. Merely changed its direction."

And that was a metaphor for him changing the path of my life with the power of his allure.

He looked conflicted. "I'm not meant to have this kind of life."

"What kind?"

Those crystal blue eyes held mine.

"You had your heart broken?" I asked.

"How can you make a choice when you don't know what the question is?"

My violin case was heavy, so I leaned it against the wall. "You're still not making much sense."

A train roared by and it sounded so close that I leaped forward to hug him, squishing my face against his chest. He felt like the shelter I'd not known I'd needed.

"Other side," he shouted over the noise.

Relaxing in his arms, I breathed in his heady cologne and closed my eyes, feeling his fingers stroking my hair to comfort me.

The sound of the train receded into the distance, and I peered up at him. "No one has ever been this kind to me."

He curled his hand against my cheek. "I feel like I'm touching something sacred when I'm with you."

"You were bold enough to alter the direction of that train," I said, pulling away. "I raise you my own dare." I turned away from him, facing the wall with my palms pressed on the cold brick, my spine arched in a seductive beckon.

"And you're trying to change the direction of my life, too, apparently," he said huskily.

Far away on another track there came a rumbling of another train, but the noise was pushed out of my mind when I felt the sensation of Xander's hand running down my spine.

Slowly, he eased up my tartan mini-skirt and hitched it above my waist, groaning as he looked at my tight ass.

Metal was screeching on metal somewhere and the vision of sparks glittered in my imagination.

He tugged on my panties. "Can I pull these down?"

"Please." I looked over my shoulder. "Fuck me."

"Anything for you, Em."

My panties were eased down until they reached my ankles. I

stepped out of them. From behind came the noise of a zipper being pulled down. The tip of his cock pressed against my folds as his hand explored between my thighs, his long fingers strumming my clit to make sure I was wet.

He pushed inside me a little, and it made me feel flustered that he was so tall and strong behind me, and I was so vulnerable in this desolate place. I moved back against him so I could bend over more, my breath coming out in ragged gasps.

"Emily," he whispered. "God, how I want you."

This was madness. I was reckless and yet my body screamed to let me have this, have him, to surrender. This kind of thrill was all I'd ever desired and I wanted to believe someone as magnetic as Xander could be mine.

Our scandalous rendezvous was the same scenario I'd fantasized about during those nights when I'd believed he was gone forever.

He shoved all the way in. "Em, you feel more amazing than I thought possible."

The tight feeling of discomfort eased, and my inner muscles clenched him as he began to thrust himself deep inside me.

All those hours I'd spent playing my violin had been me beckoning to him. This was my moment to savor. "Harder."

My palms scraped against the brick, but all I cared about was this slow, steady burning rhythm, the feel of him inside me. I held on to every second, not wanting it to end.

Xander's hips acted like a brilliant piston, verging on violent as he forced himself all the way in and then pulled out, keeping a perfect pace that had me quaking with pleasure. My breasts were swollen, nipples beaded tight, legs trembling from his deep penetration. I felt my slickness dampen my thighs.

He slowed a little and his breaths came short and sharp. "You like me fucking you in the filthy depths of London?"

"Yes."

He reached around and his fingers resumed strumming my clit. The sensations felt delicious.

"We're not meant to be," he purred in my ear. "That's what makes you feel so good."

The titillating sounds of our bodies clashing echoed around us.

Chasing after the high of coming, my legs weakened as Xander wrapped his arm around my waist to hold me against him as he continued his hard thrusting.

My flesh ignited, my mind letting go as my climax caught me up in a frenzy of need as I rode blissful waves of ecstasy.

"How can you make a choice when you don't know what the question is?"

I couldn't finish that thought, couldn't catch my breath, couldn't fathom how a ride on a train had brought me to this erotic encounter. No one could hear my moans in the darkness and I wouldn't have cared if they did. I let go, escaping the here and now...

Afterward, I leaned against the wall, catching my breath and marveling at how this man had come back into my life. It was fitting really, that we'd found each other again like two meteors randomly clashing together.

But not by chance...by careful seduction; both of us equally guilty in this dangerous dance of temptation.

Xander caressed my skin as he pulled my panties back on and tugged my skirt down. He spun me around and pulled me into a hug.

I swooned with happiness.

Us. It felt so right.

"I see *you*, Emily," he whispered. "And I really like what I see."

A rush of contentment made my heart soar. He saw the real me and not the shy student who could appear standoffish. All I yearned for was the chance to connect.

"Promise me you'll never ask about my past."

I didn't hesitate. "I promise."

He held me tightly against him. "Us, like this, is all I can give you, Emily. Will this be enough?"

It already is.

Chapter 6

Six Months Ago

XANDER PAUSED BEFORE HIS FRONT DOOR WITH HIS KEY POISED, AS though reconsidering.

"Everything okay?" I whispered, looking for a sign he'd changed his mind about bringing me home after our incredible sex in the Underground an hour before.

I'd played my violin hoping to see him again and the spell I'd cast with my music had led me here. I was anxious to see where he lived.

Just a few days ago, I'd found him homeless at Piccadilly, so it was reassuring he'd found a place already. I expected it to be bare. Maybe he'd let me help decorate.

Gordon House was smack bang in the middle of Baker Street. The elegant foyer had tipped me off that he'd found somewhere incredible. The inside of this building was just as grand as its street façade, the vertical columns giving away its Victorian heritage. Even his front door was carved with expensive molding.

It was more than obvious that only the rich could afford to live here.

With a twist of his wrist and a smile to lessen the tension, he turned the key and we were in.

We stepped into an open-plan design—the place was fully furnished.

Masculine tones dominated his abode. A large brown leather couch was accompanied by matching dark wood furniture. Sprawling floor-to-ceiling windows let in the street light. I counted ten chessboards placed around the room, their chess pieces scattered across squares as though he were mid-game in all of them.

"Are you playing these at the same time?" I asked.

He looked surprised at the question. "Yes."

"Doesn't it strain your brain?"

Instead of answering me, he eased my violin case out of my hand and set it on the dining room table.

"You play chess with people online?"

His eyes met mine. "My opponent is online, yes."

That made me pause. "Do you live alone?"

"No, my wife's taking a bath. She can't wait to meet you."

"What?"

Xander rolled his eyes. "Yes, I live alone," he said. "You've already asked me if I was in a relationship."

"You could have a roommate."

"That's not what you insinuated."

I shrugged, and then said, "The chessboards are a little unusual."

"So am I."

"Well, I like that about you."

His frown softened and he flashed a disarming smile.

"This place came furnished?" I asked, looking around.

"The stuff's all mine."

The furniture was arranged neatly around us, his taste classic and warm with dark brown and cream fabrics and antique leather chairs that had an "old boys' club" charm. There was a print of the world on the back wall, opposite a fireplace. A smart TV sat above it to round out the well-traveled and techy feel.

"This is lovely."

"What are you really thinking?"

"Excuse me?" Then I got his meaning. "You're wealthy."

"Does that offend you?"

"Why would it?" *But why were you sleeping in the Underground?*

"You don't come from money. There's bound to be pre-conceived ideas."

"You say exactly what you think, don't you?"

"Money means power. That can intimidate."

I smiled. "Everyone is equal as far as I'm concerned."

"Not equal in trauma, though."

"How do you mean?"

"The most powerful are the most traumatized, usually." He studied me. "It's that sense of drive that escalates them. Read any biography and you'll see evidence of deep-seated issues. Think of the last few presidents. All of them deeply affected by painful childhoods."

From what I could remember about them, he was probably right. "Have you been traumatized, Xander?"

"I'm well adjusted." He raised his hand before I could speak. "Even though you found me sleeping in the Underground."

My head eased back when his finger traced my nose. "I took it out."

"I can see that." He looked concerned. "Not because of me, I hope."

"I just fancied a change," I lied.

"For God's sake, don't change, Em." He blinked at me in surprise. "I need you to stay exactly as you are."

"I will."

He looked around his home. "They let me move in right away. And then I walked into Heal's and told them I needed same day delivery."

I loved that furniture store. I had strolled around it once hoping to have this kind of stuff in my home one day—a pipedream.

Xander took my hand. "I keep wracking my brain trying to think of how to thank you for being so kind to me at Piccadilly. You let me sleep at your place and you paid for my meal. You were there for me and you didn't even know me."

"You gave me a Stradivarius," I replied flatly.

"That was nothing."

"I've never been given a gift like this." I glanced over at the violin on the table, still stunned it was mine.

"You're a good person, Em. But I'm not."

"Yes, you are."

Guilt washed over his expression.

"What's wrong?"

"Once you see beyond the curtain there's no going back."

"How do you mean?"

"Seeing how things really are in the world."

"I know a lot of bad things happen," I replied, wishing I knew what he was really trying to tell me.

He let go of my hand, staring down at me. "The world needs more people like you."

A frisson of excitement rushed over me. I was here, with him, and the thought he was back in my life made me giddy with happiness.

"Want a drink?"

"Yes, please."

I followed him into the spacious kitchen area. Xander removed what looked like an old bottle of red wine off a rack. The glass had scratchy white writing on the side. With a pop, he uncorked the Château Lafite.

I stepped closer. "Is that date right?"

He studied the scrawled numbers on the side...1757. "Must be a mistake." He licked his bottom lip as he looked up at me. "I'm sure it tastes fine."

"You have this place looking amazing."

"You're amazing, Em. I'm impossible to catch. Yet here you are drinking my wine."

"I'm sure it's delicious, too."

"My work is everything." He handed me a glass. "Just so you know."

I held the glass by the stem. "I'm just as passionate about music."

"I love that about you." He strolled over to a door that led to a pantry. Inside was enough food to feed a family, with cheese, tubs of caviar, and heaps of cereal boxes. He brought out a packet of chocolate biscuits, opened it, and poured them onto a plate.

"You're well stocked up."

"I'm about to go balls deep into a project." He widened his eyes.

"Sorry."

"I get it." I gave him a kind smile. "Everything is okay now?"

"Yes." He gestured around him. "As you can see, I'm settled. Good to go on work and play." He bit his lower lip suggestively.

I took a sip of red wine to hide my flushed cheeks. The vintage tasted of rich blackberries with a hint of flowers. I couldn't taste the alcohol, though, and that meant it was a good wine.

He smiled. "Let it breathe."

I set it down. "Are you from London?"

"Buckinghamshire."

"Are your parents still alive?"

"Mum is, yes."

"Do you get to see her a lot?"

"Not as much as I should. How about you?"

"I owe Mum a visit. Haven't been home to Devon in a couple of months."

"She must be proud of you."

"She doesn't know I busk, though." I gave a shrug.

"She has nothing to worry about with you."

I cringed. "She kind of does, obviously."

I mean, an hour ago he'd been banging me in one of the Underground's tunnels.

As though reading my mind, he said, "Best sex I ever had." His comment lightened the moment.

I cleared my throat. "Can I ask you something?"

"Sure."

"Why were you sleeping rough?"

He considered his answer. "I was…avoiding someone."

"Who hurt you?"

"My ex-employer didn't want me to leave."

"Why?"

"Because I'm good at what I do. I worked for an organization that's very influential." He set his glass down. "Be right back."

My curiosity was piqued. I wanted to know what kinds of things a man could accumulate in two days. Walking down a short hall, I reached an office that had three sleek computer monitors positioned on a long central desk. A leather swivel chair sat before it. I imagined Xander moving from one screen to the other as he multitasked. Maybe he was into stocks and shares. It would certainly explain where all his money came from.

The back wall had two shelves. The only picture displayed was of an attractive woman in her mid-forties. She looked so much like Xander. The lady was wearing wellies and a sleeveless green vest—posing in a quaint village and looking like the ultimate country lady with a black Labrador by her side. I peered closer, squinting, and read the sign on the post office's wall. The town was Great Missenden.

With a jolt I realized Xander was standing at the door.

"I wasn't snooping."

He smiled. "I put our drinks in the sitting room."

We made our way back and I picked up my wine glass from the coffee table. Then I strolled over to the window and stared out. The building opposite was just as dramatic as this one. Below was a row of the finest stores, people hurrying by.

"It's an amazing view."

"I like it."

"This place is enormous."

"You don't make friends easily, do you?"

Feeling ashamed, I kept my focus on the street.

"That wasn't a criticism, Em." He walked over to me. "I'm the same way."

"You are?"

"When I was growing up, I'd spend most of my time in this tree-house at the bottom of the garden. At night I'd hear all these weird noises. We lived in this Old Vicarage and I was convinced it was haunted. Overactive imagination."

"I believe in ghosts," I said.

"I grew out of all that. Now I believe in science." He shook his head. "You can see why I'm crap at parties."

"Was that photo in your office of your mum?"

He flashed a wary look my way.

"She's beautiful."

"When my parents realized their son was different, they put me in boarding school."

"How were you different?"

"I learned to read at the age of two."

"You were a toddler?"

"Yes, I was solving complex math equations at that age, too."

"Seriously?"

He nodded, beaming. "I was a hoot at Tesco's, apparently. Telling everyone in the checkout line how much they could expect to be paying for their groceries."

"That's kind of funny."

"Yeah, well, Mum didn't share your sense of humor."

"What was your childhood like?"

"I'd outgrown kindergarten before I even made it there."

"So being with the other children was…"

His expression turned vulnerable, as though he was remembering what it felt like to be that little boy again.

"I suppose you're a genius," I said.

He offered no response, seemingly waiting for me to continue. "Well? Is this where you ask me to prove it?"

"No need." Balancing my wine in my right hand, I pulled him into me with my left. "Give me a hug."

"Gladly."

I rested my face against his chest. "That's for all those times you felt out of step with the world."

"Oh, Em."

"Thank you for letting me in," I whispered.

"How the hell did I find you?"

"I found you, remember?"

"Stay tonight," he said. "I like you being here."

Chapter 7

Three Months Ago

FINGERS TRAILED ALONG MY BARE SHOULDER, DRAWING ME OUT OF sleep. He played with my hair as I awakened to the dreamy comfort of our warm king-sized bed. It had been three blissful months of this...me waking up beside Xander.

"Hey." I stifled a yawn.

He gave me a heart-stopping smile. "Hey."

"It's Saturday," I realized, feeling relieved and happy.

It meant we could stay in bed longer. The day was ours.

"How long have you been awake?" I asked, stretching luxuriously.

"An hour."

And he'd just been lying here with me, content.

"What's it like?" he said softly. "Being able to play the violin the way you do?"

That made me smile. "I started so young, I don't know any different."

"No." That answer didn't satisfy him. "What's it like knowing you're the one that's creating that incredible music?"

"Oh." I tried to shake off my sleepiness. "It feels like the music is coming through my body. Like something sacred is becoming a part of me from the second my bow touches the strings, as though I'm merely a vessel."

"A vessel," he repeated wistfully.

"How about you?" I reached over and touched his beautiful face.

"I lose time when I'm in the zone."

"Me too."

His eyes lit up. "They say that's true bliss…and I believe it."

I'd been telling myself I should know more about what he did. It always sounded so vague and complex when he talked about it. One day I would sit on his lap and watch him work in his office.

"I get this sense that I was born for this exact purpose," I said softly.

"I never told you that I play an instrument."

"You do?"

He bit his lip seductively. "Yes, I play the Emily."

I giggled.

His fingertips trailed the length of my spine and rested on my ass cheek, then moved downward to caress and tease my sensitive flesh, causing sparks of pleasure. My lower body moved languidly with his strokes as he pressed two fingers through my folds and eased them into me.

"There will be more practice," he said huskily.

"Happy to hear it."

"You're so wet."

"Oh, God." My ass lifted in response to his intoxicating touch.

"How's that?" His fingers teased me.

"I have this theory," I whispered, "that before a soul leaves heaven for its time on earth it makes a pledge with God. No matter how much we beg or plead to be freed of our pain, he won't rescue us from it."

"You're very chatty this morning."

"No, listen—" It was a thought I had to get out.

Firm fingers found my G-spot as though trying to distract me from my musing.

Breathless, I continued, "Because our suffering brings us closer to the divine. And it's through the divine we create art. And through art we touch God."

"You're *my* idea of divine." His rhythm became faster now, more insistent, bringing exquisite pleasure. "I want to barricade the door and not let anyone in."

That was kind of romantic, but I didn't say it out loud. I was so enraptured with bliss I was close to forgetting my own name. His thumb was now inside me and his fingers were languidly circling my clit.

"I love you." He pressed his lips to my shoulder. "Never forget that."

I ascended once more to a dizzying height.

"Em, your music makes me transcend time."

Rising into my orgasm, I breathed, "That's how I feel about you."

Chapter 8

Three Days Before
The Savoy

I'M ENGAGED." I TOOK A SIP OF MY TEA AND WAITED FOR KITTY TO react.

My drink tasted of sweet vanilla and I mulled over buying a box for Xander before we left the café. He'd love this.

"Em, that's incredible!" Kitty smiled brightly. "Let's grab that booth over there and you can tell me how he proposed."

Kitty Adair had drawn the attention of every warm-blooded male in the café. She'd gotten her exotic looks—super high cheekbones and her tall, lean frame—from her Tibetan mum and American father. Kitty looked like a fashion model, but she wasn't. She worked as a manager at Selfridges and it was her sense of fashion that landed her the job, she'd told me.

Even when she dressed down, Kitty was well put together. My student budget wasn't as generous as her salary. Still, I was spoiled by Xander who loved to take me shopping. The ripped jeans and halter-neck blouse I was wearing at least made me less self-conscious around this glamorous fashionista.

"Okay, tell me how he did it?" She sipped her tea.

"In the Underground...where we met." No way was I going to share with her that it was in the same spot I'd found him homeless at Piccadilly.

Xander had chosen that exact place because it meant so much to him. He'd told me, while on bended knee to propose, how quickly he had fallen in love.

"Afterwards, he took me to see *Hamilton* and then we'd had dinner in Alain Ducasse at The Dorchester."

Impressed, she raised her hand. "No one can get a table in that place."

"I didn't know that," I confessed.

"How long have you been seeing him now?"

"Six months."

And I'd only met Kitty a month ago, so we were still getting to know each other. She was studying me as though trying to fish for gossip. We'd become fast friends when I'd been busking in Covent Garden. Xander didn't like me doing it so I'd finally relented and stopped, but those public performances had helped get me used to playing before crowds.

During my last public performance in Covent Garden, Kitty had stood close by and watched me play. Each time I ended a piece of music she'd thrown in five pounds.

Her enthusiastic clapping had won me over and afterward she'd invited me to have coffee with her in The Black Penny—the same café where we'd chosen to meet today.

I found it hard to make friends at the Academy and there was something about her that was so insta-friendly, I'd hardly had to try.

She wriggled in her seat with excitement for me. "No ring yet?"

"I don't wear it to music school."

"Bet you look cute together." She wrapped her hands around the cup. "What does he do again? You never talk about him."

"Tech."

"Does he work from home?"

"Yes."

"That's good. What kind of tech?"

I didn't exactly know but wasn't going to admit it. "Communications."

"Does he have a nice office?"

"Very." I sat back and looked out at the passersby. "I feel like he once had this whole different life before me."

"People do, right?"

"I suppose."

"Does he seem happy?"

"Yes, I guess." That was a strange question and I called her on it. "Why do you ask?"

"Just want someone who is upbeat and supportive of you, that's all."

"He supports my career."

"Good." Kitty peeled off a curl from her paper cup. "You're living with him now?"

"Yes, we're on Baker Street."

"Oh, I love Baker Street."

"Me too, so very Sherlock Holmes."

"Nice flat?"

"More than nice. There's a great view of the shops from our sitting room window. I want you to visit. Let me talk to him about a good day to have you over."

"I'd love that. Are you in that modern building that just sprang up in Regent's Park?"

"No, it's that old-fashioned building with gorgeous architecture. He has lovely taste."

"Oh, I think I know it." She flicked her fingers to show it was on the tip of her tongue.

I answered for her. "Gordon House."

"Oh, he's rich then!" She laughed.

"I don't know about that."

Kitty gave a thin smile. "How's your studies?"

"Great." I leaned forward. "Mr. Penn-Rhodes set me up with my audition for the London Symphony Orchestra. This Friday." Even as I spoke those words, I could hardly believe them.

"Wow. Exciting. How do you feel about it?"

"Really good, actually."

"You'll blow the competition out of the water."

"I hope so."

"And then you'll go on to the next audition?"

"Yes." I sat back. "You know about the process?'

"Let's meet for drinks on Wednesday. We're going to Dandelyan."

"We?"

"Some friends. It'll be a girls' night out."

"Oh, okay."

"It's my birthday, actually."

"Then I can definitely go." It was her birthday, after all.

"It's two nights before your audition so it won't interfere with it." She reached over and squeezed my hand. "You're talented, Em. No matter what happens, you'll always have your music."

"What does that mean?"

Kindness softened her eyes. "You'll always be okay." She looked down at her phone.

"Something important?" I asked.

"My boss wants me to call him." She pushed to her feet and stared at me for the longest time. "I have to go."

"Oh, that's fine. Are you going back to Selfridges?"

She launched the strap of her Louis Vuitton over her shoulder. "You're a good person, Emily."

Kitty strolled out without looking back.

My phone pinged. It was a text from Xander: *Dinner 8? I'm cooking.*

I squeezed my phone to my chest as a thrill made me shudder deliciously. God, I loved this man. We'd made a home with each other in his one-time bachelor pad and not a day went by I didn't thank God for this life. *For him.*

Half distracted, I watched Kitty climb into a black SUV.

The car sped off into traffic.

Chapter 9

The Savoy

I LOOKED AROUND THE RESTAURANT'S OPULENT INTERIOR, BRACING MYSELF in case I saw Xander with another woman.

The quiet place was nearly empty.

Ten or so striking men sat around a corner table, all wearing elegant suits and each nursing a glass of bourbon as they chatted. The empty bottle of liquor sat in the middle of the table.

And there he was…my Xander in his tailored-to-perfection Savile Row ensemble that included a pair of highly polished Oxfords. He lifted an ice-filled glass to his lips and finished off his drink in one gulp.

I saw him set his tumbler down, as though sensing me behind him.

Feeling embarrassed over gate-crashing such a formal elitist gathering, I spun around to bolt and nearly ran into the maître d'.

"I'm so sorry, sir," she said, capturing everyone's attention.

I cringed inwardly, facing them with a wave. "Hey."

Surprised disappointment flashed across Xander's face as his crystal blue eyes narrowed, and I saw dread reflected in those dazzling eyes. A chill slithered up my spine, my forearms prickling.

Xander threw a look of concern over to one of the men.

I followed his line of sight, blinking at the striking vision of the thirty-something man staring back. Complex emotions bubbled up inside me, a sense of my rising insignificance in contrast to the man's profoundness. I snapped my attention away from the glare of his raw beauty.

Then, daring to look back, I let his chestnut gaze capture mine and lost myself in what seemed like a multitude of worlds, all touched by privilege.

His hypnotic stare held me transfixed as the room and everyone around us disappeared. I studied his perfect features, his regal nose and full sensuous mouth. Raven-black hair framed his devastatingly chiseled features.

His intense scrutiny took my breath away.

He pushed to his feet with a deadly grace. He was tall, a couple of inches more than Xander's six-foot-two. Versace-clad broad shoulders made him stand out and when he tilted his head with intrigue, he held the silence hostage, commanding the room.

The way the other men deferred to him with reverence confirmed he had the authority. He was the only one not wearing a tie and his shirt collar fell open casually. For some reason that made him look all the more powerful...

He stood there, exuding power while looking my way, his voice deep and penetrating. "This must be Emily," he said seductively.

"She's no one." Xander shot me a look of concern.

My throat constricted and I tasted gin on a wave of nausea. Xander had virtually denied he knew me.

My fiancé rose to his feet. "Excuse me, James...gentlemen."

The female maître d' stepped up to Xander. "Sorry for the interruption."

"Go away," he snapped, grabbing my arm.

It was hard to know what upset me more—being dismissed by him in front of his friends or being man-handled.

"You're hurting me," I muttered.

"Not here." Xander pulled me out of the room and hurried me down the green carpeted hallway. He stopped abruptly. "What are you doing here?"

"It's Kitty's birthday, remember?" I pointed at him. "I could ask you the same thing."

He squeezed his eyes shut. "Your best friend is trouble."

"What? No, she didn't expect to see you either."

He looked furious. "Why didn't you tell me you'd be here?"

"Told you last night."

"You were going to Dandelyan."

"Well, we decided to come here, too." *Obviously.*

"You've been drinking?"

"To celebrate her birthday."

"You never left your drink alone, right?"

"What? No."

"I need you to go," he said. "Right now."

"Kitty's at the bar with the others—"

"I don't care."

The maître d' hovered uncomfortably. "Mr. Rothschild, can I help at all?"

He glared at her. "I told you to go away. So, go away."

She opened her mouth to reply, but then scurried off.

"Don't speak to her like that," I said irritably.

His left eye twitched and then he delivered a lie. "Emily, I will explain later."

"Why are you here?"

He sighed heavily.

"I left Kitty to find the loo and saw you. Who are those men? Why didn't you introduce me? Are you embarrassed?"

"Don't be ridiculous." Xander glanced down the hallway and cringed.

I saw why…

James was making a beeline toward us.

It was impossible not to be mesmerized by his sophistication. I wondered if he was a wealthy businessman needing Xander's help with something tech related. I'd stepped into an interview, maybe? Or a business meeting?

At least Xander's not cheating, so there's that.

When he reached us, James' light cologne stirred something taboo within me and I exhaled slowly to hide the heady effect it was having on my senses.

"I'm coming back," Xander said, before his friend could speak.

"One minute, that's all I need."

"Are you going to introduce us?" asked James.

Xander gestured towards me. "She's leaving."

James arched a brow.

No, he wasn't going to get away with pretending I was nothing to him and my glare told him that. Not when I was wearing his diamond engagement ring and certainly not when I was living with him.

"James, give us a second," Xander said.

"Only wish I could."

"Don't do this." Xander was seething.

"Disobedience is answered harshly," he replied with a drop-dead gorgeous smile.

My breath hitched and the axis beneath my feet tilted as I reached out to the wall to steady myself. It was the booze, along with the effect this mysterious stranger was having on my fiancé that had me feeling off kilter.

Xander caught my arm. "You okay?"

I nodded, but my lingering stare warned him that I didn't like his friend one bit—even if my body disagreed. In my alcohol-fueled haze, I wondered how this man's kiss would feel and if his lips would leave a bruise.

He looked like he'd take a woman roughly, in contradiction to his suaveness. My imagination went one further and played out the scenario of him peeling off that expensive suit so his ripped body could get skin to skin with the woman he'd seduced into his bed.

Oh, God.

And I was worried that Xander was cheating!

"I'm James Ballad." He held out a well-manicured hand in greeting.

Reaching out, I accepted his handshake. He held my hand for a beat too long; his touch sending tingles up my forearm. My soft flush rose at the way he fixed his masterful stare on me. The way his fingers swept over my palm as he let go caused my breath to catch in my throat.

"And you are Emily, right?" he finally said.

"Yes."

"The one you gave it all up for," James added, sending a glance Xander's way. His focus returned to my face. "Have you set a wedding date yet?"

"No," I replied.

Xander had gone pale. "She's leaving."

James looked at him. "So soon?"

"My friends are at the bar," I explained.

James smiled. "It's Kitty's birthday, right?"

Had I told him that?

"Okay, that's it," snapped Xander. "We're both leaving."

"We're not done." James' pleasant expression belied the tone of his voice.

My stare hopped from one man to the other and I couldn't work out who was more intense...Xander with his antsy attitude or James with his laser-sharp stare, which had landed back on me.

"I'm thrilled to finally meet you, Em," he said. "You've been kept hidden away."

Xander's hand shot up to me in a warning not to say anymore.

James' gaze swept over me appraisingly. "Would you like to join us for drinks?"

I flashed a wary glance in the opposite direction. "Kitty's waiting."

"Tomorrow," said Xander. "I'll come back and meet you here to-morrow, James."

"I want to believe you," he replied darkly.

I could feel the tension between them, which left me confused.

James caught it. "Xander's quite protective of you."

A sudden fear made my stomach feel queasy. *Protective?*

"That's what you do for friends," snapped Xander. "You do every-thing you can to make them happy."

"She's melted that steely heart of yours." James straightened to his full height. "I approve."

Xander leaned back casually against the wall. "Remember, I have what you want." His eyes spoke the rest.

"And you need to remember your oath, Xander."

"I am seriously considering coming back."

"This would please me. *If* I believed it."

Xander's nod carried the weight of his sincerity. "Assure me that there won't be any consequences."

His dangerous friend gave a nod of approval. "Good, then it's agreed. I'll deal with the details."

"You didn't answer me," said Xander quietly.

Something vicious passed between them, a connection so deep they could share a thought.

James zeroed in on me. "Again, it was a pleasure to meet you, Emily."

"Likewise," I fibbed.

James strolled back the way he'd come.

"Promise me!" Xander called after him.

"I'll consider it," James said without looking back.

Seeing Xander emotionally tortured made my chest tighten.

"Who is he?" I whispered.

His attention stayed on James until he was out of sight, then he pressed me back against the wall. "Emily, I need you to go to The Biltmore. Book a room for us. Wait for me—"

"What about Kitty?"

"Don't say goodbye. Don't let her see you leave. Don't tell her where you're going."

So fucking weird.

"All my things are at home," I said.

He rested a hand on my forearm. "Look, I need time to talk with James...sort things out."

"Sort what out?" *I'm not going to a hotel.*

I had my first audition on Friday with the London Symphony Orchestra. No way was I missing it. I'd spent years working toward this goal. I had to be focused and I couldn't allow any distractions to ruin my chance.

Hugging myself, I said, "Xander, please tell me what's going on."

"Take a taxi. Don't use Uber. Understand?"

"Do you owe him money?"

"No."

"Who are those men?"

"They don't exist. And if you don't leave right now, neither will you."

"What does that even mean?"

"Keep your voice down." He rubbed his brow. "Trust me…this is nothing I can't handle."

"What did you do?" I asked, my voice trembling.

"We'll talk later. I have to go."

"What did you mean about going back to work for them?"

He shrugged, looking frustrated.

I felt a stab of doubt. "When I first met you—"

"Not now—"

"You were running from someone. Tell me it wasn't him?"

"I said we'd talk later."

"You're scaring me."

He cupped my face with his palms. "Emily, I've done nothing wrong. I need you to believe me."

Even if he was innocent, he'd brought these sinister men into our lives.

He pulled me into a hug. "Don't use your phone. Don't use your credit cards. Don't order room service. Book us under the name Wells. I'll find you."

"How can I check into a hotel without money?"

He let me go and reached into his wallet, whipping out a gold American Express card. "Use this."

Accepting it, I blinked at the name H. Wells on the plastic. Then I remembered.

"As in H.G. Wells?"

"Yes. It's a secret account."

My flesh chilled. "Are you involved in something illegal?"

"I told you, no." He glanced toward the restaurant. "The Biltmore. Go." Xander pinched my chin. "Am. I. Understood?"

"Yes." It came out sounding like a question, and I had so many more as I watched him walk back to join James and the others.

I needed to know who that man really was and why he was intent on wielding his authority over my boyfriend.

A fun evening had gone downhill fast.

Turning, I headed down the hallway in the opposite direction, resisting the urge to look back. The grand foyer buzzed with hundreds of well-dressed guests as I double-checked that none of my friends could see me making an exit. Kitty was going to be furious that I'd walked out on her. Not to mention worried as hell.

I hated doing this. Walking out on my friends would be as rude as it got.

I paused in the foyer.

Do the right thing.

Heading back to the bar, I was intercepted by the same maître d' whose advice I'd rejected. I wished I'd never walked through that damn restaurant door.

She greeted me more brightly than I deserved. "Excuse me, Ma'am."

"I'm sorry for my boyfriend's behavior," I said. "He's overtired."

She handed over a business card. James Ballad was stamped in gold lettering above a phone number.

My eyes rose to meet hers.

"You're to call him," she said flatly.

A chill rushed up my spine. "When did he give you this?"

"An hour ago."

I offered it back like it was something toxic, but the maître d' spun around and quickly crossed the foyer.

I flipped over the business card and read the handwritten note.

Good luck with your audition on Friday, Emily.
—James

Clutching the card to my chest, I hurried toward the hotel's door, a fearful rush of adrenaline making me unsteady in my high heels.

The stark chill of the evening met me when I stepped outside onto the pavement, the grittiness of the city wafting like invisible smog.

A taxi pulled up and I headed fast toward it.

There was something terrifyingly provocative about James. The way he'd interacted with us had revealed his charisma. Xander had looked at him with a mixture of awe and trepidation and there'd been something else in his expression, too. Something I couldn't define. I'd never seen him like this before, full of anguish and uncertainty.

All I wanted to do was go home, climb into bed, and forget this day had ever happened.

Chapter 10

WHILE STANDING INSIDE THE FRONT DOOR TO OUR SPACIOUS FOUR-bedroom flat, I listened for a noise, wanting to make sure I was alone.

There was nothing like a threatening interaction with a stranger to sober you the hell up. Leaving Xander behind at The Savoy had been a mistake. One I'd regretted the moment I'd climbed into that taxi.

I'd also walked out on Kitty, which was the kind of thing only crap friends did. It wasn't like me to let people down. Now, I had an evening of texting apologies and trying to explain away my strange behavior—if I was willing to break the rules and use my frickin' phone. Later, when Xander got to The Biltmore and discovered I wasn't there, I'd have to face his wrath. That thought had my stomach twisted in knots.

Entering the deafening silence of the dark living room, I waited for my eyes to adjust. I knew well enough not to turn on the lights yet. Scanning the place for any evidence someone had been here, I couldn't believe how unsettled I felt in my own home.

Tonight, I'd let Xander down monumentally by allowing him to return to that room with that threatening man and his sinister innuendoes. If my fiancé wasn't back soon, I was going to back to The Savoy to find him.

A shiver of uncertainty made my skin crawl. This was meant to be our safe place, our sanctuary. Xander's one-time bachelor pad had morphed into a cozy home for two after he'd asked me to move in with him six months ago. I'd left that rented room on Gloucester Street, grateful to be swapping it out to live with my dream man in Marylebone. Xander made life close to perfect. Though, like anything that resembled perfection, it had apparently all been an illusion. Until now I'd seen no end to our contentment.

I wanted to climb into bed and not get out until I knew all this was behind us.

The ten carefully spaced chessboards remained in place. But the pieces could have been moved and I wouldn't have a clue. The furniture was untouched, as were the black and white prints Xander had taken from his travels that hung artfully on the brick walls, including photos from Paris, Milan, and New York. A constant reminder of his worldliness and the fact he'd traveled extensively, unlike me.

But now I realized there were so many things I still didn't know about him. Perhaps I didn't know him at all.

Walking from room to room, using only the dusky moonlight flooding in through the windows to guide my way, I checked each room with an unhealthy dose of paranoia.

I peered under our bed and poked around in the cupboards, then quickly moved on to the spare room to check in there, too.

Xander's office was secure and his three computer screens were still there. How he worked on all three at the same time was mind-boggling, but I'd watched him do it, swiveling in his desk chair as his focus jumped from one screen to the other. This was why he loved playing chess, he'd told me, so he could unwind from the intensity of what he did in here.

I only had a vague sense of what that was. Something tech-related, something about networks and conversations and translations and all the other things he'd told me that had my eyes glazing over. I tried to show an interest but his tech-speak was beyond me.

Finishing my walkthrough, I tossed my handbag onto one of the chairs and plopped down on the couch, dragging a throw over my legs and resting my feet on the coffee table. I didn't want to go to bed yet. I wasn't sleeping until Xander got home.

I pulled out my phone and sent him a text to let him know I'd bailed on The Biltmore. Then I rested my phone face up on the coffee table so I'd see his reply.

With heavy eyelids, I fought sleepiness, getting up only once to pee and grab a glass of water before returning to my spot on the couch. My head pounded with the stress of waiting as I replayed my interaction with James.

Half in a daze, I set the tumbler on a coaster and watched the condensation on my glass of water evaporate.

The front door slammed.

I sprang up, my heart pounding as those haunting hours at The Savoy slithered back into focus.

"Xander?" Staring toward the foyer, I waited for him to appear while mentally counting the seconds it took to walk the distance.

The wall clock showed it was eleven-thirty.

The only noise I could hear was my own breathing.

A shadow fell over the tall man's face as he appeared and a scream tore from me...

"I went to The Biltmore," Xander snapped. "That was a waste of time I don't have."

I put a hand to my throat. "You scared me." My heart was pounding. "I texted you and told you I was here."

"What did I tell you, Emily?"

I blinked in confusion. "I thought you meant not to call or text anyone else. You didn't say anything about messaging you."

"I told you not to use your phone." Xander ran a hand through his hair in frustration.

"Tell me they didn't hurt you?" I said softly.

He shook his head. "That will only happen if they don't get what they want."

"What do they want?"

His pale blue eyes stared into mine. "Me."

"Why?"

"It's the way things are."

"Can you be any more vague?"

"We can't stay here."

"Tell me what you did to make them angry."

"They're not angry. Emotions never factor into their decisions."

"Decisions about what?"

He shrugged.

"Who *are* they?"

"Look, I need to protect you and I can't do that if you're using tech." He squeezed his eyes shut. "Stay off the Internet. Don't use your phone. And for God's sake don't use your credit cards. Use the one I gave you."

"You're making me paranoid."

"Good."

I flinched, realizing he'd prepared for this. "You knew they'd come for you."

"I was careful."

"Then how did they find you?"

He sighed. "It's like trying to hide from the sun."

What the hell?

"Are you a drug dealer?" I snapped. "Or one of those people they use for smuggling...a mule?"

He burst into laughter. "No, I've never shoved drugs up my ass. Still, the night is young."

"This isn't funny."

His smile faded. "I'd gotten to the place where I believed we could have all of this. I thought James would understand."

"Do you have to sell the flat? It's okay as long as you and I are together."

Sadness filled the hard lines of his face. "Forgive me."

"Why?"

"I never meant to expose you to any of this. That's why I was reluctant to have anyone in my life."

"We can't look back," I said. "We face this together."

"Then we need to think about our next move."

"Which is?"

"Grab your passport. We'll be better off in Europe."

"I can't leave, Xander." I wrapped my arms around myself. "I've been waiting on Friday's audition my whole life."

And he knows this.

Xander stared at me. "I'm sorry, Em, you're going to have to delay—"

"James knows about my audition."

A stark silence filled the room.

"He had the maître d' give me his business card. On the back was a note wishing me good luck for Friday."

Xander glanced in the direction of the front door. "Have you got it?"

"In my purse."

"Give it to me."

A minute later, in the kitchen, I watched Xander at the sink holding a flame to James' business card as wisps of smoke spiraled toward the ceiling.

I glanced at the smoke detector, which thankfully had not gone off. "Does he know where we live?"

"Emily, I need you to pack."

"So that's a 'yes.'" My voice trembled. "When can we come back?"

His expression was apologetic.

"You burned his card so I wouldn't call him?"

He didn't respond.

"We have to pack up the flat," I said. "We can't walk away from all this."

"The stuff doesn't matter." He reached for me. "You do."

I stepped back. "I'm not missing that audition, Xander. I've put in years of practice building to this one chance."

"Em, please…"

I shook my head. "I'm calling the police."

"They own the police."

"That's not possible."

"Let me deal with this."

"You need to tell me everything."

"It's best you don't know. Trust me, right now it's the only thing keeping you safe."

I hurried back to the living room to grab my phone. "I'm calling Kitty."

He came after me.

"I need to tell someone, so they know we're in danger."

"You need to do what I say." He snatched the phone out of my hand and threw it on the coffee table.

"Then give me an explanation."

He mulled over his answer. "Think of them as the dark matter of power. And like dark matter you know it's there, there's just no evidence to prove it."

My thoughts scrambled to catch up.

"Are they politicians?"

He gave me a sad, sweet smile. "I wanted to be free of it all for a while. Clear my mind. But then…I met you."

Closing the gap between us and leaning into his chest, I wrapped my arms around his waist. "I won't let anything happen to you."

"I wasn't expecting to fall in love."

"You make it sound like a problem."

He pressed his lips to my forehead. We stayed locked in an embrace for several minutes. This…this was home. He was everything to me and falling in love with Xander had been so easy.

I would fight the whole world to keep us together.

Our first date where he'd kept me at a distance, acting elusive, now made sense.

"You understand me like no one else," he said softly.

Crushing my cheek to his chest, I said, "And you get me."

His rare intellect and my musical gift had drawn us together.

"I need you to pack a bag, Em," he said softly.

All this time Xander had been running from someone.

"I don't want it to end," he whispered.

I looked up at him. "What?"

"Us."

Would his fear cause him to revert back to that closed-off, secretive man whose trust I'd worked so hard to gain?

I broke the quiet. "How dangerous is James?"

A wave of emotion flashed over Xander's face.

"He seems reasonable." I recalled the man's suave demeanor.

Xander looked away.

Chapter 11

I BRUSHED XANDER'S HAND AWAY.

He was trying to comfort me. I was too unnerved to let him. I didn't want to be in a room at The Biltmore Hotel. I wanted to be home.

At 2:00 A.M. I should be getting a good night's sleep. I should be excited for my audition tomorrow—the one that could get me into one of the most prestigious orchestras in the world. But attending that event was uncertain now.

Xander sat on the edge of the bed and watched me pace.

We'd left our Baker Street flat several hours ago. Our suitcases were in the corner. Clothes spilled out from mine where I'd rummaged around for my toiletry bag in a fit of panic. We were on the run from some unseen force and my frustration with Xander hadn't lifted. I refused to unpack.

Denial was a safer place.

Our hotel room was lovely with its plush carpeting, king-sized bed and marble tiled bathroom, but it felt like a prison.

My stomach ached with uncertainty.

Xander hadn't given me any real answers as to what was going on with him or who those men were, and his continued secrecy had left me bewildered.

My pacing had brought me once again to the far side of the room. "I can't live this way."

"I'll upgrade us to a suite."

"I mean on the run, Xander."

My Strad was in the corner, tucked away in its case. I didn't care about my clothes, or shoes, or anything else, as long as I had my violin. But my old one, which I had a sentimental attachment to, was back home and the thought of someone damaging it made me sick.

Maybe I was looking at the situation all wrong. Maybe I should return to a place of gratitude. Put it all into perspective. Take responsibility for dating a man with a secret past. I'd known going into the relationship that there was so much about this man I might never understand, but I'd pushed that knowledge aside because I'd wanted him in my life.

He was more important than anything.

I walked over to him and put my arms around his neck, trying to remind him how much I loved him, and that I would be here for him no matter what. He was suffering just as much.

Xander pushed himself up and eased my hands off. "I'm going down to order room service."

"You can't call down?"

He shook his head.

Xander had gone cold on me again and it made me nervous. It felt like he was pulling away.

Frustration heated my face. "Are you suggesting the people you're running from will know you've ordered food if you use our room phone? How, exactly?"

He patted his jeans as he looked around for his wallet. He wasn't even going to charge the order to the room. And he was refusing to answer my questions.

One decision had brought me to this—made on the day I'd watched Xander step off the carriage in the Underground onto that deserted platform. I'd had a split-second to decide whether to join him, whether to take a leap into uncertainty. That tunnel had been more than a metaphor, it had been a prediction.

He headed out. "I won't be long."

"You have to let me go to my audition."

He stopped at the door but didn't turn around. "We'll talk about it when I get back."

"There's nothing to talk about."

Xander looked over his shoulder at me. "James knows about it."

"What can he do?" I raised my hands in frustration. "I'll attend my audition and leave."

A flash of pain crossed his face…as though in that moment he'd made a difficult decision.

The door slammed shut.

I stared at the spot where he'd been standing, knowing that his pained expression was caused by the guilt he felt for doing this to *us*. His eyes had shone with the tears he held back.

I wanted him to know I forgave him…and I should have told him this. Whatever happened we'd be okay.

Ten minutes later, a knock at the door had me sighing with relief, thinking we'd be able to talk some more. I rushed forward and flung it open.

James Ballad's foot shot forward to stop me from closing the door. "Go away!"

"Don't make a scene, Em." With a shove he pushed the door open and me back with it. The bathroom had a lock, but I refused to hide and leave my violin or our other possessions vulnerable.

With a pivot, I straightened and faced the man who was now standing imperiously in the center of our room. He was taller than I remembered, or maybe it was his threatening stance or the fact I was here alone with him.

His expensive suit appeared to be melded over his toned physique. James' gorgeous features and playfully ruffled short hair would make one think he meant no harm. His bright chestnut gaze burned through me with a profound intensity.

My heart hammered. "What do you want?"

"To talk." He scanned the room, noting our suitcases, and then his stare found me again.

He'd been waiting for Xander to leave. *I just knew it.*

"There's no easy way for me to say this, Em. Your life is about to change. I need you to face it with grace."

"How do you mean?" I drew in a sharp breath.

"You'll meet someone new."

"Get out."

"I'm here to protect Xander." He gave me an amused look. "That name does suit him."

"What are you talking about?" Exasperated, I didn't give him a chance to reply. "I was there, remember? In The Savoy when you two talked. He doesn't like you."

"Did he say that?"

"Not in so many words.

"You're out of your depth, Em, and you'll soon be part of Xander's past. Accept your fate and leave."

"We're getting married." I watched his reaction as he studied my diamond ring.

"Your engagement is over."

"You don't get to say—"

"Rest assured you'll be well taken care of."

The audacity of the man! "You can't get rid of me, James."

"Hmm." He paused. "Your audition's tomorrow, right?"

I gave him a hate-filled glare.

His eyes crinkled into a smile. "With one phone call—"

"How dare you sabotage my career."

"Actually, you didn't let me finish. With one call I can ensure you'll have a place in the London Symphony Orchestra."

"I don't want your help, and Xander wants nothing to do with you. He loves me and he's never going back to you."

"It's useless to challenge me. The decision's been made."

"I'll call the police."

The look on his face made a shiver run up my spine. "That would make things more unpleasant for you."

"Not from where I'm standing."

He shoved his hands into his pockets. "I'm trying to be your friend here, Em."

No, he fucking wasn't. "You don't get to call me that."

"Xander has shown you what he can do with technology. I, too, have those resources."

My frown gave my ignorance away.

"You have no idea what he does?" He looked surprised. "Well, there's that at least. You've had your fun and now it's over."

"Threats won't work."

"It's not just a threat. If you tell anyone about this, I will end you... and then I will end them."

The sound of a keycard being swiped was followed by the door bursting open. Xander hurried in, snapping a concerned look first at me and then to James.

"Nice of you to join us, Xander," said James calmly.

Xander studied me, as though making sure I was unharmed.

"He won't leave," I told him.

"She has a big day tomorrow." James held his stare. "She needs some sleep."

Something passed between them and Xander gave a nod of understanding.

"What was that?" I snapped.

James turned his back on me and rested a hand on Xander's shoulder for a moment before walking out the door. Xander shrugged it off and didn't even watch him leave.

A chasm opened up beneath my feet. "What just happened?" It came out as a sob, *because I knew.*

He reached for me. "Em."

I stepped back, my chest tightening at his look of resignation.

"Come here."

"Tell me what's happening."

"You know I love you, right?"

"What happened while you were gone? Did they threaten you?"

"It's complicated."

"We're going to be married."

"Em, please...when I met you, I said we could only live one day at a time—"

"Tell me this isn't goodbye."

He moved closer and pulled me into a hug. "I'm trying to protect you."

I wanted to stay in his arms forever. I held him as though I would. "Don't you dare leave."

"Forgive me."

I stared up at him with tears in my eyes. "What did he say to you?"

He looked away. "They need me."

"I need you."

"You'll never go without money, I promise."

"I don't want anything…just you." A sob escaped me as I buried my face against his chest again.

"Have the best life," he whispered, pulling away from me.

"Don't say that. You're acting like I'll never see you again."

He retrieved his suitcase and pulled it toward the door.

I blocked him.

He cupped my face in his hands. "Stay here for as long as you like."

"Shall I go home and wait for you?"

"That place is gone, Em. I'm sorry."

I grabbed his arm as he opened the door. "Stop, please."

"I'll be thinking of you during your audition. You'll be amazing."

"Don't go," I said, my voice shaking.

"You're strong, Em. I know you can handle this."

"Is your name really Xander?"

His silence was like a knife in my heart.

No…

He pulled away, hesitating in the doorway. "He shouldn't have told you that."

The room spun around me.

"I will always love you, Em. Please keep the Strad."

"I won't go to the audition." Grief tightened its noose. "Not if it puts you in danger."

He stared at me as though memorizing every line of my face.

I thought my heart would shatter over this unfathomable ending of us.

He turned away from me and walked out, shutting the door quietly behind him.

No, no, no...

He wouldn't leave me like this...

A chill surged through my body. I'd made this decision for him in the moment I'd insisted on attending my audition, my selfish words blazing a trail into my empty future. Grabbing the door handle, I yanked it open and stepped into the hallway.

Xander was gone.

Chapter 12

I STUMBLED BACK THROUGH THE DOOR AND HURRIED INTO THE BATHROOM, collapsing on the floor. I hugged my knees, staring at the pristine white tiled walls and the walk-in shower with gold-covered taps. Despite all this luxury, I felt trapped instead of privileged.

I don't remember how long I sat there, feeling numb and hopeless with my life in tatters.At some point I staggered to the bed and collapsed on top of it—still fully clothed—and plunged into a fitful sleep.

As soon as I woke, my thoughts spiraled around scenarios of how I could still save our relationship. We should have left London like Xander had suggested. We would still be together if I hadn't selfishly put myself first.

Xander had been gone for half the night, but it felt longer. How could I face the world again?

In a daze, I managed to get dressed, not even bothering to shower. I just wanted to go home, I wanted to feel normal and I refused to believe I couldn't go back to our place. If Xander was selling the flat, I still had time to at least gather my stuff.

I wheeled my suitcase out of the room with one hand while carrying my violin case with the other, and headed for the lift.On the ride down to the foyer, I tried psyching myself up so I could act casual in front of the hotel staff.

I made my way over to Reception as loneliness inched up my spine. "I'm checking out."

Alone.

The receptionist looked up from her screen. "Did you enjoy your stay?"

Not even a little.

I bit my lip. Reporting what had happened during the night could put Xander in even more danger. At least that's what James had insinuated.

"It was fine." I parked my suitcase next to my feet.

"Which room?"

"377."

She tapped her keyboard. "Huh."

"Something wrong?" I blinked at her in confusion.

She looked up. "Do you have your keycard?"

"No, sorry."

"How about the credit card used to secure the room?"

"No, but I need to make sure it's been paid for. Try looking under the name Wells."

After a few moments, she shook her head. "No one under that name either."

I lay my violin case on the desk. "Check under Emily Rampling. Or Xander Rothschild."

"So you play?" She gestured at my case.

I nodded.

"I had lessons as a child," she said. "Sounded like cats screaming."

She clicked away, and her confused expression told me she hadn't been able to find our names either.

"Has it been taken care of, then?"

With a raised finger, she gestured for me to wait as she answered a phone that refused to stop ringing.

She turned away, and I used that moment to grab my violin and suitcase and leave.

The taxi ride home felt excruciatingly long, but it gave me time to think. I knew Xander would make his way home to me somehow. Or he would at least call me. His walking away last night had been to protect me in that moment. It was so him—putting me first and making sure I had everything I needed.

But Xander's not his name.

I tried to ignore that haunting voice of doubt.

Relief washed over me when the taxi drew close to our building. I trudged on in and stepped into the lift, riding up to our floor in a daze.

I walked down the hall and saw that our door had been left ajar.

Sweat snaked down my spine as I nudged it open and stepped inside.

The blood drained out of my face and my breathing became unsteady. The flat was empty. It had been stripped of everything during the few hours we'd been at the hotel.

Leaving my suitcase and violin just inside the door, I ran from room to room and checked each closet. The furniture, wall-hangings, every last item in Xander's office—everything was gone. My photos, my musical sheets, and my beloved old violin, they had been taken as well.

This wasn't a break-in—they had wiped out my life.

I reached into my handbag and pulled out my phone, pressing the power button to turn it back on. Despite James' threats, it was time to call the police.

I stared down at the screen in disbelief as it failed to come on. It didn't make sense. I'd charged it back at the hotel.

The terror I felt made it hard for me to breathe.

I walked by the sitting room and noticed a black duffel bag on the floor in the far corner. I approached it cautiously. Kneeling beside it, I unzipped the bag and my throat tightened. Hundreds of bank notes were inside.

Catching a sudden movement in my peripheral vision, I spun around.

James leaned casually against the doorjamb, his tall frame filling the space easily. My fateful mistake was falling for his gentlemanly demeanor when we'd first met. The Savile Row suit and his sophisticated pose reflected a man who always got his way.

He'd followed me back.

I wondered how he'd react when I set his money on fire.

I pushed to my feet. "Where is he?"

"Five hundred thousand pounds—" He gestured to the duffel bag.

"Don't want it."

"You're going to need it, Emily. Your bank account no longer exists."

"You don't have that kind of power."

He gave me a humorless smile. "The money is enough to pay rent for a few months and take care of—"

"This is my home. I'm staying."

He pushed off the doorframe and strolled toward me. "That's not going to happen."

"What have you done to him?"

He chuckled.

"This isn't funny."

"You're very dramatic."

"You just kidnapped my boyfriend."

"He came willingly."

"Didn't look like it."

"That's because you don't have the full picture."

"I need to talk to him."

"Ah, but he doesn't want to talk with you."

"I don't believe that."

James looked around at what had once been our home. "He used this as leverage."

"What do you mean?"

"He warned me he would start a new life if I didn't give him what he wanted. Xander can be very stubborn. You're the collateral he used."

"What are you talking about?"

"This was what he wanted all along—to come back on his terms."

"No. He didn't."

"That money is a small sum to get you resituated. If you follow my instructions to the letter there will be more. A lot more."

"I told you I don't want it."

"I'm willing to place three million pounds in a deposit box at Coutts."

"Fuck you and your money."

"You'll change your mind."

I pointed to the bag of cash. "I'm going to take this out back and burn it."

"At least donate it. A lot of mouths can be fed with that."

I stomped toward him. "If you don't let me speak with Xander I'm calling the police."

"That would be an unfortunate waste of time. Mine and theirs." He moved closer. "Not to mention the punishment you'd earn from me, Emily Rampling."

I swallowed the lump in my throat. "How did you find him?"

"You were Xander's weak link."

"How? I did everything he told me to."

He gave a shake of his head. "I'm glad that's not true. Or we wouldn't have him back."

I couldn't see how this could be true. "What do you intend to do with him?"

"He merely works for us. And he's well rewarded."

"Please, let me see him."

He reached out and tipped up my chin. "Be a good girl and stop asking questions. Let me get you to a hotel."

I slapped his hand away.

"Cross me, Emily, and you'll walk through hell."

"I'll keep going."

"I'm fond of Churchill myself, but if you're going to quote him at least have some grasp of what his job entailed."

"Oh, like you do?"

James looked at me with a sympathetic expression.

"I won't let you get away with this."

"The only reason you're still alive is because Xander used it as a bargaining chip. I have agreed to his terms for now...as long as you follow my instructions."

My chest heaved. "I need to see that he's okay."

"He's not coming back." James reached out and took my hand in his, holding it tenderly. The comforting gesture surprised me.

Then he pulled off my engagement ring and tucked it into his pocket.

"Give that back to me!"

"Your life with Xander never happened, Emily."

"I have friends who'll believe me."

"They never met him, right? He's simply a figment of your imagination."

He walked out of the sitting room and headed toward the front door.

I followed him, caressing my ring finger. A faint dent in my skin was the only evidence I was engaged. "Can I stay here tonight?"

James pivoted and held my stare. "No. This is your last chance to accept my offer to get you into a nice place."

"Fuck off."

"We're changing the locks to this flat within the hour." He headed out and left the door open behind him.

My breathing was so erratic I knew I was close to having a full-blown panic attack.

I slammed the door shut and collapsed against it, letting my body slide to the floor.

Even with James gone, his presence lingered.

I hugged my knees to my chest as I replayed his words. How had I helped them find Xander? There'd been no sharing of photos on social media, no sharing of phones, no breaches in privacy with my friends. But James was right...Xander had never met anyone in my life.

We were both in danger because of me.

And I'd never forgive myself.

Chapter 13

I STOOD RESOLUTELY IN FRONT OF THE CRIMSON VELVET CURTAINS ON THE grand stage of the Barbican Theatre.

It had been my audition to seize, my moment to shine.

Becoming a member of the London Symphony was a real possibility for me now—but only if I'd somehow managed to impress my austere audience of six with Chopin's "Nocturne" in C-sharp minor.

I'd played my Strad like my life depended on it. And in many ways it did. The dream and agony of loss had left each sweep of my bow like silent tears for my lost lover.

My life had been stripped to nothing.

If felt like years, but it had only been two nights ago that everything had begun to fall apart after I'd left Kitty in the bar at The Savoy. I'd hunted down my wayward boyfriend after seeing him walking into Simpson's-in-the-Strand. And a day later James Ballad had swept in and out of my life like a tornado, taking my boyfriend with him.

Finally coming down from the adrenaline rush of my performance, I braved a look around the grand auditorium, only now noticing the beauty that surrounded me.

This had been my one chance to accomplish my dream.

With my Strad by my side, I tried to read the faces of the judges.

The place was empty other than the men and women who sat in the front row...the gatekeepers. They would decide who would continue on to the next stage of the submission process. All of us who played today wanted a coveted place in the string section. Only one of us would be chosen.

Maybe it was the lack of sleep, or the fact my life had been ripped apart. But I felt small in the vastness of the theatre. All those empty seats rising into the dark, waiting for people who would probably never hear me play.

The agony of possible failure resonated through every cell of my body. Had I failed to bleed out the notes needed to win my place amongst them?

There came a nod from Patrick Woo, the senior conductor...the man I'd needed to impress above all others. "We'll be in touch, Ms. Rampling."

With my instrument clutched to my chest, I hurried to the edge of the stage and stepped down into the dimness of a hallway.

"Is that a Strad?" asked Salme, a fellow student at the Royal Academy.

The dark-haired Baltic bombshell proudly held her precious Carrodus Guarneri, a violin known to have been played by Paganini himself. After relaying this fact to the class, she had made it a point to mock our instruments.

Usually I avoided her. She was about to audition, and God, she looked like a star in that short, glittering dress.

"I've never seen you play that violin in class," she said, looking surprised. "Is it yours?"

I nodded, trying to rise out of my melancholy.

"What a waste." Her posh accent sliced through my dignity.

Putting her cruelty down to nervousness, I walked away.

"I'm surprised you had the guts to audition," she called after me.

I turned to face her.

"Stay away from the bridge." I nodded to her violin. "I heard you practicing earlier and thought you were playing a horror score. Then I realized you were attempting Mozart."

"Go back to serving tables, Amelia."

"It's Emily. And I teach violin."

"Then I feel sorry for your students."

"Aren't you keeping them waiting?"

"I'm just giving them time to recover from your dumpster fire of a performance."

I stood there staring after her as she mounted the steps to the stage. Then I took a calming breath and hurried away.

Halfway down the hall, I peered into the room where the others were waiting. They were probably going to throw all sorts of questions my way, and I wasn't ready to face anyone. I continued on.

Over a decade's worth of lessons...four years at the Royal Academy of Music...a lifetime preparing for one moment.

All of it leading here, to these last fifteen minutes.

And I just knew I'd fucked it up.

Inside a darkly lit room, I placed my bow and violin on a corner armchair and then headed over to a long wooden table. Pushing myself onto it, I lay back, stared at the ornate ceiling, and tried to clear my thoughts.

I'd only slept a few hours since Xander had walked out of our room at The Biltmore. I hoped no one discovered my hiding place.

Nothing to see here.

Just a girl with no talent.

Before visiting The Savoy, I'd been happy with my life. My relationship wasn't perfect, but Xander was wonderful to me and I loved him completely. A part of my soul was missing. He'd taken it with him.

How could I be expected to carry on as though none of that had happened? I'd been forced out of my home after my boyfriend had left with no explanation. And all I had to my name was that suspicious bag of money.

I'd shoved it into the cupboard of the room I'd booked at the Travel Lodge in Covent Garden. I'd placed a permanent DO NOT DISTURB sign on the door until I figured out what to do with all that cash. *If* I was going to keep it.

Why must they keep these places so cold? I mused, shivering.

Digging my fingernails into my palms, I drew the pain from my chest into my hands. My life was spiraling into the darkest place and I had no idea what to do next. Finish college? Then what? I sure as hell wasn't going to be a member of an orchestra; that was for sure.

"Well, I've heard better." The familiar voice came from the doorway.

I didn't need to lift my head for a look to know who it was.

"Come to gloat?" I continued staring up at the ceiling.

"I wished I'd bought ear buds. Let's put it like that."

I turned my head to glare at James.

He'd gone for a three-piece suit again—the kind that made him look Brooks Brothers suave, not like a man who enjoyed wrecking lives. His black hair framed stunning sharp features, the raw beauty hiding his sinful leanings.

I huffed out a sigh. "Do you enjoy ruining everyone's lives?"

"Are you blaming me for your poor audition?"

"Just for the kidnapping of my boyfriend. Things like that tend to fuck up one's performance."

"How many times do I have to say it? Xander came back to us willingly."

"We both know he was forced to. And Xander's not his name, apparently."

"He likes to play hard to get." He shrugged. "It's his thing."

"He looked scared."

"That's because he likes you."

"He still loves me."

"Of course he does."

That didn't help. "So now that you've ruined our lives, what else is on the agenda?"

"Would you be surprised to hear that I want you to do well?"

"You're a bit late."

"Em." His tone carried sympathy. "Where are you staying?"

"I'm sure you already know." My throat tightened. "I want him back."

"I know."

"I have nothing left."

"You have everything to live for." He closed the gap between us.

I refused to look at him. "I don't even have the will to get up and leave this place."

"You'll adjust. Everything will work out."

I shook my head wearily. "I failed monumentally."

James grabbed my ankles and pulled me toward him. "I have a message from Xander. He wants to see your dream realized."

Oh, yes. "Why isn't he here?"

"I'm a master at saving the day." He stood between my thighs glaring down at me. "Do you want me to make it right?"

What?

"How much do you want this, Emily?"

"Take a wild guess."

His long fingers hoisted up the hem of my skirt until it was above my panties.

Raising my head to look at him, I said, "What are you doing?"

"Making your dream come true."

Surely, he wasn't going to…

He eased my panties away from my crotch and leaned low.

Oh, God.

His tongue flicked between my folds, circling and masterfully lapping until I was writhing in pleasure, my jaw slack from surprise, my groin grinding against him as I took short, sharp breaths.

My moans echoed around us.

I was letting him touch me.

Him, the bringer of all my heartache.

"Don't stop," I burst out.

This is what a girl looks like when she's lost everything, when she's given up and wants to have the pain fucked away.

"Like it?" His warm breath purred against me.

"Yes." I spread my thighs wider for him, not caring if someone walked in and caught us. From the way James was focused on me down there, he didn't care either.

What the hell was I doing letting the enemy close? Yet this forbidden seduction was wiping out all those thoughts and fears of failure. All I wanted was this…him teasing me, his tongue flicking my sex with a fierceness that sent my mind reeling. We'd fallen into the abyss of other possibilities.

I arched my back and rocked against his chin as his mouth possessed me completely.

Xander no longer wants me.

And that wasn't even his name.

It didn't matter that James was overpowering me. I no longer cared. I had lost everything...my dream...my lover. My world had crashed and burned, leaving only memories that brought nothing but hurt.

All I had left was this impending climax.

James raised his head and looked at me. "Want me to continue?"

"Yes."

He suckled my clit with that dangerous mouth of his, keeping me poised on the precipice.

I may hate the man, but damn he's good at this.

The enthused noises he made down there as he lapped away sounded taboo. I suddenly felt embarrassed by our reckless tryst. I focused on the ceiling's ornate plaster, the design a beautiful thing.

My back arched violently. *This pleasure is a beautiful thing.*

A sigh escaped my lips, and then I flinched as negative thoughts of self-loathing consumed me. There was no talent in my hands. I didn't deserve to have my dream realized.

My body went rigid.

James stood up straight. "Well, there's your problem, right there."

I looked at him, feeling dazed. "What is?"

"You're not letting go. Not surrendering. Not allowing the moment to steal you away so your soul can sing."

"What are you talking about?"

"We're going to try this again, Emily. Only you're going to give yourself to me completely. Let me own you, and in the depths of your soul believe it. Offer your pussy to me like it's all you have."

"It is. I failed."

"Your dream is a heartbeat away. You're going to step back on that stage and give yourself over to your instrument and forget yourself. *You* are inconsequential."

This audition process didn't allow for second chances. There were too many applicants. Still, my clit throbbed wantonly for more of his artful mouth, and he must have read my lustful expression.

"Ready?"

I nodded.

"Thighs wider, please."

I obeyed.

"Let go, Emily." He leaned low between my thighs again and passionately savaged my pussy with pouty lips and an exploring, feverish tongue. The deep affection of his mouth made me believe he might even know a thing or two about love.

It wasn't easy to believe—with my thighs spread open we'd had an artful conversation with me exposed erotically like a dancer from the Moulin Rouge.

I'd consented to this act even after he'd destroyed my life.

Yet I didn't want him to stop.

He raised his head. "Let the pain devour you, the agony of loss consume you until it's all you are." He slid two fingers inside me. "Play like this."

I flinched when he spread his fingers and the pressure inside me grew, bringing a rush of pleasure. He was doing something remarkable with his touch and I stilled for a moment, overcome by bliss and wonder. I inhaled sharply when his other hand went for my swollen nub, strumming it as he finger-fucked me in brilliant unison.

My jaw clenched as the tension built between my soaking wet thighs.

I wanted to tell him I hated him...but blinding pleasure stole my words.

"Play as though you are no longer confined."

The air left my lungs as his fingers continue to pump inside me and I felt his mouth crash down on my sensitive clit again, his tongue swirling and flicking, possessing me with a skill that made me shudder violently.

I felt too lightheaded to fight.

The notes found me...

Mozart...

A brilliant symphony, ingenious in its creation, destined to leave my strings as the music in my head rushed through me until I was nothing...the endless pleasure possessing me, freeing me until I vanished from the room.

The notes reached a crescendo.

I became aware of his hand as it covered my mouth, suppressing my moan as I came hard, shuddering violently, my body wracked with erotic pleasure.

I'd been so wantonly *his.*

My fingers ached from where I'd gripped both edges of the table during an endless orgasm.

It was in a daze that I felt him pull me up and straighten my skirt. I sat on the end of the table with my legs dangling and my heart thumping.

James lifted my chin as though gauging my reaction to what he'd just accomplished. He leaned in and kissed the tip of my nose affectionately. It was an intimate, kind gesture...just what I needed in that moment.

My hair spilled over my face and James eased apart the strands to peer at me with a smile; the kind a tutor bestows upon a student for a pleasing performance.

I watched him walk over to the chair and pick up my Strad. He carried it back to me and placed it in my arms, keeping hold of the bow.

I had nothing left to say...all words had been stolen by him in such an exquisite way that my internal muscles clenched, yearning for more.

What's happening?

James helped me climb off the table. His fingers interwove with mine as he led me out and down the hallway. I felt too shaken up to resist.

I pulled back when he began to climb the steps to the stage. "I had my chance."

"Turns out you get another."

"How?"

"You're with me."

Apprehension made my heart skip a beat. We were breaking the rules by returning to the concert hall.

With the confidence of a man who could steal a lover away and not show remorse, he guided me to the center of the stage where the spotlight shone upon us. I blinked into the darkness of the vast seating area below and was terrified to see the judges staring up at me.

James handed me my bow. "Play your Strad like *that*, Emily."

I watched him leave with a feeling of regret. I could have questioned him, found out who he really was...what he did, and perhaps get a message to Xander.

He'd left me dazed with my legs still trembling, my thighs sticky. My sex was throbbing from the pleasure he'd brought.

Stunned into silence, I looked toward the spotlight, blinking and trying to see past the front rows of seats. It was too dark. I inhaled sharply, trying to catch my breath.

Patrick Woo narrowed his gaze on me, intrigued.

I forced a smile.

"Whenever you're ready," said Mr. Woo.

Another judge gestured with an elegant hand. "You have another piece you'd like us to hear?"

"Mozart," I whispered.

This...a moment that shouldn't be.

My eyes having adjusting to the dark, I caught sight of Ballad making his way to the back of the auditorium. He slipped out of the exit.

"Let go." His words found me again.

Lifting my Strad, I placed my jaw on the chinrest and raised the bow. The first note rose...

Closing my eyes, I surrendered.

Chapter 14

Nine a.m. and London's commuters were out ahead of Saturday's tourists, who would soon be swarming the streets. The city was alive once more.

I'd made it just in time to watch Lloyds Bank open its doors to allow the queue of waiting customers to stream in. After resting that hefty bag of cash between my feet, I slipped my credit card into Lloyds' ATM, glancing quickly behind me to make sure no one was looking before tapping in my four-digit code.

Then waiting…

There was no way I could let this situation go on any longer. What kind of person sees their loved one walk away under suspicious circumstances and does nothing?

Surely no one?

And, anyway, that wasn't me. I'd never cowered under threats or bullying before.

There was no other option but to defy James and go to the police. First, I needed evidence. And as all our stuff was gone now, this was my last hope of grabbing something on paper. Xander and I had been a couple for six months. Our statements would prove we used this bank frequently. Like any other couple, we had a trail of payments from the life that existed between us.

Tapping my fingers on the side of the ATM, I tried to steady my nerves. It was taking too long.

Think of something else.

Anything but having my life wiped from the map.

At yesterday's audition, James Ballad had set my world ablaze with his brash and very erotic attack on my pussy. Afterward, guilt had settled in over the fact I'd just lain on that table letting him do those things to me. Even now, my thighs tightened together when I thought of it. He'd taken advantage of my fragility after I'd failed my audition. That man went in for the kill when you least expected it.

I needed to remember that.

I stared in horror at the ATM screen, which flashed a message greeting the next customer. Punching the panel with a fingertip, I tried to get it to respond. The damn thing had eaten my credit card.

With sweaty palms and a chest tight with trepidation, I stormed into Lloyds, the heat of anger warming my face. The length of the queue had me gritting my teeth in frustration, but I fell into line and tried to reassure myself.

It's an admin error, that's all.

Finally, a gesture to step forward came from one of the cashiers.

I tried to make eye contact with the clerk, despite the irritating smudges on the glass between us. "Your machine didn't return my credit card."

"What's your name?" Her false eyelashes fluttered.

I gave it to her. "It's a joint account. Try looking up Xander Rothschild as well, please."

She gave me a suspicious glare. "He's not coming up either. Are you sure you're with Lloyds?"

My mouth went dry. "This is the branch where we opened our joint account." I recognized the fake tree in the corner with the large pot it stood in as though it would one day grow into it.

"Did you open it with another name?" She glanced over my shoulder at the other people in line.

It was worth a try. "Wells?"

"Sorry, no account under Emily or Xander Wells, either."

"James, you bastard," I mumbled.

"I'm sorry?"

I shook off my misery. "Can you check one more time?"

"Do you want to open an account?"

"I have one."

"Then it must be under another name."

"I need my card back, please."

"The manager will be here at ten. She'll have you fill out a form."

"I can't wait 'til then."

"We don't have access to the ATM. Now, if you'll excuse me, I have other customers waiting."

I hoisted my bag of cash. "I'd like to open a safety deposit box."

She studied the bag. "You need at least two hundred pounds to reserve a small box, and five hundred for a large."

"So half a million pounds will cut it, then?"

She swallowed hard, her arrogance dissolving.

I forced a smile. "Let's do it."

After opening a large safety deposit box and stashing the money in it, I tucked the key into my purse and headed out. With Ballad circling my universe, there was a fifty-fifty chance the money would still be there when I came back.

The only man who knew what to do in a situation like this, other than Xander, was Harold. He'd been there for me when I'd hit rock bottom. I didn't want to put him in danger, but I couldn't face this alone. At least he'd believe me.

Harold's motto was "every problem has a solution," and it was this attitude that had dragged me out of a slump when the flat I was renting had been bought out by contractors. My eviction had threatened to leave me homeless until he'd offered me a place to stay for a reasonable rent.

And I was due a visit.

As I set out on the Tube, everything began to blur together in my mind—all the weirdness, all the lies, all the deceit.

What the hell was Xander's real name? This deception hurt the most. Didn't legal names come up when you went to sign a contract like a marriage certificate?

Ballad had wiped out all trace of our finances. The man I'd let touch me yesterday in an intimate way, whipping me into a frenzy, had destroyed the last fragment of proof that Xander and I ever existed. He'd arrogantly gone down on me knowing he'd just closed this account, too.

Before I could squelch it, I felt a vague sense of gratitude towards him for getting me all relaxed for that second chance audition. *But still.*

It was good to be back on Gloucester Street. I needed the familiarity of my old home, where I'd lived for three years. I needed a friend.

Being back in this neighborhood brought me comfort. I'd visited Harold less and less as my relationship with Xander had grown more serious. There was guilt over that, but Harold had a busy life, too, working in the accessories department at Liberty London, and spending time with his close-knit family.

Life had been harder back then and yet so simple.

The gate squeaked when I nudged it open and it was nice to have this moment of normality.

I remembered finding Xander sitting on the stone steps waiting for me after I'd rescued him at Piccadilly. I wouldn't take back our time together for anything.

What the hell?

A SOLD sign stood in the center of the garden.

Harold hadn't mentioned he was selling his house. There had been no email from him with a forwarding address or even a phone call. This home had been his mum's once, and that was why he'd never wanted to leave—there were too many memories.

Peering through the front window into the living room, I couldn't help but cringe when I saw that all of the furniture was gone. The carpet had been ripped up, exposing the century old flooring. The walls were bare. No trace of Harold remained.

And there'd be no trace of me here, either.

I walked along the right side of the house and made my way into the garden, where more memories flooded back. All those quiet times I'd relaxed in the sun, reading books and sipping tea on the rickety old lounger, which was now missing. Overgrown weeds revealed this place had been deserted for well over a month.

I should have called Harold. I'd been wrapped up in my happiness and time had dissolved around me. There was always tomorrow, or next week. And yet that had been an illusion.

Rising on tiptoes, I peeked through the large kitchen window. The room was empty other than a roll of paper towels on the floor.

My stomach flipped when I thought that this could be *his* doing…a stripping away of my present, the erasing of my past.

I left the place that had once been my refuge and rode the train to Westminster Tube station. Within an hour of leaving Harold's, I was standing inside the reception area of New Scotland Yard, ready to bury James with accusations of what he'd done to me and Xander.

My adrenaline surged even as I took a seat in the waiting area. Waves of dread rose inside me when I thought of how long it might take the police to find Xander.

Or whatever his name was.

I leaned back in the chair, as I replayed James' threat that going to the authorities would get me in a world of trouble.

Really?

Because what he'd done was going to see him locked up for a very long time.

I was escorted out of the waiting area and into a sparse interview room. If they were going for intimidating, they'd hit the mark. The scent of sweat and suspicion lingered in the air.

I tried to relax and act natural without throwing up. Others who'd waited in here had felt similar frustration apparently, as evidenced by the scratched-up table I sat at. On my right was a two-way mirror and I wondered if anyone else was watching from behind it.

A smartly dressed forty-something woman entered in civilian clothes, her ponytail twisted in on itself like an afterthought. She smiled brightly to greet me. It was the kindness I needed after all I'd been through.

"Emily? I'm D.I. Stewart." Her Scottish accent lent a friendly air to her demeanor.

She took a seat on the other side of the table and pulled out a frayed notebook.

I smiled nervously. "Thank you for agreeing to speak with me."

"Of course. Just to confirm, your last name is Rampling?"

"Yes."

"What brings you here today, Emily?"

"I'm worried about my boyfriend, Xander Rothschild."

"You were living together?" She turned her notebook for me to read. "At this address?"

"Yes, and I'm here to report him missing."

"I'm with CID. Sergeant Warren, who took your report, mentioned he was concerned about you."

My heart hammered. "I'm fine, but I was threatened not to come here. I was warned not to talk with you."

"Really?"

"Yes, by the same man who forced Xander to leave. His name is James Ballad." I pointed at her notepad, expecting her to write it down. "You need to find him."

"James Ballad?" The tip of her pen stilled as she hesitated.

"That's right. I was there when he ordered my fiancé to leave with him."

"Xander left with…James?"

"He didn't want to."

"Where were you when this happened?"

"The Biltmore. James came to our hotel room."

"When?"

"Wednesday night. I mean, Thursday morning at two A.M."

"Where did they go?"

"Don't know. I haven't seen Xander since." I bit my lip, deciding not to tell her that wasn't his real name.

"Has he contacted you?"

"No."

She paused, tapping her finger on the file as though mulling over what I'd told her. "How have you been feeling lately, Emily?"

I shook my head. "I can't believe this is happening."

"How have you been coping with things?"

"It's hard, but I've been managing."

"Have you experienced any depression, or any mental health issues?" She threw in a smile. "It's a question I have to ask, you understand."

"Sure. No, I'm fine."

She seemed to be waiting for a confession.

"Look, this really happened. You have to find Xander."

"To clarify, your boyfriend Xander Rothschild left with…?"

"James Ballad."

She glanced toward the two-way mirror. "Tell me more about Xander."

"We've been living together for six months. We're engaged. He's a tech expert. I think that's why he's so important to them."

"Them?"

"The men who took him."

"I thought he left with one man?"

"When I first met James at The Savoy, he was with several other men."

"Do you have their names?"

"No. I didn't speak to them." I leaned forward. "James made it sound like Xander could do something special for him…some special skill."

"In what field?"

"Computers?"

"Can you be more specific?"

"Not really, no. He didn't like to talk about his work."

"What did Xander say about James?"

"He confirmed he'd worked for him once."

"Were there any clues as to what Xander did for them?"

I hesitated because not knowing exactly what your boyfriend did in his day job or otherwise was a firm ten on the Richter scale of weird.

A knock at the door made me jump.

The sergeant peeked in. "Ma'am, Ms. Rampling's barrister's arrived."

"I don't have a lawyer," I said.

Stewart pushed to her feet and joined the sergeant in the hall.

Maybe they called a barrister for people who were being interviewed, though somewhere in the far reaches of my mind that didn't ring true. A lawyer could stop you from talking.

When Stewart reappeared, she looked thoughtful. She sat on the edge of the desk and peered down at me. "How do you know James Ballad?"

"I told you. He took my boyfriend away."

"Can you be more specific?"

"He's the man who kidnapped my boyfriend."

"Was there a violent struggle between them?"

"No."

"So Xander left willingly?"

"He didn't want to."

"Did you argue with Xander before the incident?"

"No."

"When did you last see Mr. Ballad?"

Oh, God. Yesterday…at my audition.

She studied my face. "Emily, Mr. Ballad is here."

The two-way mirror.

"He says he's your lawyer."

I shot to my feet and backed away.

"He wants to talk with you."

"He's not a lawyer."

Her mouth twisted in frustration. "He presented his I.D."

I tried to follow her words. "Don't let him in."

"That's not up to me. You're his client and he has a legal right to see you."

A chill slithered up my spine.

James Ballad strolled into the room with a confident swagger, his long woolen black coat and neatly combed dark hair giving him the air of a gentleman. A sleek briefcase hung by his side.

Despite his calmness, danger emanated from him. "How long has my client been here?" he asked with an edge.

"You're *not* my lawyer," I snapped.

James raised his hand. "Em, I've got this."

Stewart moved closer to him. "Let's talk outside, Mr. Ballad."

He stared at her. "Why are you interrogating my client?"

"Ms. Rampling appears emotional, Mr. Ballad. Want to tell me why?"

James looked around the room. "This isn't exactly The Savoy."

"That's the hotel where your client states she first met you." Stewart held her ground.

He glanced over at me. "I saw her there once."

"I was there with my friends," I clarified. "And with Xander."

James arched a brow. "Em, it would be best if you remained quiet. You could be held on alleged suspicious behavior outside Gordon House."

"You mean the place I used to live?"

Stewart pivoted toward me. "Emily, there's no record of you living there. Though there is footage from CCTV cameras outside Gordon House of you coming and going. There's no footage of the man you describe as Xander. And I need you to remain calm when I tell you this—" She swapped a wary glance with James. "There's no record of a Xander Rothschild living there either. In fact, we can't find proof he even exists. No birth certificate. No social security number. No driver's license. No tax records. No property records. No footage of him leaving or entering the building...ever."

My mouth went dry as I realized there were no bank records.

"There's no evidence of the man you describe at The Savoy," Stewart added. "Or The Biltmore."

"No footage at all?" I stuttered.

Her tone was sympathetic. "So why do you like hanging around Gordon House so much?"

James shrugged it off. "Let's take a closer look at that footage."

My knees went weak, but I forced myself to remain standing.

James turned to face Stewart. "May I see it?"

"Sure."

"I appreciate that, Jenny. First, I need a moment *alone* with my client." He placed his briefcase on the table.

Stewart glanced my way. "Not sure she wants that."

"Are you trying to keep me from doing my job?" he said flatly. "Let's not break the law before lunch."

"Do you need me to stay?" Stewart's expression was sympathetic.

"Why would my client refuse to talk with her attorney?" James' intensity was infused with manipulation. "Unless you told her something that would be misconstrued—"

"Everything has been conducted by the book," Stewart said quickly.

James gestured to the door. "Then please bring me the footage."

With a final glance back, Stewart stepped through the door and closed it behind her. We were left alone with nothing but tension between us.

James pulled the chair back from the table and motioned for me to sit down.

"I'm fine." I wasn't, of course. My emotions were about to spiral out of control.

He gripped the chair. "I won't ask you again."

I hesitated for a moment, then walked over and sat down.

He reached into his pocket, pulled out a smartphone and tapped the screen. "Now there's no way for them to hear us."

My gaze flittered to the two-way mirror.

"They can't watch us," he said. "That would be an offence. She'd go from D.I. to beating the pavement as a constable if she listens in."

Panicking, I sprang from my seat toward the door.

He cut me off.

I retreated three steps, but he kept moving until his body pressed me against the wall.

James rested his hand on my chest to keep me in place. "They can't see or hear us, Emily."

"I don't believe you."

"This is where you listen."

"Where's Xander?" I gripped his wrist. "Tell me you didn't hurt him."

"Calm down."

My hand slid to my side. "Tell me."

"Xander's fine."

"Where is he?"

"We're not talking about that right now—"

"Xander's using a false name, but he's real." I tried to comprehend what kind of technology could erase a life. "How did you remove him from the footage?"

"It's called 'deepfake.' It's the kind of tech that can save or decimate a life."

I smirked. "They're listening to us right now."

"I scanned for body heat behind the glass," he said, glancing at the mirror. "And checked for listening or recording devices."

A tremor ran through my body. "I…hate you."

"You didn't yesterday, though. When you came twice against my mouth?" He gripped my chin. "Right, Emily?"

"That was different."

"You were compliant. I need to see the same obedience now."

"What do you want?"

"You and I will leave together. You will not speak to anyone. You won't make eye contact—"

"I'm not leaving with you."

"There will be consequences should you disobey."

"You're a criminal."

"Actually, I'm not."

Shaking my head, I tried to ignore the rich scent of his cologne. Those dark notes of seduction reminding me of yesterday…

My limbs tingled, an ill-timed arousal from the way he'd crushed me against the wall. My nipples hardened thinking of the way his voice vacillated between kindness and ruthless power, seducing me with a dark-edged sin.

The memory of his kiss…down there.

I stared up at him. "Who are you?"

"I'm the one who calls the shots, Emily."

"Are you even a barrister?"

He dared to answer with a smile.

"What you're doing is illegal."

He leaned forward. "I don't break the law," he whispered. "I fucking massacre it."

No, no, no. His behavior wasn't going to be rewarded by me getting wet at the sound of his voice…or the controlling power of his tone. Or the way his palm sat squarely between my tits while pressing me against the wall. An unwanted memory flashed into my mind of how incredible his tongue felt against my skin.

As he leaned in, I felt his hardness against me, a sizable threat that was devilishly pressed into my stomach.

I drew in a sharp breath. "What do you want?"

"What was it I told you, Em?

"I wasn't to come here."

"And yet…"

I lifted my chin, fighting the urge to bite his lip. "I didn't know what else to do."

"You do as you're told."

"Tell me Xander's safe."

"Of course he is. Now…are you going to be a good girl?"

"Go fuck yourself."

"Sure you want to defy me?"

I gave my head a slight shake, my lips trembling.

"Better."

This felt like descending into madness. "What do you want me to say to them?"

He stepped back. "Nothing."

The absence of his warmth felt like a terrible loss, his body a protection I hadn't asked for.

The sergeant came back in. "Sorry, sir, we're having issues locating the footage of Ms. Rampling outside Gordon House."

James turned to me with a smug smile. "I see."

I'd lost my chance to speak with Stewart in private.

"My client and I will be leaving now," said James.

Stewart appeared in the doorway as the sergeant left. Her glare flittered to me then back to James. "I just need to ask Ms. Rampling a few more questions."

"How does the footage look?" James asked.

"It appears there is no footage." She shook her head. "Or at least we can't locate it now."

His glare served to chastise their incompetence.

"We have our forensic computer team on it," she shot back.

"I'm sure you do." James gestured towards me. "Em and I are leaving."

The metallic taste of blood filled my mouth. I'd bitten the inside of my cheek.

Stewart frowned. "Emily, will you be okay?"

I nodded reluctantly.

She closed the gap between us and leaned in, whispering to me, her words rippling into my consciousness and providing hope.

"What are you saying to my client?" snapped James.

"Just letting her know I'll be here if she wants to talk."

"What a generous entrapment." He picked up his briefcase. "Time to leave."

My legs refused to move. If I stayed, that footage would be reinstated, and if I left with him…

"Emily, shall we go?"

Chapter 15

LEAVING THE SAFETY OF THE POLICE STATION WITH BALLAD WAS INSANE. I'd risen to a new level of recklessness.

The look I'd given D.I. Stewart on the way out told her I knew this was a mistake. But seriously, I had no choice. Xander was in danger. And I'd already jeopardized his safety by coming here and spilling my secrets to the police. I'd also jeopardized my own life.

With an ironclad grip on my arm, James led me out of Scotland Yard into the chill of the late morning air. I was walking away from possibly my one chance to convince someone this shit was real. Had his grip not been so tight, I would have run back into the police station.

My life was ruled now by his endless threats.

Waiting conveniently, not to mention illegally, on the curb was a sleek black Jaguar. Standing beside the flashy car was a tall policeman. Instead of handing over a ticket to James he tipped his hat to prove he'd been guarding the Jag.

James gave a nod of thanks to the officer. Then, with the same arrogance he'd shown while extracting me from the station, he ushered me into the front passenger seat.

This was one of those expensive cars where you couldn't hear the engine running. The interior was all cream leather and maple wood. I would have admired it more if I wasn't being kidnapped right under the nose of London's finest.

"Put your seatbelt on." James threw his briefcase on the backseat. "Don't want to get you arrested."

"No, that would be bad." I rolled my eyes.

He smirked as he steered the Jag away from the curb, following behind a double-decker bus as he navigated into traffic.

I fastened my seatbelt and glanced over at him. "You're evil."

"I'm flattered."

"Xander told me you were sinister. Now I have proof of what kind of technology you use."

"As in?"

"You deleted proof that Xander ever existed. I just got the mother of all demonstrations."

"So, Ms. Rampling, what I'm hearing is you don't need to be locked up and the key thrown away?"

Folding my arms, I refused to comment further. *Asshole.*

He chuckled. "Shall I elaborate?"

"As long as it doesn't mean you'll have to kill me afterward."

"Very dramatic."

"Xander told me anything is possible with tech."

"This is how it works. If we want to own you, we do."

"And…?"

"I own you."

"What do you want from me?"

"I want you to obey."

"Didn't I just leave the police station with you like a *good girl?*"

"It's a start."

"Maybe I'll leap out of the car."

"You're tainting my mood."

"This is who I am."

"And you're not without your qualities."

"What did you do to Harold?"

James looked surprised. "Nothing."

"He sold his house. Totally out of character for him. He loved that place."

"We offered him double his property's value."

I turned in my seat to stare at him. "Making sure there's no one else left in my life to confide in?"

"You have Kitty."

"If you touch her…"

"Now, now, don't be tedious." James pressed the accelerator and I shot back in my seat.

"You're going to get a speeding ticket."

He shook his head, amused.

"Where's Xander?" I snapped. "Get him on the phone."

"How did your audition go?"

"Something tells me you already know."

"I want to hear it from you. I'd have thought you'd be in a better mood."

"A detour to New Scotland Yard sabotaged my celebrations. That and losing my boyfriend."

"Congratulations on making it to the final round. I imagine you played beautifully."

"What do you want? You want me to thank you for persuading Mr. Woo to give me another chance?"

His smile widened. "You're welcome."

My thighs squeezed together, remembering what he'd done to prepare this flighty violinist—his tongue going rogue on my clit and flicking me into a heady climax.

I could see why Xander was drawn to him. James was captivating and multifaceted. He had probably cultivated his superior attitude at one of those universities like Oxford or Cambridge.

I'd seen the way Xander looked at him with respect mixed with trepidation. He'd known all along his time with me was limited. Seeing James at The Savoy had proven it. That night my life had taken a nose-dive into chaos. They could wipe cameras but not my mind.

"What do you do for a living?" I said. "I mean really?"

"Want to see?"

My throat tightened as a series of images cycled through my mind, imagining what he might show me. A floating corpse in the Thames? A news report of an innocent public figure having committed a crime? Some strung-out woman who had once lived a happy sub-urban life now exposed to her worst nightmare because she'd crossed

James Ballad? The possibilities were endless.

My hands curled into fists. "Are you going to wipe me off the map, too?"

"Annoyingly, you're everywhere, Em. You'd take an extra day to wipe out."

"Do you get off on this?"

A ghost of a smile crossed his face as he glanced in the rearview mirror. He was playing with me.

"I'm up for anything," I said cheerfully.

"Love your spirit."

"Take me home. Fuck me. Then fall asleep and see what happens."

"I'm aroused quite frankly."

The way he held the steering wheel irritated me—his strong hands showing masterful control. He glanced over and gave a sexy smirk to reveal he was enjoying every second of torturing me.

"Why have we stopped?"

He unclipped his seatbelt. "We're here."

James had parked the car next to a tall building. A few policemen mingled nearby.

The sign for Downing Street was up ahead. We were close to the headquarters of the British Government and the Prime Minister's home. Security matched the location. Either he was as reckless as hell or had total confidence I'd not make a scene.

James climbed out and rounded the front of the car—probably to do the gentlemanly act and help me out the Jag.

I shoved my door open before he could. "Where are we going?"

"You're so intrigued with what it is I do for a living that I thought I'd give you a glimpse behind the veil." He stepped back onto the pavement.

Xander's words came back to haunt me...

There's a veil. Once you see beyond the curtain there's no going back.

I hesitated by the side of the car.

"Consider this an olive branch, Em."

"In what way?"

He stared down the street as though mulling over how best to answer. "It's what I promised Xander."

"What exactly did you promise him?"

He gave me a kind smile. "That I'd help you forget him."

I squeezed back tears, feeling that old familiar ache of loneliness.

I wasn't ready to let Xander go. How could I after all we'd shared, all we'd planned? The man heading off down the pathway was a wedge between our happiest years. I had never hated anyone more.

If I wanted to scream, now was a good time.

James walked along the side of a grey brick building with a tall brass fence around it. It looked like we'd be walking directly past Number 10.

I caught up with him. "Aren't you nervous about all these people seeing me with you?"

"No."

"You like danger, don't you, James?"

"I'm not the only one." He flashed a grin. "I know all about you."

"Are you referring to my need for an adrenaline rush during a good fuck?"

"You might want to keep your voice down. Don't want the Prime Minister hearing. He might get overexcited."

The fact that Xander had shared such an intimate detail about me burned like hell.

I stopped abruptly.

James had led me directly to the highly polished black door of Number 10.

The door swung open and he stepped into an entrance hall. With a pivot, he gave me another heart-stopping smile. In a daze, I followed him in and gave a nervous nod to the policeman who doubled as a doorman.

What the hell are we doing here?

Beneath the long red rug we stood on was a checkered floor and to my right was a large fireplace. Elegant antiquities hinted of another time. This was like a British museum and every painting, ticking clock, and dark piece of wooden furniture had been lovingly cared for. The lemony scent of furniture polish permeated the air and gave the place an old English atmosphere, a bit like a church where the voices are hushed, carrying a reverence as thick as the green velvet curtains.

The way James strolled down the hallway made it obvious he'd been here before. The respectful nods he received from those we passed showed they recognized him, too. I followed quickly, realizing his influence went all the way to one of the highest offices.

What have I gotten myself into? No, what has Xander gotten us embroiled in?

James pointed toward a leather chair. "Churchill's."

"He sat there?" I moved closer to study it.

"Those marks on the armrests are where his fingernails scratched the leather in frustration." James tilted his head to get me to keep following. "Quite a burden carrying Europe through a war."

We navigated around the staff streaming in and out of various rooms.

James flashed a warm smile my way. "What did the inspector whisper to you before we left the station?"

"She was available to talk if I wanted to come back." I stared straight ahead to hide the lie. "Where are we going?"

He paused before an office. "Here." He opened the door and entered the room.

Standing in the doorway, I questioned whether we were even allowed in here. The gold plaque on the desk announced we'd walked into the Prime Minister's private office.

He'll get me arrested.

In the center of the room was a generously sized redwood desk. To prove this was the Prime Minister's office, and to curtail any doubt to my addled brain, there was a photo on the desk of the PM himself, Charles Wildwood. He and his pretty wife were posed happily with their two children in front of a Christmas tree in the foyer here. Behind the desk sat his high-back swivel chair. The one *he* actually sat in when making those tough decisions. The very man I'd seen countless times addressing the nation.

I'd voted for Wildwood—stood in a booth and ticked the box for the Conservative party, and it had made me feel so grown up. Never had I considered the possibility I'd ever be in his bloody office.

My flesh chilled as I tried to fathom why I'd been brought here.

A large gold-framed mirror hung on the wall and from here I watched James watching me. The floor was made up of intricate white tiles and I wondered who had stood on them before us. Probably visiting dignitaries and all the others members of State who had made their stamp on history.

The ceiling was just as ornate with its white piping. The office was messy but still looked organized. There were keepsakes placed here and there from visits to other countries. Like the curved sword sheathed in silver. There were photos taken with other world leaders. He'd played a round of golf with the American President, and the photo of them relaxing on the green proved they were good at faking that they liked each other.

James was proving how powerful he was.

That's what this visit was about.

He strolled behind the office chair and held the backrest. "Sit."

"I'm not sitting there." I closed the door behind me. "What if he comes in?"

"Then he'll see you sitting in his chair."

"I don't trust you."

"That's probably wise. Now sit."

Approaching the chair, I ran through the different scenarios that could play out, but it was hard to focus while being trapped in here with James. This man was full of surprises and not the good kind. Yet he oozed a dangerous sophistication that made him magnetic and it was hard to pull my stare away from his regal stature. I'd seen how his charisma impressed the police back at New Scotland Yard. Even here, walking the endless hallways in the most reverent of places, he inspired a quiet awe.

My jaw tightened with frustration. "What point are you trying to make?"

He pulled the chair out to give me room to sit.

This, this was surreal. A moment in time that would never be repeated, and one I'd never envisioned. It was something I'd have loved to have told Xander about. Now, thanks to this man, there was no one left in my life to share this story with.

As though reading my mind he said, "Tell no one about your visit here. Understand?"

I gave a shrug.

"No, Emily, not even your mother."

If James threatened my mum, I'd stab him with that fancy marble letter opener.

I sat in the chair, resting my hands on the armrests, and soaked in the atmosphere. There was a grandeur to it with the many files neatly stacked in their leather binders, a green desk lamp to the right for those late-night sessions. In the center of the desk rested an impressively large Apple monitor. And there, on a coaster, was a half-finished mug of tea. Proving the PM even worked on a Saturday.

This was as close as I would get to a brush with a world-renowned figure.

James leaned forward and took my hand, placing it on the desk and then wrapping his fingers around my wrist. His touch made my skin tingle. The way he held me there was intimidating.

And precariously erotic.

"I get it," I said. "You have friends in high places."

When his grip tightened it sent a thrill through me.

"You're partly right," he said huskily.

"You influence his decisions?" I peered over my shoulder at him. "How?"

James let go of my wrist. Gripping the back of the chair, he spun me around to face him. "What do you want above all, Emily?"

"What do you mean?"

"I know you want to join the orchestra. Well, you're one step closer. What other aspirations do you have?"

"You know what I want."

"A house in Belgravia? Give me a day and you'll be walking through your new home in the most luxurious neighborhood in London. Money? I can have millions in gold bars placed in that safety deposit box you opened today at Lloyds. If you're thinking grander, I'm listening."

I felt a stab of anger at the humiliation I'd endured at the bank because of him. His knowing smile told me he'd followed my line of thought.

Blinking up at him I asked, "Did you help the Prime Minster get elected?"

James cupped my face with his hands. "He had a vision, Em."

No. Surely, he wasn't this influential…this powerful.

And my life was in his hands.

I closed my eyes. "James."

Tilting my head, I leaned into his palm and drew his thumb into my mouth. I suckled, nipping the tip and moving my head suggestively to deep throat it while holding his gaze.

"It's important you know," he said darkly, "I can outthink you. Outmaneuver you. And out manipulate you. Flirting is endearing. But it won't work." He pulled his thumb from my mouth and gripped my throat. "I own the man who sits here. I made him. I keep him in power. I can remove him."

His words resonated in the stillness.

It was a profound revelation that I wished I'd not heard. My throat began to ache and whether he intended it or not, I became aroused in response to his aggression. A shudder of pleasure shot up my spine and emanated to my limbs at his show of dominance.

"Interesting," he said.

Raising my chin higher, I gave him a look that told him I didn't care if he threatened my life. I wasn't going to change my mind about Xander.

I pulled away. "You can't hurt me any more than you already have."

"The Lord giveth and the Lord taketh away."

He wouldn't.

His threat to ruin my musical career made my blood chill like ice. "You're the devil."

"I own the devil."

"What are you going to do?"

He studied me with a calm expression. "Everyone has a price."

"You know what mine is."

He shoved a hand into his trouser pocket and stood there with the pose of a man who was used to dishing out advice and getting his way.

James broke the tense moment with a confident smile. "The walk back to the car will give you time to think about what's best for you."

I rose from the chair and followed him out, turning briefly to take a mental snapshot of one of the most famous offices in the world.

We retraced our steps to the front door.

A sprinkle of rain met us on the other side.

In silence, we walked along the pathway with him glancing at me now and again. Probably to see how such a visit had affected me. Maybe hoping he'd scared me into compliance. James opened the car's passenger door and gestured for me to get in.

With droplets of rain on my eyelashes, I peered into his Jag. "This is where we part ways, Mr. Ballad."

"Am I going to be able to trust you?" he asked.

"Yes."

"Are you certain?"

"If Xander wanted me, he would have fought for me."

The expression in his eyes turned kind, as though his empathy could touch my pain.

I closed the gap between us and wrapped my arms around James' body, resting my head against his chest, his woolen coat scratchy against my cheek. I didn't want James punishing Xander for my recklessness. This was me betraying myself to save him. Showing I was ready to let this go.

Let it all go.

James held me in a masterful hug.

Everything about this man screamed a desire to control and an obsession with power. Even his expensive cologne enveloped my senses, possessing the air around us.

My memory drew me back to that dimly lit room in the Barbican center yesterday. That private space where I'd mourned my dream having slipped away, minutes before James had stepped into the room and made me forget my failure.

Forget even myself.

Then, he'd given me the chance I thought I'd lost. My career was holding on by a thread. He could cut through it if I didn't comply.

This was it then—a choice between my dream and my boyfriend.

"Xander will be proud of you," he said soothingly.

"If he really exists," I whispered.

James' firm lips pressed against the top of my head in a gesture of affection. My body shuddered at the thought of his mouth lavishing me down there, swirling and teasing and luring me into an endless orgasm that he owned with precarious potency.

Peering up into his dark eyes, I whispered, "Look after him."

"He can look after himself."

With a shake of my head I said, "Promise me."

James relented with a nod.

"You pervade everything, don't you, Mr. Ballad?"

"Now you understand."

He released me from his embrace.

I turned and walked away, feeling his stare follow me as I kept going.

I rounded the corner out of his sight and then leaned against the wall, exhaling the breath I'd been holding since leaving him behind.

Chapter 16

THEY COULDN'T STEAL MY MEMORIES—THOSE PRECIOUS MOMENTS I held onto with all my heart. Our love was sacred.

The time I'd spent with Xander had helped me evolve into the person I was today. There was no avoiding that or pushing that truth aside. The life we'd built together meant everything. And he needed me.

No one was going to break us apart without facing the consequences.

I may have told James I'd accepted my fate but that had been a boldfaced lie. The hell I was letting him win—and no way was I giving him the power to ruin us. My love for Xander was all I had left. Each snapshot of the time between us was absorbed into my consciousness and held up as a shield of truth.

I'd make this right.

This wasn't me doing anything suspicious.

This was just me remembering the photo in Xander's office of his mum standing in front of a village post office. This was just me taking a train from Marylebone Station all the way to Great Missenden.

He'd told me he grew up in an old vicarage. As far as I knew, most towns like this only tended to have one of those. It should be relatively easy to find.

Great Missenden was as English as it got with its sprawling fields, blackberry bushes, and family owned stores dating back a century or more. Even the token red phone box outside the old-fashioned post office was a quaint touch. I recognized it from the photo and a jolt of excitement hit me. Maybe, just maybe, I'd find my way back to him.

If Xander's mum still lived here she may even have heard from him.

Coming here was the ultimate act in defying James.

What did he expect? I would pretend my boyfriend never existed? That a man disappearing under suspicious circumstances would simply be ignored? He had underestimated me. James had thought I'd be intimidated by the visit to Number 10 Downing Street. He'd meant to scare me off.

Yeah, not going happen.

I knocked on the front door of the vicarage, finding comfort in knowing Xander had once lived here. He'd told me this was his childhood home—he wouldn't cut his mum out of his life, surely?

I glanced back at the quiet lane behind me with a heavy dose of paranoia. I'd made my way out of the city, jumping from train to train to throw off anyone who might be following. I'd worn jeans and a hoodie and had kept my head covered for the entire journey. Still, that lingering sense that Ballad would know I was here made me doubt the wisdom of my actions. Maybe I should go home.

You've come too far.

There was no response from my knock. I made my way around the back of the property and stepped into a bright garden with rows of colorful flowers. At the end, a line of lush trees with swooping leaves. It was nice to take a few seconds to imagine Xander playing over there as a boy. Then I saw it, the tree-house resting in the enormous trunk. The one he'd told me he liked to hide in to avoid the strange noises of this old house. He'd also told me he'd spent precious mid-summer days playing out here when he'd been home from boarding school.

He'd not shared much more, though, other than his parents were away a lot of the time living in far-off places while his dad served as a senior diplomat abroad. Places they were reluctant to take Xander. Later, he'd attended the University of St. Andrews in Scotland, rounding out his education in computer science that enhanced his natural flair for tech. He was so smart I imagined he wowed his professors.

This place was a connection.

I miss him.

I should be here with him.

There'd been so many memories left to make.

I suddenly spotted an older woman in a sunhat kneeling over a patch of dirt. She dug a shallow hole with the trowel and threw in a seed, scraping the ground to cover it.

"Mrs. Rothschild?" I called over.

It was her—the woman from the photo. She was a little older, but it was definitely Xander's mum. She peered at me from beneath her floppy hat. She had Xander's golden sun-kissed complexion and his high cheekbones and bright eyes. Even the elegant way she rose to her feet and walked toward me reminded me of him.

"Sorry to bother you." I stepped forward.

There were stains on her jeans from where she'd been kneeling. This irreverence revealed her earthiness. It reminded me of the way Xander would become engrossed in his work, too. Very often I'd see his hair sticking up from pulling an all-nighter in his office, in the morning appearing as cute at hell in his creased PJs. He'd stand in the kitchen munching on a slice of buttered toast and sipping tea, his good morning smile so endearing, making me feel so at home.

God, I missed him.

"I'm a friend of your son."

"You are?"

"He told me about this place."

She had his intelligent eyes, the way they assessed a situation before lighting up when he smiled...just as she was doing now. Disarming, but I suppose that was the point.

"I'm sorry I didn't call first."

"That would have been wise." Her accent sounded Norwegian.

I pointed to the treehouse. "He told me he used to play in there."

"Yes, what can I do for you?"

"I was wondering if you've heard from him recently."

"Didn't catch your name?" She pulled off her gardening gloves and threw them on the grass.

"Emily." Not calling him Xander was a challenge, but I didn't want to freak her out by using the wrong name.

"Our family is very private, Ms…"

"Rampling." I gave her a kind smile. "Did he tell you about me?"

Her expression made my gut tighten with doubt.

"Where do you live?" she asked.

"London. I took the train down."

"It's my recommendation you take the train back immediately."

"Just tell me if you've heard from him. Tell me he's…" *Don't scare her.*

"How do you know him?"

"Did he ever talk to you about his work?"

She scratched her jaw as though needing time to think it through. "My son's not here."

"Will you ask him to call me next time you speak with him?"

"Why have you not addressed my son by his name?"

Shit.

"Sweet girl, he obviously wants nothing more to do with you."

I waited for her to deliver another scathing strike, but she didn't.

"We live together," I said.

She frowned, as though this was news to her. "Evidently my son has his reasons for saying goodbye to you."

"He didn't say much about you either."

"Do you see what's missing?"

Looking around at the well-tended plants and flowers, I tried to catch her meaning.

"Chrysanthemums," she said flatly. "The flowers one gives on the occasion of the death of a loved one. They are only used for funerals."

"I don't know what you mean."

"Then you don't know my son."

"You're saying his work is dangerous? He's protecting me."

"I'm protecting him," she clarified.

"I would never do anything to put him in danger."

"And yet you are here."

"I didn't mean…"

"Trust his judgment. He's let you go."

"I don't believe that. Not after what we had." I didn't want to say anymore and alarm her. "We were going to get married." My fingers caressed where my ring had been.

A mask of sadness fell upon her. "You should go."

"Tell him I love him. Tell him…I'll wait for him."

I would wait a thousand lifetimes if that's what it took. I would forgo children, and a home where a family would thrive, and a place where love would reign. My heart was his and it always would be because Xander was too extraordinary to forget.

My stomach ached and I rubbed it to soothe the knots.

I wanted to spend more time here…see family photos and talk about what kind of son he was and hear funny stories she was bound to have. Like when she went shopping with him in Tesco's when he was a child, and he'd surprise the other shoppers at the checkout when he guessed how much the stuff in their cart would cost them. I wanted to soak in as much of Xander's history as I could and keep this connection strong.

His mum peered up at the sky as though assessing the weather and there was something uncanny in it. "There's a shortcut to the station over the field. It's dense woodland. The coverage is good."

Was she hinting we were being watched by satellite?

My body felt chilled despite the warmth of the sun. "You know about *them*, don't you?"

She pointed to where she'd been gardening. "I'm planting peonies."

"Please, Mrs. Rothschild, I'm concerned for Xander."

"Xander?" She stared at me with sorrow.

That's not his name.

"What's your favorite flower?" she asked.

I gave a nod of resignation. "Lilies…or roses? I'm not sure."

"That's because you're too young." She gave me a warm smile.

"Mrs. Rothschild…"

"Use the gate. I'd hurry if I were you."

"I'm fine with taking the same way back."

She looked surprised. "Dear girl, my advice is equal in its standing to that of my son's."

"He told me the wrong name."

"Ah."

"What's his real name?"

"He always loved secrets."

"Did you know he's a chess master?"

"My son showed extraordinary talent for many things at a young age."

"Like what?"

"He had an uncanny ability to read people. Something tells me you're very special."

"I miss him," I said, pressing a hand to my heart.

"Whatever he has done it is to protect you."

"You know about them, don't you?" I stepped forward. "He might have gotten caught up with some sinister people. It's not my intention to upset you. I don't know who else to turn to."

"I'm sure it will all work out."

"Do you know James Ballad?"

Her lips twitched, revealing that she did. "True power is hidden."

"I've seen a little of his influence."

"You've seen nothing." She drew in a sharp breath. "And anything you have seen you would be wise to forget."

"He's really that powerful?"

"My husband was a diplomat, working in some of the most dangerous places on earth. He'd say his happiness, his safety, his contentment was not important. What he did was for a greater purpose."

"You know what your son does, don't you?"

"That's why I'm telling you to use the gate."

I refused to give up trying to find Xander. "Thank you for your time, Mrs. Rothschild."

"Do you have somewhere to stay?"

"Yes."

"And money?"

"I'm fine."

She hesitated, and gave me a look of sympathy. "It's probably best you don't return to Great Missenden."

I heard what she said, but I didn't look back.

I made my way along the side wall and out the front gate, feeling crushed that I'd not been able to persuade Mrs. Rothschild to help me.

Walking along the sundrenched pavement back the way I'd come, my hand ran along the leaves of a hedge as a sob shuddered through me. I'd hit the ultimate dead-end. Her words haunted each step I took with their scathing clarity—Xander wanted nothing more to do with me and I would never know why.

Out of the corner of my eye, I saw the blur of an SUV as it pulled up next to me.

A rush of terror left me paralyzed.

Four men in combat gear poured out of the vehicle, trapping me between them and the hedge. My heart hammered against my chest as adrenaline spiked through my veins. With unsteady legs, I bolted left to round the car and escape...

Brutal hands dragged me to the back of the car, violently forcing me onto the rear seat. I bashed my head when I hit the other side, trying to get out.

The men trailed in behind me.

One of them snatched at the hair at my nape, keeping my head still. I looked into the angry eyes of one of my attackers. His buzz cut suggested he was military.

"Careful of my hands," I begged.

I should never have come here...

"Keep still."

"Get off me."

"Shut the fuck up," he snapped.

The scent of expensive cologne seeped under my skin and I tried to inhale another breath. My scream sliced the air.

The barrel of a handgun was shoved between my lips, bruising my mouth as it crushed my tongue. Squeezing my eyes shut, I tasted the cold tang of metal and froze.

Oh, God, he's going to kill me.

"Blowjob, metal edition," he sneered, with a chuckle.

He let go of my hair as the gun was withdrawn. I wiped saliva off my chin as I gasped for the air I'd lost. Turning my head, I refused to look into the man's dead eyes.

The SUV swerved, wheels spinning, and gravity pulled me onto the floor as we sped off.

Military Man held a boot to my stomach to keep me down.

"Careful with her," said a gravelly voice from the front seat.

"She defied the boss. I'm letting her know she made a big mistake."

"That wasn't the order," came a warning from one of the others.

"He won't know." Military Man tucked his gun away.

"*He'll* know," came that same gravely tone.

I dragged in air, my eyes stinging from hot tears. I was drenched in sweat and being blasted with air conditioning, causing me to shiver uncontrollably.

"Not sure why you care," said my attacker. "Ballad's not exactly going to be gentle with her."

Chapter 17

BREATHE.

Just breathe.

I hung from shackles with my feet barely supporting my weight, a blindfold pulled taut over my eyes. My lips felt bruised from having a gun shoved into my mouth. Regret filled my every thought, and this time I felt a good dose of rage along with the fear.

"Ballad's not going to be gentle."

Trembling, taking deep breaths, I tried to judge how many hours I'd been in this place. I'd lost all sense of time and direction, but it felt like evening. My limbs were battered from the way they'd manhandled me in and out of the car. We'd been driving for what felt like hours in that SUV.

When the vehicle had finally slowed, I'd heard marching, the sound of boots on the ground and a man shouting out orders. If we'd driven through a military checkpoint the guard had failed to see me in the back, bound and blindfolded.

Or perhaps that sort of thing wasn't out of the ordinary here.

Motivated by frustration, I managed to work the blindfold off my eyes by scraping my face along my forearm.

I looked around at the sparse interrogation room.

Only minutes later, I inhaled sharply as my kidnappers filed in.

One of them lit a cigarette. He offered a drag to his gun-wielding buddy who'd bruised my lips. After inhaling the smoke, he handed it back and then swaggered over to me with a threatening, arrogant expression.

I flinched when he touched my face.

The bully blew cigarette smoke into my face. It stung my nose and left me coughing.

My terror morphed into anger. My defiant stare showed no remorse—not after they'd kidnapped me. Not after I'd done the right thing.

"Who do you work for?" he asked.

"I don't work for anyone."

He grabbed my chin. "Lie again and see what happens."

"Does Xander know I'm here?"

"Who?"

I swallowed the lump in my throat.

"This will hurt. Brace yourself." He punched my stomach.

Stars blurred my vision and agony flared in my gut as all the air left my lungs. Pitching forward, my wrists snapped in the shackles, stretching my arms painfully wide.

"I'm sorry I went to Great Missenden," I huffed out.

He pulled his fist back, ready to punch me again.

The door opened and *he* appeared like a vision of intimidation in his black tuxedo, his striking features seemingly even sharper—perhaps because his fury was only barely contained.

He strode powerfully across the room toward us. "Why is she shackled?"

There came an uncomfortable exchange of glances from the others.

James snapped his attention to me. "You're making quite a habit of defying me."

"So you resort to kidnapping a girl," I bit out. "Bit tacky for you."

He straightened his back. "As far as everyone's concerned, you're in London."

"I told a friend."

"You don't have any."

I had Kitty. She'd report me missing. Or at least look into why I wasn't answering my phone.

James smiled as though reading my mind. "Kitty Adair works for me."

Might as well have been punched a second time. "I don't believe you."

"Well, reality seems to be a problem for you."

"Is setting your thugs on me protocol, too?" I snapped.

"I hate it when my victims yell at me, Emily."

"I promise not to go back to Great Missenden."

He rolled his eyes. "Oh? That makes everything splendid."

"Does Kitty really work for you?"

"She's actually rather fond of you."

"Are you going to kill me?"

"Quite honestly, I'm undecided."

Fear slithered beneath my skin.

"Ms. Rampling, I need to see remorse."

"I'm sorry."

"Well, that's a start."

I looked over his shoulder at the other men. "I'll never disobey you again."

"I'm not convinced."

"I mean it this time, I promise."

"Do I need to threaten your family—?"

"Don't."

"I'm doing the talking right now."

Swallowing hard, I cursed myself for not thinking this through, for putting everyone around me in danger. My mum, Harold, and even Xander.

"What will it take to persuade you to forget Xander and go away, Emily?" he said darkly. "Do I need to step out of the room?"

Nausea made my stomach churn. "James, please, I just need to know he's happy."

He stepped back with a sigh. "Maybe the only way to convince you is to have him push you away." James pivoted toward the door.

I drew in a sharp, hopeful breath as Xander appeared.

His expression was as complex as when I'd first met him at Piccadilly...and just as beautiful. My beloved, the one who'd know how to get me out of here. Maybe we'd be able to leave together.

He, too, was dressed in a tuxedo that contrasted greatly with the rough surroundings. Really? They were both wearing posh suits fit for fine dining or an evening mixing with other elites—while I'd been imprisoned and abused in here.

Xander came towards me and I flinched at his glare of disappointment.

He looked conflicted. "What are you doing here?"

"I went to see your mum," I admitted.

He shot James a look of concern.

"I'm afraid she did," said James.

Xander slipped into the man I once knew, wrapping his arms around me and resting his forehead against mine, his warm breath against my skin. I clung to hope, but at the same time grief wracked my body at the thought of losing him forever.

With his firm body crushed to mine, I couldn't imagine him not being in my life. Xander was more than a part of me. This was both sublime and unbearable as I prolonged the agony of him leaving again.

His fingertip caressed my mouth. "Who did this?"

I felt too dazed to answer.

"Em, who did this to you? They cut your lip."

Trembling uncontrollably, I tried to speak but no words came out. I was too drenched in panic.

Xander spun round. "Who?"

"Step back," said James.

"I'm going to rip every last one of you apart," Xander yelled.

"Enough," James said coldly. "Stay calm."

If terror bore a name it would be Ballad. His intensity burned white hot, as searing as a furnace of wrath.

The men observed his every move and even Xander gave a nod of compliance and stepped back. Even now, after what Ballad's men had done, Xander deferred to him.

"Who has the key?" asked Xander. "I want her out of these."

James raised his hand to quiet him. "My orders were clear. No one touches her." He assessed the cuffs, reaching up and running his hand along the metal. "Who put her in these?"

The one with the cigarette threw it down and extinguished it with the heel of his boot. "We used the necessary force."

"There are four of you," James replied.

The man with the gun tapped his holster. "She made a scene. We made sure no one heard."

James blinked. "You pulled your gun on her?"

The bully shrugged. "No one saw."

My teeth clenched. "You threatened me."

"Emily, your silence is appreciated." James turned to face the man. "Show me."

"Show you what, sir?" he replied.

"What you did with your gun?" James closed the gap between them. "You cut her lip."

"I made her quiet down, sir."

"Give it to me."

The gun was unclipped from its holster and handed to James. It happened fast, with James grabbing the man by his collar and shoving him to his knees. There was no struggle, just compliance from his victim to prove Ballad owned this room and everyone in it.

James shoved the gun into the bully's mouth. "Is this what you did to her?"

The man's eyes went wide as he tasted the metal barrel.

"Nod to answer," added James.

The air seemed to crackle with tension.

James looked at me. "Close your eyes, Emily."

"No, don't, please."

"I asked you to close your eyes."

I didn't want to look, didn't want to think my actions had led to murder. Xander's hand came up and his palm covered my eyes.

James' voice broke the quiet. "If I give an order, follow it. Don't get creative, Samuel. Am I understood?"

My eyes squeezed shut beneath Xander's palm. "It's my fault," I blurted out.

"Are you taking responsibility?" asked James.

I shifted my head to see his expression. "Yes."

The man remained kneeling with his head bowed. No one tore their attention away from the sinister scene.

"I love you," Xander whispered to me.

And it felt like goodbye.

This was the man I loved, the person I had given myself over to in every conceivable way, and seeing him again, being this close was all I had needed in this moment to survive.

Uncertainty hung in the air like invisible smog.

James rested his palm on the kneeling man's head. "Key."

Samuel reached into his pocket and offered up the small cuff key he'd used to secure me.

James took it. "We leave in fifteen minutes."

I let out a sigh of relief that he was going away.

No arrogance remained in my attacker's expression. He looked up at Ballad with gratitude and respect. Then he rose and strode quickly to the door, leaving without looking back.

"Everyone out," ordered James.

The other men followed. The door shut behind them.

I inhaled deeply, trying to calm my trembling limbs.

James handed Xander the key and he used them to unlock the cuffs. As soon as I was free, I fell into Xander's arms and he embraced me tightly. My limbs ached as my circulation returned. More bruises marked where the metal cuffs had chaffed my wrists. I stretched my fingers, relieved they were unharmed.

"You shouldn't have gone there," Xander whispered.

"I needed to know you were…." Tears stung my eyes. *Still alive.*

"Did they do anything to you?" He tapped near my lip. "Other than this?"

"No."

James shoved his hands in his pockets with his usual stance—confident and unshakable. "I couldn't have been clearer, Em. And to be transparent now, no one has ever gotten more than one pass from me. You're the exception. But I'm done giving second chances."

"Hurt me and you'll lose Xander."

James faced him. "You know what needs to be done."

"I can handle her," said Xander. "And it'll be my way."

"Because so far you've done a stellar job."

"I can deal with her."

James looked angry. "I've yet to see her convinced."

Xander rested his hand on James' shoulder. "Trust me. I've got this."

"Meet me at the rendezvous. The pilot has already burned through enough fuel."

I stared at James. "I'll never forgive you."

"Raise the stakes," James said sharply. "If you think it will help."

"Does he know?" I asked. "Does he know what you did to me at my audition?"

He turned to face me. "Yes, he does."

It was a strike to my heart.

"Then you're both as bad as the other," I snapped. "I'm going to go see D.I. Stewart. I'm going to tell her everything."

Xander flinched. "Em, shut up."

James turned to me with a dangerously serene expression.

"I have evidence that Xander exists," I said. "I have it hidden. I'll show her those photos and she'll believe me. She'll investigate you."

"I've failed you," said James. "My men were too harsh. I should have been more…"

"She doesn't mean it." Xander rubbed my arm.

"Show her what you're capable of, Xander," Ballad said darkly.

My gaze snapped from James to Xander.

Xander looked away from me, his expression conflicted. "It's better if it's me, Em." He eased me against the wall and reached his hand down, unzipping my jeans.

"What are you doing?" I stuttered.

Firm fingers slid along my panties, finding and flicking my clit, bringing a jolt of pleasure. "I need you to listen to us," said Xander. "Say you understand the danger you're in."

It felt good. *It felt wrong.*

They were trying to scare me. Make me regret defying them.

Having James watch Xander finger-fuck his girlfriend was a walk into a realm that was forbidden and twisted and yet darkly beautiful.

I gave a whimper of pleasure.

Muscles tightened around fingers that were a fierce piston as he plunged inside me in a steady rhythm, faster and more insistent. The pressure of his thumb on my clit was bringing me closer to the edge.

I turned my head away, confusion raging in my mind at the way these two men were trying to scare me.

What I wanted from them both would scare them more...

Rising out of the depths of my imagination was the fantasy of Ballad touching me, too—of both their fingers playing with my clit, both fingering me, bringing me to a heady climax. I wanted it to be Ballad's lips on mine and Xander's on my pussy. If I was brave enough to let my thoughts fly free with what I truly wanted, it would be Xander's intensity and Ballad's fierceness capturing me between them.

Xander withdrew his hand and I cupped my sex at the loss of his touch, a near climax never to be realized. When I opened my eyes, Xander was showing me his wet fingertips.

"Lick it off," ordered James.

My face flushed wildly. Xander's fingers brushed my mouth and I suckled them, tasting my sweetness, arousal flooding through me like the rush of a drug.

A frisson owned my being and it felt like perfection, a poetic need as potent as life itself that couldn't be denied. A soft moan escaped me as a shudder wracked my body. I needed to come and being denied this pleasure felt crueler than any words.

They'd teased me to the edge of an orgasm and denied me fulfillment in a final punishment.

I shoved Xander's hand away and narrowed my accusatory stare on James. "I hope you die a devastating death."

He headed for the door.

Xander called after him. "I'll have her sign an NDA."

"The time for such reasonable actions is behind us. See you at the flight pad."

Even though he'd left the room, James' aura haunted the seconds that lingered, and his presence still saturated every molecule of air.

Xander reached into his pocket and withdrew a phone. "Let's get you out of here."

What kind of man follows an order to touch his girlfriend in front of another? Xander would never know what was in my thoughts...he wouldn't guess my secret longing.

They couldn't break me.

Xander held his iPhone to his ear and barked an order. "I need you to fly me off base." He listened carefully. "I'll tell you the location when we get there."

A slither of dread snaked up my spine.

Xander hung up and shoved his phone in his pocket. "We have three minutes to get to the pad."

"Where are we going?" I held my breath.

"I'll do what I can to get you away from here."

I sprinted toward the door.

He wrapped his arms around my waist, his strong grip refusing to relent.

I tried to wriggle free. "Let me go."

"You won't get off this base without me."

"Where are we?"

"Doesn't matter. You won't be coming back."

Shaking off his grip, I made another mad run for the door.

He trapped me against the wall. "I need you to listen."

"What's your real name?" I said on an exhale.

"I don't want to put you in any more danger."

"Tell me," I seethed. "Or I'm not going anywhere."

His eyes squeezed shut. "Xavier."

"Xavier," I whispered.

"Look, I know how to convince Ballad to give you another chance."

"Why did you leave him?" I tried to make sense of it.

"I wanted something he couldn't deliver."

"And he can now?"

"Yes."

"And you believe him?" I tried to read the truth in his eyes.

He looked away. "I need to get you somewhere safe."

Xavier led me out of the room and down the whitewashed hall-way. With each step we took, I couldn't help but feel I was trading one trap for another.

Chapter 18

THE HEAT INSIDE THE MILITARY HELICOPTER WAS OPPRESSIVE—THE noise so loud it almost drained out our voices.

Exhaustion pulled me down, my body aching, reminding me of my harrowing journey from Buckinghamshire and the rough treatment from my kidnappers. The view below gave me no clues as to our destination. Far below, sprawling homes and endless woodland merged together in a blur until there was nothing but open land.

"Water?" Xavier offered.

I studied his face. All this time I'd been living with a man and I hadn't even known his real name.

I shouted over the chop of the blades, "Are we going back to London?"

"Somewhere a lot safer," he replied.

I just wanted to go back to my hotel in Covent Garden. Seeing my boyfriend again came with a catch. The cut on my lip was a reminder of that. It hurt each time I tried to talk. There was an upside of having nothing to smile about.

Behind where Xavier sat was camouflage paraphernalia wedged behind mesh to keep it in place. Ballad had connections to the military. With each interaction, I learned more sinister facts about him...and this one was truly terrifying.

"I left my Strad in the hotel," I called over.

Xavier loosened his necktie.

"Where were you going tonight?" I gestured at his tuxedo. "I've been in a living hell and you've been living it up with the boys."

"You shouldn't have gone to my family home, Em."

"You don't get it, do you?"

He shook his head. "You've complicated everything."

"What are you talking about?"

"You should have gotten on with your life."

I leaned forward. "What kind of girlfriend would that have made me?"

"I told you I was going back to them. I asked you to forget me."

"I've been out of my mind." I pointed at him in frustration. "You... you never loved me. I was just a girl you used for a distraction until you were ready to go back to them."

He sat back in surprise. "I've been trying to protect you. I think of you every second of every day. Seeing you hurting like this is ripping my heart out. Don't accuse me of having fun while you're out there living your life. What I do is impossible, and you were the only respite from that."

"Why didn't you explain?"

He drew in a calming breath. "If saving you means I have to do the unthinkable..."

"What does that mean?"

But he punished me with silence.

"If you really love me..."

His gaze rose to find mine. "There's only one way this can work."

"You and me? How?"

"If it doesn't, we're both fucked."

What the hell did that mean?

"Do you know where all our things are?" I asked. "Our passports?"

He ignored my questions, glancing down at the scenery below. "We're here."

Beyond a strip of land on the horizon I made out a dense forest. As we banked left over the woods, an estate came into view with a great lake surrounding it. A magnificent vision—we were flying towards a castle.

My jaw tightened. "Where have you brought me?"

"Hold on. We're landing."

The helicopter touched down, the blast from the blades bending the trees on the edge of the forest. Xavier unclipped his buckle and came over to help with mine. With my hand in his we leaped out onto a grassy bank, then bent over while hurrying to avoid the bluster from the blades above.

Hand in hand we ran toward a drawbridge. When we made it to the edge, Xavier turned and signaled to the pilot. The helicopter rose off the ground.

I watched my last hope of escape fly off over the trees and bank left until it was out of sight. We walked across a wooden bridge to reach a medieval gate.

I pulled my hand from his. "Are you sure James won't find us?"

All he had to do was ask the pilot where we were dropped off.

Xavier whipped out his phone. "That's always a possibility."

"What's the plan?"

"Let's get inside."

Looking down at the moat surrounding the castle, I had an uncomfortable vision of me swimming across it if the bastard found us.

"Who is opening the gate?" I followed its rise into the stone archway.

He'd punched a series of digits on his phone. "This place is teched-out."

"You've obviously been here before."

Another layer of his life was peeled away, and it dug the knife of betrayal deeper.

My lungs filled on a panicked breath. "I don't feel good about this."

In fact, it was hard to recall my last settled thought.

I walked beside him down the ancient stone pathway towards the entrance. A click signaled he'd unlocked the big door ahead. I only hoped it was as easy to get out.

The door was as heavy as it looked. Xavier gave it a shove and it opened into the castle's grand foyer.

The décor was as I imagined it would be. Everything reflected old-world England with impressive antiques and a well-worn stone floor. Two regal knights stood frozen in time at the foot of the sweeping staircase, which swept up to an impressive upper floor with ornate railings. From upstairs, one could easily view the entire foyer below.

I could hide out here for a while. Maybe this wasn't so bad.

Crisscrossed jousting lances hung on the wall of a hallway that we strolled down as though we were on a tour and not two people being hunted. I tried not to think about the reality of our situation, choosing instead to admire the brass chandeliers that hinted at the centuries that had seen this place once lit by candle flame.

"How old is this place?" I asked.

"Sixteenth century."

"You know your way around well enough."

He led me into a modern kitchen that still had an ancient hearth with a large empty pot hanging within.

Xavier pointed to a bricked area. "They still make their own bread. It's delicious."

"When was the last time you were here?"

"Been a while."

Over to our right was a long antique dining table, surrounded by several high-back chairs. He shrugged out of his suave black jacket and threw it over the back of one of them.

"How can you be so calm?" I snapped. "After what just happened?"

"I think better when I'm calm."

"We need to devise a plan," I said. "We need to think about leaving the country."

"We should probably eat something first."

I was still running on adrenaline. "Where's the staff?"

Xavier unbuttoned his cuffs and rolled up his sleeves. "He releases them for the weekend."

"Who owns this place?"

Xavier headed for the fridge.

"You brought me to *his* home?" My heart rate took off and my legs wobbled at the rush of panic I felt.

"This is as safe as it gets."

"Are you sure he won't suspect us coming here?"

"How do eggs sound? Scrambled on toast? Your favorite."

We'd just escaped Dr. Evil and fake name here wanted to play house. Xander...or Xavier...had always been quirky, but this was veering off toward madness.

He was keeping something from me.

Leaning on the central island, I watched him open the fridge and grab a wire basket filled with eggs, a jug of milk, and a tub of butter. He placed them on the central island. Then, he grabbed a pan from a cupboard.

"Xavier," I began softly, "the pilot will tell him where he brought us." My fingers gripped the edge of the island.

"We're locked in."

"He can't get inside?"

He broke into a warm smile. "He listens to me."

"Why have you bought me here?"

He carried over three plates he'd retrieved from a cupboard and set them down on the island. "You could live here for weeks and not need to leave."

My flesh chilled. "How do you know this?"

"I've stayed here before."

"I gathered that."

"Don't be pissy."

"I'm a sitting target."

"He would never hurt me like that. We have too much of a history."

"Who is this man to you?"

Xavier refused to look at me, and, in that moment...*I knew.*

"Your friendship with Ballad is the only reason I'm still alive?"

He chose his words carefully. "He hides his kindness."

"Let's leave."

"There's nowhere you can go he won't find you."

"Do you really believe you can protect me?"

"Yes."

"Just come out and say it."

He went to say something and paused. "I don't want to hurt you."

"I'm in the middle of nowhere, Xander."

"Xavier."

"How do I even know *that's* your real name?"

"It is."

"What about when we got married. You'd have to tell me then."

"I was going to deal with it."

"I can't stay."

"Running is futile." He reached for me. "Come here."

I refused with a wave and my thoughts returned to my suspicions.

It had been the way Xavier deferred to James, the way they'd swapped glances, the way James had relented to his will and Xavier to his.

Xavier gripped the edge of the island. "I've got this."

"What's really going on here?"

"I will tell you this much...Ballad always gets what he wants."

"And he wants you?" My voice trembled as I watched his expression, watched him fail to deny it. "Did you..." *Have an affair with him?*

A kind smile reached his eyes. "I need you to understand—"

"Why didn't you tell me?"

He ran a hand through his hair. "When we met, I warned you that my life is complicated. Told you not to ask about my past—"

"I didn't expect your past to include...him."

"You once told me that seeing two men together was hot."

I ignored that. "Your past has caught up to you, Xavier." Rage spiked my adrenaline.

He rounded the counter and came over to embrace me.

My hands pressed his chest to prevent him from pulling me close. "I can't think straight."

"I tried to avoid this."

I peered into his eyes. "Why did you leave him?"

A chill washed over me as my gut told me I was close to the truth.

"I wanted...more." His fingers touched his mouth as though remembering a kiss—not mine. "I told him I would only come back if..."

My lips trembled. "You're lovers again?"

"I met you, Em. I wasn't expecting to fall in love. You came into my life and I fell hard for you." Xavier shook his head adamantly. "Things have changed out there in the world since I've been gone. They need me back. This is not about a relationship. It's about doing the right thing."

"Why won't you tell me what it is you do? It would make all of this easier to understand."

"I'll talk to James."

"Wait. Do you set fires with your mind?"

He burst into laughter. "You're the only person I know who'd say that. No, no fire starting. Nothing like that." He was grinning now.

"I want you back."

"I don't get to decide that, Em."

"Ballad does?"

"Let's eat."

"I'm not hungry." I caressed my aching stomach. "How does he have so much power over you?"

"I have power, too. I'm not without my influence."

"Like how?"

"I'm the one they need."

"But Ballad has the ultimate power?"

"He knows if anything happened to you, he would lose me."

Thoughts of them together swept across my vision and played out in real time. I tried to grasp this heartbreaking truth that Xavier belonged to James...*like that.* I was in a fight of my life for the one I loved.

"We've not been intimate since I came back."

I swallowed back tears. "Tell me about him."

"Not a good idea."

I looked around to make my point. "He's aristocracy."

"Obviously."

"Is that where he gets his power?"

"Yes and no."

"Elaborate." I needed to understand the man whose wits I had to go one on one with.

"History robbed him of his title."

"What title?"

Xavier looked surprised. "King."

"Of England?"

"Great Britain and the sovereign of fifteen countries." He lowered an accusatory stare on me. "Did you even pay attention in school?"

"Did you ever consider the danger you were putting me in?"

"Yes, that's why I walked away from you on the London Underground. I tried to lose you. You persisted. And then you let me fuck you up against a brick wall in a tunnel. I was surprised you stuck around."

I slapped him.

"I deserved that," he admitted. "I didn't mean it. This is hard on me, too."

I shook my head. "Why do you insist on pushing me away?"

"Because I'm not the man you think I am."

"Who are you then?"

"My ability…is unusual." He brushed a hand over his cheek. "Once people hear what it is, they're scared of me."

"I love you."

"I don't want to argue."

"I'm sorry." I fell against him and crushed my body to his.

"Do you hate me for Ballad?"

"I didn't know you were into men."

"Him…it's him."

Breaking his stare, I understood more than I wanted him to know. James had this magnetic way about him, an enticing suaveness and dark sophistication. His stark beauty affected all those around him… his regal features carried a social influence that saw him getting his way.

"When did he last kiss you?" I had to know.

"The night before you and I first met at Piccadilly."

"Nothing since?"

"No."

"Who beat you up the night I met you?"

"We had a scuffle. I left." Xavier stepped forward and wrapped me in his arms. "What can I tell you to make you feel safe?"

"How do we leave?"

He held me at arm's length. "We have to see this through."

"How do we survive him?"

"I need to earn your trust back."

Easing away, I let him know it was too late.

"Did you see my favorite tree?"

Blinking up at him, I realized what he was saying. "In Great Missenden?"

He nodded.

"I thought of you in that garden," I admitted.

"I'd hide in that tree-house with novels I'd found in my dad's library. He had a thing for sci-fi. I wanted to be just like him. Anything he read I wanted to read."

I gave a shrug. Him letting me in now felt like a wasted effort.

"What about you?" He kissed the top of my head. "Tell me something I don't know about you. That if we'd spent more time together, I'd have found out."

"What's the point?"

"There's a chance for us."

My gaze met his, tendrils of happiness trying to ensnare me. "Promise."

"I promise."

The room swirled and I replayed his words while holding onto this chance he was offering.

"I have a thing for dinosaurs," I whispered.

"Impress me with something I don't know about the world two hundred and forty-five million years ago."

"No."

"Humor me."

"The chicken is the closet known modern relative to the T-Rex."
I pointed to the eggs. "You're about to tuck into a dinosaur's relative."

He broke into a smile. "I love you so much, Em."

"Love you, too," I said, blushing. "You knew that about dinosaurs
already, didn't you?"

He grinned, and said, "Congrats, by the way."

I peered up at him. "You heard I got through the first audition at
the London Symphony?"

He looked full of regret. "I wish I could have been there."

Outside the window I heard the sound of blades slicing through
the air—a helicopter was landing close by.

I felt a chill of terror. "What have you done?"

"I don't expect you to understand my reasoning."

A cold sweat snaked down my back. "Is that him?"

"The only way to survive this is for him to fall for you like I did."

"What?"

"Win him over, Em."

I shoved him away. "I hate him."

"Fighting him is dangerous."

"I will not have that man anywhere near me."

"It's not your decision."

"Well, it's definitely not yours."

"You asked why I brought you here."

"You'll get me killed," I stuttered.

"Em, listen to me—"

I bolted out and down the hallway, veering left, recalling every
piece of décor that served as a landmark—all the way to the front door.

The handle refused to turn.

I spun round and jolted at the sight of James strolling toward us
through the east hallway, his long coat flapping behind him. He came
into the foyer looking even more vicious.

From the west hallway, Xavier appeared at a run and stopped
abruptly when he saw him.

James glared at him. "I failed to make it to the dinner, Xander.

Apparently, someone hijacked my helicopter."

"Ah."

"Want to tell me why that seemed like a good idea?" he seethed.

"I brought her here."

"I can see that." James stepped closer. "I had a flight to catch."

"You shouldn't be meeting with Iv—" He caught himself before saying the man's name. "Send someone else."

"He didn't know I was coming. Or so I thought." James ripped at his bowtie to undo it. "It should have been me."

"Bad idea."

"Did I ask for your opinion?"

"Not this time, no." Xavier ambled over to him. "What happened?"

James closed his eyes and seemed to be steadying himself. "We'll discuss it later."

"Something happened?"

"Later," snapped James.

"You forced my hand with Em."

"You think this helps her?"

"The alternative?"

"She's to be questioned here then?" James didn't hide his disapproval. "By me. This is what you want?"

"If that's what it takes, yes."

"Your order was simple. Clear. Unfuckable." Ballad's eyes narrowed on him. "Protocols are there for a reason."

"There's always another way. You taught me that."

"Want to join us, Xander? See the consequences of your actions?"

Icicles surged through my veins.

"Ms. Rampling." James pivoted to face me. "If you have nothing to hide you have nothing to fear."

My legs wobbled beneath me. "What's happening?"

"Who did you speak with about us?" asked James.

Oh, shit. I'd mentioned him to Xavier's mum. "No one."

James gestured for me to follow. "Sure about that?"

"Where are you taking me?"

"We're going to explore how willing you are to obey."

"I'm not hiding anything," I said.

Ballad reached out for my hand and took it, squeezing with a firm grip as he wove his fingers through mine. "You've been up to no good, Em. Let's crack that secret open."

Outraged, I said, "I know his real name."

"Yeah, might not want to piss me off any more than I already am," James warned.

Chapter 19

MY EYES ADJUSTED TO THE ROOM.

No, not just a room…a dark chamber with torture devices—like the ones on display in the London Tower. This was James reminding me of his threat against my life.

Still, he couldn't know what I'd done. Unless he'd gone to Lloyds bank and checked out my safety deposit box. And I had the only key.

"Nice place you've got here," I said with false bravado.

"We've kept many of the rooms the same to preserve our history," James told me with a cold smile.

Walking past Xavier, I headed for the door. "Show me what else you've got in the way of medieval paraphernalia. Love those tapestries. How do you ever leave this place?"

"Emily." James shrugged out of his jacket. "Shut the door."

Despite my doubt and apprehension, I closed it, leaning back against the wood. This man was the reason I'd lost Xavier. Whatever he needed my boyfriend for could be done by someone else. He'd manipulated him back into his life with some contrived story and Xavier had believed it.

I was going to fight for him.

So, I stayed put. "Xavier told me you have royal blood?"

James shot him a quelling look.

"It was important to establish trust," Xavier explained. "Share a bit about you."

"What else did you tell her?"

"Apparently you could have been king?" I answered for him.

"I imagine my ancestors are more upset than I am."

"Your ancestor, Richard of York, was entitled to the throne," added Xavier, as he leaned against the frame of a rack.

"What happened," I asked.

"You've heard of the two princes who disappeared in the confines of the Tower of London?" said Xavier.

"Yes."

"What do you remember about them?"

I recalled my shaky history lessons. "Two Princes were held in the Tower as prisoners. Was it in the fourteenth century?"

James gave a nod. "They were there to be protected."

"They were brothers?"

"Yes. Edward V, King of England, and Richard of Shrewsbury, Duke of York," said James. "Ages nine and twelve. They were lodged at the tower for their protection so Edward's coronation as King could go unhindered."

I remembered. "But they died before he was crowned king—under suspicious circumstances."

"They disappeared," added Xavier.

"I thought their bones were discovered in the late seventeenth century," I said. "Two workmen found them under the stairs of the Tower? Didn't Charles II have them buried in Westminster Abby?"

"She does know her history," said Xavier. "But what you couldn't know was animal bones were mixed with adult bones."

"To make it look like they died?" I realized.

"The false bones were placed in the box to protect the boys." James sat on the edge of the rack...an intimidating move on his part.

I ignored it. "I thought the boys were murdered?"

"The princes survived," said Xavier.

The weight of this revelation had me staring at James. "They lived?"

Xavier pointed to him. "You're looking at Edward V's direct descendant."

"So they went into hiding." I studied James' regal features. "What does this mean? You'll challenge the crown?"

James laughed. "Not on the agenda."

I glanced from him back to Xavier.

This could work—us being civil and clearing the air, having a rational conversation even if James was using this place to intimidate me.

A window let in just enough light to throw shadows over the faces of these two gorgeous men. The mood was changing…sinister undertones bubbling to the surface.

I wondered if anyone had died in here.

James pushed to his feet. "I have shared something deeply personal with you, Em. A secret kept over centuries. I'm giving you the same chance to be honest."

My mouth went dry with nervousness. "How do you mean?"

James patted the rack. "Let's talk about the note."

All the air left my lungs.

James motioned to the rack. "Or we can chat here, sweetheart."

"You took me to number 10 Downing Street," I said breathlessly. "I didn't ask to go there."

James lifted his hands, palms up, in a gesture that didn't seem sincere. "To prove I trusted you to be reasonable."

I reached behind me for the door handle.

"Don't try it," ordered James.

I licked my lips nervously, trying to swallow my panic. "I admit reporting Xavier missing at the police station was a mistake. I'm sorry."

James gave me a severe look. "The inspector whispered something to you before we left. What was it?"

"I already told you…she told me I could return to the station if I wanted to talk with her."

James came closer. "The truth."

If I ran, I'd be confessing my guilt for hiding the truth of what the inspector really told me. If I ran, I'd never make it out.

I moved close to Xavier and wrapped my arms around him. "I don't like this."

He pressed his lips to my forehead. "You know how much I love you."

James folded his arms across his chest. "Em, how was your trip to Great Missenden?"

Fear welled inside me. "You would have done the same."

"I'm flattered you expressed such an interest in me to Xavier's mum," said Ballad. "Let that be the last time you use my name in public."

The way Xavier's expression filled with concern sent a slither of terror up my spine.

I let go of him and backed away. "I didn't speak to anyone else."

"That note," asked James. "Who was it intended for?"

Xavier stepped toward me. "Just tell us, Em."

"There was nothing about you in the note. I left it in the safety deposit box. I'm the only one with a key."

I'd left it there in case something happened to me...

James forced a smile. "Actually, I have it here."

My back hit the wall as I watched him unfold the note I'd left with the money in the safety deposit box.

He read some of it and then looked up at me.

Fuck.

I'd laid it all out on the piece of paper he was holding. Named names and written down the timeline of meeting James and all that had transpired since. James was reading those parts with a brow arched in curiosity.

"Let's get her to open up a little more," he said.

Xavier reached out and pressed his hand against my lower spine, pushing me across the room towards the rack. "Don't fight it."

He lifted me off my feet and laid me on the contraption. Looming above me, they both strapped my arms above my head with rope and did the same to my ankles at the base.

I knew struggling would be futile, but I did anyway—until my body gave up when the binds tightened.

My wrists stung from the the rope holding me in place.

James leaned over, cupping my face in his hands. "We removed the money when we retrieved the note, Emily. You were warned."

Somewhere in the far reaches of my mind I knew this torture

device was designed to stretch a body to a painful extreme and then snap a spine. Who cared about losing half a million pounds in the scheme of things? I never wanted it anyway.

James tipped up my chin. "Last chance to confess, Em, and then you get to see how much of a bastard I can be."

"Let me go," I pleaded, staring at him wide-eyed.

"The truth."

Swallowing hard, I tried to assess if their threat was real. "The inspector didn't believe me."

James gave the lever a nudge and my arms were pulled taut and my legs stretched uncomfortably.

"Did you call her back?" asked James.

"No."

"Sure?" he pushed the lever farther.

"No doubt you've monitored my phone records," I said. "You already know I didn't." My body was wrung out with the pressure of being pulled too taut.

"Have a think about what you remember." James rose up and grabbed his jacket. "Xavier, after you."

"She's telling the truth," snapped Xavier.

"Don't leave me," I begged.

Xavier flinched. "I'm not leaving her."

James shook his head. "We need to talk."

"We'll talk later," said Xavier

James' jaw twitched. "They shot the Puma out of the sky."

"You were meant to be on that flight." Xavier looked horrified.

"So were you."

"Was Samuel on that helicopter?"

Ballad's nod came with a flash of sadness across his face.

It was as though I wasn't here as they dealt with their unspoken grief for the man they'd sent in James' place.

"No one knew about the flight," whispered Xavier.

"Someone knew," said Ballad, and he glanced at me.

"She wasn't out of my sight."

James gestured to the door, indicating Xavier was to leave with him. "Let's give her adequate time to think about her future…and how she'd like it to play out."

"Ten seconds," said Xavier. "That's all I need. Then I'll be out."

James gave a nod and headed for the door. "I'll be outside."

With James gone, Xavier hurried over to me and his mouth crashed against mine. He was stopping me from speaking, worried that Ballad would overhear.

His kiss was firm and passionate, his tongue lashing mine. His affection soothed me in this dark, foreboding place. His touch at my wrist made me jolt until I felt him loosening my binding.

When he made it to the door, he glanced back with a look that told me this was it—my last chance to escape.

The door slammed and I heard the sound of a key turning. They'd locked me in.

I tried to ignore the rusted shackles on the walls. That cage for a human. A cupboard-like structure that looked like a person would be shoved inside. My jaw tightened as my secret burrowed deeper.

I worked my way out of the binding and with a free hand was able to get my left wrist undone, too, and then the rope at my feet. With shaky legs, I pushed off the rack and hurried to the door. Despite the echo of a key turning, I managed to pull the rusty door open. Xavier had rigged my escape.

There was no time to explore.

Hurrying along the hallway and up the winding staircase, I made it to the vast foyer and sprinted to the front door.

It was locked.

I'd find another way.

Voices carried…theirs.

No, I couldn't do it…couldn't leave Xavier behind. If I could just get his attention, I might be able to draw him away from James.

Tiptoeing down the hallway, I closed in on what sounded like an argument. Pressing my ear against the door, I tried to make out their conversation.

They were talking about a land to air missile. It had taken down that helicopter. My heart skipped a beat at their anger revealing someone had attempted to assassinate James. Or even Xavier. My being at that military base had prevented their trip. Xavier was making this his argument to prove my innocence. Telling James he should set me free.

The door flew open. I staggered back.

James jolted to a stop when he saw me.

Shit.

I bolted down the hallway to escape him and heard his footsteps behind me fast approaching...

Sprinting around the corner, I skidded precariously on the floor, hitting the wall with outstretched hands. My focus snapped up to the jousting stick fixed on two hooks, and I eased the long wooden pole down as it wobbled dangerously.

Heaving it under my arm to balance the thing, I gripped it to still its teetering and readied it to point at Ballad.

Come and get it, fucker.

Chapter 20

J AMES RUSHED AROUND THE CORNER AND CLOSED IN ON ME.
His hand knocked away the tip of the joust as he skidded
past, swearing as he dodged it.

Xavier followed fast at a blur, unable to slow down in time to stop.
I watched in horror as the point of the joust struck his abdomen. A
huff of pain escaped his lips and he doubled over, collapsing to the
stone tiles while clutching his belly.

The joust fell from my grip with a loud clang.

James slumped to his knees beside him and reached for his shirt.
"Let me see!"

Xavier went still.

A scream tore out of me as I hurried to my fiancé's side.

I scrutinized his body, trying to see the severity of the wound,
vaguely aware of James' angry glare on me. The one I deserved, the
one that told me I would regret this for the rest of my life.

"Please, no," I sobbed.

"What were you thinking?" yelled James.

Xavier opened an eye and laughed, rolling onto his back and pulling me down on top of him. "That hurt."

I let out a howl of relief and pressed my cheek to his chest. "I'm
so sorry."

Xavier rubbed his stomach. "I'm okay."

James sprang to his feet and grabbed me by the back of my shirt,
hauling me off of Xavier with momentum and dragging me along-
side him down the hallway. My legs were almost off the ground as he
forced me to run at his pace.

"James," Xavier called after him. "I'm fine."

"Not the point," James growled.

"It's kind of funny," Xavier said, hurrying after us.

"There's nothing funny about it." James kicked a door and it flew open.

He dragged me into a grand dining room with a long table surrounded by high-back chairs. The decades in here were as preserved as this man's fury.

He lifted me up and thrust me down forcefully on my back. Searing agony shot down my spine as I landed wrong, my legs dangling off the edge. My body shuddered under the fierce pressure he exerted when I tried to rise.

It happened fast—James left my side for a beat and then quickly returned with a sword. I heard the grate of metal against metal as he unsheathed the weapon and brought the silver edge to rest at my throat.

I froze, the blood draining from my face.

My flesh chilled with terror. One slice through my neck...

James gripped the hilt with white knuckles. "Want to play, little girl?"

Xavier raised his hands to caution him. "Don't."

The sword's edge pressed deeper into my neck and I tried to swallow as the cold metal dug into my skin.

"James, you promised you wouldn't," said Xavier.

"She could have killed you."

Xavier stepped closer. "Put it down."

"This is not a game, Ms. Rampling," James seethed. "This is life or death and I'm done playing nice. This is where your privilege ends."

"I'm sorry," I managed.

James pressed harder.

Rage filled every cell of my body as my hate soared for this man. "Kiss me first." I held his gaze triumphantly.

James shot a frustrated look at Xavier.

Xavier gave a shrug.

James studied me for a few moments. Then he leaned in and pressed his lips to mine, not lifting the sword but keeping it there as an ever-present threat. His tongue was a savage, forceful persuader, battling mine. I found his kiss different than Xavier's—it was arrogant and controlling, and full of rage. It stung my cut deliciously in an arousing, terrible way.

He pulled back. "Time's up."

I pressed my lips together to soften the burn and soothe the cut. "I've already told you the truth."

James wore an incredulous expression as he stared down at me.

Then he rested the sword on the table and his hand moved to my chest to hold me still. "Speak."

"There's nothing to say." I pleaded with my eyes.

James stepped back and stood straight. "Look behind you."

Warily, I glanced at Xavier and then followed his line of sight, turning my head to see a violin resting on a corner cabinet—my Stradivarius.

I sprang up, but James moved too swiftly, making it down the side of the table before me and reaching for my violin. He held it by the neck, lifting it above his head so I couldn't grab it from him.

"Give it to me." I leaped for it.

"There's about to be one less Strad in the world."

I struggled to reach it. "Xander, you gave it to me. It's mine. Tell him."

"His name's Xavier," said James dryly.

My efforts were futile against his towering height. "Please."

"How much is this thing worth?" James looked thoughtful. "Couple of million?"

"You wouldn't." Drenched in terror, I froze before him.

James admired it. "Not to mention the craftsmanship."

Sweat snaked down my spine. "James, please, I'll do anything!"

He closed his eyes in fake appreciation. "The music this instrument makes is like no other."

"No, don't."

James grasped the neck with both hands and swung it toward the wall.

I inhaled sharply at the sight of my beloved instrument being flung toward the stone at lightning speed, stopping just short of obliteration.

"She said she believed me." I drew in a deep breath. "The inspector told me to get her evidence. She'd seen something like this before—people disappearing from cameras. She said you were untouchable without it."

James held the violin poised an inch from the wall. "That it?"

"Yes, I promise." I reached out for the violin.

James handed it to me.

I stepped back with the instrument clutched to my chest like it was a lifeline, my heart still hammering and my flesh clammy.

James smiled pleasantly. "I'm going to make dinner. Come with me. I need to keep an eye on you."

You can piss off.

"That's an order," he said.

Falling against Xavier's chest with my violin pressed between us, I tried to catch my breath.

"It's over." Xavier pried the violin from my hands. "Em, let me put it somewhere safe." He took it from me and placed it in its case.

"You broke into my hotel room and stole it?" I asked James.

"You mean the room I'm paying for," he snapped.

I went over to the violin case and rested my hands on it protectively.

"Em told you what you wanted to know." Xavier glared at him. "Now we can all relax."

James straightened. "We'll have dinner and then decide what happens next."

"Seriously," snapped Xavier. "A little more reassurance, please. And if you ever threaten her like that again…"

"She's conspiring with outside forces," said Ballad.

"You mean the police?" I said furiously.

"I lost a man tonight," said James.

"I know," soothed Xavier. "I'm sorry."

"It could have been you." James tugged on his left sleeve and then his right to straighten his pristine white shirt.

I stared at the sword resting on the table, a reminder of just how fucked in the head Ballad was.

James saw me looking at it and walked over and picked it up. After sheathing the weapon, he carried it over to the wall and hung it back up.

"I want to go home," I said.

James mulled over it. "It's on the agenda. But I could change my mind."

I hugged myself, trying to warm my chilled flesh. "I want Xavier to take me."

James gave a shrug. "I'll consider it."

I looked up at Xavier. "How's your tummy?"

"Fine." He hoisted his white shirt out of his trousers to show me. There was a faint mark on his toned abs.

Feeling guilty, I reached out and caressed the contusion. "I'm so sorry. It was meant for James."

Xavier cringed. "Not a good thing to admit."

James scoffed at my admission.

"I'm going to check on something," said Xavier. "I'll be right back."

I hated seeing him walk away, leaving me alone with this man. "Can I come?"

He offered me an apologetic look. "Go with James."

Reluctantly, I followed James back to the kitchen, wary of the man who'd almost destroyed my violin and sliced open my throat with a sword.

At least Xavier was coming around. Our escape was thwarted this time, but we'd get another chance.

While I cleared the island of the unused eggs and milk, Ballad set about uncorking a bottle of red wine and filled three glasses. Xavier's drink was going to be waiting for him when he came back, which reassured me that he'd be joining us soon.

"Where did he go?" I asked.

James lifted his wine glass and sipped. "I taste berries. How about you?"

Poison, probably.

I took a sip. "Grapes."

He faked a horrified expression. "Heathen."

James fitted the mold of a man who would like fine wines and all the other luxuries that went along with high-brow living. I imagined him attracting the cold, beautiful types.

"Are you a Lord?" I asked.

He looked up from his glass. "Earl."

I needed to learn as much as I could about this man so I could find him again if I wanted to. He was my way back to Xavier if we were ever separated again.

Sitting at the kitchen table with my fingernails digging into my palms to center me, I watched James chop vegetables, peel potatoes, and prepare other dishes with the confidence of someone who loved to entertain. He made this look like I was a guest he'd invited over for dinner.

The two men had secrets between them…a history and a shared love. I had to find out what I was up against and make him think my defenses were down.

I tried to make conversation. "How long have you known Xavier?"

His smile was filled with the warmth of pleasant memories. "A long time."

"He told me you met in the Army. You were stationed together?"

James looked up. "We weren't stationed together."

"Oh?"

"No, I was in the same vicinity as him at some point during a mission."

"So vague." I leaned back. "Why are you smiling?"

"Because you're fishing for clues about me and it's endearing."

My shoulders slumped in frustration. "Why are you so secretive?"

"My past reflects my future."

"How so?"

"How's your wine?"

I took another sip. "Mysterious."

His lips quirked in amusement as he picked up the wine bottle and came over to me.

"I get sleepy if I have too much."

"Well, we don't want that."

Peering up at him I said, "I know about you and Xavier."

James filled my glass and then topped up his own. "What do you know?"

My suggestive look told him.

He set the bottle down and leaned over to kiss the top of my head. "He's in love with *you*."

I felt an odd flutter in my stomach as his provocative cologne wafted towards me, and forbidden thoughts ran through my mind once more. My breath stuttered as though he'd done more than just kiss me. And then I recognized the scent he was wearing—it was the same one that Xavier had once worn.

Knowing that they'd shared the same cologne brought on more feelings of uncertainty. Even when he'd been far away from this man, a part of James had remained in Xavier's thoughts.

I watched Ballad walk back over to the kitchen counter.

I wish he wasn't so damn... What was the word? *Enigmatic.*

He exuded a seductive aura that seeped beneath my skin and made it tingle. Somehow, some way those sensations made their way down between my thighs.

"What are you thinking?" He interrupted my daydreaming.

I swallowed hard. "Are you going to let us continue to see each other?"

When he hesitated, my lips quivered with the thought I was about to lose Xavier all over again.

"Do you forgive him?" he asked softly.

"For leaving me and going back to you?"

"For answering the call to serve his country." He raised his glass in a toast. "This time as a civilian."

"You make it sound so noble."

"It is."

I sighed. "Thank you for letting me go back to my life."

"You may take your place in the orchestra. You worked hard to get there. You deserve all the success you have coming your way."

How nice of him, I thought, managing to avoid an eye roll. "I need to make the final round."

"You will."

"And find a place to live."

He wiped his hands on a cloth and threw it on the counter. "We can help."

"No, thank you."

"Why not?"

I nibbled on my bottom lip. "I want to make my own way."

"Listen, Emily, a love life is incompatible with what we do."

"It worked for you."

"Until it didn't."

"You admit it?"

He scratched his neck as though mulling it over. "Xavier shouldn't have shared that with you."

"I kind of guessed."

"We put ourselves last and the work first. Just as it should be."

"Do you love him?"

James grabbed his jacket off the back of a chair and for a second I thought he was going to leave. Instead, he brought it over and wrapped it around my shoulders. "Castles are cold, drafty places," he said softly.

I tugged it around me, grateful for the warmth. Any more pushing for answers on my part could hinder my return to a life I cherished. With an unbearable heaviness crushing my chest, my thoughts fast-forwarded to a future where I'd spend my days alone. "Let me have one more night with him."

James reached for his glass and took several sips. "Leaving behind the ones we love is the hardest thing we ever do."

"You loved someone once?" At his look of surprise, I added, "A woman?"

"Yes."

"What happened to her?"

His eyes darkened and a flash of sadness crossed his expression.

"You put the work before your wife?" I said.

"Who told you I was married?"

It had been the way he'd touched his ring finger. He realized his mistake and shook off a thought.

"I'm sorry it didn't work out," I said.

He finished off his drink in one big gulp, and with that he shut down my line of questioning.

I pushed to my feet and approached him. "Let me have one more night with him, James, so we can say goodbye."

He gave a subtle nod to show he would allow it.

Reaching for the bottle, I refilled his glass this time, the red liquid swirling all the way to the brim. "I want you to be there," I said. "I want you to see how much we love each other."

Looming over me, he looked devastatingly handsome. The moonlight poured in through the window, cutting across his chiseled features and illuminating his eyes.

His jaw flexed as he considered my offer. "You don't want me in the room, Em."

"Why not?"

"My control bleeds into those around me."

I suppressed a shudder. "I want you to see what you're tearing apart."

James' focus moved to the doorway. "Xavier, I cracked open the Chateau Margaux. It's had plenty of time to breathe."

I turned to see the man who had once been the center of my world. Xavier looked beautiful standing there, his dark golden hair shimmering in the soft light, his eyes reflecting kindness.

"Thank you," Xavier said. "Are you both getting along?"

"Yes," said James.

"No," I countered.

Xavier grinned. "Yes, you are." He was holding my Strad in one hand and the bow in the other. "Play for me."

My eyes shot to James to let him know I wanted him to see the pain he was causing Xavier…causing us both.

Xavier strolled in and handed me my violin. "I want to hear the music you played the day we met."

The same music I'd played in the Underground when he'd been lying in a ball on the cold tile because of something Ballad had done to him. I thought it best not to voice that thought, though, and gave him a smile and a nod instead.

"I'll play for you, too, James, if you wish."

"I would like that," he said softly.

The tension crackled around me as a prelude to the pain. The hours that followed would have me seeing these two men through a different lens. Knowing what they once were to each other, sharing glimpses of their past together, witnessing silent words spoken with smiles and knowing looks. I could already see the scorching history that sizzled between them.

Playing my Strad meant I could convey the agony that inflamed my soul in a waywords had failed to do. My heart was breaking, and nothing could be done about it.

I gave James a challenging look. "Oh, that other offer still stands… if you're man enough to accept it."

He smirked. "The question is Emily, are you prepared for the consequences if I do?"

Chapter 21

HOW DO I PUNISH A MAN WHO HAS DEVASTATED MY LIFE?
Take away what he wants more than anything.
So it began like this…

I was directed to one of the castle's many bedrooms, where I freshened up after grabbing a quick shower. I put on my bra and panties and nothing else. Damn the cold. This was my war and I was ready to fight.

Then I placed two chairs in the middle of the grand ballroom for my audience of two. I planned to invite them to attend their own personal concert with me as the main act—performing in nothing but my underwear.

Let James admire the curves he'd never touch, lust after my beaded nipples pushing through this skimpy bra. He may have tasted me but that was where our intimacy began and ended.

Next, I'd bewitch him with ethereal notes flowing from my Stradivarius—played by a vixen whose talent was going to blow him away.

Maybe James would even notice Xavier, the tortured man sitting beside him, who was about to lose the love of his life.

And, of course, I'd play for Xavier, to stir a need so powerful he wouldn't be able to contemplate ever being parted from me again.

To taunt James' desolate heart, I began with Vivaldi's "Four Seasons," beginning with "Winter." I looked over to see the blackness in his eyes fade to grey as the notes flowed and resounded ethereally.

This was my voice…my unique form of expression. My violin was a living, breathing entity that was in touch with each emotion surging through me.

Starting out, my Strad seemed moody from having been separated from me, but now, as though offering forgiveness, it came alive in my hands—the strings bounding with joy.

I transitioned into Niccolò Paganini's "Caprice No. 24 in A Minor" and caught that ghost of a smile on Xavier's face as he recognized the piece from when we first met—the memories of that day still vivid.

His beautiful face drew me to him even now—the way he earned his place in the room beside James, the way his expression shared his admiration for me.

Both of us were balanced precariously on the verge of unbearable heartbreak.

Lowering the violin, I paused to read Xavier's reaction.

"Not that I don't appreciate the view," he said, "but aren't you cold?"

I ignored that. "Why did you ask me to play 'Caprice'?"

Xavier looked wistful. "It takes me back to when we first met."

"You were homeless," I reasoned. "How can that be a happy memory?"

He sat up straight. "Because I met you."

"And why were you homeless?" I whispered.

He swapped an uncomfortable glance with James.

I raised my Strad and dragged my bow over the strings dramatically, creating a horrible screeching sound. "You were running from… him." I glanced at James.

Xavier pushed to his feet. "Thank you for playing for us."

I refused to be shut down. "Why did you leave Pervade?"

"What?"

James looked amused. "I think that's what she calls us."

Xavier gave an exasperated sigh. "This is old news, Em."

"Pervade London, here," I said, pointing at James, "runs the organization like a monastery."

James crossed one long leg over another. "It's best you don't try to define us."

"I'm sure you feel that way," I said tersely. "I'm just trying to wrap my head around what it is you do."

"That information is revealed on a need-to-know basis," he said.

I looked at Xavier. "You left because James wouldn't give you what you wanted...which was him."

James glanced at Xavier. "We don't need to rehash the past."

I pointed my bow at him. "Your past is ruining my present."

"Emily," Xavier said. His tone held a warning.

Still pointing my bow at James, I said, "You missed him as much as he missed you."

A pained expression flashed in James' eyes revealing there was truth in my assertion. "Our work is far reaching."

"What are you fighting for?" I snapped. "What are you sacrificing everything for if not so people can be with the ones they love?"

"You don't see what goes on behind the scenes, Emily," said Xavier. "No one does."

James raised his hand to quiet him. "It's irrelevant."

Xavier stood and walked over to me. "Sometimes the world must be put first."

"What do you do?"

"I gave you up," Xavier snapped back. "That is what I do."

"Love isn't allowed at Pervade." I let that sink in.

It was James' rule.

"You didn't expect to meet me," I reasoned. "You didn't expect to fall in love. You were just waiting until James came around and accepted your terms. I was collateral."

James gestured to my hands. "You play beautifully."

I ignored him and stared at Xavier. "I can have one more night with you. James has permitted it."

Xavier opened his arms to me as if that would be enough. "Em."

I pressed my Strad to his chest. "I'm dying here," I said.

"That hurts me more than you know," he admitted.

"You love him, not me."

He stepped back. "Em, it's not like that."

"Then say you love me more."

His expression showed his conflicted emotions, and it wrenched my soul.I shoved the Strad into his hands.

Pivoting fast, I sprinted out of the room.

If I couldn't have Xavier, nothing mattered. I didn't care about playing in an orchestra, didn't care about where I would live, none of it mattered because my heart was shattered irreversibly.

We were over.

I ran blindly through the maze of hallways, rounding sharp turns, continuing on and on to put distance between us.In my head, the ghostly notes from my violin still played, the music haunting me with each step into the unknown.

Chapter 22

SOMEHOW, I WAS ABLE TO FIND THE SAME BEDROOM I'D USED BEFORE. After crashing through the door, I hurried over and flung myself onto the bed, burying my face in the pillow to hide my tears.

Minutes later, I heard the door open and felt the mattress dipping, then comforting fingers stroked my hair.

"Emily, please," Xavier said, his voice shaky. "I can't bear to see you like this."

I braved a look at him. "I love you. I don't understand why we can't be together."

He rose from the bed and paced the length of the room.

I pushed myself up against the headboard. "I want to spend every night with you. Wake up with you. Be there for you."

"Me too." He paused and offered me a smile. "More than anything."

"Don't you trust me?"

"With my life."

I swiped away a tear. "I believe you when you say your work is important. If this is what you want…if this will make you happy…"

"Oh, Em."

Putting a hand to my chest, I whispered, "It just hurts so bad."

He stared at me with a conflicted expression. "I talk to computers." He gave me a rueful smile. "Stupid, really. Here you are in front of me…real, authentic, good."

"I don't understand. You mean you code?"

"No, it's very different. When computers talk with each other, I interpret what they're saying."

"Computers talk?"

"Artificial intelligence."

"What do you mean by that exactly?"

"Computers have evolved. They make decisions. Some even take action."

"What's it like talking with it?"

"With them." He shrugged. "Intense."

"You were talking with the AI at home? You played chess with it...I mean, them?"

"Yes."

And I'd had no idea...

I was hit with the realization that Xavier's far-reaching skill was why James was so possessive of him.

"Are they dangerous?"

"Potentially."

"People need to know."

Xavier shook his head. "That would cause chaos."

A shadowy figure appeared in the doorway. It was James, and he looked furious.

Xavier turned and faced James' wrath. "She knows."

"You told her?" A muscle in James' jaw twitched.

"Now she can be in my life," said Xavier calmly.

"That was not the plan," said James. "You were to let her go."

"I changed my mind."

The air between them crackled as tension scorched the air. I got off the bed and stood closer to Xavier.

"Why did you bring her here?" asked James. "To seduce her into something she doesn't want?"

"She wants it." Xavier raised his hands. "And so do you. I see the way you look at her."

"Don't even go there."

"I knew that once you tasted her, there'd be no going back for you."

"You're recklessly playing with lives," he replied coldly.

"You always get what you want, James," said Xavier. "I learned from the best."

"Is this what you want?" James moved forward quickly, grabbing Xavier and shoving him up against the wall. "This?"

"I want you to take her hard."

"If I refuse?"

Xavier cupped James' balls. "This tells me all I need to know."

James pressed his lips to Xavier's in anger. A moan tore from Xavier as they kissed. It was savage and cruel and forbidden, and this could have been hate playing out if not for the searing passion between them.

James pulled back. "Want more?"

"Fuck, yes."

Both men struggled violently through another kiss, with Xavier resisting and then attacking James' mouth with equal fervor, their tongues warring for dominance as James fondled Xavier's cock.

I approached them.

I should have been consumed by jealously, but this was like stepping into a dream. I was seeing two strong men reveal their fierce chemistry as James thrust his pelvis forward to lock Xavier's hips in place, while Xavier rubbed James though his trousers as they continued their sensual attack.

Their aggressive affection felt different, authentic...and even sacred.

They were beautiful together. Two fierce alphas caught in a violent tryst. Watching them made me feel voyeuristic, and caused my nipples to harden and my loins to ache with arousal at the view. My fingers traced my lips as though they were kissing me.

At last they broke apart, panting, and turned to face me as though only now remembering I was here.

Xavier shoved James off and sauntered over to stand behind me. "Give me this." He reached for the catch at my bra strap and unhooked it, throwing it to the ground.

I stood there with my breasts exposed and swollen. Glancing over at James, I saw his dark lust. The way he drank me in made my body tingle. He looked gorgeous with that foreboding stance, those broad shoulders both a threat and a promise that made my blood heat and skin flush.

Xavier knelt behind me and tugged down my panties. I let him, wantonly giving him the control to strip me in front of this man.

My body shuddered as Xavier reached around and pinched my nipples, tweaking them.

James watched it all, transfixed. "This is dangerous."

Xavier cupped my sex. "The room is yours to control."

"I've always given you what you want," said James. "Made concessions for you. But this is…too much."

"Why?" asked Xavier.

"Because it's temporary," he replied.

"Be honest." Xavier wrapped his hand around my throat and gently squeezed. "Your cock has never been so hard."

James' eyelids became heavy. "You can't sustain this."

"Emily knows that it's temporary, don't you?"

I managed a nod, aroused, feeling the dampness between my thighs.

"I'll meet you downstairs," said James. "We need to talk about finding her somewhere to live."

"There's more than enough time for that," chided Xavier.

James walked toward the door.

Xavier gave my butt a slap. "On the bed."

I followed his command and sat on the edge facing them, naked and vulnerable, my focus bouncing from one man to the other.

Xavier looked defiant. "I'm giving you both what you need."

James scraped his fingers through his hair as his gaze swept over my nakedness, lingering on my pert nipples.

My toes curled in anticipation.

Xavier placed his hands on my thighs and widened them. "Ballad, let go of your past and embrace this. Embrace us."

Now they would see how wet I was.

"I'm sorry it's cold in here," whispered Xavier.

Despite being naked I didn't feel the chill. I was too enraptured by these passing moments of daring eroticism.

"For you," Xavier said softly.

Mesmerized, I watched James stroll over to the fireplace and lift a box of matches from the mantle. He removed a match and lit it, throwing it into the fireplace. A burst of orange danced in the hearth, a crackle of flames.

He turned and faced us. "This is why you had me go down on her in the theatre," James spoke quietly. "You manipulated us then, too."

"And ever since that day you've thought about how she tastes," teased Xavier. "How she feels against your mouth when she comes."

James raised his chin. "This will be on my terms. Do you understand?"

Xavier offered him a smug little smile. He'd won.

James approached me, moving in a seductive, predatory manner as he unbuttoned his shirt and pulled it off, revealing ripped abs. He unbuckled his leather belt and slid it out, letting it drop to the floor.

He knelt between my legs with an air of dominance, resting his hands on my inner thighs and easing them apart. Those same firm fingers parted my labia to reveal wet folds. His exploration caused delicious tingles to reach my core.

I shot a look at Xavier, expecting to see betrayal in his eyes even though he'd instigated this...

Yet I only saw approval in his eyes. "You both need this more than you realize," he told us.

James ran a fingertip along my clit. "What was yours is now mine."

I shuddered at his touch, my sex throbbing with need.

"Ours." Xavier unbuttoned his shirt as he watched us with lust-filled eyes.

James' strumming fingers over my pussy brought wave after wave of pleasure, and I felt my slickness beneath his touch. The scent of my arousal was so erotic all I could do was shudder through each breath.

My thighs opened farther and I welcomed his probing fingers as they slipped inside me, the pressure bringing a new thrill.

It could have been the flames that had sucked the oxygen from the room. It could have been James' threat of control, or maybe it was the promise that Xavier would be taking me again soon, but I had no anger left.

Xavier gave me a knowing look and licked his lips suggestively. His delicious teasing made me pulse with need.

"Kiss her here." James' fingertip tapped my clit.

Obliging, Xavier knelt beside him and leaned in, pressing his mouth to me and flicking his tongue over my sensitive nub, sparking intense pleasure that had my thighs shuddering in response.

James held a hand to the back of Xavier's head so he stayed in place between my thighs, lapping fervently.

"Oh, please," I moaned.

"No coming yet," ordered James. "I own both your orgasms, understand?"

"Yes." My head fell back, every cell in my body shuddering with delicious sensations. I lifted my hips, begging for more pressure.

James' palm pressed my pelvis down, reminding me who was in control.

Xavier lifted his head and gestured for James to take over devouring my pussy.

James willingly took over, flicking me rhythmically with the tip of his tongue. Then he paused to look into my eyes, his lips shiny from my wetness. "You will obey me in all things, Emily."

"Yes," I whispered, moaning. "I will."

Xavier moved to the end of the bed and stared down at me, hypnotized by the way James teased my clit.

"Emily, you want more?" asked James.

"God, yes," I exhaled breathlessly.

"We're not offering permanence."

Those words shot into me like those flames bursting up from the hearth.

No, don't mention one of us leaving. Not now. Not after this.

I went to rise.

James held me still. "If you leave, this moment will never be repeated."

The pleasure they brought was too intense to resist. I managed a nod of resignation, and then spread my thighs for Xavier. He sunk between my legs and resumed his brilliant suckling. I refused to give up these precious moments I had earned by staying.

And we'd only just begun...

I ran my tongue over my lips, my face flushing with the vulnerability I felt. I squeezed my internal muscles tightly, knowing they'd see my yearning for them there...a silent plea to be taken.

James rose to his feet and removed his trousers. His thick, erect cock was exquisitely lined with veins, the purple head shiny with a bead of pre-cum.

He saw me staring. "Are you ready for my brand of fucking?"

I didn't know what that meant, but I wanted it. My head crashed onto the bed and at that moment nothing else mattered but giving myself over to them.

"Get undressed," he ordered Xavier.

Xavier slipped his pants off and was soon standing naked with his erection devastatingly hard and rising to almost touch his abdomen.

He stroked his cock. "You want us both, Em?" he asked, his voice husky.

"Yes," I whispered.

"Are you sure you know what you're asking?" said James. "Your pussy stretched around us as you scream our names?"

"I need it, please." I moaned.

James slid a finger into me.

Bucking, I responded to the tightness as he added another finger. I squirmed with delight at the sensation of being finger-fucked so brilliantly.

Xavier leaned in and grabbed my left breast, squeezing the nipple, shooting an electric jolt into the bud as his mouth captured it, his fingers pinching the other nipple with determined tweaks. Pleasure rippled through me as though a fine-tuned string was connected all the way down to my sex.

His hand was nudged away by James whose mouth clamped down on my other breast, his tongue matching Xavier's swirl for swirl as they both possessed an areola each, greedily nipping, their mouths drawing in and letting go.

Crying out at the intensity, my hand reached around and pressed the backs of their heads to hold them in place against my breasts, wallowing in this carnal play.

I reached low.

James' hand caught my wrist to stop me. "Did we give permission for you touch yourself?" he asked.

With ease, they flipped me over onto my chest and strong hands lifted my butt in the air. James picked up his belt and brought the leather up behind me. With Xavier gripping my wrists together and my ass in the air I was helpless to pull away. I clenched my jaw, preparing for the first strike.

A warm hand examined my buttocks, running over the smooth skin as though testing its endurance.

Strike.

I jolted forward as the agony shot into my flesh and then I froze as the warmth flooded my skin.

"You've been naughty, Em," James taunted. "Show me you accept your punishment."

"What did I do?" I shot him a defiant look.

"That note, for one thing."

I looked straight ahead and swallowed my fear. I raised my bum in the air to invite another round of punishment.

Several more strikes from the leather had me quivering on all fours, the pressure from where Xavier clutched my wrists becoming almost unbearable as he pressed my hands into the mattress.

I felt firm lips trace over the blemishes before trailing between the crack of my cheeks. The tip of a tongue circled the rosebud, then pushed through and probed the soft tissue.

My face burned with embarrassment, and yet I wailed, "Oh, please."

"Go get the lube," barked James.

Xavier climbed off the bed and hurried out.

"Soon," James soothed, as his hand brushed over my cheeks.

Within a minute, Xavier was back, and he threw the bottle of lube on the side table. The fantasy of seeing them using it on each other burned up my imagination, arousing me even more and becoming an overpowering need.

When the two men climbed on the bed at the same time and presented their cocks, I knelt before them, my butt rising in the air, still feeling the heat from the sensational burn of the leather.

I dipped my head low to take one cock and then the other into my mouth, hungrily sucking and gripping each erection at the base. Lavishing attention on each one, my tongue rimmed Xavier's purple head and then lapped at James', giving them both equal pleasure and delighting in their moans.

Peering up I saw the erotic scene reflected above…

James reached around and grabbed a scruff of Xavier's hair at the nape of his neck, clutching him violently. "Happy now, Xavier?"

"God, yes." Xavier's cock twitched in my mouth.

This was what he needed.

What he wanted.

What he longed for…James holding him in a leisurely passionate kiss, groin to groin, their hands cupping each other's faces as they greedily ravished each other's mouths.

And me spurring them on by drawing their purple tips into my mouth, squeezing them together as my lips stretched wide to accommodate them, erotically teasing them with my flicking tongue.

I shifted lower to suckle their tight balls, my fists wrapped tightly around each man's base and stroking them briskly.

It felt like I'd always been destined to belong to them.

The thought sent ripples of happiness through me.

Xavier pulled me up and turned me around, clutching my back to his chest. He hugged me so tight I couldn't escape. Not that I wanted to.

He lowered his hands and yanked my thighs open.

With one long thrust he buried himself deep inside my pussy, his fullness stretching me uncomfortably. The sensation quickly morphed into a delicious throbbing. I was imprisoned in his arms, impaled on him, my thighs spread open and my soaking wet sex exposed.

James leaned down between my thighs. "How does your pussy feel?"

I let out a long groan.

"Say it," he demanded.

My muscles clamped around Xavier's length and tightened around him. "It feels amazing."

"Good girl," said James, tapping my clit with a fingertip. "And?"

I begged him with my eyes.

"You're asking me to go down on you while Xavier's inside you?"

My breathing quickened at the thought my fantasy was becoming real.

"Do you deserve it?" he teased.

"I want to." I was dizzy with lust.

"Say you are ours," cooed James. "Admit you belong to us."

I nodded furiously. "Yes."

James gave me a satisfied smile. He reached out to ease apart my folds, his fingertips trailing along my skin. Dipping his head, he drew in Xavier's sack and began suckling him.

"Jesus," Xavier's voice sounded raspy.

Blinking down at James, his head between my thighs, his hair tickling my skin, I exalted at his desire to savor us both. His five o'clock shadow gave him an edgy beauty, making him even more mesmerizing. It made me wonder how Xavier could bear to be so close to him and not have this level of intimacy.

I had never loved Xavier more. He was giving me to the man he loved…and him to me.

My head lulled to the side and I went with these sensations, unaware of time as it passed.James trailed the tip of his tongue along where Xavier's cock disappeared inside me, circling and then flicking my clit, teasing and titillating.

My moans sounded primal, responding to a desire so pure, a need to be captured like this by these two men.

"Both of you," I whispered.

James ignored me, his intense strumming morphing into licks and kisses, a devouring that caused my legs to tremble violently as he worshiped every crevice, explored each fold, and focused on my pulsing clit, jolting bliss into my core.

My heart soared, beholden to him with each inhalation. He'd stolen my ability to breathe, to reason, to resist, and all I wanted was for time to hold its breath and keep us here.

"You have the most beautiful cunt." James pressed his lips against my sex in a long kiss. "You taste like a goddess."

"Make her ready," demanded Xavier.

In a daze, I watched James rise up and grab the bottle of lube. He returned with it and explored my puckered ass, poking a fingertip inside to test it.

Xavier lay back and pulled me with him. I lay along him with my thighs spread wide by his strong hands gripping my knees apart.

James gave a nod of acknowledgment and used the clear liquid to prepare that puckering; the slickness a strange sensation at first as he tried two fingers lathered in lube. His probing felt wrong, and yet so right.

"I'm going to help you, Em." He pushed two fingers further into that tenderness. "Relax. That way we can give you what you want."

"Both of you?" I said breathlessly.

"That's right. We'll both be deep inside you." James gave a nod to let Xavier know I was ready.

Xavier's hold on me tightened and I knew what came next.

He withdrew his cock from my vagina and then pressed the tip of it against my taut ass. James gripped Xavier's shaft and guided his friend's cock. I bucked at the pressure as he entered me.

"Deep breath, Em," James said.

With a nod, I told them I was ready for more of Xavier's penetration. He remained behind me, with my back to his front.

The dreadful burn, the cruel stretching, finally transmuting into an intense arousal and I relaxed a little when James strummed my clit to ease the discomfort.

Xavier tipped his hips to thrust deeper. My panting filling the room, my sex spasmed though empty, my anus stretched wide to accommodate Xavier's width.

James rose over us with his right hand directing his cock toward my pussy. This was really happening—both men were taking me at the same time.

Drawing in a sharp breath, I told myself I wanted this, had needed it since I'd first met James at The Savoy. That same night I'd felt the searing heat rising off both men, their close proximity to each other too terrible to bear and impossible to refuse.

Again, came that gentle tapping to test my readiness, this time it was the tip of James' cock. "How's that feel?"

I nodded frantically, clutching his shoulders. The stretching felt like I might be ripped apart, a pressure too much and yet not enough, a promise, a prayer, a deep longing.

James slid in more and I squeezed my eyes shut to endure the burn of them both inside me, a tsunami of sensations at being owned by two men.

Panic rose inside me. "It's too much—"

"Look at me," coaxed James. "That's it, breath through it. Just relax. Let me rub your clit. See, how's that? It's helping, right?"

Squeezing him with taut muscles, I felt him twitch and harden inside. I'd been captured for the sole purpose of his pleasure...*their pleasure.* Crushed between them. I felt safe and nurtured and understood as these two men gave me what I needed.

James continued to stimulate my clit. Never had I felt more connected, or loved, or believed I was quite this beautiful.

Finally, Xavier had let me into his world—all the way.

They were all the way in and if this was divinity, I believed it.

I wrapped my thighs around James' waist to hold him, not wanting these sensations to cease. Not ever...

I never wanted to be parted from either of them.

"How are you doing?" James whispered.

"So good," I said, my voice shaking.

"How does it feel?" he added.

"Oh, God," I managed.

"Ready for a hard fucking, Em?"

I gritted my teeth at the jolt of arousal his words brought. "Yes."

It started slow, a leisurely sliding in and out, James' enormous girth stretching me wider and bringing a pleasure that was close to blinding.

Between them, I was forced to remain still as these two men took the lead and rocked against me, hips a piston from front and behind, their deepening thrusts proving they were in sync.

The rhythm changed, with James withdrawing all the way out and then thrusting in all the way to completely impale me with a controlled pummeling—Xavier matching him thrust for thrust in my ass as both men sent me into oblivion.

I heard a long groan from one of them. "Your cock feels incredible—"

I was too gone to know who'd spoken. Xavier was wildly pounding me now, and James was all power and control above, perspiration spotting his brow, his strong arms holding him above us. His pecks flexed as I dug my fingernails into tight muscle.

From his vantage point, James stole glances of them both sliding in and out of me. His face filled with desire as sticky wet sounds filled the room.

The fire warmed us even though we didn't need it.

James swirled his hips in a circle, his pelvis brushing against my clit. All I could do to endure this deep pang was dig my fingernails into his back.

He bit into my shoulder. "Harder."

His teeth felt divine against my flesh.

Appeasing him, I scratched my fingernails down his back and felt him swell even more inside, pushing the boundaries of what I believed I was capable of enduring.

"We come together," James ordered.

Xavier shuddered behind me and I felt him stiffen and go still as he rose toward an orgasm, his groans revealing he was barely holding on.

"Come, Emily." James gave his order.

My nipples burst into tight buds of ecstasy as Xavier squeezed them rhythmically in time with James' thrusts, until all I knew was white-hot bliss, a burning pleasure in my sex that I fell into as we came together.

The two men became frenzied in their pounding, delivering strikes so bold all I could do was grip onto James and give myself over to them completely.

I had a vague sense of them spilling their heat within me.

I saw stars as a violent shuddering took hold of me, my orgasm stealing my thoughts, my sense of time and place.

It was my groaning that drew me back into the room as a second climax prevented me from catching my next breath. Then I felt nothing but the pressure of two bodies…filled completely by them as they came down from an indescribable high.

I relished the feeling of their kisses on my shoulder, cheek, breasts, and mouth—saying a silent prayer for time to swallow me into its center and hold me between these two men forever.

"Fall asleep, Em," coaxed James. "With us inside you."

My thighs fell apart as I melted in their arms, spent and satisfied, willing to do anything they asked of me.

And fully aware that my feelings of lust for James had changed, teetering on the edge of something more.

Chapter 23

THE TABLE HAD BEEN TASTEFULLY SET WITH FINE CHINA PLATES AND crystal glasses for this late-night dining experience. The room's décor—now that I had a moment to take it in—was regal and elegant. A line of high-back upholstered chairs surrounded a long oak table—the same one I'd been thrust on hours ago.

Silver domes covered three plates, a glass of red wine placed at each setting.

After showering, I'd found my clothes—the ones I'd put on this morning for my trip to Buckinghamshire—on the end of the bed and they'd been washed, since my experiences in the holding cell hadn't been kind. Xavier had been the one to wash them; spoiling his girlfriend was a habit he'd yet to break.

It was hard to look down the table at James after everything we'd done together. Trying to make sense of these swirling emotions, I looked over at Xavier. He sat at the other end offering me a look of reassurance.

Turning my attention away from the medieval weaponry on the walls, I admired the massive stone fireplace. Bright red flames crackled in the hearth. Not unlike the fireplace that had warmed our naked bodies as we'd tumbled around in ecstasy.

Along the walls were paintings of chivalrous-looking knights. One of them actually resembled James.

He sat at the head of the table, the distance between us an ocean apart. This formal seating plan seemed like a punishment, as though we were returning to the status of what we had once been...enemies.

With a nod from James, I lifted the silver dome to reveal a meal of roast chicken, assorted vegetables, and the deliciously aromatic scent of rosemary.

My stomach grumbled with anticipation. "Nice going on the seating plan."

James lifted his crystal glass and took a sip.

"Considering what the three of us just did."

"It was…" James bit his lip before continuing. "A detour."

Which made me swallow nervously as a recollection of being squished between them raced through my brain, holding me suspended as I replayed the scene.

"Try your roast chicken, Em," said Xavier.

"What? Oh, yes." I cut into the sumptuous meat and took a bite. My smile revealed how amazing it tasted. "James, you're a great cook."

"He considers himself a chef," said Xavier.

"Ah, I see." I paused, and then reached for my glass. "Are we allowed to talk about the AI?"

Ignoring James' glare, I took a sip of wine. Flavors of blackberries and grapes danced on my tongue.

"I'm sure it's a more comfortable conversation than what we did to you in the bedroom," James said, arching a brow.

My cheeks blushed wildly.

Thoughts of me going down on them at the same time sent a shiver down my spine; two kneeling men before me, all alpha power and taut muscular bodies. I squeezed my thighs together, trying to ease the pang.

The way James was staring at me proved he'd enjoyed teasing me. I took another big gulp of the smooth wine.

He topped up my wine glass.

"Thank you."

"Better be careful," James said, topping up his own. "We all know what happened last time you had more than one glass."

"You mean I played my violin for you?" I threw in a cute smile.

James picked up his fork. "Yes, of course I meant that."

"Any chance of a tour?" I asked.

"I'm sure we can arrange that." He looked relaxed for a man who had the weight of the world to consider. The sword on the wall was a reminder of how far he'd go.

He saw me staring at it. "It was used at Trafalgar Square."

Several more swigs of wine and I was still trying to read him. "You get off by threatening women?"

"Only the ones that need taming."

Xavier laughed. "You can be a bastard, sometimes."

"Really?" said James. "And you're the master of unseen moves."

I raised my hand in the air. "I had the most incredible time with you both."

James grinned and so did Xavier, and I sensed their relief that I'd finally broken the ice.

"Endear me to you, James," I said. "I mean, what you did upstairs was enthralling, but I need to know more about you."

"He was a naval officer," said Xavier.

I turned in my seat to look at him. "Not an attorney?"

He threw off a salute. "I'm not as fascinating as Xavier."

"Oh?"

"Don't talk about me," ordered Xavier.

"If we're going to enlighten Ms. Rampling," James said, licking his lips, "let's go all the way."

Xavier looked nervous. "You want her to hate me?"

Sparks flew from the fireplace, making me jump.

"Did he share the level of his I.Q. with you, Emily?" added James.

I let out a sigh. "He's well read and..."

"Well over 350."

"Not sure why that's relevant," said Xavier.

"Considering that, before you, the highest recorded I.Q. was 300," said James. "To put it into perspective, Emily, Stephen Hawking's IQ was 160 and Einstein's 190. William Sidis, an American child prodigy, scored 300."

I tried to fathom why Xavier hadn't shared this with me. "And you're good with languages."

"You could say that." James looked amused.

"You're a linguist, too," Xavier piped up.

"A little French," admitted James. "A little German."

"Fluent Russian," Xavier added.

"And you have a good memory, too, Xavier," I offered.

"That's an understatement." James skewered a carrot on the end of his fork and brought it to his mouth. He chewed elegantly as he stared at Xavier. "It's photographic."

My gaze bounced from one man to the other. "I knew you were special."

Xavier grinned. "Glad we cleared that up."

"How about a demonstration?" said James.

"Of what?" Xavier acted innocent.

"Of when you first met her." James placed his fork down. "Tell her what you remember from that day."

"She found me in the Underground." He shrugged it off.

I noticed the seductive narrowing of James' eyes. He was trying to coax Xavier into opening up.

"He remembers," I said in his defense. "We often talk about it."

James gave him a wry smile. "Show Emily your gift."

"Well, she already knows I'm special." Xavier grinned.

"You haven't touched your wine," James said smoothly.

"I'm looking forward to a second round with us all in your bed." Xavier winked at me. "That's the only party game I'm interested in."

I set my glass down. "I'd like to see a demonstration of your talents."

Xavier took a sip of his wine. "I don't want to scare you, Em."

"No fire starting, then?" I smirked at him.

"No, a little more...memorable."

"What would be more memorable than—"

"I remember everything."

"But that's normal, right?" I reasoned.

"He is able to recall the number of commuters in the Underground that walked by you as you talked with him," said James. "He'll be able to tell you what you wore that day, down to your earrings. He has the ability to replay, word for word, your conversation. Each flicker of an eyelid, each reaction you showed during your time with him is remembered in minute detail."

I was stunned. "You remember every word from that evening?"

Silence fell…

"Traffic's slow," Xavier began. "I can catch him." Xavier's eyes glazed over as he continued…

"He got into a taxi."

"You saw him? Which way did he go?"

"It's too dangerous for you."

"Tell me."

"I'll get it back for you if you promise to buy me a meal."

"Seriously?"

"I was joking. But I am pretty hungry."

"Bring me my violin and I'll treat you to a three-course dinner."

Xavier studied me. "It went something like that."

"Huh." I managed.

He'd replayed our full conversation—the one we'd shared on the pavement outside Piccadilly during those seconds he'd offered to retrieve my violin from a thief.

"That's impressive," I muttered.

"One hundred and twenty-three people passed us on the street while we were talking," added Xavier. "And two dogs walked by with their owners. A Lab and a Corgi. Shall I read off the number plates of the cars caught in traffic? It's a bit boring."

I shot to my feet, staring at him.

"How about dessert?" said James. "Xavier, go grab the key lime pie from the fridge. Bring three plates, please."

"I scared you," whispered Xavier.

"It's unnerving," I admitted.

"And forks too, please," added James.

We both watched Xavier push to his feet and head out. Even with him gone I was still staring at where Xavier had been sitting and replaying what had just happened. Pivoting toward James.

"That's another reason he plays chess," said James. "It soothes his mind from every single second that gets recorded in his brain."

"How can he bear it?"

"It's what makes him quirky."

"You're using him. His talent. His ability to talk with…AI." I gave him an accusatory glare.

"Please sit down, Emily."

"I need to check on him."

"He left so we can talk. So, let's talk."

"I'm fine."

"I told you to sit."

I sank back into my seat. "I still know him better than you."

"My job is to protect him. Make sure he has everything he wants and needs so he continues to work for us."

"You make it sound cold. He's not a machine."

"Work for *us*, Emily. Not the Russians, not the Chinese, not some billionaire with money to burn. Us."

"He would never betray England."

"I would hope not."

"You're keeping him prisoner."

"He's free to come and go. Relationships, however, are…"

"Because he's the only one who can do what he does."

With an elegant hand, James removed his necktie and laid it before him on the table. "Can you continue to love a man so potentially dangerous?"

"You?"

"I'm talking about Xavier."

How dare you.

Pushing to my feet, I closed the gap between us. With a shove, I moved his dinner plate aside and squeezed myself between him and the table, lifting myself up to sit on the end with my legs dangling. It was an interesting vantage point that had me looking down at him.

Bringing my high heels up, I rested them on his thighs, then grazed his groin with one pointed tip, letting him know I could use it like a weapon—like that sword on the wall.

He grabbed my ankle and moved it away from his cock. The thrum of his firm touch sent a tingle into my calf.

"Tell me more, Sir Ballad." I reached forward and lifted his tie, running it through my fingers to tease him.

James stared up at me. "I'm his guardian. I help ensure that his brilliance soars."

"He's priceless to you."

"You can only imagine my concern when I thought you'd impaled him on a jousting pole."

"Maybe you shouldn't leave such dangerous weapons hanging around."

"Put your hands behind your back."

"I'm in control here, James."

He pushed to his feet. I caught the tip of my tongue between my teeth in response.

James was now looking down at me. "You want to feel connected. I can give you that. You want to be cherished, nurtured, spoiled or fucked within an inch of your life. These things I can give you."

"But not him?" I fluttered my eyelashes and threw in sarcasm. "Perhaps I can just have you?"

He leaned in and his lips brushed mine. "It's within my power to crush you. Wipe out any evidence of your existence. Scorch the earth bare where you step. One wrong move and your name might as well have been written in water."

"You don't scare me."

His jaw clenched. "It seems to me the only way to handle you is to have you."

"You don't want me. You just want to make Xavier happy."

There had to be a way to figure out if James felt something for me. If I relented and let him take me again, I might be able to discover his true feelings.

"Place your wrists behind your back."

Raising my chin in defiance, I delivered my response. "My greatest revenge is going to be making you fall in love with me." I placed my wrists behind me anyway.

He leaned around my body and secured my wrists together with his tie. "Feel that? This is me taking back the power. Your fate rests in my hands."

I felt a twinge of apprehension, but it was too late. I was bound.

James' fingers trailed down my chin and then my throat, bringing a tingling as they brushed my shoulder, and then circled a nipple. "You are the greatest treasure."

I was coming undone...

He rubbed his thumb over my lips, making them plump. "This moment with us, here, will change your life forever."

"How?"

"I don't want to do this."

"Do what?"

James looked over my shoulder. "It's best if I deliver the poison with some sugar."

Turning to follow his gaze, I saw Xavier. He was focused on us as though trying to read what was unraveling.

James smiled over at him. "I'll take one of those."

Xavier approached and placed a dessert plate near us on the table. Then he walked over to a seat nearby and pulled it out with his foot. He sat down and placed the other two dessert plates in front him, quickly digging into the pie with a silver spoon, his full lips smacking together in delight.

James reached toward the dessert, lifting the small silver spoon and using it to scoop up some of the creamy pie. He brought it to my lips.

Opening my mouth, I tasted the sweetness of cream and the tang of lime, both dancing on my tongue. I savored the sensations.

"Em, when you do that thing with your mouth," Xavier said softly. "You are so..."

Ballad turned my attention back on him with a tilt of my chin.

My pleasure was his to deliver. "I wish I'd stabbed you with that joust," I taunted.

Xavier chuckled.

"She's certainly beguiling." James scooped up more of the cream and again brought it to my mouth.

I pressed my lips together in protest.

"Open." The spoon was eased into my mouth.

"What did you mean, poison?" I said through a bite.

"What I'm about to share will leave a bitter taste." James wiped cream off my lip with his thumb and licked it off his finger. "It's about that night when I came for Xavier at The Biltmore." He dabbed my mouth with a napkin. "We needed him urgently."

A chill slid up my spine.

"Two computer systems belonging to two opposing countries were talking...with each other. Two foreign entities classed as enemies. The governments had installed AI to monitor and *control* their weapon systems. Bad idea, as you can imagine."

My brain went into overdrive, my wrists tugging on the restraint behind my back.

"The AI systems were communicating for over a month before anyone noticed. Though no one knew what was being shared between them at that time," he continued. "Specialists tried to shut them down. They failed. Each respective country went on high-alert. The U.S. and Great Britain went on red alert. We were called in. I needed my expert. Who was currently hunkered down with a violinist at The Biltmore getting his rocks off." He flashed an affectionate smile at Xavier.

"We were hiding," I threw in.

"You can't hide from me, Emily."

I ignored that. "You needed Xavier to interpret what the AI were saying to each other?" I cringed at the memory of my temper tantrum at The Biltmore when James had turned up. "What happened?"

"Xavier has quite the knack for translating AI language." James broke into a smile. "He talked them back from the ledge."

I realized the danger. "Oh, God."

"He's certainly close to that, yes."

"Which countries?" I had to ask.

"As you can see—" James looked over at Xavier. "We need him. With no distractions."

My mouth went dry.

James' focus returned to me. "How's the dessert?"

"Sweet."

He tipped up my chin. "There's good in this world. We're trying to preserve it."

"Thank you for trusting me with that." The words slipped out quietly as I glanced at Xavier.

He looked so innocent licking cream off his spoon, so sweet-natured, and the thought he'd potentially saved the world from a disaster was mind-blowing.

James untied my wrists. "That was to stop you from running."

"What happens now?"

"You go to bed. And you try to sleep."

"With you, right?" I said softly. "With both of you."

Chapter 24

I AWOKE TO THE PRESSURE OF BEING SQUEEZED BETWEEN TWO MEN—ALL firm muscles and heat. Wiping the sleepiness from my eyes, I saw that James and Xavier were still passed out. Them being here brought me the comfort I needed, along with a feeling of trust.

I'd climbed into James' bed last night after drinking too much wine. My world had been rocked by revelations that still made my head spin. I'd believed the more booze I drank the clearer things would get and the more I'd understand.

But it had just made things fuzzier.

James' right leg lay over mine and Xavier's arm was wrapped protectively across my chest. Easing them off, I sat up trying not to wake them.

I looked over to see if either of them had a glass of water on their side-tables. There was only a small clock announcing we were an hour away from dawn.

My thirst was too intense to ignore. Scooting to the end of the bed, I climbed off and headed into the bathroom. I caressed the finely woven material of the robe I found hanging there, and pulled it on, breathing in the delicate scent of James' cologne.

Wrapped in an enormous amount of warm snugness, I walked back into the bedroom and glanced over at my two lovers, who were still asleep.

Those two gorgeous and very secretive men had a history. The sleeping beauty of a man lying beside Xavier was the one who had launched my life into chaos. But after last night's revelation, everything had fallen into place. The reason for his possessiveness had finally been revealed, and had brought about an understanding that made enduring all this a little easier.

Before now, I had touched the veil but never seen beyond it. Faced true power but not truly comprehended it. And found love but was destined to never reach its pinnacle.

I'd fallen under James' spell—just like Xavier, who was caught in the web of his mentor's allure. I was being drawn toward this man like the pull of centrifugal force, no matter how much I tried to resist. There was no going back.

What now?

Weeks of pleasure before they sent me away? Even with the knowledge that pain waited for me on the other side of this decision to stay, I'd refused to deny myself these precious moments…these unbidden pleasures from those two charismatic men. Quite simply, after everything, this was what I'd needed to heal.

All that was left was to savor every erotic interaction, every inspiring conversation, every stolen kiss and kind word that I hungered for.

Time spent with James was enlightening. Most of all it was opening my heart again so I could play my violin with the kind of passion that would see my ambition realized. Those days without Xavier were too terrible to bear.

Those who have been burned up, obliterated and renewed, are the fearless ones who blindly fly toward the stars because they have nothing left to lose.

I wasn't going back to that place of loneliness where I would have to be without Xavier. I was going to find a way to keep us together.

Ballad had asked me what I wanted that only he could deliver. I wanted to play my violin for the masses—*that was my dream*—but I wanted to make it on my own terms.

More than this…I wanted to marry Xavier.

I was willing to do anything to see this become a reality.

Barefoot on the cold stone floor, I retraced my steps back to the dining room, the location of where those secrets had become known.

James had finally shared it all with me—or as much as possible, though his motivation was still unclear. Perhaps he wanted me to have a greater understanding of his actions. Perhaps he needed to be remembered as a man who was good, who had dedicated his life to a greater purpose.

The demonstration of Xavier's astounding memory had nearly overwhelmed me. My own memories were now tinged with another perspective, one that included knowing he had lived through our mutual experiences differently. He'd held onto our shared moments with a clarity that I could only barely comprehend.

All evidence of our dinner here last night was gone. The room had returned to its pristine state. James had returned this space to order. And that, I realized, was what he needed—to control his universe and everyone in it.

My imagination ran wild with what they had done when I had gone to bed. They'd possibly shared a late-night drink and talked some more, or shared a kiss, perhaps they'd made love.

I felt a twinge of jealousy, but pushed that thought away and continued on to the kitchen.

I grabbed a glass from a cupboard and held it beneath the refrigerator door's dispenser. Gulping the water and finally quenching my thirst, I took time to admire the modern appliances that tastefully blended with the ancient décor.

Memories of what we had done together in this vast place was etched in my mind, and I clung to them for the comfort they brought. Each kiss from them meant we were becoming more. Surely this was a beginning and not an end?

Wiping my hand across my mouth, I had the vague thought that James woulddisapprove of my uncouth gesture.

Although he'd promised to show me around, it was too enticing a place to wait to explore. After placing my glass in the sink, I left the kitchen, enthused by a rush of intrigue that made me long to see more.

The dark wood hallways were lined with grand oil paintings of serious-looking figures, all of them having been immortalized by talented painters over a century ago. Antique pieces of weaponry hung along other corridors, enhancing the medieval atmosphere and proving that Ballad had gotten his lust for blood from his ancestors.

It made me wonder how he felt about never being able to inherit the crown.

He'd taken the power anyway.

I entered another hallway and noticed that the door at the end was standing ajar. I stepped into a vast office that doubled as an impressive library. Thousands of books were stacked in dark wooden floor-to-ceiling bookshelves. A sofa rested in the center of the room, facing four leather chairs, all of them positioned upon a red and gold weaved rug. The scent of pine needles emanated from a giant stone hearth, atop which was carved a shield with two lions on either side and a crown above them. I assumed it was Ballad's family crest.

Nearing one of the bookshelves, I fingered the ancient spines as I scanned the many classics. Easing one of them out, I opened it and saw it was a first edition dating back a hundred years. James' rare collection would make historians dizzy with envy.

Time dissolved as I breathed in the antique book smell that was a heady combination of earth and burned vanilla, wood and smoke.

Continuing on around the room, I admired the other antique objects, like the rusty keys that were displayed in a glass case. A feather pen was showcased, it's end stained where it had been dipped in ink. Beside it, leather-bound folders were stacked high on a tall table inlaid with leather, and a strange white rope behind a glass frame hinted that the item was of a nautical origin. Reaching a desk, I noticed a thick book, its pages filled with military submarines from around the world.

My fingers trailed along the edge toward the left drawer…

Something moved in my peripheral vision and I let out a yelp.

James was standing across the room.

Dressed in jeans and a white shirt, he looked surprisingly awake. Only his tousled hair gave away the fact that he'd just woken. He was holding two mugs, wisps of steam spiraling up from each.

"Can't sleep," I said by way of apology.

"Me neither. Xavier, on the other hand."

"He does love his sleep."

"When he's asleep his mind is quiet."

"But he has dreams."

"He does."

There was only one way he'd know that. I wondered if he still dreamed of me.

James came closer. "Warm enough?"

I looked down at the robe I was wearing. "It's cozy."

"Glad you like it."

"I should have asked to borrow it."

"I'm glad you felt comfortable enough to wear it."

Okay. Who swept in during the night and gave this man a personality transplant?

"Something wrong?" he asked.

"You made tea?"

"Milk, no sugar, right?"

I nodded.

Hours ago, he'd been intent on making my life hell. I liked this new version, the one where he gave me blinding orgasms and made us tea. He was coming around to like me more, it seemed.

He seemed to read my thoughts. "I feel we made progress."

"Oh?"

"We've established that you want what's best for Xavier. And for the country."

I reached out and accepted the mug, welcoming the heat against my palms. "I love him. I would never hurt him."

"It's the letting go that's the problem."

"It was hard for you, too, then?" I dug at his heart.

His gorgeous face wore an unreadable expression.

"This place is endless," I said, changing the subject.

"It is."

"How much time do you spend here?"

"A good amount."

"Did you grow up here?"

"I spent a lot of time abroad."

"Where?"

He hesitated and then said softly, "In sunnier climates."

"Like where?" *Mr. Mystery.*

He caught his bottom lip between his teeth to stop himself from answering. He even made uncertainty look sexy.

I took a sip of my tea and it was warm and refreshing.

"Your father worked there?" I pushed.

"No."

My mind searched for the reason he'd grown up away from England.

"Are you warm enough?" He gestured to the fireplace. "I can light it if you like. If you want to stay and read."

I gestured to the bookshelves. "Have you read any of them?"

He looked surprised. "Of course."

"It would take a lifetime."

"I started young."

"You live alone?"

"There are staff."

"That's not the same."

"They're like family." James gave me a smile.

With each passing second, I saw why Xavier liked him. It was as though he was finally pulling down his wall and letting me in—even if some of the details were sketchy.

"How do you feel about us being together again?" I asked.

He mulled it over. "It pleases him."

Still. "Xavier seems happy now."

He looked away and sighed. "Well, he got what he wanted."

"Are you only sleeping with me for his sake?"

"I don't think it was the sleeping together that necessarily pleased him."

"The fucking then."

He avoided answering me, instead taking a sip of his hot tea.

"I'm the only one who truly gets him," I chided.

"If Xavier was a country, you would merely have visited the capital."

"I lived with him."

"His biggest fear?"

"He doesn't seem scared of anything."

"His biggest fear is of anything happening to you."

I raised my mug in a toast. "And you threaten him with that to control him."

"Anyone close to us is at risk."

"Find someone else who does what he does."

"There is no one."

"Are you jealous of what he can do?"

"God, no. His gift is a curse."

"How do you think of him? Simply as a genius?"

"He's even beyond that. He's unique."

"You knew where he was the whole time. You spied on us."

"I gave him the time he needed to decompress."

"Then you came for him."

James smiled. "I let him have you. I allowed you to have him."

"How generous."

"I have my moments."

"We share the experience of knowing what it is to love him," I said. "The intensity of his affection."

He strolled over to one of the bookcases and paused before it. "How adventurous are you?"

"Turns out I'm really adventurous."

He thumped the bookcase with his fist.

It made me jump and tea swooshed around in my mug. Nothing spilled out, thank goodness, as I was standing on a Persian rug.

A door swung open revealing a dark passageway. A throwback to when the castle was at risk of being under siege.

"Where does it lead?"

"Want to find out?"

Heading into the dark unknown with him was potentially a bad idea. "What about my drink?"

"Bring it."

I blew off a niggling feeling of doubt and followed him into passageway, a chill meeting us as we entered the darkness. James walked beside me with the confidence of a man who knew every inch of this place. The only noise I heard was our footsteps and my shaky breaths. Even if danger loomed, I was mad for letting him put distance between myself and Xavier. Enough distance to silence my screams. And yet... this was exhilarating.

He was exhilarating.

James gave a panel a punch and another doorway opened. We stepped into a living room that was cozily decorated and modern and for the first time I had a sense of James' true taste in furniture and the arts.

He shut the door behind us.

I wanted to trust this moment, trust *him*, but he was a hard man to read and that hint of the sinister about him put me on edge. Despite that, it was wrong of my thoughts to go there, back to the way he'd touched me in the bedroom. The way he'd tasted, or even the way his body felt crushed to mine. This was me craving more time with him. I was being honest with myself, at least.

"These are your private rooms?" I said.

"My living quarters."

The thought of him never taking me hard again filled me with dread. If he could read me as well as I believed, he knew this, too. He'd welcomed my submission, allowing him to lead us to this place he controlled. Like he controlled everything.

"I'll show you around."

The room lit up as sensors detected our movements.

We stepped into another study, its walls covered with photos of Officers in the Royal Navy. Each frame held a picture of military men in a line-up, dressed in their fine uniforms. Something told me if I searched their faces, I'd see his.

Neatly stacked files rested upon a simple desk, with a sleek computer monitor rounding out the modern feel. The computer was unplugged, and now I knew why. He didn't want an AI system hooked up in here.

Strolling over to one of the photos, I read the inscription above it that revealed this formal shot was of a line-up of submarine captains, James being one of them. He looked younger, but that firm jaw and his dashing aura made him easy to spot. And God, if he didn't look hot in uniform...

"You worked on submarines?"

His smile reflected a time in his life he'd enjoyed.

"You were the captain of one?" I said, impressed.

He gestured. "This way."

The thought of him mastering one of those impressive vessels made my flesh tingle with pride for him. Or maybe it was the way my arm brushed over his as we entered through the doorway, too close to avoid each other.

James led me to his bedroom.

A grey and white themed decor complemented the low bed with its high-backed headboard.

His real bed...

From the way he kept his distance, I could tell he had no intention of taking me on it. Not yet, anyway.

I couldn't resist strolling into his walk-in wardrobe for more clues. James followed me in and I flashed him a wry smile, running my hand along a row of bespoke suits. In the center was a chest stacked with expensive-looking shoes.

"Why did you leave the Navy?" I asked.

"I switched careers."

"You joined Pervade?"

He gave me a reluctant smile.

I pulled out a drawer and peered in at a fine selection of watches. Farther down were more drawers filled with elegant ties.

"What's in there?" I pointed to a steel door.

"My doomsday collection."

"Supplies? Are you serious?"

"You'll never know."

"Until you let me in there."

"*If* I let you in." His words sounded seductive.

"When the world falls apart, I'll come here."

"I'm afraid it's already fallen apart."

"And whose fault is that?" I teased.

"I'll come get you…how about that?" Shadows danced over his devastatingly handsome features.

As though picking up on my scrutiny, he raked a hand through his hair. With that stubble peppering his jaw, he oozed a sensual masculinity that was dangerously alluring. Thoughts of how he'd controlled Xavier and I in his bed flashed through my thoughts, taunting me.

Luckily, the heavy material of his robe hid my beading nipples. I squeezed my thighs together as the delicious soreness in my pussy throbbed, reminding me of what he was capable of.

"Welcome to my private chambers, Ms. Rampling." His lips curled in an erotic smile. "Only the elite get to see it."

"Elite?"

"The ones I like to fuck."

In that moment I knew Xavier would never give him up. James was too devastatingly gorgeous, too charismatic. Whatever had brought them together had forged a bond that made the one I had with him seem pale in comparison.

I stared into his eyes. "How long were you lovers?"

"Don't do this to yourself."

"It helps to make sense of everything. My heart is breaking."

"I know."

"Where did you meet?"

James stilled and then said softly, "The Far East."

"How?"

"I was commissioned to escort him to a location."

"While you were in the Navy?" I mulled it over. "Why did you say you were a lawyer?"

"I'm allowed to lie." He arched a brow.

There was too much information being exchanged and I nose-dived from exhilaration to terror. If he was willing to share these details it could mean he no longer saw me as a threat. And there was only one reason for that...

"Pervade is part of the Secret Service?"

"Careful..."

"I'm intrigued."

"I'm telling you as much as possible without endangering you."

"Why would it be bad for me to know more?"

"People want to hurt me."

"That helicopter crash..." I narrowed my gaze. "They thought it was you."

"Apparently you saved my life, Emily. You pulled me back here to deal with you. Obviously, I'd rather fuck than be shot out of the sky."

A chill descended over me as his words hit home.

"I may or may not regret letting you take me," I said.

"Always the charmer." He winked.

"You didn't like him at first?"

James looked surprised. "I thought Xavier was...complicated."

"What happened to cause your attitude to change?" *For him to fall in love.*

"I saw what he was capable of. The good he could do."

"You gave him a pass for his behavior?"

James gave a shrug. "My preconceived ideas were torn down. He gets anything he wants."

"But not you?"

"Evidently that plan is skewered."

"I can't live without him."

He set his mug on a table and took mine and placed it next to his. "Want to see something cool?"

As though rising from a dream, I realized these unfolding moments had given me insight into understanding *them* a little more. What they had and how they had evolved into something greater. I wanted to know more about the Far East, and what they'd done there.

My eyes stung, but I refused to let a tear fall. There was still hope that James would come to trust me completely. And let me stay with them.

"I have something fun to show you."

I shook off the self-doubt. "As long as it's not skeletons in your closet."

"Close, actually."

That devilish grin revealed his playful side.

Hand in hand, we continued along the winding hallway until we reached a chrome door. After deactivating a security system, we went through it and I realized we were standing in a temperature-controlled chamber.

James lifted me up and sat me on the edge of a long table. "I'll bring them to you." He handed me a pair of white gloves.

Intrigued, I slid the gloves on and watched him approach a chrome cabinet. After he punched in a sequence of numbers on a panel I heard a click. James pulled on a pair of gloves himself and reached in to remove a small tray, upon which rested an arrowhead, its worn down point proving it had been used back in its day. James lifted it from the tray and carried it over to me, leaning forward so he could show it off.

"How old is it?"

"1271. From a crusade stronghold." He let it slip into my gloved palm.

I held it reverently. "Where was it found?"

"Scotland. More specifically, in the ribs of a skeleton."

"How come you have it?"

"It's part of my family's treasures."

"Your ancestors are Scottish?"

"On my dad's side."

There was something else I had to ask. "Have you ever killed anyone?"

James blinked in surprise. "How would you feel if I admitted I had?"

"I would be sad for you."

"Me?"

"That you had to live with that."

His expression changed, becoming somber. "If you knew innocent lives had been saved because of it you would not judge me so harshly."

"Enough lives to make it worthwhile?"

"That's the idea."

"Did you like doing it?"

His brow furrowed, but it was in response to my robe falling open, revealing my breasts…and my sex. I let it stay like that to distract him.

I studied his face. "I don't judge you."

"Yes, you do," he said, as his jeans brushed my bare thighs, sending a jolt of arousal through me.

"You want to ruin my life." I leaned forward and brushed my lips against his.

He stepped back, biting his lip seductively. "Want to see something special?"

I tried to keep my mind on the ancient artifact in my hand.

His gaze fell to my lips. "I'll get it." He lifted the arrowhead out of my palm with care.

After he stepped away, I drew in a sharp breath, trying to erase the effect he was having on me. But there was no denying that my clit was still throbbing from the way he'd brushed up against me in a devilish tease.

He pressed a button and the arrowhead was returned to its drawer. From the same cabinet he withdrew a gold crown inlaid with emeralds and rubies.

I reached out to take it from him. He pulled it out of reach.

I rested my hands in my lap. "Sorry, it's just so pretty."

"It was destined for Queen Anne Boleyn."

"It's so beautiful."

Mystical even, the way the fluorescent light bounced off the jewels, transmuting them into shards of colorful light. My thoughts raced over what I knew about Henry the Eighth's second wife, who had fallen victim to his passion for beheading his women.

My thighs widened again to give James the room he needed to get closer and he confidently stepped between them. I exhaled sharply as I felt the pressure of his erection through his jeans. It gently rubbed against my clit, causing my lips to quiver at being kept in a climactic holding pattern.

"Dazzling," he whispered.

We both looked down at the crown he was holding.

"Anne and I belong to the same club," he said matter-of-factly, "both of us were destined for the throne."

"She was beheaded." My voice sounded breathy.

"I fared better."

"Does it make you sad you aren't king?"

He looked amused. "I fulfill my role in other ways."

"How?"

"I ensure Britain remains a sovereign state."

"It's not the same as being king?"

He leaned in. "I still rule."

It was the way he held my stare that titillated me. More than this, it was the way he was causing a delicious arousal to burn through me with each move of his pelvis. I'd never been one to chase power, but he was mesmerizing.

"I want to see a demonstration," I said breathlessly.

"Of my authority?"

"Yes."

"I doubt you'd like what you see."

"Why?"

Sadness flashed across his face. "'I am death, the destroyer of worlds.'"

The spell shimmered toward a nightmare...

I swallowed hard. "That's a quote from Oppenheimer? The man who created the atomic bomb."

He gave a nod. "It comes from the translation of the Hindu scripture the *Bhagavad Gita*."

"What does it mean?"

"Despite personal concerns or views, one honors his duties. One remains a warrior. Does what is needed."

"You're saying..."

"No one gets in my way. No one."

Until me.

His jeans pressed against my sex and he held himself there. A heady mixture of pleasure and fear slithered up my spine.

I readied for his deadly kiss. James' lips were parted and near, so full of promise, so ready to deliver that final strike of power.

Shuddering, I was being drawn into the flame of his sensuality, not caring if it singed my wings, unable to resist him. Unable to deny myself what only he could give. *Yes* to him pushing me back. *Yes* to him ripping open my robe all the way. *Yes* to his cock pressing into me and him fucking me hard on this table.

Yet my body remained rigid as though my mind was his to control, only my gasps revealing my rising climax brought on from the pressure of him against me.

"You are breathtaking," he whispered huskily.

"James."

"Not without Xavier." His warm breath on my lips.

I dipped my head. "I don't know what I was thinking."

"We both know what you were thinking." He broke into a heart-shattering smile.

"What must you think of me?"

"This." Raising the crown, he then lowered it to rest on the top of my head.

Wearing such a priceless piece made me self-conscious. I reached up to touch it and then pulled my gloved hand away respectfully.

James pulled off my gloves. "Touch it."

"What about keeping it preserved?"

"Anne would want you to enjoy it."

My fingers curled around the bejeweled spikes. "Her memory is captured in this."

"So is yours, Emily."

"I see the good in you," I whispered.

His irises darkened. "It's inevitable that at some point I will shatter your heart to smithereens."

"Then I better make the most of it."

"That's my recommendation." He leaned forward and kissed the end of my nose.

I wanted to tear his heart apart like he was threatening to do to mine, but all I could do was surrender to these sensations that were making my face flush.

"I will be inside you again soon," he whispered. "With Xavier present."

I gave a nod and tried to look casual at his sensual promise.

James grinned. "Looks pretty on you."

"Wish I could keep it," I said. "Though I don't know when I'd wear it."

"Keep it on." James reached for my hand to help me down. "Xavier will enjoy fucking you while you wear it."

"Then I'm never taking it off."

"I love that plan." He weaved his fingers through mine. "Let's go to the battlement."

"What?"

"Roof."

With me still wearing this precious crown, we wound our way up a stone staircase until we reached a door.

We stepped out into the crisp early morning air and strolled along a turreted wall.

"It's cold," I said.

"I have just what you need to warm you up."

Turning a corner, I saw what he meant.

Staring out at the horizon was a vision of loveliness—Xavier.

He'd carried the duvet up with him and had wrapped it around his shoulders, the mound of material swamping him as he snuggled within its sumptuousness. He turned to look at us and his face lit up with a smile.

Rushing forward, I fell against the warmth of his naked chest. PJs were his only clothes, and he was barefoot, too. He welcomed me beneath the generous duvet and hugged it around us, then kicked it out so we could stand on the trailing material.

Facing the wall, I stood with my back against his chest and peered out at the dramatic vista with its oranges and yellows and bright reds lighting up the morning sky as dawn ascended along the horizon.

Xavier looked amused as he glanced over at James. "Is her crown from *the* collection."

"Yes," he replied.

I leaned back against Xavier. "It was Anne Boleyn's."

"Oldest trick in the book," joked Xavier. "Make a woman your queen and she'll do anything."

James gave us an indulgent smile. "I'll come back with coffee."

"Stay," I told him.

Xavier pressed his lips to my shoulder, as though thanking me for saying it.

James turned to go. "Take the time you need."

We watched him disappear from view.

"He cares so much for you," I said softly.

Though James' need for Xavier was multi-layered, and he had to know this.

"How are you feeling?" Xavier leaned forward to look at my face. "That was a lot to take in yesterday."

"I'm doing okay."

"Sure?"

I drew in a sigh of happiness at being back in his arms. "So many questions."

"Ask me."

"The secrecy has lifted?"

"Some."

I needed to mull over what I'd seen and heard. Needed to come to terms with what I believed was happening with us all.

"Our second date," I began quietly. "What did I wear?"

His sigh matched mine. "Black halter-neck dress. Strappy shoes. A thong that snapped easily. You'd removed your nose ring. Which told me you were already addicted to my cock."

My elbow hit his ribs. "Earrings?"

"Gold studs."

"What else do you remember?" I asked wistfully.

"I wanted to impress you, so I took you to Hide, that restaurant in Mayfair."

"I was already impressed."

"We had oysters. You wanted to know how pearls are made. I told you over a bottle of oaked chardonnay."

"Xavier," I coaxed.

His grip tightened. "Are you sure you want me to go there?"

"Yes."

A raven flew low and landed on a tree in the distance.

"You blinked over one thousand three hundred and ten times during the first hour. That was another way I knew you liked me."

"What?"

"The average is one thousand two hundred."

"You counted?"

"Not consciously. That would be tedious. I can recall at will."

"What must that be like?"

"I don't know any different."

My mouth went dry. "Something else."

He tapped his hips against me. "You're as bad as James."

"I need this."

"Remember our table at Hide? We sat near the window. Watched the commuters scurrying by."

"It was raining."

"Two inches fell." He chuckled. "Two point four, to be exact."

That was six months ago. I felt a chill through my bones.

"On the back wall of the bar were the spirits. I can tell you the amounts in each one, if you like. All twenty of them. The vodka bottle was empty. Rum half-full. Jack Daniels had a torn label from when the cap was opened. Wine bottles lined along the top of the bar. Ten of them. A row of white and then red. The barman had a lime stain on his tie. He checked his wristwatch seven times during the last hour of his shift. He looked like he was going to meet someone. He'd check his reflection too many times for him to be merely heading home that night."

"Something else." Hopefully something I would remember.

"The couple sitting to our left," he continued. "Remember them? The woman wore red. She played with her silver cross necklace. Nervous. We'd guessed it was their first date."

"I remember."

"He received a text from his wife during dinner."

"You saw that?"

"I saw her face. Then his. It was disappointment that he'd gotten caught. He'd already taken Viagra."

"You saw that?"

"He went to the restroom to take it. The tablet needed several swigs of water to wash down when he got back to the table. The drug kicked in at the thirty-minute mark." I turned my head to look back at him and he added, "His pupils dilated. He adjusted his trousers. Twice."

At some point in the evening I remembered glancing over to see the woman in the red dress looking deflated. I'd guessed the dinner wasn't going well. This fit my memory of it.

"She left after dessert," said Xavier. "Took a cab. The advert on the side of the car was for the musical *Wicked*. The driver opened the door for her. Across the street a couple were arguing. A pedestrian was struggling with his umbrella. He never did open it in time for his Uber to arrive."

"Tell me something else," I said.

"You're beautiful when you sleep."

"You watch me?"

"It replaces my need for chess."

"Oh, Xavier."

"Want me to go on?"

"Maybe one more?"

"I know when you lose an eyelash."

"Seriously?"

"And Emily, I recall every single orgasm you've ever had in minute detail. Their length, their power, and those times where you came more than once."

"Oh, God."

"Obviously I know when your period's due. That's easy. I make sure we have in your favorite meringue pudding. The one from Marks and Spencer."

"Ha."

"The one you like to dip your finger in and then lick off the cream." He tapped his hips playfully against me.

"I want that life again," I whispered.

"We have it."

"Permanently," I said, testing him.

"I'll always watch over you."

There it was, the possibility of us ending swinging around again. I refused to believe it.

I refused to let my hope die. "Do you know how to stop time?"

"It's my superpower."

"I wish we could hide out here forever."

He pulled me closer. "Nothing can touch you."

Together, beneath the warmth of the sumptuous duvet, we watched the sun rise. Beautiful and cruelly unstoppable—a profound vision of blazing colors drenching the landscape in purples, reds and golds, the brightness dancing over the trees and fighting off the grey. As the colors burned into being, my heart was scorched with the inevitable.

Xavier squeezed me tightly. "You're my greatest love."

"What about...him?"

He dipped slightly to kiss the nape of my neck, his lips staying there as the sun continued to rise over the landscape. "We're perfect together. All three of us."

His fingers trailed down my abdomen and then dug in as he gripped me to him possessively.

This crown felt wrong. Like an omen, or a portent to something in my future—as though Anne Boleyn's fate was somehow aligned with mine.

"I love you, Emily Rampling," Xavier whispered.

I felt a rush of warm happiness, which was quickly swallowed by a swell of concern. James was standing a little ways off and he was looking out over a turret.

The helicopter flew low over the fields, banking toward us.

Chapter 25

I'D BEEN PISSED OFF WHEN I'D FIRST ARRIVED AT BALLAD'S CASTLE. NOW I didn't want to leave. The irony was not lost on me.

With the noise of the chopper blades above us, our voices were virtually drowned out. We'd had to put on headsets and that had made it possible for me to listen to the chatter between James, Xavier, and the pilot.

The castle turrets faded from view.

After the rush of adrenaline dissipated from our rapid take-off, I was lulled by the thrum of the engine and the view of James and Xavier sitting opposite me. Our civility hid what we'd been to each other back in that ancient fortress.

What we'd done with each other.

What they'd done to *me*.

I squeezed my eyelids closed for a beat, enjoying the soothing memory of being wrapped in their arms. I already missed spending time alone with them.

My experience at the Ballad estate had been flawed at the start, but the threat of torture had morphed into carnal pleasure. Even now, hours later, my body thrummed from our lovemaking.

No, love wasn't part of it. It had strived to be something darker, something forbidden. A ménage-à-trois that took fucking to an entirely new dimension—the forget-you-exist kind.

It was hard to tear my eyes away from James—the architect of my pleasure and pain. That wicked mouth had delivered blinding pleasure, his charismatic presence placing him firmly at the center of the universe. It made me wonder what drove him, what spurred him on to place himself as king of everything. Or, who made that decision for him.

Gone were the jeans and shirt from before—he had donned a designer suit, a shiny pair of brogues, and had even put on an expensive watch. His tousled hair had been arranged in a sophisticated style.

I hate him.

Hated how he'd drawn me into the center of his flame.

Had I gone willingly?

His promise to take me again soon with Xavier present alighted my being, burning me from the inside out. The attraction I felt for him was intoxicating, and even though uncertainty plagued me, I couldn't walk away. This craving for more of them—more conversations, more shared meals, more passion—was impossible to deny.

I needed it…needed them.

As though sensing my stare, James looked up from the screen. He didn't smile, though, and there was no reassuring gesture. No kindness. With each beat of his heart, he was transforming back into the man I'd first met, reasserting his control.

Xavier's eyes were closed as he relaxed during the flight, as though us being whisked away was perfectly normal. He'd gone for a more casual look, wearing jeans and a Polo shirt—and wearing a different pair of shoes than the ones he'd arrived in. He kept clothes back at Ballad's castle, and I found it unsettling.

Xavier opened an eyelid for a split second and offered a smile. His way of saying there was nothing to fear.

I knew better.

Xavier was my home—which made James the wilderness that led away from him. There was no escaping this experience. No escaping James. My feet were already entangled in the brush and I was tripping to get away.

And yet my attachment to them always pulled me back.

From the arrogant glance James gave me, exuding his authority, he could see I was falling for him. *If* we were ever intimate again, I'd bite his lip and make him bleed—bleed like he was making our hearts bleed for him.

James eased a sleek briefcase off the seat beside him and pulled out a laptop. He rested it on his knees and cracked it open. He typed away with his focus on the screen.He was missing the picturesque scenery of winding country lanes and endless hedges, the vast stretches of greenery along with the richest tapestries of color.

I watched him work, hoping there was no end in sight to our ménage-à-trois. My chest tightened when I allowed my thoughts to drift there.

The helicopter dipped.

Neither of them flinched. I was the only one gripping my seatbelt like it made a difference and could actually save me if this thing went down—like the Puma that was shot out of the sky because they'd believed Ballad was on board.

Jesus. I hoped they'd not gotten intel about his latest movements. I'm sure there were perks to his lifestyle, but this sinister threat didn't make them worthwhile.

My violin case sat securely on the empty seat on my left. James had strapped it in to keep it from shifting during the flight. Its aged case and what lay within was a reminder of the responsibility of owning it. That Strad brought the promise of a brighter future. Something I could trust.

This was what my life had become…helicopter rides, castles, and revelations that the world was not as it seemed. And these two enigmatic and complicated men who had vague job descriptions and even greyer connections to power.

The thought of the last twenty-four hours brought on a tidal wave of emotions. Tendrils of doubt burrowed deep inside me.

Xavier undid his seatbelt and came over to me, sitting on my right. He took my hand in his and brought it to his mouth, kissing my fingers. Then he offered me a drop-dead beautiful smile. He rested our clasped hands in his lap as though sensing my nervousness.

Puffs of billowing clouds dissipated to reveal the River Thames twisting through the landscape.

"You're missing it," I told James.

He looked up at me and blinked, as though replaying my words. Then he turned to look out at the scenery, a curl of a smile at the corner of his lips.

"What are you working on?" I asked.

"A speech."

"When do you have to give it?"

He gave me a rueful smile.

"Can you read some?" I threw in a cute grin.

James' long fingers reached for the mouthpiece. "Microphone off, please, Carl."

The pilot's voice crackled through my earpiece. "Got it, boss."

I readied myself for the upcoming lecture he was about to deliver—something about not asking too many questions.

He gave his laptop screen a slight nudge and drew in a breath. "What is the cost of one life?" he began poetically. "Even one life is too high a price to pay. We know this, we feel it in our souls as profoundly as we comprehend it. However, the winds of change have turned against our allies and we are again reminded of our profound history. And, like before, when we refused to bow to tyranny, or cower in the face of evil, we took action. We refused to allow our allies to crumble beneath savage attacks, from savage people. We cannot expect our brothers and sisters, our allies, to endure this on their own. We cannot abandon them. We will not abandon them. It is with a heavy heart, but a strong heart no less, that I say...we must do what is good, what is right, what is honorable..." James' gaze rose from the screen. "I'm still working on the last line," he said, using his usual tone of voice.

"Did you write that?" I breathed.

"It'll do." Xavier winked at him.

"What's it for?"

James tapped his lip thoughtfully. "To persuade."

I watched him close his laptop.

"Seatbelt, Xavier," said James firmly, sliding his laptop into his briefcase.

Xavier clipped in his seatbelt and then turned and gave mine a customary tug.

London came into view.

And just like that James shut down, as though his connection to this city once more drew his full attention.

We landed in Regent's Park, where a black SUV waited for us. We left the helicopter and trudged the distance across the grass to our car, with Xavier carrying my violin case and James leading the way with his briefcase in hand.

Sitting in the backseat of the car, I turned to Xavier. "Where are we going?"

"You'll love it."

I wanted to ask why we'd left the castle so quickly, but as I'd not been meant to see it, I chose not to remind James how much I'd learned within those mighty walls.

Recognizing the scenery, my thoughts began to race, wondering what we were doing here. This was a stone's throw from Camden Market, and one of my favorite towns to visit: Primrose Hill, a quiet village just north of Regent's Park. It offered visitors the quaintest coffee shops, bookstores, local boutiques, along with picturesque walkways.

The car slowed to take a corner and I recognized the eclectic homes lining the winding street. The terraced houses and their bright colors made it easy to forget we were still in the city.

There was a history here. *Ours.*

Xavier liked this part of town because H. G. Wells had based his book *War of the Worlds* in this location. He loved that novel. He got a kick out of walking along the green where the aliens were meant to have landed. It was such a geeky thing to do. Now, I realized he'd been looking for a way to escape those nightmarish details in his head.

I couldn't fathom how he endured it.

It was also during our first trip to Primrose Hill that he'd introduced me to the poems of Sylvia Plath—his way of broadening my education after learning of my compromised one in that secondary school in Devon. Crooking my neck, I could see Plath's old home, No. 3 Chilcot Square. Fans of her poetry could often be seen outside paying homage to her.

We, too, had our moment with Sylvia Plath outside her home— both of us huddled beneath an umbrella while I read "Lady Lazarus," setting her words free into the late evening, relishing their rhythm and flow, both of us glancing at the place she'd lived as though some part of her spirit still resided there.

The car idled at the curb not far from her former home. I gave Xavier a curious glance, a silent question as to why we were here. He gave me nothing.

The driver opened the rear door for us.

With me clutching my violin protectively, we got out and walked the short distance to a house that was three doors down from Sylvia's. The elegant facade and arched windows provided a dash of character. I wondered who lived here.

This expansive home was in the same style as the others lining the street, except it had elegant brass balconies above the ornate windows.James pulled out a key and threw me a disarming smile before he unlocked the door.

A lemon-scented foyer greeted our entry. Each of us wiped our shoes on the doormat before walking into the elegantly furnished sitting room. Everything looked new.

I gave a sideways glance at James and got a wink back.

I tried to process what was happening.

"Let me show you around," said Xavier.

He led us through the generous upscale living spaces. Warily, I left the masculine décor of the lower floor and followed them to the upper level. We walked in and out of the bedrooms—all six of them.

"Who owns this place?" I asked.

"Better than a hotel, right?" said James.

"It's yours?"

"*Ours*," said Xavier.

My mouth went dry. I wished I'd finished that coffee before we'd left James' estate. We'd been rushed out of there like the place was on fire.

"Why did we leave the castle so quickly?" I asked.

"I'm needed here," said James flatly. "I have an appointment in The House of Commons this afternoon."

His admission reassured me that he trusted my confidence at least. I suppressed a smile at the thought as I parted the blinds and peered out at the extensive garden, its privacy protected by a sweeping line of trees.

"Do you like it?" asked Xavier.

"You'll stay?" I asked.

Xavier glanced at James.

James approached the window and peered out. "For now, yes."

"How long?"

Xavier pivoted to look at me. "Garden's nice, right?"

"We can change the décor." James shoved a hand in his pocket and turned to look at me. "You'll continue to act under my guidance, of course."

I glared at him. "Under your control?"

"Yes."

"I can come and go?"

"With certain limitations. You may attend your final audition."

"What about teaching?"

"Cancelled, for now."

"But my students—"

"They've been provided with another tutor." James shrugged it off.

"You can't do that."

"Yes, I can."

Xavier came toward me. "Afterward, you'll own this place outright."

A rush of excitement dissolved as I replayed his words. "After what?"

"Why don't we all go into the kitchen?" said James. "I'll make breakfast."

Xavier smiled. "I'll make coffee."

"I don't want anything," I lied. "When did you find this place?" I ignored their attempt at playing Martha Stewart to distract me from the news that I was essentially their prisoner. "When did you stock the food?" I added.

"We move fast." James smirked. "It's our specialty."

"This is a temporary fuck-pad," I bit out.

James didn't flinch.

"I'm a temporary plaything?" The sarcasm dripped from my tone. "Instead of playing chess, you get to fuck me."

"Don't," said Xavier.

I studied them both.

"You know why," said James.

Hurrying out, I descended the hardwood steps, gripping the banister as I went, and quickly made it to the front door.

"Emily." James thundered down the stairs after me.

I spun to face him. "I need to know what this is!" Because I was seconds from walking out.

James glanced back to see that Xavier had followed us. Turning to me, he said, "This is essentially a slow goodbye."

"Slow?"

"I need to reacclimate you after all you've learned." He shrugged. "Nothing has changed, Em."

"Not even after..." That night when we'd bonded on an entirely new level.

"Not even after that," he confirmed.

"Why?"

"Because you're dating a man who does not exist," he snapped.

"Xavier?"

James looked surprised. "I don't count."

"Because you're allowed to have a life. You're allowed to exist. To stroll the mighty chambers of Number 10. To wield your power around London."

"What you want is incompatible," he replied calmly.

"With what?"

"Being a famous violinist," he said sharply. "You want to rise in the orchestra. Have a solo career."

"I never told you that."

"Don't, James," said Xavier. "Not now."

James ignored him. "I'm giving you this house. How about a 'thank you'?"

"How about a 'fuck you'?" I said.

James' jaw clenched with fury.

I stood defiant. "You took our home away, remember? I once had a place...with Xavier. We had a good life."

"You can't have both, Em," James said quietly.

Tears stung my eyes.

James sighed. "Any attention on you brings attention to Xavier."

"And on Pervade?"

"Don't call us that," he said. "Please."

"I'll give up on joining the orchestra."

James shook his head. "That choice is not yours to make."

Xavier came closer. "I would never ask that of you."

"It's fine. I'll teach." I nodded as the pain of what I was offering them hit home. It would be like every bow pulled and every note struck meant nothing.

"That would destroy you, Em," said Xavier softly.

"Not to mention national security," said James.

Xavier glared at him. "Seriously?"

"Yes." James returned his angry stare. "I've been more than generous. I trust you, Em, but if I see that trust broken..."

I yanked open the door, revealing a burly man in a black suit looking down at me, an earpiece visible beneath his white collar.

James' tone turned dark. "Shut the door."

The man obeyed the command and closed it.

I pivoted to face James again. "You can't keep me prisoner."

"It's protection."

I glared at him for twisting the truth. "From who?"

"Where do I begin?" James delivered coldly.

"You act like you own me."

"Essentially, I do."

I let out an exasperated sigh.

"We can give you what you want," James said. "If you'll...submit."

What the hell did that mean?

"Do you need me to convince you this is the right decision?" he continued.

"You can try."

James held my gaze for a few moments.

Then moved on me fast...

He cupped my face with an ironclad grip and crushed his lips to mine. Forcing his tongue into my mouth, he punished me with brutal lashes that made my insides melt, setting me on fire with lust, lit by his domination.

I felt Xavier's palm at my nape, holding me in place, keeping me still so James could continue his ravishment of my mouth—letting his fantasy play out.

A moan escaped my lips, muffled by that brazen mouth of Ballad's, so harsh and unforgiving. Yet I desired his show of power. It sent tingles into my chest, shooting pleasure down between my thighs and dampening my panties, my nipples beading in response.

James broke away. "In order to fulfill my promise to Xavier, we needed someplace special. This is it."

"What about what I want?"

"Emily, keep talking. If you want to test my resolve, go ahead."

I hated him for saying it...this gorgeous man with the dangerous allure who wielded power over both of us.

My hand burned with the urge to make contact with his cheek.

He seemed to read my mind. "I wouldn't do it if I were you," he warned.

"What would happen?"

"Do you really want to find out?"

"Fine," I said, relenting. "How long do we get?"

He arched a brow. "Much better attitude."

"You *are* death," I threw his quote back at him. The same one he'd used in his chamber of horrors. Okay, there was that pretty crown in there and I hadn't seen everything, but something told me it was an array of weaponry that was still bloodied from its victims.

"Emily, shall we show you the benefit of your compliance?" said James darkly.

I stared at him, trying to resist giving an answer.

This wasn't happening…

I wasn't burning up for them, my soul wasn't yearning for their touch, my core wasn't thrumming with the promise of pleasure. My entire being wasn't demanding more control, more sensations rushing through me, owning me.

If I stayed, we'd create the co-mingling of more memories…ones that would have to last a lifetime. With these unraveling thoughts, my shoulders slumped in defeat.

If what they were looking for was submission, they were seeing it.

The promise of the cruel yet luscious way James would direct each lash of his tongue at my sex, each vicious fuck and prolonged pounding that I had come to desire were what I needed now more than my next breath.

Say yes.

Accept their passion…all the passion you're craving.

Most of all, I needed to accept the inevitable pain that would shatter my soul.

And maybe, if I dared to stay, I'd bridge Xavier's transition away from his old life to the one without me. This, after all, was true love.

All I had to do was splinter…

And if I survived, the coming back together again would see me rise.

I held on to that thought, because that was all I had.

All I could hope for.

Shards of light flooded in through the bay window by the door, dancing upon Xavier's flawlessness, his stark beauty reminding me of the impossibility of *us*. His expression pleaded for me to stay.

What was being asked of me was merely the giving up of my happiness.

"What do I get out of it?" I asked, even after that dark musing, a philosophical truth spilling like rain.

"You mean other than a house?" James delivered the quip.

"Yes. Do I get...?"

He tucked his hands in his pockets. "Me?"

There came no answer to whether James was part of the temporary deal, but I knew that he was.

That became obvious when he removed his hands from his pockets. "Show me."

A frisson of awareness captured me, causing addictive tingles in my chest. *Damn him* for having this effect on me. Damn him for making loving him possible.

Unzipping my jeans, I pulled them down a little.

His hand came down on mine and together we eased my jeans lower to expose my underwear.

He focused between my thighs. "It seems you like to argue."

Oh, God. That spot of wetness on my panties revealed how much this man turned me on. How much they both turned me on. Quickly, I zipped up my jeans.

Thoughts of the past with us all wrapped together in a tangle of bodies and sweat were too enticing to push away, the erotic imaginings of what else we'd do together too alluring to ignore.

"How does your clit feel?" He leaned in. "Is it throbbing? Are you fantasizing about my tongue on you again? Just like you were in the helicopter on the way here?"

Yes.

He continued in that husky tone. "Is your cunt hungry for me *again?* Your ass clenching with need to be filled by Xavier? Is us taking you at the same time all you can think about?"

I turned my head away sharply, cheeks flushing, even as his thumb continued to rub my bottom lip. My tongue licked his thumb as I glanced at Xavier, relieved when I saw his nod of approval.

"I own your pleasure, Em." James drew me back to him.

Instinctively, my bite came down hard on his thumb in rebellion.

"Very good," he said with no response to the pain, merely shoving his thumb deeper into my mouth and running it back and forth along my tongue like he was fucking me with it.

"I like it when you show strength," he added. "That we can use."

I swallowed my saliva as best I could despite the tip of his thumb nudging my throat seductively.

He removed his thumb. "Take them off," he demanded.

Obeying, I kicked off my shoes and then leaned against the wall, dragging my jeans all the way down over my hips and then stepping out of them.

I felt his warm hand on my hip, and then heard the snap of my panties as James ripped them off.

"Spread your legs a little," he ordered.

Again, I obeyed, watching him as he reached down and began thrumming my clit with a swift fingertip. Glancing up, I saw Xavier watching in awe.

"Eyes on me, Emily," snapped James. "What do you say?"

"Thank you, sir."

"Very good."

Breathing sharply, my clit spasming at his touch, I looked down to see his speed increase, nudging my folds with his frantic rhythm.

Remembering his command, I broke my stare from what he was doing.

"Part your labia," he ordered. "Show us more of you."

Obediently, I parted my folds, the exquisite tingling sensation feeling extraordinary.

"That's it, Em," Xavier encouraged.

James continued flicking with panache as he said huskily, "You didn't know before you were living in my city. You had no idea how much of your life I had access to. Now you do. You couldn't have comprehended that all that power belonged to one man. You couldn't know your pussy was always destined to belong to us."

My eyes widened with that revelation.

James' tone darkened. "Come hard and show your compliance. Or don't come at all."

"I want to come," I whispered, as twinges of arousal made me breathless.

"I will allow it." James gave a nod of approval. "But before you do, agree to obey me in all things. No more rebelling—or I will burn away your disobedience."

"I promise to be good."

"Then you may come."

His chestnut irises sparkled with glints of gold. They were devastatingly hypnotic and I fell under their spell as easily as I fell into my orgasm. My thighs trembled as I disappeared into the bliss of his sexual prowess.

My deep-throated moans filled the room as I rode out the intense climax.

"Come again, Emily." His flicking once more accelerated. "Another orgasm, please. This one for Xavier."

Gasping, I surrendered—chasing after what was mine with rocking hips and endless moans, reaching down to grip his wrist, keeping his fingers dancing in place to carry me over the edge again.

And again…

Chapter 26

THE PALACE OF WESTMINSTER, ENSCONCED ALONG THE RIVER Thames, was easily the most famous and recognizable of British landmarks—the towering clock known as Big Ben a regal part of its vast gothic architecture.

James helped me out of our chauffeured town car and we headed into the palace. My body was still buzzing from that devious clit play he'd recently demonstrated so brilliantly in front of Xavier back in Primrose Hill. Our erotic show had been enjoyed by all three of us, apparently. There'd been no time for more. Ballad had a meeting that had brought him here.

All of these emotional highs and lows were making my head spin. Xavier didn't come with us, but I had been invited along.

James didn't tell me why. He'd virtually ignored me during the entire trip here while working on his laptop. I didn't really mind...it had given me the chance to stare out the windows and admire the view. Admire him, too.

This morning had seen him escalate his authority. He'd sent me reeling and it was hard to come down. It was exhilarating to be toyed with, and I relished the memory of how he'd pleased Xavier by playing with me in front him. It titillated my senses to know Xavier had enjoyed seeing it.

James was the director of all the chaos. The thought of it kept me in a constant state of arousal. Despite this, I had merely clutched my hands in my lap and remained silent for the entire ride, trying to figure out my place in all of this intrigue.

With a flash of Ballad's I.D., we were allowed entry into the Palace of Westminster, which housed the Houses of Parliament.

Not once had I ever considered the possibility that I'd be strolling along these lofty corridors one day, peering up in awe at the spectacularly designed interior.

And certainly not like this—wearing a sleek blue Chanel business suit, high-heels, and a short-bobbed wig. They'd dressed me in a disguise.

Ballad didn't want anyone to see the real me, apparently. I looked like his secretary walking beside him, carrying two folders to round out the executive assistant feel.

From the outside, Parliament was gorgeous with its triple towers, gothic architecture, and sprawling structure that included the House of Commons and the House of Lords.But it earned its palace status on the inside, too.

James led the way through the impressive lobby. Together, we continued into a familiar room—one I'd seen on TV but never really paid attention to before, since it was in huge contrast to my simple world. This was the House of Lords.

The policeman who permitted our entry had given us a cursory nod of permission to go in. We found ourselves alone in the lavishly decorated chamber.

The massive door closed behind us with a deep thud.

Red studded leather seats circled the center stage—fit for the bums of Britain's elite who scrutinized the Bills brought into being by the House of Commons, a stone's throw away. The men and women who'd found themselves a place here had inherited one of these lofty seats. That was pretty much all I knew.

Peering up at the ornate ceiling, I admired the grandness of the paneled compartments showing ancient emblems. The stained-glass windows offered intricately colored patterns. Shades of red and gold drenched us in soft bronzed light.

"Wow." My voice echoed as I turned in a circle to take it all in.

"That's where the Queen sits." James pointed to a majestic throne. "During the state opening of Parliament when she delivers her speech."

"Can I sit there?"

"No." He smirked and gestured to a long red seat. "Sit there."

I wanted to open the folders I was holding and have a peek inside—the same ones he'd told me not to look at under any circumstances. Fingering the edge, my imagination ran wild with what information it might contain. Maybe it was merely a prop for a well-healed secretary, or maybe it was a test to see if I obeyed and didn't sneak a peek.

James closed the gap between us and towered over me. "I'm going to give you *the* talk."

Crooking my neck to look up at him, I tried to interpret his words.

"There's a car waiting for you. The driver has been instructed to escort you to a safe place."

"What is this?"

"Xavier and I believe that with him present, you feel pressured to stay."

"James—"

"I need you to listen. To understand that if you stay, even though it may be temporary, anything you see or hear must remain confidential."

"I can do that."

He knelt before me. "Emily, the danger's real. It's as insidious as it is unpredictable."

"What are you saying?"

"If you stay there'll be consequences. Lives will be threatened. Lives—including yours—will change beyond all understanding."

"How would that be my fault?"

"Because of your association to me...to us. That's why you've been disguised."

"I'll be careful."

He studied my face, looking unconvinced.

My eyes pleaded with him. "I want to stay."

"The cost is high. Perhaps too high."

"Will they hurt you because of me?"

"That's a frequent threat. But it's not me I'm concerned about."

Reaching up, I caressed his jaw, my fingers trailing over his cleanly shaven face and cupping his cheek with affection. "Let me stay."

His hand rose up to take mine and he brought it to his lips, kissing it tenderly.

"Why are we here?"

James pushed to his feet. "For the truth."

The air left my lungs as I sank deeper into the seat with my heart racing.

"Pervade?"

James straightened his back. "We exist to protect humanity."

My flesh chilled at the change in his stance, that domineering nature slipping back into being as his eyes darkened.

"Do you do bad things?"

"Yes."

"Do you have a license to kill?"

He gave me a wry smile. "Do you think I'm James Bond?"

My lips turned up in amusement. "I was beginning to wonder."

"I'm on the side of the angels. But I've already told you that."

I processed his words. "Why are you letting me in now?"

He mulled this over. "If you stay I'm going to use you."

Struck by his honesty I said, "How?"

He leaned low and tipped up my chin. "Your beauty, and your talent, would be useful to us."

Knocking his hand away, I got to my feet. He held his ground, keeping a small gap between us, looking down at me with the authority this place gave him.

Glancing at the door I said, "You want me to stay for Xavier's sake?"

"For now, yes."

"But not for you?"

A flash of raw emotion darkened his vestige. "I want you to know you have a choice. Xavier doesn't. And I'm giving you the opportunity to walk away. Xavier will always watch over you."

It would never be enough…

"I don't want to know any more secrets," I said sharply. "Don't tell me anything that will put me or you or Xavier at risk."

"Emily, you went to Great Missenden. It's a mistake that cannot be reversed. My advice is this—retrace your steps down the hallway, all the way back to the car. Don't look back."

"And you trust me to remain silent about all of this?"

"All of what?"

"Right." I exhaled slowly. "Did you suspect I was a spy?"

"Yes."

"That's why you were angry when I turned up at your castle."

"Concerned, yes."

"But not now?"

"No."

"How would you know for sure?"

"It's part of what we do. We needed time to turn over every leaf. Search every connection. Retrace every step you've ever taken."

My lips trembled at his confession.

"I've yet to totally violate you. If you stay, however, violating you will be my pleasure…"

"That's a monstrous thing to say."

"You're still standing here."

"Because of Xavier."

"Because of me. Admit it. Then, and only then, can we move forward."

"You want me to tell you I have feelings for you?"

"Don't insult me with such banality."

"Love, then?"

"You fell in love with me back at the castle."

"Arrogant…" I bit back the rest.

"If I have no hold on you in that regard, leave now."

"I'm staying for Xavier."

"Honesty, please."

"I find you compelling. Charismatic, even. And love and hate are such similar emotions I find I'm having difficulty telling them apart these days."

"What is your answer?"

"Don't make me say it." Don't make me betray Xavier.

"Emily. Look at me."

I held his stare, my expression telling him what he wanted to know, how I really felt. Yes, there was love in my heart for him and I couldn't remember the exact moment it had happened or even why, all I knew was that this man had a hold on me.

Though I hated him, too.

"I approve," he said coldly.

This was madness...this giving in and letting go. Perhaps my walking away would be the most sensible thing I'd ever do.

Yet...

"Thank you for giving me the chance to decide." I studied him. "You already know my decision."

"Agree to obey me in all things. It's the only way I can keep you safe."

"Yes..." I let out a shaky breath. "I agree."

"I'm about to test your promise, Em."

How?

I shivered, but there was no real fight left in me. I was too consumed by this heady mixture of affection and intrigue.

"Thoughts?" he pushed.

"You're a complicated man, James."

"You have no idea."

He'd entrusted me with more details, even if the veil still covered my eyes.

"What's your part in all this, Sir Ballad?"

"Small steps, Emily."

A knock at the door drew my attention. We both stared off at the man who'd poked his head in.

The policeman threw me a respectful nod and then gave one to James. "Sir, I've been told to advise you that Hawk has arrived."

"Good." James gave him a thin smile. "Thank you."

When he left I turned back to James. "Hawk?"

"Let's grab a tea first."

"Where is that?"

"Down the hall."

After a quick stop-off for a cup of tea—which was so James—we made our way down the sprawling hallways and on through another grand door. His comment that he could *use me* should have scared this undergraduate who'd once had a simple life. But intrigue was too strong a pull for my ego, which was being caressed by a promise that I could offer something more to the world than just making music and playing in an orchestra. I could play a part in something even greater.

Halfway down the hallway, I realized my mistake.

"James, the folders!" I said, panic-stricken.

"You left them in the ante-room," he said calmly. "On the coffee table."

"Yes." I went to turn back. "I'm so sorry."

His strong arm wrapped around my waist and he hugged me to him. "You'd make a lousy spy, Ms. Rampling."

He seemed unperturbed and continued on into the House of Commons with me by his side. Scanning his face for signs of anger, I considered pulling away from his grip and hurrying back for the folders. Maybe they were empty after all, merely props to deceive others.

James took my hand in his and led me up the steps toward the back wall. We made our way along the rows of seating until we reached the end. He'd chosen the upper most area, far from anyone and private enough to allow us to talk.

The place was quiet. Only a handful of men and women sat on the lowest seats, talking softly. We were far away from them in the lofty seats and they seemed not to notice us.

James sat close to me, his arm pressing into mine and my left hip crushed against his so that I felt his body heat through that sharp suit. The sensations were almost too much for me to handle...these electric pulses of excitement from our intimacy. His subtle cologne filled my senses with a potent mixture of *him*.

I tried to distract myself by looking down at the grand sight below. The chamber was easily recognizable from when I'd watched Charles Wildwood, the Prime Minster, debate members of the opposition. This was where chaotic shouting occurred during the speeches, a cause for anger, bravery and much swagger from men and women born of privilege, and others who'd clawed their way up to the highest ranks of politics, all fighting over policy, change, and ideology.

I'd not really watched them debate on TV for any length of time, to be honest. I often found myself changing the channel because of the disruption from politicians shouting at each other over their podiums. Or worse still, the terrible jeers from the members of the opposition.

My pulse spiked when I saw him.

Tall and lean and handsome in that academic way, his coattails flapped behind him as though he'd just stepped out of that preppy university in Oxford that he'd once attended. I was looking at *the* Charles Wildwood, the Prime Minister himself.

He glanced furtively around at the few people in attendance, his gaze flitting to James but not showing recognition, which I found strange. After all, we'd been in his office. I'd sat at the Prime Minister's desk as James had told me that he owned this man.

That grand PM stood about ten feet away from the podium, checking his phone. Glancing over at Ballad, I was surprised his ego hadn't been bruised that he'd not received a wave from the Prime Minister.

With a loud bang the doors were closed by a young man wearing round glasses, looking preppy in his duffle coat. He approached the Prime Minster.

My breath hitched when I saw it—a folder that looked startlingly like the two I'd carried and then left behind on the coffee table. Even from my vantage point, I could see where I'd worried the corner with fretful fingers.

"James," I got his attention.

His hand came down on my thigh. "Shush."

"It's your folder."

The warmth of his palm soaked into my skin and I was calmed a little by this, and by his seeming serenity. I had to wonder if our pause for tea had been planned all along.

The young man handed the Prime Minister the folder. It was carried off by the PM with an air of assuredness as he stepped up to the podium.

"This is all very impressive," I muttered.

"I'm giving you a code name." James lowered his sights on me. "In public, I'll address you as Ms. Kingston."

"Why?"

"It's what we do."

"Can't I choose the name?"

"Hush, now." His palm slid to my inner thigh.

His touch ignited a flame inside me. My skin quickened beneath his caress, legs opening farther so he could slide his palm higher. The pleasurable sensations caused my nipples to bead.

"These things can be tedious," he whispered.

I bit my lip suggestively. "Don't want you to get bored."

"I'm afraid it's unavoidable."

Shielded by the seat in front of me, I hoisted my skirt to show James I wasn't wearing any panties. "I want to please you."

My body shuddered as he cupped my bare pussy. "Well done, Ms. Kingston."

"Do it again…what you did back at the house."

He rested his palm against me, still and firm.

"Will Xavier mind?" I whispered.

"I'll let him punish you," replied James, turning his focus back on the Prime Minister.

The PM was reading from that folder now, his familiar voice sounding eloquent as he practiced his speech, readying it to deliver to Parliament when the time came.

After several minutes, James drew my attention back on him. "You're nice and wet." He patted my pussy to show his approval.

My thighs shaking from tension, I tried to focus, tried not to shiver through this intense arousal wetting his hand.

James continued to stare straight ahead, listening intently to the speech, nodding occasionally, narrowing his gaze as though focusing in on a phrase or a word.

Drawing in a sharp breath, I ran through my options. There were none, not really. I needed to obey this man and please him, so I could prove that my promise was authentic...so I could stay.

Leaning back, I spread my thighs wider, our dirty secret concealed by the high-backed seats in front of us.

"Good girl," he said softly.

Waiting...

And waiting...

"James."

"Patience."

With a dry mouth, I held my pose as my humiliation rose. Yet I was painfully aroused, my clit throbbing deliciously beneath the pressure of his touch, my muscles aching for relief.

Finally, his firm fingers trailed along my folds, exploring, opening, teasing...causing my breathing to hitch. My body went rigid and my internal muscles clenched when he slid in, beginning a slow, steady finger-fucking.

"So wet," he teased.

"For you."

"Silence." He pressed the base of his palm against my clit to emphasize his point.

With my teeth embedded in my bottom lip, I tried to endure the pleasure quietly, tried not to grind my pelvis against his hand now that it had found its steady rhythm, my right hand clutching the end of the seat to hold on through this erotic punishment.

All the while the cheerless words flowed from below.

Familiar...

The PM emphasized each sentence as he read from the page before him.

"Even one life is too high a price to pay. We know this, we feel it in our souls as profoundly as we comprehend it. However, the winds of change have turned against our allies and we are again reminded of our profound history. And, like before, when we refused to bow to tyranny, or cower in the face of evil, we took action. We refused to allow our allies to crumble beneath savage attacks, from savage people."

This was James' speech.

"We cannot expect our brothers and sisters, our allies, to endure this on their own. We cannot abandon them. We will not abandon them. It is with a heavy heart but a strong heart no less, that I say...we must do what is good, what is right, what is honorable..."

It was the same speech James had written in the helicopter. The same one he'd read out loud to us. These thoughts and others filled my mind as I rose and rose and rose into the stratosphere, hovering near an orgasm as James' fingers expertly manipulated me.

"I'll only come when you say," I said breathlessly, barely holding on. I knew this would please him. This was what he'd meant when he'd asked for my submission.

James' fingers delved deeper. "You'll wait until the end of the speech, understand?"

"Yes, sir." I bit my lip, trying to endure the intense longing for release.

His thumb joined the fray and rubbed my clit with lightning speed. "You're exquisite. Was it Xavier's idea for you to go pantiless?"

"Mine."

"Why?"

"I want to please you."

He gave a nod of satisfaction, though his focus stayed on the man giving the grandest of speeches. It was a speech about war...a speech about changing the world.

"I can't wait," I whispered.

The rhythm slowed, bringing me a continued buzz, one I could only barely endure. "Thank you, sir."

I glanced down as his soaked fingers strummed my glistening pussy, my clit swollen beneath his touch. It sent me close to the edge again...

Mercifully he whispered, "Come."

Shuddering, grinding against him as slowly and surreptitiously as possible, I squeezed my eyes shut and disappeared into the nothingness, drenched in pleasure, absorbed by light and warmth as I chased after waves of release.

In his hands I was a tight bud desperate to flower. A young woman obsessed with the two men in her life who owned her every waking thought.

This was outrageous and forbidden and daring and filthy and I reveled in it. I was a dirty girl with dirty thoughts doing dirty things with a regal man in a bespoke waistcoat. The ultimate exhibitionist's high. If Ballad wanted to prove he knew my darkest fantasies he'd landed on more than truth—he was fulfilling my darkest needs and satiating all of my secret desires.

My orgasm tore through me as I gripped his wrist so tightly it had to hurt.

He didn't seem to mind. "Good girl."

The air in my lungs finally found its way back as his fingers continued caressing me to bring me down slowly, proving he truly cared about my pleasure.

I leaned back, completely out of breath.

The Prime Minister seemed happy with the speech.

He strolled out of the chambers with the same dignity with which he'd entered. The few other men and women who were present trickled out behind him.

James whipped a handkerchief out of his pocket and wiped off his fingers, then slipped it back. He tugged my hem down as I sat up straight again and tried to pretend I'd not just had the best public orgasm of my life.

The warmth in my cheeks remained and my body shuddered as though the memory of his touch was too much.

"I love you," I managed.

His voice was unemotional. "For my purpose it's pleasing to hear."

"Why are you so cruel?"

"Why do you crave my cruelty?"

I don't know.

Reaching over, I grabbed his hand and his thumb brushed over my palm as though to reassure me. It wasn't enough, I needed more.

"Say something," I pleaded.

"Xavier will be pleased with how well you've done."

I threw my head back in frustration, though hearing Xavier's name brought some reassurance. I'd probably fall at his knees in relief when I saw him.

This had all been too much…that speech written by Ballad, and his gift of pleasing, proving his possession. The fact he'd been arrogant enough to do it here. And I wanted more, craved more of him…

Even as his coldness endured and he shut me out.

"You passed the test, Emily."

"You passed mine, too," I said, pouting prettily. "I look forward to more of the same."

He gave me a crooked smile as though this was all business as usual and pushed to his feet. I followed him down the stairs and out of the House of Commons into a grand foyer. We carried ourselves with the kind of grace that would fool everyone. No one would believe that we'd just committed some naughty act in the seats of Parliament that probably carried some ancient punishment.

My thighs were sticky, and I couldn't ignore the feeling. I looked around for a place where I could freshen up.

A familiar face came into view.

Mike Todd, the burly Labor leader and head of the opposition, strolled by us, his rosy cheeks and waddle unmistakable. He was heading into the House of Commons.

At least this time James received a nod of recognition from him.

Todd paused before entering the grand chamber that we'd just left to exchange courteous words with the young man in the duffle coat who had handed the Prime Minister one of our folders.

Todd was handed the other one.

With a nod of approval, the Labor leader accepted it and then headed into the House of Commons.

James grabbed my hand to get my attention. "Don't stare, Emily, it's rude."

I turned to look at him with wonder and trepidation burning my soul in equal measure. James Ballad seemed to be the man pulling the strings on *everything*.

Chapter 27

"**H**EAD FOR THE TESLA," JAMES SAID.

"What happened to the other car?"

"Walk faster."

I spun to look back at the Houses of Parliament. He grabbed my elbow with an ironclad grip and guided me over to a flashy car idling on the curb. The blacked-out windows prevented anyone from seeing inside the Tesla.

I paused next to the vehicle, replaying what had just gone down inside those hallowed chambers. "Who gave you that level of authority?"

"God, I suppose."

"God?"

"Fate, then."

"My vote means nothing?"

"It's not that cut and dry."

"Your man always gets in?"

"Or woman, yes. Undoubtedly."

"Who else is in on it?"

He gestured to the car. "Get in, Emily."

"Who are you, really?"

He yanked open the Tesla's rear door and shoved me inside, then climbed in and sat beside me.

I felt a rush of relief when I saw who was behind the wheel.

Xavier turned his head to glance back at us. "How did it go?"

"The speech needs some tweaking," said James. "But we're close."

Xavier's gaze lingered on me. "How did it go for you?"

Glancing cautiously over at James, I wondered if now was a good time to share what we'd done. "We were about to discuss the ethics of it all."

"Drive," snapped James.

"We can talk more later," added Xavier.

"I'd rather talk now," I said. "Help me understand this shaky democracy."

"Well, royalty gets some say," said James. "Drive, please."

Xavier pulled away from the curb and pressed his foot to the accelerator. "You had fun?" he asked.

"I finger-fucked her," said James dryly. "In the House of Commons."

"You have no heart." I turned in my seat to face him. "You don't know what love is."

He focused on the view of the Thames.

"You've gone rogue," I blurted out.

"Know what's criminal? Politicians using war for their own political advantage. When they have a sketchy history it's easy for a foreign country to control them. Some men will do anything to get the attention off of them after a scandal, including and not limited to starting a war."

"It still seems unfair."

"We know things, Em," James said, his tone firm.

"You play the all powerful role?"

"I don't play it. I am it."

Xavier glanced at us in the rearview. "Do your Jamaican accent for Em."

"Seriously?" snapped James.

"Yes, I want Em to see your playful side."

"It's retired." James tugged on his shirt sleeves. "Along with my patience."

I studied his face. "You like playing God, or more accurately, the Devil. What made you that way, Earl Ballad?"

"I don't know. Why don't you reflect on that in silence?"

"Honesty," I whispered. "That's all I've asked for."

He looked out the window again, and ran a hand through his hair.

"I need to keep you safe. There's a balance between that and giving Xavier what he wants. What I want."

"You want there to be an us?" I asked wistfully.

James looked conflicted. "Our time together is…"

"What are you afraid of?" I reached for him.

He swept my hand away. "This is futile. You are futile, Em."

"Have you ever loved anyone?" I seethed.

He glared at me. "I loved my wife."

"And you divorced her."

"Never," he said, pausing with a pained expression. "I was two thousand feet below the surface when I got the news."

An icy chill raced up my spine as we turned in the opposite direction away from Westminster Bridge, leaving the murky Thames behind.

"What happened?"

"She was assassinated." Grief filled his eyes. "She was in her car outside our home."

That was undoubtedly why he'd left the Navy.

I swallowed hard. "I'm so sorry. I didn't know."

"How could you?" He shook his head. "I shouldn't have told you this."

"You and I—"

"I'm merely the liaison between you and Xavier." He blinked in frustration.

"No, you're much more." Scooting over to him, I cupped his face and kissed his cheek tenderly. "Thank you for telling me this," I whispered.

"It was a long time ago."

I reached for his hand and brought it to my lips, kissing his fingertips to let him know I wanted him to find peace.

"How the hell did this happen!" he yelled at no one in particular.

"You mean us?" I said. "What we have?"

James leaned back against the headrest and stared at me, giving me a sensual look that bared his thoughts.

"Let me soothe you." I reached for his zipper.

His hand came down on mine to stay me. "I either need a stiff drink or…"

"I know what you need," I coaxed.

His dark countenance hinted at conflicting emotions, as though he were struggling with ghosts that had found him again.

Finally, he gave me a slight nod of approval.

I began to caress him through his trousers, feeling him grow stiff beneath my touch as I pulled his zipper all the way down to free his hefty length. Leaning low, I licked the frenulum and then laved the ridges of his hardening shaft, massaging the base with my palm.

My tongue moved to the tip of the head, lapping at his pre-cum.

Stroking him I whispered, "Harder?"

"Yes." James' eyelids squeezed closed. "Should I give you more of my cruelty, Em?" he asked huskily.

I gave a nod. "I want that, sir."

My sex throbbed as his hands fisted my hair with painful force, pressing me down on him, my throat opening and constricting around his tip and taking his full length as he moaned with pleasure. This was what I needed to hear more than anything…his arousal and his impending relief—his happiness.

Mercifully, he let me come up for air, only to push me down once more and guide me at a forceful pace. With a taut mouth I gave him the same aggression he shared with me, my palm burning from the strain.

"Xavier," he called out.

Ballad's firm hands went around my waist as he turned me to face forward, pulling me onto his lap and pushing my skirt up around my waist. I cried out as he entered me with one powerful thrust, his full length burying deep inside. He lifted me up and down aggressively so that our fucking was frenzied and forceful. It felt vicious and cruel, and was everything I needed in this moment. Everything *he* needed.

Blinking in surprise, I watched Xavier unbuckle his seatbelt and slide through the gap in the two front seats to join us.

The car was still driving.

"We'll crash!" I gasped.

Xavier maneuvered onto the floor of the backseat as I braced for an accident.

Wait…it's a self-driving car.

Of course it had to be, because Xavier was kneeling on the floor of the backseat between my thighs as I rode James. He took James' balls inside his mouth, suckling and lapping at them.

And we were still moving…

My focus veered from the action happening below me as our car changed lanes, avoiding the Mercedes in front of us. It picked up speed, navigating its way through traffic.

"Jesus," growled James.

His strong hands slowed my rhythm to a leisurely pace. And when Xavier's mouth rose to my clit, I let out a primal moan, thrashing as I rode James like a woman possessed, bouncing and breathless.

James pulled out of me and I looked down to see his erection between my thighs, slick and throbbing. Xavier moved in and captured James' shiny shaft in his mouth, a moan escaping them both as he wrapped his full lips around his lover's shaft, his head bobbing between my thighs in a dazzling display of male power as he deep-throated James' length with verve.

James shuddered behind me, his gasps and moans and shaking thighs proving he'd allowed himself to be swept up into the vision of us.

Reaching low, grabbing a handful of Xavier's hair, I controlled his bobbing head on that impressive cock, taking away their ultimate power. It felt divine and deliciously addictive.

The grand pillars of the National Gallery came into view. Trafalgar Square was opposite, its regal lion statues surrounding Nelson's Column.

"Put me back in her," demanded James.

I felt the fullness of him enter my pussy once more, making my limbs quiver. Xavier was now focusing his tongue on my swollen clit and I loved him for it.

James put a hand around my throat, holding my body captive. All

I could do was stay still as James pounded into me with shocking speed while Xavier teased my pussy, interfering with my ability to breathe.

I let out a moan of joy when I saw Xavier pull out his rock-hard cock and begin stroking himself as he devoured my folds possessively. Then he slid his lips down to tease James' balls once more, playing us one against the other.

The rapture is consuming us all.

With James thrusting into me from below and Xavier licking and flicking my clit expertly, my surroundings faded and I seemed to be floating, overwhelmed by pleasure. I was only vaguely aware of the erotic sounds we were making.

Xavier shot pearls of white over the three of us. My moans rose and mingled with their groans.

James grabbed my hair and turned my head, crushing his mouth to mine. My pouty lips widened to accept his tongue as he fucked me fervently, our mutual keening quieted by our kiss.

The Tesla left Buckingham Palace in our rearview.

"I want her," breathed Xavier.

James lifted me off him. "Here, take your girl. Fuck her hard."

"She's our girl." Xavier's tongue ran along my inner high, lapping at the creamy silkiness he'd left there, his half-hooded eyes lusting for more. His cock grew hard again, ready for me.

"Yes," James said softly. "Ours."

I was on all fours now, being pounded from behind by Xavier, his hand reaching around to strum my clit as I knelt to draw James' slick cock into my mouth. This was more than perfect, it was a union that had always been destined.

As the car hugged a tight turn, my body wracked with pleasure, the heart-stopping climax sweeping me away. Consumed by this frisson, I continued to lavish my affection on James.

Beholden to these remarkable men.Our decadent love-making was all we needed.

In my heart, I knew we'd find a way for us to be.

The three of us were perfect together.

Chapter 28

DAWN BROKE THROUGH THE BLINDS AND SCATTERED LIGHT ACROSS the bedroom. I didn't open my eyes. I was in bed with my beloved Xavier, and I wanted to hold onto this feeling of being nurtured.

There came an awareness of an ache between my thighs, a soreness reminding me of yesterday when I'd been taken hard in the back of a Tesla by two men with furious appetites for the wildest love-making. The self-driving car—with "special upgrades"—had carried us through the city while we'd done dirty things inside, as though our actions were perfectly normal for a Tuesday afternoon.

Afterwards, there had been time for mutual pampering, sharing hugs and kisses as we'd laughed all the way back to Primrose Hill.

For my part, it was mostly relief we'd not crashed the car. For Xavier, it seemed it was what his complex psyche had needed…being flanked by two lovers who could ease his existence.

As for James, his motives were still unknown. Yes, he'd hinted this was all for Xavier, but I sensed he was coming around to wanting more. I sensed he'd needed that mind-blowing threesome, and I'd loved seeing him relax—seeing glints of happiness find their way through the cracks of his steely shell.

My heart soared even now despite the risk of possible heartache, my feelings morphing from trepidation to contentment remembering each kiss and each caress.

With my eyes closed, I replayed my time at Parliament. In my mind I heard the conversation with James in the House of Lords and his haunting words. My eyelids fluttered in remembrance of what had followed in the House of Commons.

Stretching, I pried an eye open and glanced over at Xavier. He was wide awake and sitting up against the headboard, focusing on his Kindle.

He reached over and caressed my naked shoulder. "How are you feeling?"

"Pretty special, actually," I replied, smiling. "What's the time?"

"Only six. You can go back to sleep."

I rolled over to rest my head on his lap. "How are you?"

"Great." He played with my hair and it tickled my scalp.

"What are you reading?"

"Just jumping around the Internet."

With a gentle tug I grabbed the end of his Kindle and turned it to face me.

"Chess?"

He gave a resigned nod.

I sat up. There was more going on in that beautiful head.

With a squeeze of his arm I asked, "Can you share what you're thinking?"

"Not right now."

"Is it what we did yesterday? Together?"

He raked his fingers through his hair. "Nothing to do with that."

"Are you playing chess with an AI?"

"Maybe."

"Yesterday…"

"I want to do it again." He glanced at me. "How about you?"

"Only if it pleases you."

"Emily," he said, trying to force the truth from me.

"I'm going to hop in the shower." I got out of bed and made my way into the bathroom, feeling the burn of his stare on my back.

I was reminded that he noticed everything…every flutter of an eyelid, every curl of a lip, every frown. Nothing was off limits. I was constantly being "scanned" by this man.

Luckily, I loved him, and part of me felt like he could see into my soul.

A few minutes later I was standing beneath the torrent of hot water, turning my attention on what might happen today. I'd missed a week of study at the Academy and was going to have to go back to class with some made up excuse. The thought made my stomach churn.

It wasn't exactly my fault, though. James had prevented me from attending classes. As cruel as that was, it also meant I'd been able to hang out with the two of them, which brought its own privileges. Compared to my old life, when I was scrambling around for lost change in order to eat, this was preferable—though my life before all of this had seen me at my happiest. My dream was hanging on by a thread and it felt like a lifeline, no matter how tenuous.

Either way, I was going to have to play my violin later today—if for no other reason than to get my music fix.

I rummaged through the bag of toiletries on the counter. There were tampons, face wash, face cream—everything a girl could want while being held captive…but no deodorant.

Standing in the bathroom doorway wrapped in nothing but a towel, I called over to Xavier, who had popped in ear buds.

He saw me and eased a bud out.

"Can I use your deodorant?" I asked.

"You'll smell like a man."

"Don't mind." *I'll smell like you.*

"You will when someone mentions it at the Academy."

I brightened. "I can go in?"

"Don't see why not." He slid his finger along the screen of his Kindle. I assumed it was a chess piece he was maneuvering.

"Deodorant," I reminded him.

"Down the hall. We should have everything you need in the last bedroom on the left. Your clothes are in there, too."

I didn't want to point out that this felt like a violation. Not yet, anyway.

Trudging down the hall, I tried to comprehend that this house could one day become mine. But I'd give it all up for reassurance that

Xavier would always be in my life.

I felt myself relax for the first time since my world had been turned upside down and broken into a million pieces, scattered to the four corners of the earth.

With a nudge, I opened the last door on the right.

A blur of movement made me pause.

My vision adjusted to the dimness in the room and I saw a man lying in the bed in the corner. He had a gun pointed in my direction.

All the air left my lungs…

James sat up, bare-chested, and lowered the weapon. "Shit, Em. What the fuck?"

My heart hammered against my ribcage as I struggled to breathe.

"I'm sorry." He gestured for me to come closer as he shoved the gun beneath his pillow. "You startled me. I was asleep."

"Why do you have a gun here?"

He brushed a hand over his tired eyes, letting out a sigh of frustration. Then he glanced to the expensive watch on his wrist.

I swallowed hard. "It's early."

"Yes."

"I should have knocked?"

"You should have."

"Xavier told me my stuff's in here."

James blinked at me. "You turned left when you exited your bedroom."

"Oh."

He broke into a smile. "Climb in."

"Where were you last night?"

"Working. I didn't want to wake you."

"I missed you."

He patted the bed.

I let the towel slip from my body as I padded over to him.

He drank me in and then whipped up the sheet. "In. Now."

I eased beneath the duvet and snuggled against his warm body, resting my head against his hairy chest.

"There you are," he soothed. "Much better."

I breathed in his heady cologne, my heart rate finally slowing.

He pressed his lips to my head. Maybe he was replaying our close call and needed a minute to recover, too.

"I'm okay," I reassured him.

He exhaled slowly. "I keep it under my pillow."

"Good to know. Um…why?"

"In case stray girls come looking for their panties," he said sarcastically. "The threat is real, Em."

I didn't want to think about the danger. I stared into his dreamy chestnut eyes.

"Can I attend music school today? Any more time off and I could be in trouble."

"Stay with us."

Letting out a moan, I rested my cheek against his chest. "God, I want to."

Then I remembered there was gun beneath the pillow. The thought that he might have to use it on someone made my skin crawl. My body stiffened against him.

He said softly, "I'll have a car take you in and bring you home."

"I can make my own way."

"I'm the boss."

"Yeah, I remember."

"You did very well yesterday."

"In Parliament?"

"Yes, in there, too."

"The coffee room was the drop off point for your speeches?" Feeling intrigued, I recalled that young man handing the folder to the PM.

"Watching you orgasm in the House of Commons was a delight. Might add that to your job description."

I ignored that. "Does the PM know you write the speeches?"

"Afterward…in the car with Xavier." He shook his head as though remembering. "You are an exquisite gift."

"You can tell me," I insisted, refusing to abandon the subject.

"Everyone knows I write the speeches, yes."

"The PM pretended he didn't know you."

"I get that a lot."

"Do you ever talk to the President of the United States?"

"My little spy," he teased.

"I forgot your folders, remember? I'd make a crappy spy."

"Artists often do. We need scientists, mathematicians, techies— people who aren't driven by their imagination but can act on it."

"You knew those files would be picked up by a member of your team?"

He broke into a grin. "Sure you're not a spy?"

"You've spied on my life. You probably know me better than I know myself."

"You're too extraordinary. Spies need to appear boring so they can remain invisible."

"Xavier's interesting… and so are you."

"We're not spies."

"Then what are you?"

"Someone who pervades." He smirked at that.

Oh, God, he was magnetic…so charmingly dashing it was hard to look away.

"To be honest, you'd be an asset," he continued. "You're obviously not a spy, so it'd be an ideal disguise."

"Where did you go last night?"

"Whitehall. Made a decision. Gave an order. Came home."

"Home?"

He caught himself and snapped his gaze to mine.

My toes curled. "Did you miss us?"

"More than you know."

He sounded sincere. I rested my cheek on his chest, feeling the intensity of his closeness.

His fingers trailed through my hair. "Do you like the house?"

"Of course." I raised my head to look at him. "Do you prefer your castle?"

His head crashed back on his pillow and he stared at the ceiling. "Anywhere you both are…"

"You like what we have?"

His lips quirked. "Don't you?"

My fingertips trailed lazily along his chest and then ran over his firm abdomen, venturing lower.

"Careful, Em."

"Because I'm not allowed to without Xavier?"

"It's only fair."

"What if I did this?" I reached low and teased his length with my palm. He grew hard against my hand as it glided up and down his fullness.

He grabbed my wrist.

"How about this?" I pulled away to kneel beside him on the bed, lowering my head and running my tongue along his erection. I let out an erotic moan as I rimmed his purple tip.

James grabbed a fistful of my hair and held me suspended above his cock, close enough to see the ridges and veins of his perfectly taut head.

"I'm a bad girl," I whispered, licking my lips as I tried to get close.

He held me firmly, not letting me up and not letting me have what I wanted. What I needed.

Him.

Oh, to taste that silky skin stretched over his steeliness, his scent filling my senses and driving me wild.

"You are bad, aren't you?" he said darkly. "You know what happens to naughty girls?"

"They get what they want?" I asked breathlessly.

With ease, James yanked me across his lap and his hand came down in a series of strikes on my bare ass. My skin burned as arousal flooded through me at this sensual attack. He caressed and pinched and squeezed and then spanked my hot flesh again. It felt raw and honest and, despite my squirming, I liked it.

His erection grew harder beneath me and the feel of it pressing against my stomach was intoxicating. I wriggled some more.

"Hold still."

"Can't."

There, peeking out from beneath his pillow was the handle of his gun. James seemed to notice me staring at it.

He pulled me off his lap and I lay beside him. "You liked that?"

I let out a moan and pressed my mouth to his chest, feeling the burn worsen.

Rolling on top of me, he grabbed my wrists and raised them above my head, pinning them against the mattress. A shudder ran through me at the pressure of his weight, his firm chest on mine. My nipples beaded beneath his hardness and my thighs parted. I wrapped my legs around his waist.

"Caught you," I said triumphantly.

Surprise flashed across his face. "Why must you be so beguiling?"

"Why must you be so dominating?"

"This is nothing compared to what I want to do to you."

I let out a provocative moan.

He stared down at me. "Owning you is a privilege I accept."

I felt the wetness between my thighs and shuddered at the promise of pleasure.

"Show me how to make you happy," I whispered.

His eyelids squeezed shut as he pressed his hips against mine. Then he drew his cock along my wet folds and ground his pelvis in a circle.

"Yes," I said. "I need this."

"You know what I want?"

"Tell me." *I'll give you anything.*

His expression showed he was mulling over a decision. "Coffee."

James climbed off the bed.

The loss of his weight and warmth felt shocking.

I stared after him as he strolled across the room and entered the bathroom, shutting the door behind him.

"Dark roast," he called through the bathroom door. "Go make it, please."

I heard the sound of the shower coming on, and then water splashing.

Sliding out of bed, I shivered as the chilly air hit my naked body. Moving silently across the room, I paused to pick up my discarded towel as I headed for the bedroom door.

And then I remembered the gun.

Chapter 29

THE GUN FELT HEAVY IN MY PALM.

Turning it, I wrapped my fingers around the grip and raised it to peer through the sight. I wondered if he used a silencer.

James Ballad was above the law. That much was true.

But he was also just a man. A man who'd had his life torn apart when his wife was murdered. A man who had dedicated himself to making the world a better place—in his mind, anyway.

And God, he was devastatingly alluring.

Here he was in this small house—small by his standards—in Primrose Hill, a man whose authority reached the upper echelons of our government. A man who kept a weapon beneath his pillow.

I wondered if Xavier knew about it.

Examining the hard metal, I ran a finger along the barrel. It was beautiful and deadly at the same time...so very Ballad.

James called through the closed door. "Put the gun back were you found it, Emily."

I shoved it beneath the pillow.

"No sugar in my coffee," he added. "I like it strong."

Make your own fucking coffee.

I was an open book. He, however, was uncharted territory. Of course, I knew his Navy background had contributed to his love of adventure, a need to explore, and a willingness to risk his life. And there was so much more to discover.

With a turn of the handle, I eased open the bathroom door.

I shouldn't have.

It would've been wiser to go downstairs and brew some dark roast in that posh Keurig. But there was something compelling about him. And having James on top of me had stirred an arousal I couldn't shake.

Still, I had an agenda, and nothing was going to stop me.

I stood before the shower—*his* shower—staring through the glass at this naked and very soaped-up Royal Highness. Streams of water drenched his dark hair and splattered over his face as he tipped his chin into the stream, the downpour striking his ripped torso and splashing over his taut thighs and pert ass—the same one I liked to squeeze and dig my fingernails into.

He noticed my presence, and wiped his eyes so he could see me better.

Moving closer, I dropped my towel and pressed my palms to the glass.

My eyes swept over his erection, full and long, and I felt a swell of pride that he was hard because of me.

The only words that slipped from my lips were honest ones. "I want to watch."

Conflicting emotions flashed across his face and perhaps he, too, was considering if watching could be construed as intimacy.He turned his body to face mine, his intense focus making the atmosphere thick and erotic, like molecules were shifting and dancing around us, joining us together.

All I could do was press my forehead and both hands to the glass. Despite my nakedness, I had lost all feelings of self-consciousness. With him all barriers dissolved.

He pressed his forehead against the glass, his eyes staring down into mine. James wrapped his hand around his shaft. He slowly began to stroke himself, soon quickening the pace, and I watched his erection grow in size.

His dazzling dark eyes watched me watching him.

James was all hard muscle wrapped in sophisticated, devastating allure. My mind flipped back to the moment I'd first seen him. I'd looked away because his refined beauty had been blinding.

Now, I couldn't look away.

It was impossible not to be captivated by his erotic expression as he brought himself closer to the edge.

His long groan echoed within the four walls of his shower, and I felt the distance that kept us apart. I desperately wanted to wrap my hand around the hard length of him and ease his strain as his hips rocked. I wanted the chance to feel the warmth of those silver steaks as they became glistening ribbons.

I loved the way his lips pouted, the way his rigid body rode out the bliss with shudders...the way his eyes rose to meet mine as though to say *it's because of you.*

Because of you...

Our hands mirrored each other's on the glass—pressed together to keep a connection as though neither of us could bear it to end. Neither of us was willing to break this heady spell.

"You shouldn't be in here," he said softly.

Blinking, as though awaking from a dream, I stumbled out, grabbing my towel on the way. I hurried down the hallway and entered the room I should have chosen.

I found my clothes and more toiletries and shoes and all the things I would ever need. And all of them had been brought here by James, I just knew it. Some were new, some from my old life, and the thought that he'd touched these things sent a wave of excitement through me. The way everything was hung or folded or tucked away in the chest of drawers showed Ballad's touch.

Thinking quickly—though not clearly—I slid into my underwear. My mind was still in James' bathroom, replaying that sensual scene over and over. I chose my old jeans, pulling them off a hanger, along with a satin shirt. That long cardigan would give me the artsy bohemian look I craved because it was from my old life, the one where I had some say.

Though crave was now a word reserved for the way I felt about Ballad.

Heading downstairs, I gripped the banister. Perhaps one day I'd know every creak on every step and every inch of every room. In a daze, I made it to the kitchen.

I understood now…

I finally realized why Xavier had done what he had to get this man back in his life in this intimate way, why he'd blackmailed him. All because James' love had been denied, and for Xavier, it might as well have been oxygen James was holding hostage.

Moving swiftly, I placed a filter into the coffee maker, and then found three mugs, the milk and the sugar, all those movements helping me keep my mind busy…

Arms came around my waist.

I turned, peering up to see Xavier towering over me. He was my port in the storm. My one true love.

But was I his?

He looked fresh and gorgeous and as complicated as he always did. This morning he'd dressed down in jeans and a jumper, which he wore over a white shirt to round out his casual style.

Reaching up to cup his face, I gave him my forgiveness. I bestowed upon him absolution for his past, forgiving him for returning to James—and for taking me to that castle in the middle of nowhere, and for everything that transpired within its ancient walls. And I also forgave him for this…a continued unknown.

Because I truly got it now…more clearly than I ever had.

"You okay?" he asked.

"Just making coffee." Because it didn't feel right to tell him I was shaken from bathing in his friend's aura.

The delicious aroma of dark roast and vanilla filled the room.

Xavier's attention drifted to the door.

We watched James stroll toward us. In contrast, he was wearing a white shirt and a waistcoat and jeans. He hadn't shaved that stern jaw. He seemed to be going as an alternate version of himself, oozing a devilish suaveness.

"What?" He noted our stares as he stopped at the kitchen table.

Surely he knew how devastating he was? How that swagger and

decadent smile made time stand still.

"Nice waistcoat," said Xavier.

James gave him a look of disinterest.

"I'll make toast." Xavier got to work preparing breakfast.

I poured us all a coffee and handed them out. When my hand reached James', it trembled, and I hoped he'd not caught it as the mug was passed to him.

James accepted his drink with a nod of thanks and sat down at the kitchen table.

I, the moth, had flown directly into the flame unknowingly. I stared at him and he offered me a smile. I could tell it was meant to reassure me that what had happened in his shower was no cause for guilt. Not for him, anyway.

A chill ran through me as I noticed that Xavier had been watching the two of us. My heart rate sped up as I wondered if he'd caught that special moment. The one that revealed I'd walked into the wrong damn room this morning.

After joining James at the table, I played with the Special K in my bowl. Xavier remained standing as he ate his muesli while running his thumb across the screen of his Smartphone. It made me wonder if that chess game was still going on.

James bit down on a slice of buttered toast covered in Marmite and then took a sip of coffee and gestured for us to join him.

The silence was awkward.

From James' wink my way, I could tell he felt it, too.

Xavier didn't move. "How can you eat that?"

James paused mid-bite. "Marmite?"

"Yeah."

James bit off a corner and then slipped into a cute smile. "An acquired taste."

"Your tastes are unusual," chided Xavier.

"As are yours," James quipped.

"I would say you're looking awfully dapper today, but I'm sure you're aware."

"Did you get out of the wrong side of the bed this morning?" asked James.

"Why?"

"No reason."

Xavier grinned. "Do your Jamaican accent for Emily."

"Playing games so early?"

"You love games…"

"Did you live in Jamaica?" I asked.

James ignored me.

"You're both so serious this morning." Xavier bit his lip. "What brought this on?"

James nodded at his phone. "How's the weather?"

Xavier looked at the screen. "The usual."

"Do I need an umbrella?"

Xavier gave a shrug.

James leaned back. "I miss my London Times."

"Read it on your phone."

"Not the same."

Xavier's gaze rose to meet mine briefly before once more landing on James.

"What happened this morning between you both?" he asked.

My cheeks burned as I watched them parley.

James studied him. "Any more coffee left?"

"Come here," Xavier said to me.

My chair scraped the floor as I stood. "I'm looking forward to going into the Academy today."

Xavier grabbed my mug from me and placed it near the sink. Then his large hands gripped my shoulders and he pushed me back against the counter. He peered into my eyes to assess my reaction.

"What?" I whispered.

"I'm trying to work out what happened this morning."

James set his mug down. "She needs to get ready for school."

Xavier's steely glare fixed on me. "Something scared you."

I swallowed hard.

"What happened, Em?"

"She came into my bedroom," admitted James. "She got turned around."

Xavier arched a curious brow.

James let out a sigh. "I was going to tell you."

His chin raised in suspicion. "Confess your sins."

"Don't," snapped James.

"I gave you permission to finger-fuck at will." Xavier glared at him. "That's it."

My breath left me, and I looked from one man to the other, struck silent by the tension coming alive, turning into something more between them.

"I'm sorry," I said.

Xavier smirked. "Guilty."

James sipped his coffee. "No need to be jealous."

Jealous of whom, though? My thoughts raged with this question.

James reassured him. "It was quick and unimaginative."

With wide eyes, my mind contradicted this as the scene played out in my memory of that beautiful man in the shower, all ripped and gorgeous and coming in his clenched fist.

Xavier caught every flicker of an eyelid, every dilation of a pupil, every quirk of a lip.

"I shouldn't have followed him in there," I stuttered. "His bathroom."

"That's why we're in this place," Xavier soothed. "To bond."

"I just looked."

"At what?" He furrowed his brow. "What scared you?"

James pushed his plate away. "I pointed my gun at her."

Xavier flinched. "You pointed your fucking Glock at my girlfriend?"

"Obviously, I didn't know it was her."

Anger blazed in Xavier's eyes. "Be. More. Careful."

James took a swig of his coffee, dragging out the tension.

"And after that you did something sexual?" snapped Xavier.

"Seriously? While she was feeling vulnerable?"

"Stop judging me."

"Let me clarify what I'm picking up," snapped Xavier. "To make up for almost shooting Em, you displayed your dick in the shower?"

"Yes, I shower naked."

Xavier blinked at him. "You jerked off in front her." It wasn't a question.

Jesus, how did he do that?

"We had a moment," admitted James.

Xavier slid into a devilish grin. "Has she melted your black heart, Ballad?"

"And your point is?" snapped James.

"Wish I could have been there," said Xavier with a wry smile. "I wouldn't have let you spill a drop."

James finished off his coffee and set the mug down. "Em, what time do you need the car?"

"Eight, please."

James nodded. "I'll tell the driver to be ready." He looked at Xavier. "Give Emily her new phone. Our numbers are in it, Em. Call anytime. For anything."

I felt a great rush of relief that I was getting a phone.

"Whenever you're ready." James raised a finger in the air as he walked toward the door.

"I'm not going in," Xavier called after him.

He paused but didn't turn.

"I want a day off," added Xavier.

"Very well. Plans?"

"Haven't decided."

James looked back at him over his shoulder. "Escort Emily in and then go do something fun."

"Don't patronize me."

James pivoted to face him. "Want to talk about it?"

Xavier's stare snapped to his phone and at that moment I realized he was reacting to something he'd seen on there.

"Get your fucking AI off my back," said Ballad.

Xavier gave him a thin smile. "I'll meet you later to brief you on what I know."

"And what's that?"

"What you're plotting, Ballad." Xavier smirked. "You need me to sign off on it."

"Actually, I don't." James flashed him a smug smile. "You left your queen exposed. You know better."

"Thought we agreed there'd be no games."

"Good, then. Glad we go that cleared up."

"Wait." Xavier walked over to the kitchen table and reached for James' mug. He carried it over to the counter and poured fresh coffee into it, then closed the gap between them and handed it back.

James wrapped his fingers around the mug. "If this is a peace offering, it's accepted."

"It is."

"Much better attitude."

"See you later then."

Ballad's eyelids became heavy as though affected by his words. "I look forward to it. Keep me abreast of your movements." James looked at me. "Emily, no straying from the Academy. You go in and then come home."

"I don't want to be followed," I said.

"That's a shame, Em. Have fun."

James seemed to be considering what else to say, but then spun around and left.

"What's wrong?" I asked Xavier quietly.

He was staring at the spot where James had stood seconds before. "He spies on me. I spy on him."

My face blanched. "Why?"

"We've got each other's back."

"And?"

Xavier broke into a smile. "We're just watching out for each other. That's all."

"Is everything all right between you?"

Xavier raked his fingers through his hair. "What did he say to you in the House of Commons?"

"Why?"

"You were rattled when you got in the car, yesterday."

"He controls the government. It's mind-blowing. He didn't want me to talk about it in the open. He got all controlling and bossy."

He waved that off. "Before that?"

I swallowed, not liking the bitter aftertaste of the coffee. "He gave this long speech about how…"

"Say it."

"He might find me of use?" I said softly.

"Those were his words?"

"Yes."

Xavier rubbed his eyes in frustration.

"Do you regret this?" I asked.

"No. It's just…there are always consequences with him."

"That's what he told me."

"He hasn't shown you how possessive he can be. Not even close."

"He's like that with you?"

He shook his head. "I've done worse."

Was he referring to running from James and living with me? From the way Xavier shook himself out of his daydream, I felt this was the only conclusion. But James had hunted down Xavier until he was back under his command, so they were both guilty for their freefall into chaos.

"Your relationship with him is complicated," I whispered.

"He owns my soul, Em. Sure you want that?"

"What should I do?"

"Ballad's falling for you." He gave me a rueful smile. "Use that to your advantage."

"You love him," I said.

"Fervently."

"Has something changed between you both?"

He pulled me into a hug. "We're wrong and yet so fucking right. You've merely glanced at the black star that is Ballad. I'm inside it."

And once you were caught in the gravitational force of a black hole, there was no escape.

Xavier looked down at me. "He's gotten to you."

"Why do you say that?"

"I recognize that look in your eyes. Same one I had after I met him."

"Does it bother you?"

"I'm hiding you beneath his wings, Em. Safest place."

"I'm sorry about the shower thing," I whispered.

Shame scorched my cheeks.

His hands wrapped around my waist and he lifted me up onto the countertop, his fingers working the zipper of my jeans.

I stared at him. "What are you doing?"

"You're going to talk while I go down on you."

"About what?"

"What happened in his bathroom...tell me everything in precise detail. Leave nothing out."

"You mean..."

"Describe how he looked. What you saw him do." He yanked my jeans off and dropped them on the floor. "And I'll do this."

He slid my panties down.

Chapter 30

I T WAS GOOD TO BE BACK IN CLASS AT THE ROYAL ACADEMY OF MUSIC.
The familiar presence of my classmates had restored some
normality to my life.

I sat clutching the Strad to my chest like it was a baby, trying
my best to concentrate on the class. It was like trying to traverse two
worlds—one with two men who consumed my every waking thought,
and this, my old life of lessons, practice, and big dreams for a future in
music.

I felt caught between these two worlds.

Stifling a yawn, I returned my attention to our instructor.

"Am I boring you, Ms. Rampling?" said Charles Penn-Rhodes, a
retired orchestra conductor out of Vienna whose accent was as thick as
his round-rimmed glasses.

Cringing, I said, "Sorry."

Salme raised her hand. "We strive for perfection," she answered
his question brightly. "We become the violin."

Penn-Rhodes awarded her a smile. "In the beginning, we must be
prepared to fail. With failure comes learning. It's only with constant
practice that you can become a maestro."

Salme Baker came from royal orchestra stock. Her mom was a
senior cellist in the London Symphony Orchestra and that meant she
had the advantage over us lesser mortals—not to mention owning a
multi-million pound violin. She played well and I didn't begrudge her
that. It was the fact she'd taken a dislike to me for no obvious reason.

But today, my wielding a Stradivarius made me a worthy
opponent.

"Ms. Baker, play without worrying about perfection," said Charles. "Don't try. Do."

Salme rose to her feet with the grace of a dancer.

With her bow raised and her chin high she swayed to the music as the beautiful strains of Wolfgang Amadeus Mozart's "Concerto No. 3" filled the room. I imagined that's how Mozart had imagined it being performed when he'd scribed those notes on parchment, proof to the ear she played exquisitely. If this was meant to represent her not trying, she'd just been anointed star pupil.

Charles had influence at the London Symphony Orchestra, the kind of pull that made us all sit up when he walked in. His assignments were taken seriously by students who wanted to make a name for themselves.

I'd just committed professional suicide when I'd stifled that yawn. I muttered a self-scathing remark under my breath and then realized everyone was looking at me.

"If you think you can do better," chided Penn-Rhodes.

"No, I was…somewhere else." That sounded just as bad.

"Up you get," he invited me to play with a sweep of his chubby arm.

I pushed to my feet and hurried into the center of the room, waiting for permission to begin.

"Emily." Charles raised his hand to stay me. "Let's try something else."

My gut clenched with tension at the unfairness of him favoring her. Something told me I was about to endure a humiliating test.

A test. Unlike the one James had given me in the House of Commons…

"Emily, focus, please." Penn-Rhodes gave a nod. "Show us how you scale without obvious change in the note." He bowed respectfully. "Let's not shame that Stradivarius."

The look on his face was pure speculation, a silent question as to how I'd gotten hold of this instrument.

Positioning my chin on the rest, fighting a case of nerves and feeling self-consciousness mixed with doubt, I slid my bow across the strings and produced an A-major 3-octave.

"Again, please." Penn-Rhodes shook his head. "This is your time to impress, Emily."

Was that a hint he'd put a good word in for me at the orchestra?

Salme was tapping her foot and it was an off-tempo rhythm. I pivoted away to avoid being put off.

"Face this way, please," said Penn-Rhodes. "Eyes open."

This meant Salme and her tapping foot was directly in my line of sight. I raised my violin again and repeated the single-note scales and arpeggios and increased the tempo.

Penn-Rhodes raised a hand to stop me.

Laughter rose from the class.

"Again, please," he demanded. "Trust your violin. It knows more than you."

The rest of the day went the same way—in each class I felt progressively off-kilter. Perhaps I'd fooled myself into thinking I had any talent at all.

I finally headed out of the Academy, my violin case feeling heavier.

The weight of defeat?

Farther down the pavement, I saw Salme chatting with a group of friends. I had to walk past them to get to the waiting SUV—the one with the bodyguard waiting beside it. He wasn't the same driver who'd brought me here, which caused me to feel uneasy.

Swallowing my pride, I put my head down and hoped Salme wouldn't see me.

"Hey, Emily," she called after me.

"You played great today." I tried appeasing her.

"Where have you been?"

I was surprised she'd noticed my absence. "Just…around."

"I think you might need to give up the Strad." She glanced at the SUV. "It's not working for you."

"Excuse me?"

"Your violin is pushing back." She smirked. "It's alive, you know, and it senses the person playing doesn't deserve it. It's a bit like a horse. It knows when the rider is scared."

I'd find my stride again.

She raised an envelope in her hand. "Did you get one?"

I blinked at her and stared at the embossed envelope. "What is it?"

The waver in my voice made her smile.

"Penn-Rhodes' top students have been invited to play at the Russian Embassy. We've been chosen to entertain a visiting dignitary." She stepped forward. "Peramivir will be there."

"Who?"

"The Russian Ambassador." She beamed with pride. "You didn't get one?"

"When is it?"

"Tomorrow night."

Taking in their faces one by one, I could see they were enjoying this. These were the elite students who'd been bestowed with the honor of performing at the highest level. Each of them held the same envelope.

"Congrats." I tried not to let my mortification show.

"Another VIP is going to be there." She combed her thin fingers through her dark hair.

"Who?"

She glanced at her friends, amused.

"Ms. Rampling," the bodyguard called over. "We have an appointment."

Salme studied the man and then the car. "Looks like you got yourself a sugar daddy. Is he the one who gave you the Strad?"

"What?"

She burst into laughter. "Someone paying your rent?"

My face flushed brightly, which let everyone know she was close to the truth.

Except it was two men, not one, and they were far from her description. Of course, I'd never be able to say anything about them. That was the rule.

I couldn't think of a clever retort. "I have to go," I said, as I headed for the car.

"What happened to your other violin?" she called after me.

I turned to look at her. "Why?"

"You might want to play that one instead." She pointed at my case. "Give someone with talent the chance to do it justice. It's wasted on you."

Her friends laughed.

A rush of humiliation mixed with doubt nearly overwhelmed me. Closing my eyes for a second, I thought of Xavier. The memory of his love calmed me like a warm embrace. She couldn't touch me now...no one could.

"Good luck for tomorrow," I told them.

With confident strides, I hurried over to the driver. He opened the rear passenger door and I leaped in. The vehicle was different from the one that had driven me here. It made me wonder if James had a car park full of them.

I pulled my seatbelt on.

The driver turned to look at me. "Do you know him, ma'am?"

"Who?"

There was a rap on the window.

Penn-Rhodes was standing there signaling to get my attention. A jolt of hopeful uncertainty tore through me. I reached for the button and nothing happened. "Can you lower the window, please? That's my tutor."

The glass came down.

I knew immediately what Penn-Rhodes was holding in his hand as he passed it through. "I get to go to the Embassy?"

"You know about it?" he asked.

"Salme told me she's going."

"I was looking for you." He glanced inside the car. "This is nice."

I took the envelope. "Thank you."

He pointed a finger at me. "Play your heart out tomorrow."

"I will. I'm sorry about today."

"Not everyone can access their heart like you, Emily. That's a gift. The world makes accessing our soul that much harder. Don't let it change you. You'll soon be leaving us, and I wanted to say that, at least."

That was the first time he'd addressed me by my first name.

"Thank you so much."

As he headed back into the Academy, the car window wound its way up. We took off into traffic. It filled my heart with happiness to know that a musician as prestigious as Penn-Rhodes considered me worthy of playing at such an event.

"I have to make a call, ma'am," said the driver, holding my gaze in the rearview.

I felt terrible I'd not asked his name. The screen between us came up before I had the chance, hiding him from view. I made a mental note to ask him as soon as he lowered it.

Peeling open the envelope, I read the gold embossed invitation stamped with the white, blue and red of the Russian flag. The invitation included the dress code required—black-tie for the men and evening gowns for the women. We were expected at seven P.M. and scheduled to perform an hour later. Leaving us all enough time to make it through security and get set up.

This would be my moment to shine.

In the envelope was a list of music Penn-Rhodes had chosen for us to play. I'd have plenty of time to rehearse these. Salme was probably heading home to an evening of practice, ready to get ahead of us all.

I noticed the driver had turned the wrong way. Instead of choosing Prince Albert Road, the car was driving through Marylebone and heading in the opposite direction, away from Primrose Hill.

I rapped on the glass. "Excuse me, we're going in the wrong direction."

Primrose Hill was only ten minutes from the Academy—a thoughtful touch by James to have me so close. He'd not mentioned us meeting anywhere else later today, though. In fact he'd told me to come straight home.

The glass remained between us as we picked up speed, swerving past Bond Street. Selfridges passed by in a blur on our right. Panic-stricken, I reached into my handbag and pulled out my phone, turning it back on.

The screen took forever to appear. I tapped James' number and put the phone to my ear.

My heart pounded against my ribs as it rang and rang.

"Ballad," he answered sharply.

"It's me," I said quickly.

The call dropped.

My fingers tightened around the phone as I went to redial. The car came to a jolting stop and I looked out, recognizing nothing.

Chapter 31

THE CAR DOOR FLEW OPEN AND I SAW A YOUNG MAN STANDING ON THE pavement looking in at me. His Middle Eastern features reflected a sharp intellect.

He made a sweeping gesture, inviting me to climb out of the vehicle. "This way, Ms. Kingston."

I wasn't moving. "Where are we?"

"Mayfair. You're joining Sir Ballad."

"He's here?"

The young man glanced behind him.

Leaning low, I tried to look beyond him and peer through the Park Room Restaurant's window, but I couldn't see James.

"I'm Akmal," the man said, making eye contact with me. "Nice to meet you."

With a shaky hand, I grabbed my violin and then let him assist me out of the SUV, all the while glancing around at the passers-by as though they could help.

He eyed the violin. "You can leave that with me," he said.

I clutched my case tighter and shook my head. "I'll hold onto it."

No way was I giving a stranger my Strad.

He shut the door behind me with a slam and gave a wave to the chauffeur.

"How was the drive?" he asked.

Terrifying.

"Fine."

The concierge opened the door to the restaurant for us and Akmal motioned for me to go on ahead. I walked in carefully, eyeing the other diners.

We were led down a narrow hallway. I stopped suddenly when I saw a bodyguard positioned in front of one of the doors, that telltale wire spiraling from his earpiece.

"She's with Ballad," Akmal told him.

"They're expecting her?" asked the guard.

"Yes."

"Open the case, please," the guard demanded.

I laid it on a nearby table and reached for the catches, flicking them open while thinking of different scenarios. No way would James allow any harm to come to me. He'd seemingly made every provision. I took a calming breath.

"Slowly, please." The guard stepped forward to watch me open the case. "Take it out."

I did as he ordered, gently easing the violin out, and then flashing a wary glance at Akmal.

"Protocol," he reassured me.

I wondered who else this man was guarding in that room and a shudder of nervous excitement slithered up my spine. I couldn't wait to see Xavier. Hopefully it was him.

"It's fragile," I told the guard as he took the violin from me.

He held it up to the light. "Looks old."

"As in two centuries…"

"Whoa," said Akmal. "Careful."

With a nod I was handed my instrument back and I re-secured it in the case.

The guard opened the door for us and Akmal escorted me in.

James sat at a corner table. He was still in that waistcoat and jeans and his hair was playfully ruffled in an attempt to look less intimidating. It didn't work. He still oozed a deadly suaveness.

He was accompanied by a sophisticated looking blonde in her forties. She looked familiar and I tried to recall where I'd seen her. My heart sank a little when I saw Xavier wasn't with them.

The room was classically designed in a minimalist style, with hardwood floors and black and white prints of London's landmarks. There was only one dining table. It was a discreet setting in the heart of Mayfair for private functions and meetings.

James stood and pulled out a chair for me, then took my violin case and placed it on the seat beside mine. "Ms. Kingston," he said warmly. "How was your day?"

"Fine, thank you."

We both sat and it felt reassuring to be close to him again.

James smiled. "Allow me to introduce Ms. Kingston." He studied my face for a few moments and then gestured towards the woman. "The Right Honorable Agatha Parish."

"Nice to meet you." I reached over and shook her hand.

I recognized her now. Agatha was a senior member of the government, a woman who frequently held court with the press announcing her doom and gloom policies on behalf of the Prime Minister.

Her stare grew cold as she clutched my hand for the longest time, assessing me.

"It was good to see you again," James told her.

She finally released me and leaned back in her chair.

"Home Secretary," said Akmal, "I'll see you out."

She offered him a strained smile and then turned her attention back on me.

"Didn't catch your first name?"

Ballad pushed to his feet. "Have a safe trip to Chequers Court."

She'd be heading to the Prime Minister's country estate, I knew that much. It was where he got to relax, and only the top members of the cabinet had the privilege of knowing what went on there. This included Ballad, apparently.

"Thank you, I'm quite looking forward to it." She rose elegantly and reached for a large red case embossed with a royal crown and the initials E.R. beneath it. Her intense stare landed on my violin case. "You play?"

"Yes, ma'am," I said respectfully.

Her lips formed a slow smile. "Ballad, you've been keeping this jewel locked away."

"You have no idea." He winked at me.

"Now, regarding the matter at hand," she said, her expression stern, "the Prime Minister—"

James interrupted her with a confident wave. "Inform Charles nothing has changed. War is off the table—"

"But the speech—"

"He'll appear to be the reasoned one. Let the United States carry this. They owe us."

"You're making a mistake," she chided.

"I'm fully aware that you have your sights set on becoming PM."

"A rumor."

"You're a hawk, Agatha. Some would call you bloodthirsty."

"I'm merely putting the country first."

"I suggest you visit the countries where you want to send more troops. Check out all the amputees. Then move on to the graves at home."

"Don't be crass."

"Don't throw away lives for political gain."

"You're no saint, Ballad."

"That's the most insightful statement you've made."

Agatha sighed and sent a condescending glance my way. "She's very young, James. Doesn't she bore you?"

My forearms prickled in response.

He arched a brow. "Look at her one more time in that manner, Home Secretary, and you'll be serving your country from Siberia."

"Well, I must admit," she said, her tone softening, "she is quite lovely."

He gave a nod. "I'm grateful for that change of attitude. Please give Charles my regards."

She walked away in a cloud of expensive perfume, glancing back nervously as Akmal led her out and closed the door behind them.

James turned in his chair to face me. "Wine?"

"Yes, please."

He signaled the waiter. The bottle was ordered and the table was cleared.

"She looked like she was scared of you," I said. "The Home Secretary."

"That's because I can have her on a plane to Siberia tonight if she crosses me again."

"Oh, the heady power." I gave him a cheesy grin.

James grinned back at me as a bottle of wine was delivered to us.

"We're having dinner later," he said. "But I can order you an appetizer if you like."

"No, thank you." I rubbed my stomach to ease the ache.

"I would have shared with the Home Secretary that you're the most exhilarating woman I've ever met, but I didn't want to stir up any more intrigue."

That made me breathless. "Of course."

James pulled his napkin off the table. "How was your day?"

"Fine." I looked toward the door where the Home Secretary had exited. "What was your meeting about? Was it to discuss a possible war?"

He flashed me a mega-watt smile.

I flashed one back as he poured the golden wine into our glasses.

"You're here to clean my palate." Seeing my confusion, he added, "I need to cleanse myself of the bitterness of politics and have my fill of something pure."

"I'm flattered."

He studied my face and then leaned back. "Did something happen today?"

The car ride had rattled me, but I chose not to tell him that. Instead, I used his conversation with the Home Secretary to segue into mine. "So, sending her to Russia would be bad?"

"The KGB are still a thing."

"Is it okay to talk?" I arched a brow, glancing around the room.

"Yes, this place was swept for bugs. The location was chosen spontaneously so there would be no time to plan something nefarious."

"Good to know."

"What's up?"

"What are your thoughts on Russians who are on our home soil?" I went for it. "As in the Russian Embassy?"

"Are you fucking joking?"

"No, why would I be?"

He waved a hand in the air. "The Russians have a thing for poisoning operatives…ours and theirs."

I frowned. "Which is bad, obviously."

"They've also developed a tsunami bomb. The last thing Europe needs is a thousand-foot high wave coming at it. One could go as far as to say they're the biggest threat to national security. But I'm sure you're aware of this from the news?"

"Uh, sure." I decided to change the subject. "So, is Xavier joining us?"

"Yes. He has a surprise for you. In the meantime, I thought I'd get a read on how you're doing?"

"Without Xavier here?"

"Yes, no pressure."

He continued to stare at me, so I added, "I'm still getting used to everything…the idea of living in Primrose Hill." I smiled. "It's close to the Academy, which works out great for the commute." I could be there and home in a heartbeat—back with my boys.

James straightened in his chair. "How does it suit you? Us all being there?"

I grinned. "It suits me fine."

He was trying to read me. "You're okay with me staying there with you?"

"Yes." I reached over and placed my hand on his. "More than anything."

"I'm glad." His smile faded and he pulled his hand away. "You were given an envelope by one of your instructors. What was in it?"

I raised my hand defensively. "I was going to tell you. Actually, it was the only good thing that happened today." I took a sip of wine.

"Tell me more," he said.

"I'm not sure about…" I shook my head, trying to find the right words. "There's a student in my class and she plays beautifully."

"Same instrument?"

"Yes." I glanced at my violin case. "Her name's Salme. She has no self-doubt at all. She's confident and is never scared of performing and she has no flaws."

"That's a flaw, Emily."

I let out a sigh. "I just wish I had her balls."

"You question yourself? Your talent? Your ability to play at the top of your league?"

"Constantly."

"Keep on doubting and questioning yourself. That way you'll always be evolving and striving to be your best." Seeing my skeptical expression, he added, "You're in great company. Extraordinary artists who doubted themselves in the past were Raphael, Rembrandt, and even Leonardo da Vinci." He drew in a dramatic breath. "Even Pulitzer Prize-winning author John Steinbeck was plagued with self-doubt."

"But—"

"No buts. Don't change. Be you. For goodness sake, Em, when God made you, he dropped the mic."

I let out a laugh and clapped my hand over my mouth.

Oh, the way he spoke, so poetic and masterful and seductive. It was all I could do to sit here sipping chardonnay and not throw myself at him.

"Feel better?" he asked.

"Much."

It made him smile. "Salme's going to trip on her sense of greatness. She's stunted and will never evolve because in her mind she's perfect. And perfection is an illusion."

Wait.

Was that why Penn-Rhodes had asked her to play without chasing perfection today, because he'd detected this? I had to wonder what he heard with a maestro's ear when she played.

"The envelope, please." James held out his hand.

I reached into my handbag and rifled around. "You won't like it."

"You have no idea how many times I hear that each day."

I pulled out the envelope and handed it to him. "Say I can go."

His brow furrowed.

"It's important. It pertains to my career."

James opened the envelope and used his napkin to pull out the card. "From Penn-Rhodes?"

"You know him?"

He read the invitation and then used his right hand to pick up his phone, lifting it to his ear. "Akmal, I need to see you."

Akmal entered the room immediately and strode over to our table. "Yes, sir?"

Still using the napkin, James slid the invitation back into the envelope and handed it to him. He obviously didn't want his prints getting on it—or perhaps he didn't want to smudge the ones already there.

"Usual protocol, sir?" asked Akmal.

James nodded.

I shot to my feet. "Where are you taking it?" Panic had my stomach tied in knots. "I need it to get into the embassy tomorrow night."

Akmal walked off with it.

"Sit down, please." The order came swiftly from Ballad.

Plopping down with a huff, I said, "If I don't go it'll look strange. Penn-Rhodes will be there. He has contacts at the orchestra. He can put in a good word for me."

"That location is out of bounds, Em." James shook his head. "What part of 'thousand-foot high wave' don't you understand?"

"No one there will know about us."

James' gaze snapped to the door. "Xavier, great timing."

Xavier strode in confidently with fresh-faced brightness. His sexy ripped jeans and blue jumper giving him a friendlier, more causal air than Mr. Serious, here.

Xavier greeted me by kissing my cheek and then moved over to pat James on the back.

"I got invited to the Russian Embassy," I bit out. "I have to go."

"You don't have to do anything," said James.

"This is my career."

"Let me look into it." Xavier stood next to me and consulted his phone. "Hmm… interesting."

We both studied him, intrigued.

Xavier glanced at James. "Peramivir is an hour away from arriving at Heathrow."

Slowly, Ballad pushed to his feet. "His embassy didn't notify us of an official visit."

Xavier nodded. "He'll regret that when the home office doesn't provide the level of security he needs."

"Well, he has his beloved KGB with him, right?" But what the hell did I know about such things…

Both Xavier and Ballad turned to stare at me as though I'd misspoken—as though those very words had set off a landmine. Then Ballad began to pace the room.

"Is Ivor Mikhail with him?" he asked.

Xavier frowned. "I'll see if he's on the same flight."

The expression on Ballad's face worried me.

"Who's Ivor Mikhail?" I asked, pushing to my feet.

Xavier approached James and grabbed his shoulders. "It's not happening. Let's go see Em's surprise and grab a pizza. Then we can go home and sit this one out."

My stare bounced from one man to the other. "I can get you in."

I was sure the embassy would allow for an escort. Or maybe I could have James double as a tutor.

Xavier glared at me. "I need you to step out of the room, Emily. Right now."

"Why?"

"Leave us." Xavier turned an accusatory stare on James.

Tension was razor-sharp between them.

Leaving my violin behind, I rushed out of the room and pulled the door closed, then pressed my ear against it.

"Step away, please," said Akmal.

The bodyguard had left with the Home Secretary, so I assumed Akmal was now tasked with guarding the door.

I glared at him. "Where's my envelope?"

He gave me an apologetic smile. "You'll have to discuss that with the Boss."

Voices rose from inside the room. I turned and listened...

Xavier's tone had turned dark. "Because you threatened to *use* her, Ballad. Of course that's my first conclusion when I hear Mikhail's name."

"Not like that," James said. "Use her in other ways."

"Other ways?"

"For me," James snapped back. "For my pleasure. And yours."

His words set off a firestorm of desire within me, but my erotic thoughts scattered as the sparks continued to fly between the two men.

Despite feeling the burn of Akmal's glare, I pressed my ear to the door.

"Very convenient," snapped Xavier.

"This has nothing to do with me," James responded. "Your conspiracy theory is off base."

"Why don't I believe you?"

Silence fell, and then I heard angry whispers.

Akmal grabbed my arm. "Step away from the door, Miss."

"But...I have to check on them."

Akmal led me away.

Chapter 32

"THE DIPLODOCUS WAS ONE OF THE LONGEST DINOSAURS TO walk the earth," Xavier announced to us in the deserted museum.

I mulled this over, trying to forget the last hour when things had gone off the rails. Five minutes ago, we'd walked through the main doors of the Natural History Museum when an amiable botanist had let us in after closing. She'd invited us to wander the exhibits without a guide.

This would be considered the date of the century—me with two hot men in South Kensington, wandering around one of the most interesting places in the city.

With Xavier by my side, I crooked my neck to stare up at the vast skeleton of "Dippy," the dinosaur showcased in the main entrance. The exhibit was taking up most of the room, proving just how long its body was.

Our dramatic surroundings reminded me of a cathedral with its arched stained-glass windows and carved stone walls. All this beautiful architecture was inspiring and totally free for the public to enjoy.

I'd be in my element if it hadn't been for James sabotaging my career back at the Park Room Restaurant.

He was standing a few feet behind us. His mood hadn't changed from when we'd left the private room in that Mayfair restaurant. We'd driven here in complete and very icy silence. I'd decided chatting about what had happened in such a wide-open space was a bad idea, so I'd joined them in remaining quiet. But my mind was buzzing with a million thoughts a second as I tried to think of a way to persuade James to let me go to the Russian Embassy tomorrow.

What would Penn-Rhodes say when I told him I wouldn't be participating? What would my fellow student think if I turned down this chance? Salme would win again. The thought of her smug smile made my stomach churn with anxiety.

"There's other ways to get you where you want to be," he muttered, moving forward to stand beside me.

My frustration was evidently burning a hole in the stratosphere— as well as my aching stomach. Rubbing my tummy didn't help ease the pain.

Was I really willing to let these men dictate what I could and couldn't do?

Don't let them know you're scheming.

"Dippy," Xavier repeated his name.

"How many bones?" I assumed he'd counted them without trying. He didn't even have to look at the description.

"A lot." He glanced over at James, who rolled his eyes.

"These aren't the real bones," James informed me. "They're plaster cast replicas of the fossilized ones." Seeing the surprised look on my face, he added, "They don't bore holes into prehistoric animals if they can avoid it."

"None of them are real?" I asked.

James raised his brows. "Take this as a lesson in life. There's so little you know about the truth."

Xavier glared at him. "Can you take it down a notch, please?"

"It's fine," I said. "I'm open to learning—if you're willing to talk."

"Well played," said James. "But no."

James' alpha moves aside, it was nice to think we had the run of the place. Museum security would be tracking us but we could walk around and not have to stand in line for any exhibits. "James, how did you pull this off?"

"*I* pulled it off," said Xavier. "How do you like your surprise?"

"I love it." I moved closer and wrapped my arms around him.

He embraced me tightly, and I wanted to swoon when he kissed the top of my head.

"You were telling me how much you love dinosaurs back at the castle," he said. "I made a call to an old buddy who works here."

"Of course you remembered," I whispered.

"See? I was listening."

"More like mentally recording," muttered James.

I stepped away from Xavier and stared at Ballad. "Do you want to talk about it?"

"Not here, no," he said flatly.

"I should be the pissy one," I said. "Considering the fact you're sabotaging my career."

James moved forward and took hold of my hands, his thumbs caressing my skin.

"I can get you into that place you've always dreamed of," he said softly.

I yanked my hands away. "I want to get in on my own merit."

"Tomorrow can't happen."

Raising my chin, I said, "Nothing has been decided."

Xavier cringed. "It's been decided, Em, and we need you to accept it."

"We're talking about my career," I whispered.

Xavier looked at me sympathetically, but James spun round and headed off.

"Oh, look, this way to the Tyrannosaurus," he called back.

We followed him, strolling up to the enormous T-Rex skeleton with its short arms and big head—and that grimacing jaw. Somehow knowing it was a plaster cast took the shine off seeing it. "How accurate is it?"

"Very." Xavier stared up at it admiringly. "To me it's the sexiest of all the dinos."

"I'm more of a Spinosaurus kind of guy," James chimed in.

We turned to look at him.

Xavier piped up, "That one's ugly."

"Yeah, but he's capable of ripping your T-Rex to shreds, so there you go."

Their rivalry amused me—along with the fact that James' sensitivity was showing, finally. He knew his refusal to allow me to perform at the Russian Embassy was hurting me, and that seemingly hurt him, too. Reaching out, I gave his hand a squeeze to comfort him. He responded with an affectionate smile and then brought my hand to his lips and kissed it.

Xavier nudged between us and looked at me. "Did you know the T-Rex had an extensive vocabulary?"

I thought about it. "In what way? You mean the noises they made?"

"No, they liked to read the Thesaurus." Xavier grinned at me and winked.

I let out a snort of laughter, which caused James to laugh at me.

With the tension defused a little we continued our tour, strolling through the Darwin Center and then onto the treasures of the Cadogan Gallery with its objects that were over 4.5 billion years old. We got up close to a meteorite and then a dodo. Next, we explored our ancient relatives, the cave men. The male of the species hadn't really changed, I secretly mused. They were still chest-beating alphas. James was probably a direct descendant of the one at the back—all crazy-ass ruggedness, hailed as the leader of the tribe.

It was impossible to forget that an hour ago, Xavier had accused James of setting me up to play at the Russian Embassy. Or that's what I'd deduced from the snippets of conversation I'd heard while eavesdropping.

Lowering my voice, I said to James, "Can I ask you something?"

"Sure." He peered into a glass case containing fossilized tools. Right then he looked like any other person and not someone with the weight of the world on his shoulders.

"The moon landing fifty years ago," I said quietly. "Did it happen?"

James blinked in surprise. "Are you about to launch an interrogation into conspiracy theories?"

"Yes." That earned me a scowl from him—probably because he'd figured out I'd overheard their conversation at the restaurant. "It's just that with your influence I'm sure you're privy to these things."

"Aliens are real." Xavier waggled his eyebrows playfully.

"Seriously?" I felt a rush of excitement, and wondered what else I should ask about.

"Global warming is real," began James, "and the world isn't flat. Stop the madness."

I waved my hand through the air. "I know all that."

James looked amused. "But did you know there are a series of tunnels and secret passageways beneath London?"

My eyes went wide. "Really?"

"Yes, right beneath your feet."

"What about the pizza conspiracy theory?" asked Xavier.

"Haven't heard that one," admitted James.

Xavier brightened. "Apparently, the female of the species can devour an entire pizza on her own."

"That's not true," I said, defending woman-kind.

"Let's go get some and test the theory." Xavier led us back the way we'd come.

Outside the museum, the weather had turned drizzly. We quickly shuffled toward the curb where the car was scheduled to pick us up.

I looked up at James. "Who is Ivor Mikhail?"

Sadness flashed across his face. "I need you to forget you ever heard that name."

Xavier took my hand in his. "You're going to have to trust us."

James threw a wave to the driver as he approached the pavement.

"I know it's hard." Xavier patted him on the back. "But you have us now, James. We're your family."

James shrugged. "What hurt is you thinking I would use Emily to get access."

"Maybe I had it wrong." Xavier reached for the car's passenger door handle and opened it.

James stepped back. "It's that doubt that's pissing me off."

I climbed into the backseat and watched them matching off with each other, the tension rising.

"Go ahead," James said. "I'll see you at the house."

"Where are you going?" asked Xavier.

"I'm going for a walk." James shoved his hands in his pockets. "I need to think."

"We'll have food waiting when you get home," I called out to him.

He gave a nod and strolled away. Within seconds he was lost in the meandering crowd.

Xavier climbed in beside me and our car navigated into heavy traffic.

I didn't ask because I didn't need to—Ivor Mikhail had something to do with James' past. It was the tortured look I'd seen in his eyes.

I grabbed Xavier's hand to get his attention. "Tell me what's happening."

He yawned. "Nothing for you to worry about."

"Mikhail is an old enemy," I whispered. "From the cold war."

Xavier laughed hysterically. When he'd recovered, he said, "Ballad's not that old, Em."

Right... A Google search later would provide some answers.

As though reading my mind, Xavier snapped, "Don't fucking Google anyone."

"I'm out of the loop on everything."

"Best place to be, trust me." He took a deep breath. "I envy you."

Primrose Hill was a welcome sight as we drove along the familiar roads. We made it home within the hour. Xavier had ordered dinner and we'd stopped off for a family-sized, deep-dish pan pizza from a restaurant on the way.

We headed into the house and it felt good knowing we could make a home here together. His faith in our endurance was something I held onto with every part of my being.

I would always love playing house with him no matter where we ended up.Xavier brought out two beers from the fridge and pried the caps off so we could drink from the bottles. Within minutes we were sitting at the kitchen table with a slice of pizza each on our plates and sipping cold beer. My taste buds lit up with the flavors of tomato sauce and cheese.

The carbs did nothing to dull the ache inside. I couldn't think of how I should have done things differently. I would always want Xavier in my life.

Tomorrow, I'd have to face Penn-Rhodes and I dreaded the thought. He was the reason I'd gotten into the Academy. As senior admissions officer he'd granted my scholarship and navigated me through years of training. I bit off a corner of thick crust as I mulled over how I'd be wording my excuse for not attending. Two more slices and I was close to proving Xavier's pizza theory.

A ring of the doorbell made me pause halfway through a bite.

"I'll get it." Xavier pushed to his feet and headed off to answer it.

When he came back he wasn't alone.

Kitty was behind him.

She'd dressed formally in a business trouser suit and her hair was pulled back in a ponytail. No make-up, though she was no less pretty for it.

I pushed my plate away. "What are you doing here?"

"I invited her," Xavier said softly. "It's good to have friends, right?"

I glared at him. "She was never my friend. She only pretended to be."

"We got along great, Em," she said. "I know our dynamics changed but we liked each other a lot. That means something."

Xavier shot me a sympathetic look. "I don't want you to feel isolated, Em."

I took a swig of my beer, stalling. I couldn't get there, to a place where I could pretend she'd never betrayed my trust. Then again, James had been a royal asshole and I was sleeping with him.

I pivoted in my chair toward Kitty. "Tell me something, that night I first met James in Simpson's-in-the-Strand, did you know he was there meeting Xavier?"

She blinked.

"Was the directive from James to let me see him?" I continued. "He knew I'd follow Xavier into the restaurant?"

She didn't need to say yes.

I didn't disguise the bitterness. "That's why you arranged for us to go to the Savoy. Was it even your birthday?"

She gave Xavier a nervous glance.

I wiped my hands on a napkin. "You realize that was the night James dropped a bomb on my life?"

"I'm sorry," she said softly. "But it all worked out, right?"

The elephant in the room had never been dealt with—Xavier had lied about his name. And James had pressed a sword to my throat in a castle I probably couldn't find again if I tried.

Our history was as shaky as our future.

The event tomorrow night would be what would save me when they left this house.

When they left me...

Xavier's kind expression told me there was hope. He was fighting hard for our love, scheming behind the scenes and doing what had to be done to find a way.

His ability to read my thoughts was uncanny.

"I love you so much, Emily," he said. "I'm sorry for the hurt we've caused."

"I'm sorry for my part, too," admitted Kitty. "When you're dealing with situations of this sort, there's bound to be a few bumps in the road."

These were not bumps, these were craters.

"It's good to talk." Xavier pulled a chair back for her. "Want a beer, Kit?"

Her hesitation gave her away.

"You can't drink can you?" I pushed away from the table and walked by her. "Because you're on duty."

I headed up to bed.

"Emily." Xavier called from the bottom of the stairs.

He ran up the steps and closed the gap between us. "Listen, I want our life to be like a meditation. As enlightening as it is peaceful."

"I want that, too," I whispered.

"I just wanted to say that," he whispered. "Before tomorrow."

Tomorrow…the day I'd missed that all important concert.

"Go to bed." He leaned in and kissed my forehead. "I'll join you soon."

As I made my way down the hall to our bedroom, his words resounded in my head like a prayer.

Chapter 33

Penn-Rhodes peered at me over his round-rimmed glasses. "You're going to have to help me understand, Emily."

His office was tucked away in the rear of the music department. I wondered how he could bear such a small room—though most of his time he was out teaching in the classroom. He graded papers in here and did all those other things instructors do when they weren't wrangling students.

This man was a renowned violist and had toured the world with the Vienna Philharmonic, one of the finest orchestras in the world. So yeah, he deserved a room with a window.

I met his perplexed gaze. "It wasn't an easy decision."

"Are you serious about your career, Stellina?" He'd softened his chastisement by calling me his little star in Italian, the way he did once before—the day I'd been accepted into the Academy. Penn-Rhodes had been the one who'd told me I'd landed a scholarship within these hallowed walls. The warm memory of that day stayed with me. These were the weeks that counted, when the end of our time here neared and we were meant to spread our wings and make the school proud.

"There's some things going on in my personal life," I began.

He studied my face. "Who gave you the Stradivarius?"

"A friend."

His scrutiny stayed on me.

"I'm working through something," I admitted. "Just need time."

His hand shot up to stay me. "You can't let anything get in your way if you want a professional career."

"It's just that…"

"Say it." He snapped off his glasses. "Is it Salme?"

"No, I mean she's…you know."

"Oh, I know." He sighed heavily. "I deserve an explanation."

"I'm sorry I can't make it, but…I'm not comfortable with the location. "

He rose and rounded the table, standing closer to me.

"You have a fear of water?"

"What?"

"You don't like boats?" He laughed. "It's not taking off, Emily. The yacht will stay in the Thames."

I pulled my eyes away from the sauce stain on his tie. "It won't take place at the Russian Embassy?"

"The location was moved. The event's being hosted by Renaldo Zane on behalf of the embassy. He's arranged a lavish party on his yacht."

Zane. That name made my flesh tingle.

"What kind of people will be there?" *Russians?*

"There will be lots of guests. Americans. Members of the British government. Patrick Woo."

"Patrick Woo?" I said wistfully.

The music director of the London Symphony Orchestra, the man who'd already seen me audition. The elite conductor could open the door to my professional future.

"You see how important it is for you to be there."

Still, James had told me this couldn't happen. Even if the location seemed safer.

"I'm sorry." I stepped over to the office door.

"Emily, I'm so surprised by your decision."

Clutching the knob, I inhaled a deep breath. "I'm sorry to let you down."

"I just assumed you'd be thrilled to see her again."

I looked back at him. "Who?"

"Diana Zane." He slid his glasses back on and stared at me. "I thought you were a fan."

"She'll be there?"

"Of course. She's Renaldo Zane's wife." He paused, then said, "If you go, she'll hear you play, Emily. Wasn't that your dream?"

Chapter 34

XAVIER LEFT THE KITCHEN AND CAME OVER TO GIVE ME A HUG. "I'LL see you out."

We strolled through the front door toward the SUV idling on the curb.

I wished I could think about anything other than the events of the next few hours. Only yesterday, Penn-Rhodes had informed me who would be attending the event tonight. Diana Zane would be there, my childhood hero, for goodness sake. And Patrick Woo, the man who held the keys to the kingdom.

My heart was breaking…the decision far from made.

"I'm glad you came around." Xavier opened the rear passenger door of the SUV. "Kitty really likes you."

"Talking it over helps."

"You eat and come home, okay?"

"Right."

He leaned in and called to the driver. "Chez Antoinette in Covent Garden, please. No detours. And Gary, don't take your eyes off them."

He gave an informal salute off his chauffer cap. "Got it, sir."

Xavier leaned in for a kiss, and then made me uneasy by pulling back a little.

It was as though he was trying to read me better, the way he assessed me with his laser-sharp perception.

"I'm nervous about seeing Kitty again," I said quickly. "I was a bit mean to her yesterday."

"Nothing to be nervous about."

I reached for the seatbelt and clipped it in.

"You'll have a great time."

"Yes."

He started to turn away, and then looked back at me. "Are you hiding something, Em?"

"Did you know?" I asked, gazing at him steadily. "That she was spying for James."

Xavier gave a cautious glance over at Gary and continued in a low voice. "I should have taken the time to meet her."

"You didn't want to meet my friends."

"We'll talk more when you come home."

He leaned in and kissed me tenderly, his soft lips as yielding as mine—as forgiving as they were comforting.

"I love you," I whispered.

His eyes crinkled into a smile and then there came a change in his expression, an uncanny reflection of doubt in those pale blue irises. Then he pulled away and walked back into the house.

Had I just given myself away?

After unclipping my seatbelt, I leaned forward to get Gary's attention. "I forgot something."

He let me out and I ran back, ducking by the front window. I accessed the garden with a turn of the key and then quickly picked up my violin case, along with the canvas bag that was resting beside it. Sneaking along the wall, I exited the garden and hurried back to the SUV.

After settling into the luxurious passenger seat, I braved a look into the rearview mirror and found Gary staring back at me.

"We can go now," I said.

"Ma'am, I thought you were having dinner?"

"I am."

"Then why are you bringing your instrument?"

"Kitty's never seen a Strad."

His brow furrowed. "What's in the bag?"

I glanced down. "A gift."

His fingers tapped the steering wheel as he thought this through.

I stared through the front window, trying to act casual. "How's traffic?"

Giving me one last suspicious look, he relented and started the engine.

Don't do it.

Let the future you dreamed of become something different...filled with love.

Yet I knew the three of us had an expiration date. James had threatened me with it too many times.

So there you are.

We arrived at Covent Garden in less than thirty minutes. I loved the West End's theatre district. I'd done pretty well when I'd busked here. The place was always bustling with tourists who meandered around its elegant piazza, with its market, teashops, restaurants, and luxury fashion stores making it one of the most popular shopping destinations.

And a great place to get lost in.

With strict instructions not to have Gary take his eyes off me, Xavier had upped the ante on my Svengali escape act.

But I knew Covent Garden—more specifically Chez Antoinette. I'd busked in the courtyard and snuck in there on my breaks to take a pee. It was easy to get lost in the shuffle in this thriving place. But there'd be no tasting their delicious meals today.

Gary took a spot in the corner with a good view of my table. Luck was on my side because we were early. I pretended to peruse the menu as I waited for Kitty, while trying to keep my limbs from trembling.

I let a few minutes pass before pointing at the loo so Gary would know that's where I was heading. I brought my violin case and the bag along, too, all under the intense scrutiny of my bodyguard.

Around the corner, I rushed into the loo and changed into an elegant silver halter-neck evening gown and heels. I stuffed the other clothes in the bag and stashed it in the bin.

I made a beeline for the back of Chez Antoinette. With a quick glance toward the dining room to make sure I'd not been seen, I headed for the exit.

As soon as I stepped outside the restaurant, my bare flesh was stung by the chilly evening air.

Carrying my beloved violin case, I hurried away.

Chapter 35

A BRISK BREEZE BLEW BRUNETTE STRANDS ACROSS MY FACE AND CAUSED my silver gown to cling to my body as I stood on the landing peering up at Renaldo Zane's super-yacht, *The Venetian*. My grip tightened on the handle of my violin case when I saw her. She was leaning on the balustrade, staring out at the view.

Diana Lucia Zane looked elegant in her stunning chiffon gown with her hair up in a chignon. She was a musical goddess, this woman whose words had changed my life in so many ways—whose music owned my soul.

Growing up, I'd devoured interviews and articles about her, my imagination filling in what was not shared of her private life. I devoutly scoured the pages of *Vogue*, *Elle*, and *Vanity Fair*, and all the other magazines, to see what fashions she favored and the exotic places she visited, getting rare glimpses of her. More than this, I loved hearing about the theatres she performed in and the musical pieces she adored. She'd married billionaire Renaldo Zane in her late forties.

Diana's words to the little girl I used to be all those years ago had led me here tonight, an opportunity mixed with all the complexities of life.

Penn-Rhodes' words repeated like a dark promise, *"Diana will get to see you play."*

"Are you a musician?" a voice rose in the dark.

I looked up at the towering guard. "Yes."

"The musicians are tuning up in the staffroom." He gestured to the ramp. "I was about to secure the boat. Head up through the security check-point. Do you have your invite?"

I grimaced, my eyes telling him *no*.

He answered in kind with a look that said, "Then you're not getting on."

I glanced up at the balustrade. Diana was no longer there. It felt like a piece of my heart had been ripped away, my chance lost. Hearing her play live was a gift. Diana hearing me play was now a dream that would never be realized.

My stomach twisted in knots.

At least Xavier's trust wouldn't be quite as shattered if I didn't make it on board. I'd lied to them both about meeting with Kitty. I'd left Gary to shoulder the blame. I'd been selfish, but I'd not asked for their political intrigue and strict rules.

Seeing the hurt in their eyes would crush me, I knew. Worry and guilt tightened my throat.

Not getting on the yacht was probably for the best—even if it meant the ruination of a lifelong dream.

"Emily?" Penn-Rhodes waved to me from the bridge. He scurried down the boardwalk.

"She's with you?" asked the bodyguard.

"Yes, she's my student. She's with us." Penn-Rhodes led me onto the boat. "So glad you found a way to be here."

My opportunity returned like a dark and magical promise. Maybe my two lovers would understand...and forgive me. Maybe the consequences James had talked about were merely imaginary concerns.

"This way," said Penn-Rhodes. "Hurry."

Dutifully, I followed him up the steps and we were waved through the security check-point.

I'm really doing this...

At the rear of the yacht I saw the raised platform where we'd be performing. Arranged before it were a hundred or so chairs waiting for an audience. I could see why security was high. The soirée was an elegant affair with the male guests wearing tuxedos and the women adorned in sweeping gowns, all of them sipping champagne. I scanned the glamorous crowd, searching the faces for Patrick Woo.

Penn-Rhodes led me down a twisting staircase. "Remember when I had you play your violin facing the other students?"

He'd forced me to face Salme and her tapping foot.

"When you perform there are always distractions," he said. "Ignore the audience, their restlessness and their cell phones. Ignore it all. Do what you were born to do."

"Thank you, Maestro."

He went on ahead.

I braced my palm against the wall, trying to balance my shaky legs as I remembered Xavier's accusation that James wanted me at this event. Would James have known I'd refuse to miss this chance of a lifetime? Was I the equivalent of one of Xavier's chess pieces being moved at will?

"Forget something?" asked Penn-Rhodes.

I shook my head, trying to push the trepidation away. My heels clicked along the polished floor as we headed toward the sound of musical notes emanating from a room. I heard the erratic plucking of violin strings and the chatter of excitable students.

Ignoring a glare from Salme, I found a spot in the private cabin and turned my back on her.

I flipped open my case and eased out my Strad, then began the methodical process of drowning out the noises in the room so I could concentrate on fine-tuning my violin.

The fine hairs on my nape prickled when I saw Penn-Rhodes move from student to student handing out nametags. He handed me one. Reluctantly, I stuck it to my dress.

With a dry mouth, I focused on a string that wouldn't give. It was too new. Too perfect. Too resistant to my trembling fingers.

Salme appeared at my side. "What did you do?"

Her dress was bright red like her lipstick. I noticed that she'd overdone her rouge and eye shadow. My eyeballs began to burn as her obnoxious perfume singed my retinas.

"You have no right."

I blinked past the sting. "I have no idea what you're talking about."

"Penn-Rhodes chose you."

The heat in the cabin intensified.

"You're supposed to play the second set." She glanced at my violin. "Hope they brought their earplugs along."

That would mean I'd be front and center.

I suddenly needed air…

I rose abruptly with my violin and swept past Salme, retracing my steps up the winding staircase until I made it to the upper deck. Clutching my violin and bow as though a gust from the Thames could steal them away, I leaned my body gratefully against the balustrade and drew in great gulps of air, its scent tinged by river water.

The memory of my time with James and Xavier weighed heavily on my spirit. So many thoughts swirling through my mind made it hard to think straight. There were other orchestras, other opportunities, and, after all, James had offered to help with my career. Turning him down meant I would lose *him*.

My pride had set me up for a fall.

I stared out over the rippling water without really seeing it. I knew that both worlds contradicted each other. Xavier was too precious with his rare gift. James too powerful to be compromised.

Boarding this yacht had sealed my fate.

Love would no longer be mine to cherish.

It was over.

All this time I'd believed it was them who held power over my future. A sob wracked my body at the realization that I'd thrown away the greatest love I'd ever have.

A waft of delicate perfume took me back in time. In a daze, I followed the delicate fragrance around the corner. Diana Lucia Zane was leaning casually against the railing, staring out at the river bank.

I approached her hesitantly.

She smiled when she saw my violin. "I hear you're to play after me, Bella?"

"Yes," was all I managed.

She'd hardly changed from when I'd watched her as an eager child in the front seat of a concert hall. I noticed that the fine lines around her eyes only brightened her smile. She was still just as glamorous and beautiful as I remembered.

"I met you once," I whispered. "When I was a child."

Her lips quirked, her expression kind.

"You were so...perfect."

Her smile turned sad.

Consumed with awe I said, "You told me I have the hands of a violinist. It's why I play." I held up my Strad.

"Darling girl."

"You changed my life, Signora Zane."

She gave me a concerned look. "You must leave. Right now. Get off this yacht."

"But..." I glanced back to see my fellow students pouring out of the stairwell door and trailing over to the other side of the boat.

Diana reached up to trace a delicate finger along my jaw. "Bellissimo."

She entranced me with the way her delicate fingers first traced the strap of my dress, that same hand capable of so much profoundness when she played, and then glided to my chest, landing on my nametag. She ripped it off.

Wide-eyed and full of confusion, I watched Diana stroll grandly away as though she'd not just spoken those ominous words of warning, her chiffon dress billowing around her in the breeze like an exotic sea creature.

I saw the last student exit and trail around the corner. My heart began to pound against my chest as stage fright devoured me, causing my hands to shake so much I didn't believe I could play.

Suddenly I felt the boards beneath me quake, and my terror intensified when the vessel began to move.

The yacht was heading down the Thames.

Chapter 36

MY THROAT CONSTRICTED AS I WATCHED THE CITY'S LANDMARKS passing by, Diana's haunting words replaying in my mind as we glided beneath London Bridge's towering metal structure.

I took deep breaths, trying to calm my racing heart. With trembling fingers, I touched the place where my nametag had been. I knew Diana's actions had nothing to do with jealousy. Somehow, she knew certain people here tonight shouldn't see my name.

Penn-Rhodes signaled for me to follow him. The time had come to step onto the stage and perform. Reluctantly, I hurried around the corner and stopped abruptly when I saw Patrick Woo standing in front of the raised platform.

Just breathe…

I'd played for him once before. No, it had been twice, since James had somehow arranged for me to have a second chance to impress the guardians of the orchestra.

Why did Diana want me off this yacht?

The seats quickly filled with guests as we took our places on the stage. I scanned the many faces. A line of dignitaries sat in the front row. Peramivir, the Russian Ambassador, sat amongst them, and beside him, a burly man with a grumpy face and thinning hair…Ivor Mikhail.

I tore my gaze away, recalling James' visceral response in the Park Room Restaurant when he'd heard the man's name. Remembering his pained expression caused dread to shudder through me. I'd felt compelled to do research on Mikhail sooner rather than later, because I'd never seen Ballad look so tortured before.

Diana took her place before us.

In a daze, I realized my feet were resting upon the same stage as hers. My beloved idol was mere feet away and playing Mendelssohn's "Violin Concerto in E Minor." These lowly students bathed her in grandeur as her soul poured forth musical notes from her Mary Portman Guarneri violin. Yet again she reminded everyone why she was hailed as an iconic star. She moved elegantly, playing with the ease of a world-famous violinist.

Afterward, there came the thunderous quake of awed applause.

Penn-Rhodes signaled it was my turn.

I, Emily Rampling, was to follow the greatest violinist of the twenty-first century. My talent would pale.

With a kind nod of support from Diana, I hurried forward, raising my violin and bringing up my bow, positioning my chin rest.

Brahms' "Violin Sonata No. 3" sang from my Stradivarius as my heart chased after each note, my body moving with the music, my soul cracking into a thousand shards of misery. The melancholy piece had been written to honor the creator's forbidden and unrealized love. Ignoring the audience, and the many faces focused on me, I played with every fiber of my being. I had once desired to perform in public, but now I struggled to keep control of my confused emotions and self-consciousness.

I wasn't meant to be here.

I'd stolen this moment that was never destined to be mine. This realization cried through my strings to convey what I was incapable of saying. Each note, each draw of my bow was a plea for forgiveness.

Pulling my love for Xavier out of the ether, I played for him, recalling the first time we'd met in the Underground…the way he'd bravely chased after my violin to rescue it. The fact he'd given me this one in its place was as astonishing as it was profound. He and James had gifted me with a beautiful home. In return, I'd betrayed their trust and lied to them.

A future with the three of us together was never going to happen.

Destroyed by these thoughts, I let go and gave myself over to the music completely, as only a true lover can.

Just as James had taught me.

And then it was over. I stirred from my melancholy, lowering my bow and staring out at the sea of faces looking back at me, and then snapping my gaze over to Penn-Rhodes.

He gave a nod. "Whatever is ailing your heart, cling to that."

The clapping grew louder until there was a standing ovation.

Awed by their reaction, I managed to smile. Their fervent applause to my performance made my heart sing with joy.

Exhilaration took hold of me. This was a memory I'd always hold on to.

The evening progressed with my fellow students showing off their talent and lending their youthful brilliance to this esteemed setting. Diana played once more to end the evening's recital—again reminding everyone present why she was hailed as the queen of the international stage.

Afterward, we huddled in the corner congratulating each other on a concert well done. Penn-Rhodes's tutoring had been honored.

A hand rested on my shoulder.

Pivoting, I saw Diana.

"You play beautifully," I said breathlessly.

"Come with me." She spun around in a cloud of chiffon-filled elegance and strolled toward the staircase. "You're to play for a VIP, Bella."

Glancing back, I realized I had no choice but to follow.

She led me down the staircase. "You have been summoned."

"Who by?" Less than an hour ago she'd warned me to get off this yacht, and now she was leading me into its depths.

She looked back, offering me a thin smile. "You don't get to say no."

My uncertainty rising, I clutched the neck of my violin, my bow's strings burning red lines into my palm.

"You warned me earlier," I whispered. "Why?'

"It's too late now."

Oh, God. Could they know about me and James?

We entered a dark room.

The rich scent of cigar smoke hung in the air, filling the space of the small cabin. I noticed a spiral of white smoke rising out of the far corner, and the figure of a man who was cloaked in shadows, only the tip of his expensive brogues revealed in the dimness.

A shudder of cold slithered up my spine as I realized Diana was leaving.

The door snapped closed behind her.

"Играй за меня, маленький котенок," he said, his voice a low whisper.

"I don't know what that means," I admitted, straining to see his face.

His hand swept towards me, revealing the cigar he held, its smoke snaking closer.

"Signora Zane said that you want me to play for you?" I wrinkled my nose at the unpleasant scent in the air.

He didn't answer.

"Modern or classic?" I offered.

His voice sounded like sandpaper when he spoke. "С первого момента, как я встретил тебя, я влюбился в тебя."

"Okay, modern it is." I raised my bow.

The violin sang out its revolt. "The Devil Went Down to Georgia" seemed like the perfect offering for this mysterious and arrogant asshole. I dragged my bow across the strings to reveal the high notes of this rebellious song, letting him hear proof that I'd sensed his cruelty, his dangerousness, his foreign power. The reckless notes flowed and danced around us.

Xavier didn't know I was here.

Neither did James.

Nor Penn-Rhodes. Or any of my friends. Only Diana, who had told me to leave.

I'd ignored her advice—a terrible mistake.

My only anchor to these dreaded moments was my bow sweeping

the strings to express my outrage that this man had demanded I play. I wouldn't have cared if he was the leader of Russia itself. This talent was mine to give to those worthy of hearing it—not those who demanded or threatened or intimidated.

This may be the lion's den, but I was a lioness.

Afterward, breathing heavily from my physical performance, I glared at him through the smoke.

I heard the hiss as his cigar was snuffed out.

Chapter 37

SILENCE FELL OVER THE ROOM AS THE LAST WISP OF SMOKE FADED AWAY. The man uncrossed his legs and rose to his feet.

My chin lifted in defiance.

He strolled out of the shadows, taking the few short steps needed to remove my violin and bow and carry them over to the side table where he gently placed them down.

Oh, God.

James walked up to me and brushed his fingers through a lock of my hair.

"You speak Russian?"

"Russian, Italian, French, Spanish..." He gave a slight shrug, as though these were just a few.

Somewhere in the far reaches of my mind I remembered Xavier telling me this. It had been in that castle, where James had threatened my life and forbidden me to leave.

I squeezed my eyes shut as his palm cupped my cheek.

"You can't help but defy me," he said darkly.

"Patrick Woo is here and he's—"

"I know who he is."

"And Diana Zane."

"I pulled you out of danger."

His words struck a nerve so deep I couldn't catch my breath. It was that look of disapproval, the way he towered over me threateningly, and the lingering scent of his rich cigar.

My heart fluttered in my chest. "If that's why you pulled me in here, then what's the reason you made me play?"

"Quite frankly, it's often a struggle to resist asking you to play."
He sighed, and then continued. "Our paths have met at a treacherous
crossroads. When we return to the deck, don't even look my way."

Those men up there were dangerous...

"Does Xavier know I'm here?"

"Yes."

Doubt flooded my mind. "Did you change the event from the
Russian Embassy?"

"Anything to secure your safety."

"You're not Russian, are you?"

James chuckled. "No."

Moving in, I wrapped my arms around him and rested my head
against his chest.

"I need you to do exactly as I say. Will you agree to that?"

"Yes."

"You're going to return to the cabin where you tuned your violin.
Stay there until the yacht docks. Disembark with your friends."

I nodded.

He tipped my chin up. "I'll be close."

"Say that afterwards, it won't be goodbye." My heart cracked with
his look of uncertainty.

"We'll talk."

"Ivor is here," I whispered.

"I know."

I read the painful truth in his eyes. "Did he kill your wife?"

He looked away. "I don't blame you for coming here tonight."

I shook my head. "You were always going to leave."

"Let's get you home safe."

I moved quickly to block the door. "I can't be without you, James."

He trapped me between him and the exit, peering down with an
intensity that burned me up from the inside out. Cupping my face and
leaning in, he pressed his lips to mine. His tongue slipped inside my
mouth, searching and comforting, then he nipped my bottom lip before pulling away.

Don't let this be goodbye.

"What will you do?"

"You're my priority. I'll remain in the shadows." He opened the door and motioned me ahead. "I'll be right behind you. At the top of the stairs, head left. That's the way back to your cabin." His lips quirked in amusement as he handed my violin and bow back to me. "And Em, go *left*."

It made me smile.

Leaving him was the hardest thing I'd ever done, or so it felt. The distance feeling eternal with each step I took as I ascended the staircase. I turned left and made my way along the back of the boat, my precious instrument clasped tightly against me.

A shadowy figure strolled around the corner.

Ivor Mikhail.

I flinched under his stare.

His face wore an amused expression as he came closer. "Ah, the violinist," he said, his accent thick as he checked around to make sure we were alone. "Do I know you?"

This I'd read about—the men of the KGB were capable of anything from blackmail to kidnapping to assassinations, and he was one of them.

He rapidly closed the gap between us, backing me up against the balustrade and towering over me.

He glanced at where my nametag should be. "Why are you looking at me like that? Like you know me…"

A voice from behind us snapped, "Get away from her."

Ivor spun to look at James. A flash of recognition.

James threw a look of reassurance my way. "This was inevitable."

Ivor's gaze snapped back to my face as though trying to connect us.

"Step back," seethed James as he placed a fingertip to his ear. "Do you copy?" He gave a nod as though hearing confirmation. "Three minute window. Stern. Portside."

Ivor's attack on James was swift. He maneuvered closer, first throwing a strong punch and then swinging a kick that proved he'd been trained in hand-to-hand combat.

James landed a strike to Ivor's gut. The man doubled over and then sprang up, knocking James against the wall and landing a blow to his jaw.

"I'll get help," I called out.

"No," snapped James.

The men gripped each other's collars as they spun violently toward a wall. Ivor tripped and his phone slipped from his pocket. He went to grab it and James pulled him back.

They tumbled through a doorway that opened up into a deserted dining room.

James leaped to his feet in one sleek move and swung his leg up and around in mid-air, aiming for the man's neck.

Ivor jumped aside and then leapt at James, flinging his entire weight on him. They fell to the ground and skidded along the highly-polished floor until Ivor got the upper hand, straddling James, grabbing him by the throat and strangling him.

It was impossible to watch.

James' face flushed with blood as Ivor banged his head onto the deck.

I rushed into the room and laid my violin and bow on one of the tables. Then I reached for the back of a chair. When my hands slipped off, I realized the thing was secured to the ground. Desperately, I looked around for another object to use.

James snapped his hands straight up and outward, breaking the man's grip and shoving him off. They wrestled each other out the door toward the back of the yacht. A sharp punch to James' jaw tipped him back. Ivor hoisted him up onto the railing as James fought for balance.

I saw his terrible look of realization—he was going over.

I grabbed the neck of my violin with both hands, raising the Stradivarius into the air above my head and rushing forward, bringing it down hard on Ivor's skull. A loud crack rang out as the violin splintered, spraying pieces of precious wood around us.

Ivor slumped forward onto James, only dazed.

I dropped the one recognizable piece of my violin—the neck with its strings dangling like stray wires.

I went for Ivor's phone, but he saw what I was doing and rushed towards me.

James grabbed Ivor from behind and picked him up, using the momentum to hoist the man onto the balustrade. "You've outstayed Her Majesty's welcome."

James pushed him over.

I clapped a hand over my mouth, muffling a scream.

Breathless, James looked back at me. "You okay?"

I managed to nod my head, my hands shaking.

"Just sent him into third class." He forced a smile and then his expression changed when he saw my shattered violin.

He looked horrified.

"Best moment of creativity I ever had." I gave a strained chuckle.

With a sympathetic expression, he retrieved the pieces of my instrument, along with the bow, and threw them into the Thames to hide the evidence of our struggle.

From the stern, we stared out at the water as it swallowed up the pieces of the Strad into its greyness. It felt like icicles were forming along my forearms, a dreadful chill soaking into my bones.

James brushed broken glass off his trousers and then straightened his tie, looking calm and well-put together and nothing like a man who'd been in a deadly fight. But I knew that fairly soon, bruises caused by Ivor's blows would appear on his face.

Sadness swelled in my chest. "He deserved it."

Ballad drew in a steadying breath.

"Is he...?"

"The fall killed him." He straightened his back and stretched. "Let's get you to the cabin."

He escorted me the rest of the way. When he opened the cabin door, he gestured inside and asked, "You know everyone?"

There were several students milling around inside.

I scanned their faces and nodded. "Yes."

He held out his hand.

Reaching into my jacket pocket, I withdrew Mikhail's phone and handed it to him.

James turned it off. "Once they realize he's missing they'll track it." He handed it back.

What? No.

My fingers tightened around the phone as I realized what he wanted.

He watched me carefully. "Hide it in your violin case. Carry it off the yacht. Kitty will take it from there."

"She'll meet me?"

He gave a nod. "Make sure the phone leaves your side within sixty seconds of stepping foot off the ramp. Understand?"

My wide-eyed stare conveyed I was having a "what the hell" moment.

He gave me a look of sympathy. "They won't suspect a student. The phone can't be on me. Everyone goes through security when we disembark."

"Won't I?"

"No." He smiled. "You're the entertainment."

"Where are you going?"

"I can't be seen with you." He went to touch my face, but then drew his hand back.

"I'm sorry for it all," I whispered.

"I'll meet you on the other side," he said, and then slipped away.

Hurrying into the cabin, I made my way over to my violin case, drawing in a deep breath as I unclipped the lid and flung it open. With a sigh, I ran my fingers over the soft velvet where the Stradivarius should have rested. It was only then I noticed my hand was trembling.

The reality of this evening was starting to sink it. But I didn't have time to dwell on it. I was still in danger.

I still had to get off this yacht.

Chapter 38

SIXTY SECONDS.

It seemed like a reasonable amount of time right up until I had to stroll down the walkway to disembark, shuffling beside the other meandering students who were getting in my way—trying to appear like I didn't have a dead member of the KGB's phone in my case.

Glancing back, I saw James being patted down. Cars were parked along the pavement ready to collect passengers. Desperately, I searched for Kitty.

I had to get rid of this device.

"Emily," Penn-Rhodes called to me.

I spun round to see him behind me.

"Patrick Woo wants to talk with you," he said. "He was impressed with your performance."

I continued to walk backwards. "Can I meet him later?"

He looked baffled.

Forty seconds.

"Did you enjoy the event tonight?" His frown deepened.

"Very much so. But my lift home is here." I turned and hurried toward the pavement.

Penn-Rhodes came after me and quickly caught up. "Emily, this is your career we're talking about. Five minutes of your time could change your life."

30 seconds.

"I'm sorry." The crushing injustice of it all made my chest ache.

I saw Kitty standing beside a sports car. Scurrying away from

Penn-Rhodes, I made my way over to her. She took the violin case from me and rounded the other side of the car, where she was now hidden from the crowd.

A motorbike roared towards us and swerved by where we were standing. The pick-up of the phone was as discreet as it was fast. The driver sped off.

I looked back the way I'd come, and saw Penn-Rhodes talking with Patrick Woo next to *The Venetian's* ramp.

Another chance slipping away…

"Get in," snapped Kitty.

Reluctantly, I leaped into the front and was thrust back as we zoomed away. Only now did I realize that sweat had snaked down my back, causing my dress to stick to my spine. My hands were shaking.

After a while, The London Eye came into view and I focused on the exquisite colors as they changed from blue to purple and back to blue.

Kitty pulled the car over and we came to a stop.

I swung a worried look her way.

All I could think of was Patrick Woo's disappointment as I'd turned my back on him, refusing to speak.

Kitty narrowed her eyes at the rearview. "Your ride's here." She nodded for me to get out.

"Who is he really?" I had to ask. "James?"

"Your worst nightmare." She flashed a sexy smile. "Serving Her Majesty's every whim, no less."

My hand reached for the handle. "Sorry I stood you up tonight, Kitty."

"Goodbye, Emily."

I flung the door open.

I hurried toward the town car behind us. The rear passenger door opened, and James gestured for me to join him. Slumping in the seat beside his, I tried to calm my racing heart, realizing I'd left the violin case with Kitty—not that it mattered now.

"Primrose Hill," James ordered the driver.

The glass divider rose up between us and the chauffeur.

We were going home.

He pulled me into a hug, and I rested my head on his shoulder, Kitty's words about his nightmare reputation haunting me.

"How do you know Diana Zane?" I looked to him for the answer.

"Need to know basis, Em." He flashed me a dazzling smile.

"You know what she means to me?"

"I know."

This man was intoxicating, and after seeing how he'd handled his attacker, I had a renewed sense of respect for him.

We pulled up outside the Primrose Hill house. James sat looking straight ahead, seemingly deep in thought, making no effort to get out of the car. His delay and our silence were too painful for me to endure.

Finally, I broke the quiet. "You're not coming in, are you?"

He sighed deeply. "Every student is about to be placed under surveillance by them. We can't stop it. Only monitor their actions."

"When will I see you again?"

He shook his head, letting me know I wouldn't get an answer.

I peered at the house, hoping Xavier was at least still inside. "I'm sorry."

He took my hand and brought it to his lips, kissing my fingers tenderly.

"My mum's sacrifice...that she would never hear me play," I continued softly. "I could have been a dancer. Could have studied anything other than music. I could have chosen something she could have enjoyed."

"Her happiness comes from seeing you happy."

"I just threw it all away."

"British lives are sacrificed every day for a greater purpose, Emily. You've joined the ranks of heroes who put their own dreams on hold to make the world a better place."

"Me? How?"

"Mikhail's phone." He gave a firm nod. "You just changed the course of history."

I let out an uneasy breath. "Do you think you could have ever loved me?"

He squeezed his eyes shut and said, "Xavier is my sky and you are my stars. I don't want it to end." He started to say something else and then stopped himself.

Resting my forehead against his arm, I tried to breathe through these final heart wrenching moments.

James' tone became formal once more. "Return to school and behave as normal. Don't conduct any online searches. Don't visit any of the places we took you to."

"I promise to never speak of us. Or about any of it."

He gave me a somewhat skeptical smile, but I saw kindness as well.

Tears stung my eyes like acid, but I refused to let them fall.

"It's time, Emily," he said quietly.

I got out of the car and walked towards the house, feeling like my life-force was being stripped away. With his aura still enveloping me, I made my way up the walkway to the front door.

I turned the key and stepped inside, hearing the car drive away.

The stillness within these walls was deafening.

I strolled from room to room looking for Xavier.

Finally entering the sitting room, I collapsed on the couch. Closing my eyes, I let the grief consume me, my throat burning in agony in my effort to hold back the bitter tears I wanted to shed over the loss of him—of *them*.

I'd believed these two men had captured my heart and were keeping it prisoner. But all this time it had been music that had truly owned my soul—and I both loved and hated the muse for it.

Staring down at my hands, I tried to remember what had happened to the Stradivarius, as though my mind was protecting me from the memory.

The hope of happiness had always been an illusion.

My beloved Xavier was gone.

Chapter 39

Two Weeks Later

I SET MY VIOLIN CASE ON THE STONE STEP AND ROSE TO STAND ON THE outer edge of Trafalgar Square's fountain.

The passers-by mostly ignored me, only a few looking up and then soon dismissing the girl who wasn't up to much, who was seemingly staring at the view. Though I was secretly peering at the security cameras trained on this location.

Before me stood Nelson's Column and surrounding it were the vast bronze sculptured lions positioned at all four corners. The same landmarks I'd driven by in a Tesla with James and Xavier while making love on the backseat.

It made me smile even now.

In the two weeks since James had left me outside my Primrose Hill home, my emotions had been vacillating between loss and hope. There were enough scorching memories of our love to last me a lifetime, and this was what I held onto. Though not being able to have contact with either of them was causing my hope to fade fast.

Standing straight on the stone edge of the fountain, I held my palm in front of my face, then raised my thumb, index finger and pinkie finger. Keeping my ring and middle fingers down, I moved my hand back and forth—using sign-language to get my message across.

I love you.

I love you.

I love you.

I placed my palm on my chest as though this could ease the ache in my heart. *Please, send me a sign you got this.*

It was time to return to the Academy for my afternoon class after stealing away during my lunch hour—feeling satisfied that I'd sent a message to my beloved Xavier the only way I knew how.

Since I'd seen him last, I had dutifully continued with my ordinary routine—attending classes daily and then leaving to go straight home. On the weekends, I had taken up busking in my favorite haunts in Covent Garden and had returned to the place where it all started— Piccadilly Circus.

Just in case…

Thankfully, I'd found a vast sum of money deposited in my Lloyds bank account, upwards of half a million pounds, which would last quite a while for someone who lived simply.

And my old violin—the one I used to play before I met Xavier— I'd discovered in a cupboard. I was quite happy to be reunited with my beloved instrument, having many fond memories of owning it. And it had brought Xavier and I together, after all. I was even thinking of going back to teaching music lessons.

These thoughts burned up my mind as I wandered along the corridors of the Academy. I stopped off at my personal locker to gather books for my next class. A blur of movement next to me caught my attention and I turned my head to see Kitty Adair.

She didn't look at me, only pretended to be fussing with a locker catch. "How are you?"

I played along and stared into the cavernous space that was the inside of my locker. "Fine," I lied. "Did he send you?"

She gave a subtle nod. "You have your finals, right?"

"Next week." I had to fight the urge to look at her.

I smiled, feeling that this was the moment I'd been waiting for…a message, a word, a sign that I'd see them again. And on the eve of my exams it couldn't have come at a better time.

"Em," her tone changed. "Have you heard from Xavier?"

I swallowed hard. "No."

"You're sure?"

"I think I would remember that," I bit out. "You're more likely to hear from him." A shudder of fear slithered up my spine. "Is he okay?"

She hesitated for a moment. "Yes, I'm sure he is."

I rested my violin case against the locker. "What happened?"

"Don't look my way."

"I need to speak with James," I said vehemently.

"I get that." She gave a nod as though her work was done and walked away.

I looked over at where she'd been standing and exhaled a shaky breath of doubt.

Oh, God. Had something happened to Xavier?

Salme walked by looking smug. "Hey, Emily."

"Hey." I looked over her shoulder at Kitty's back as she strolled away.

"How are you?" She smiled brightly, which was so unlike her. "What happened to your Strad?"

"Um…" Biting down hard on my lip, I tried to act casual.

"You've been playing so well. Doesn't matter what instrument you play, to be honest. You're talented. You'll make it."

I stared at her for a moment, realizing what she was insinuating…

I lifted my case. "Got to go." Scurrying away, I rounded the corner and hurried all the way to Penn-Rhodes' office.

I rapped on his door.

He was sitting at his desk munching on a sandwich. He reached for a serviette to wipe the crumbs off his fingers. "Emily."

"They chose her?"

"Salme was a strong candidate."

"But I played with all of my heart and soul." I inhaled sharply. "You said Mr. Woo was impressed with me."

But I'd snubbed him that night after the event when we'd disembarked, and I'd refused to return and speak with him. That had to be it, right?

Penn-Rhodes blew out a sigh of defeat.

I flew out of his office and ran back the way I'd come, my violin case banging against my leg. I dashed out into the drizzling rain where

I finally caught my breath, my chest tight with exertion, my mind breaking into a thousand splinters of doubt.

I'd lost out to *her*.

Salme stood beneath an umbrella on the curb waiting to be picked up. "What are your plans after you leave here, Emily?"

I sucked in a wary breath. "I don't know."

"Keep practicing. There's lots of local bands around here you can join. Pubs love cheap musicians like you. And you know what they say, if you can't do, teach."

"You never did like me," I replied flatly.

She chewed on the thought. "You walk around like you're better than everyone else."

"You read me wrong."

The sky opened up and rain poured over us. She was shielded beneath her umbrella, but I was getting drenched.

A gust of wind caught her umbrella and she fought to keep hold of it. Her violin case slammed to the ground. We both stared down at it. After a few moments, I picked it up and handed it back to her—for the sake of the instrument.

Of course, there was no thank you in return.

I headed away, off down the pavement, welcoming the downpour. Anything to hide these tears. Anything to wash away this day.

Please let Xavier be okay.

And if he was elsewhere it meant he hadn't seen my message from Trafalgar Square.

Penn-Rhodes' voice called out from behind me. Clutching a large black umbrella, he hurried to catch up.

"I wanted you to know, Emily," he said, sounding out of breath, "that Patrick Woo was very impressed with your performance on the yacht. And he told me the audition you gave, the second one at the Barbican, was the finest he's ever seen."

I swiped a damp strand of hair out of my eyes. "I don't understand. Why not me, then?"

His expression was sympathetic. "Things don't always turn out the way we want them to."

"And I wanted it so much."

"I know, and I wish there was something else I could do."

"Thank you." I gave a nod. "For coming and saying these things."

Anger flashed across his face. "Salme's father made a hefty donation to the London Symphony Orchestra."

So…Salme's father had paid for her place. Not to mention the fact that her mum was a renowned member. I'd never stood a chance. Had James known this all along?

I blinked in surprise. "How is that fair?"

"I didn't want you to think it was anything you did wrong." Penn-Rhodes shook his head in disgust. "Don't let such things change you, Emily."

My nod was weak.

I'm already changed.

With his head bowed under his umbrella, Penn-Rhodes hurried back to the building.

I trudged home.

When I entered the empty house, I immediately headed upstairs to peel off my wet clothes and pull on a T-shirt. I would have worn one of Xavier's, but all of his clothes had been removed.

Remembering the lone beer left over from when we'd had pizza a couple of weeks before, I headed downstairs. Now seemed as good a time as any to crack it open.

When I walked into the kitchen, I was stopped in my tracks by what I saw resting on the countertop—a chrome case in the shape of a violin. With trembling fingers, I unclipped the lid and pried it open. Within the velvet casing lay a sleekly designed and very modern violin, the color a gorgeous cobalt blue. The matching bow nestled beside it was equally exquisite.

A single card lay on top: *One of a kind —created from the once lost design by Leonardo da Vinci.*

In awe, I lifted out the instrument and ran my fingers along the strings. It felt light in my grip as I raised it up and slid the bow across it.

No... It sounded off...like it needed more than just tuning.

Beautiful in every conceivable way but not quite right...it was the echo that resonated. Such a shame that something so exquisite wasn't as perfect as it first appeared.

But I didn't care, because it came from him...my Xavier.

He would have been heartbroken when he'd heard what had happened to the Strad—the same one he'd left on my doorstep the night everything had changed.

I needed him like a poem needs a voice.

Xavier is my sky and you are my stars. I don't want it to end.

Oh, my beloved James.

I sighed heavily at the beauty of this remarkable cobalt blue instrument, and I had a gut feeling that if I corrected the fault its music would astound everyone.

Just behind the F-shaped hole that every violin has on either side to enhance its acoustics, a corner of something white peeked out. I pulled on the paper and it slipped past my fingers, falling to the floor.

Carefully, I placed the violin back in its case along with the bow and then knelt to retrieve the envelope.

Easing up the seal, I slid out an invitation.

You are cordially invited to
Royal Court Manor
Montego Bay, Jamaica

Hadn't Xavier tried to coax James into speaking with this very accent?

His connection to this place was now glaring as I recalled all he'd shared with me during those hours together in his castle. All that time I'd had my sights set on Xavier...

My thoughts swirled with the hopeful possibility that this invitation came from them. Perhaps they were trying to share the allure of crystal-clear blue waters, swaying palm trees, and the luscious taste of mouth-watering pineapple. All the while watching glorious sunsets as we took long walks along the pristine white-sand beaches.

More than all of this, I'd have the chance to fall into their arms again.

My beautiful men.

Coming Soon

PERVADE
MONTEGO BAY
(Duet #2)

Also from
VANESSA FEWINGS

PERFUME GIRL

&

THE ENTHRALL SESSIONS:
ENTHRALL, ENTHRALL HER, ENTHRALL HIM, CAMERON'S CONTROL, CAMERON'S CONTRACT, RICHARD'S REIGN, ENTHRALL SECRETS, and ENTHRALL CLIMAX

&

THE ICON TRILOGY from Harlequin:
THE CHASE, THE GAME, and THE PRIZE

VanessaFewings.com
Vanessa is also on Instagram, Twitter, Facebook, BookBub, Pinterest, and Goodreads.

For those wanting to chat more:
visit Vanessa Fewings' Romance Lounge on Facebook.

Printed in Poland
by Amazon Fulfillment
Poland Sp. z o.o., Wrocław

52389552R00197